PRAYER WARRIORS
THE
FINAL
CHAPTER

Other books by Céleste perrino Walker

Prayer Warriors
Guardians

Books by Céleste perrino Walker and Eric Stoffle
Eleventh Hour
Midnight Hour

PRAYER WARRIORS
THE
FINAL
CHAPTER

**A story of prevailing prayer by the author of
Prayer Warriors and Guardians**

CÉLESTE PERRINO WALKER

Pacific Press® Publishing Association

Nampa, Idaho

Oshawa, Ontario, Canada

www.pacificpress.com

Additional copies of this book are available by calling toll free 1-800-765-6955 or visiting http://www.abcasap.com

Library of Congress Cataloging-in-Publication Data

Walker, Céleste Perrino.
    Prayer warriors, the final chapter : a story of prevailing prayer by the author of Prayer Warriors and Guardians / Céleste Perrino Walker.
        p.cm.
    ISBN: 0-1863-2001-2 (pbk.)
    1. Prayer groups. 2. Prayer. 3. Angels. I. Title.

PS3573.A42525P73 2004
813'.54—dc22   2003055376

04 05 06 07 08 • 5 4 3 2 1

DEDICATION

For Joyous and Serge
Love, Celestial

ACKNOWLEDGMENTS

With thanks to all the people who make it happen and all the people who still believe in reading, especially those who have a copy of all my books. (Both of you—you know who you are.) And special thanks to Rob, for helping with the demon names. And to Josh for trying (all those who would have voted for Bernardo the Nasty can write and cheer him up). And to Rachel, because she thinks it's neat that Mommy writes books.

Thank you to my editor at Pacific Press, Tim Lale, for all his help in the refining process of this book. Work's only work if it ain't fun. Thanks for making it fun.

And special thanks to everyone who wrote to tell me how *Prayer Warriors* and *Guardians* changed their lives. It's easy not to give spiritual warfare a second thought, but that is a grave mistake. Ellen White said, "None are in greater danger from the influence of evil spirits than those who, notwithstanding the direct and ample testimony of the Scriptures, deny the existence and agency of the devil and his angels. So long as we are ignorant of their wiles, they have almost inconceivable advantage; many give heed to their suggestions while they suppose themselves to be following the dictates of their own wisdom" (*The Great Controversy,* p. 516).

Céleste perrino Walker

Prayer Warriors: The Final Chapter finishes a story that began years ago. I hope that like *Prayer Warriors* and *Guardians* before it, *Prayer Warriors: The Final Chapter* will open your eyes to the exhilaration and the danger of the spirit realm and that you, too, will find the power of prayer.

CAST OF CHARACTERS

Billie Jo Raynard:

Billie Jo Raynard and her husband, Jimmy, live in Tennessee. They have two children, Cassidy and Dallas. Jimmy miraculously recovered from a coma caused by a logging accident. Since Jimmy's accident they have been struggling to get by financially. He can no longer log, so he has a job at a plant making canning jars. Jimmy's mother, Helen, causes a lot of difficulties in their marriage by trying to control their family.

Angel: Jewel
Demon: Nog

Cindi Trahan:

Cindi Trahan and her husband, Marc, live in Tennessee. They have an adopted daughter, Esther, whose biological parents, Ray and Julia Vargas, work as nurses at a mission in Africa. Cindi has taken over the prayer list the great prayer warrior Ethel Bennington used to have. She has updated it with modern technology, calling it A Wing and a Prayer, and she now sends out the prayer requests via email.

Angel: Shania
Supervising angel: Reissa
Demons: Sparn, Rafe

Jared Flynn:
Jared Flynn was a member of Cindi's prayer list. The prayer warriors on the list prayed for his wife, who later died of cancer. He is having a difficult time dealing with the death of his wife.

Angel: Kaskai
Demon: Ogel

Shay Beauregard Okeke:
Having lost her baby in a tragic accident, Shay is recuperating in one half of the duplex her father left her in his will. It is located in New Orleans, Louisiana. Her husband, Nwibe, was killed in a Marburg outbreak at the mission. She has two adopted children, Marcus (Nwibe's son) and Madina. Shay plans to return to the mission, but she hasn't made the move yet.

Angels:
Gaius (Shay)
Ayala (Marcus)

Demons:
Jezeel (Shay)
Gorn (Marcus)

Wahabi Okeke:
Bartender in Niamey, Africa, a city near the mission outpost. Brother of Nwibe.

Deniece Daignault:
Shay's childhood friend.

Don Germaine:
Confused by a broken relationship, Don returned to the United

States, where he learned of the accident that claimed the life of Shay's baby. He rushed to see her and has remained through her recovery, helping to care for the children. He is considering asking her to marry him and would like for Shay and the children to return with him to the mission. He is on temporary leave. Cindi Trahan is his sister.

Angel: Julian
Demon: Merck

Toby and Davy O'Connell

Toby and Davy were married until a plane accident took Davy's memory. Leaving Toby, he requested a divorce and disappeared. Brokenhearted, Toby took all her money and traveled to Africa, where they'd always said they would be mission pilots. She began to develop a relationship with Don Germaine at the mission, where she, at first reluctantly, served as a nurse. When Davy's memory returned and he came looking for her, Toby broke off the relationship with Don and determined to give Davy a chance. She runs the mission in Don's absence. Davy flies the ultralight that they use to service some clinics they have planted. The recent outbreak of Marburg has made the locals wary of the mission. Some are becoming hostile.

Angels:
Lileah (Toby)
Jes (Davy)

Demons:
Lucien (Toby)
Belial (Davy)

Crazy Carol:

Carol Bennington is the mentally-ill daughter of the late Ethel Bennington. She is homeless and roams the streets with her big dog, Come Here, by her side.

Jesse Redcloud:

Jesse Redcloud came from a broken home and through foster families, running away from the last one. He planned to rob a church until an encounter with angels changed the course of his life. He is now the supervisor of a local homeless shelter.

Angel: Saiph
Demon: Balor

CHAPTER

Cindi Trahan rolled over in bed and squinted at the numbers illuminated on the dial of the alarm clock on her husband Marc's nightstand. It was only five in the morning. She knew there would be no more sleep that night and groaned. Wearily she pushed herself out of bed. She wrapped a worn flannel robe over her nightgown and rubbed her arms. The temperature had dropped again.

Moving soundlessly down the hall, she paused at her daughter Esther's room and opened the door. In the sudden glare of the light she saw the child sprawled face down, arms akimbo, legs tucked up beneath her in almost a kneeling position. Her flushed face was squashed up against the side-rails that Marc insisted she continue to use, even though Esther had argued that they were for babies.

Cindi couldn't help seeing Esther as a baby still. It was hard to believe they had adopted her nearly six years before. It seemed as though she had always been part of their lives. Cindi laid another blanket over the child and crept out of the room.

In the kitchen she filled the tea kettle with water. While it heated she went to the china cupboard to choose a pretty teacup to drink from. It was part of her early morning ritual. She settled on one with a Blue Willow pattern and returned to the stove, where she spooned loose tea leaves into the silver strainer, inhaling deeply the fragrance of tropical flowers. Splurging on handpicked and blended herbal teas was one of her necessary luxuries. As she put the tea canister back on the shelf the kettle broke into an agonized whistle. Cindi removed it from the stove and carefully poured boiling water into her cup.

With the steaming cup of tea she made her way into the living room and sat down at the computer. Its bright screen lit up the dark room, and Cindi needed no other illumination as she logged on to the Internet. As she watched, her email Inbox flooded with messages. Carefully she scrolled through them, cutting and pasting key parts of the body text into one giant email she called A Wing and a Prayer. This master email she sent once a week to a list of people who had agreed to pray for each other's concerns.

Cindi smiled as she remembered how this system had worked when Ethel Bennington, one of her former home-nursing patients, had been alive. The phone had jumped all day as people phoned in prayer requests. Cindi would write them all in a notebook, and Ethel faithfully prayed for each one.

After Ethel died, it fell to Cindi to carry on Ethel's prayer chain. And so she had. *Wouldn't Ethel be surprised*, Cindi thought, *if she could see the changes modern technology has made?* With the click of a mouse the prayer requests could be sent to hundreds of people who subscribed to A Wing and a Prayer.

Cindi had often asked herself what Ethel might have thought of such an idea. Would she scorn it as impersonal? Or would she praise it for being practical and easy? Most of the time the answer came in the remembered voice of her former patient, heard clearly in her head. "What matters most to God is that we hold each other up in prayer often and in earnest." *Yes, that's what Ethel would say,* Cindi thought.

Cindi cleaned up her Inbox and saved the draft of her mass email. The next day she would enter any final requests and then send it out. Before logging off she printed a copy of the email to use during her own prayer time. She brought up the Disconnect box, but before she could click on it, an instant message appeared on her screen. She frowned and opened the dialog box.

"Are you there?" it read. The sender's screen name was Rainman. That was Jared Flynn's screen name. She had been corresponding with Jared after he joined the email list requesting prayers for his wife, who had cancer. The list members prayed for her for six months. She had died, and this was the first time in the two months since that Jared had contacted her.

"Yes," she typed. *"How are you?"*

She hit Send and waited. There was a long pause.

"I've been better, but I can't remember when. It must have been a long time ago. Can't eat. Can't sleep."

Cindi began a reply asking him if he'd like to have the list members pray for anything specific. Before she could send it the screen flashed again.

"I lost my job."

"What do you want us to pray for specifically?" she asked, concentrating on the keys. She stared at the screen, waiting for a reply.

"Me." It was so pitiful; she felt a rush of sympathy.

"Is there anything I can do?" she asked.

"I'd like for someone to listen."

"I can do that."

Cindi waited for a reply, but none came. She assumed he was typing a long response, but the wait stretched on, and he sent no reply.

"Jared?" she typed, *"are you there?"*

Nothing. She waited a while longer in case he had lost his connection and needed to log on again. Her fingers drummed impatiently. After a minute she gave up and logged off. Her tea was cold. She prayed silently for the faceless man out there named Jared, who had lost his wife and now appeared to be losing the rest of his life.

Their light was so bright that had Cindi Trahan been able to see it, she would have gone blind instantly. Though the angels filling the room around her were as real as she was, she could not see them. They spoke to her, and she heard their words as thought suggestions, which she was free to heed or ignore. By making sentient beings, the Creator had given human beings the power to choose between good and evil, right and wrong.

Shania, their leader, stood a bit taller than the rest. Cindi was her particular charge. She had noticed through the years that whenever her charges spent time with the Master and tried to follow Him, they heard her voice much more clearly, and their choices were in keeping with the Master's holy will. When they neglected the Master, the voices of the fallen angels competed more easily with the holy angels, and a human being was likely to go either way.

The fallen angels were not given much quarter in Cindi Trahan's home. She neither listened to them nor followed them, and their voices were weak in her ears. Still, they congregated as close as they dared. This woman was an odious and dangerous adversary. She had picked up the ministry of the great Prayer Warrior, Ethel Bennington. Their leader, Sparn, was under direct orders from Prince Satan to bring her down. Besides the general havoc she wreaked with her prayers, the powerful prayer cover of Cindi and the diligent people on her prayer list sustained the Operation C.A.R.E. mission outpost run by her brother, Don Germaine. And the demons wanted to destroy the mission. At any cost.

Since they were not able to work through Cindi directly, the demons employed whomever else happened to be handy and easily influenced. Sparn had tried for months to find a chink in Cindi's armor but had come up empty-handed until now. Ogel, a demon with very little to recommend him besides his relentless persistence, had come to him with a plan, and this morning, as he observed, he was delighted to see that it might work.

Ogel had been cavorting with this particular contingent of demons because his charge, Jared, was communicating with Cindi. After Jared's wife died, Ogel had been unceasing in his efforts to take down the man whose grief had placed him in a precarious position emotionally. There were all manner of inappropriate responses Jared's grief could take. Ogel decided to concentrate on one. That very morning he had convinced Jared to contact Cindi. Sparn thought the move was pure genius, but he didn't tell Ogel.

So far, it was all very innocent, to be sure. But using Jared's weakened state, Ogel hoped to persuade him that he had more than a friendly interest in Cindi. He hoped Jared might discover that in Cindi he could find solace. After all, the Master had given human beings many wonderful blessings, and all it took for a blessing to become a curse was to convince them to enjoy it the wrong way. Sometimes that was an easy thing. Or maybe it just looked easy.

No sooner did he have Jared connecting with Cindi than that troublemaker, Kaskai, Jared's guardian angel, severed the connection. Cindi had given up on him and was now making breakfast for her family. But Ogel was nothing if not persistent. He would wait for his chance.

"Keep it up," Sparn urged. "You will succeed, and when you do, the prayer link to the mission outpost will be severed, and it will finally die as we have intended all along. Your victory will be my victory. See that you report only to me." Ogel nodded, glad, finally, to be appreciated in his work and puffed up with a sense of his own importance.

Cindi made some banana French toast and put on a fresh kettle of water for more tea. Marc liked a hot mug of apple spice in the morning, and Esther liked peppermint. She called it candy-cane tea. Marc came down the stairs while she was slicing fruit into a bowl for fruit salad.

"Morning," she said cheerfully.

Marc grunted. He was not a morning person. He slumped into a chair at the table, and she brought him a mug of tea that he alternately blew on and sipped gingerly. She knew it was no use talking to him until after breakfast.

Esther appeared at the bottom of the stairs, rubbing her eyes and yawning. "Can I get up?" She asked this every morning, and Cindi always had the same answer.

"Aren't you already up?" Esther smiled at the old joke and sat down at the table.

"Are those banana or plain?" she asked, indicating the French toast.

"Banana."

"Yum! I'll have two, please."

Cindi was often amazed at the food the small girl packed away. Yet she was willowy and tall, like her mother, Julia Vargas. Julia and Ray, Esther's biological parents, had visited the Trahans on their last visit home from the mission field. They had come to see Esther, who knew them as Uncle Ray and Aunt Julia. When she was old enough to understand she would be put in the picture and informed of her paternity. Until then, Cindi was happy with the way things had gone since the adoption when Esther was born.

Ray and Julia had been as involved as any loving aunt or uncle could be, and not the least bit possessive. They never regretted their decision to give up Esther for adoption. Russell Duffy—Julia's father and Esther's biological grandfather—was a loving, supportive presence in Esther's life as well as a dandy last-minute babysitter. All in all, she felt satisfied that they had made the relationships work, and a difficult situation had turned into a blessing for all concerned.

"Oh, by the way, I forgot to tell you, your brother Don called the other day and left a message," Marc said, scraping the last of his French toast from the plate.

"When did he call?" Cindi fought down a twinge of irritation. It was just like Marc to take a message and forget to relay it.

Marc shrugged and looked at his watch. "A couple days ago maybe."

"Well, did he say what he wanted?"

"Nope. Just said he'd call back again and catch you some other time when you weren't on the computer." Marc pushed back the chair and headed up the stairs. Cindi didn't bother to follow him. His brain was already halfway to work. He always woke up the same way. One minute he was meandering out of dreamland, the next he was charging along, full speed ahead, torpedoes at the ready.

Cindi checked the kitchen clock. Not quite seven yet. Would Don be awake this early? She debated with herself for a few minutes, wondering if it was important enough to wake him if he wasn't up. Finally she laughed at herself. If it was important, he would have called back.

He definitely would have called back.

Don Germaine stepped out of his apartment into a brick wall of heat. It wasn't even 7:00 A.M. yet and already the temperature had to be in the nineties. That was New Orleans. He would be drenched with sweat before he made it to the end of his short driveway to get the newspaper from the box. At least, that was his excuse for ambling into the heat at such an early hour. More than the news, he wanted to know if Shay Okeke and her children, Marcus and Madina, were up yet. He'd already been up for hours, and he was starved.

They had a nice little arrangement, he thought. Shay's father had left her ownership of a duplex when he died, and since her return to the States she had occupied one side of it. After the accident that claimed the life of Shay's unborn baby, Don had lived in the duplex and cared for the other two children until she returned from the hospital. When Shay came home he took a hotel room nearby so he could be close by to help out. He hadn't been there for long when the couple that rented the other half of the duplex moved into the house they had been building. Don settled into the vacated side of the duplex and had been there ever since.

Living right next door to Shay and the children gave Don an odd feeling sometimes. It was like playing at having a family. During the day he helped out around the house, sometimes watched the children so Shay could run errands, and occasionally did odd jobs or conferred with the staff at Operation C.A.R.E., the mission he was in charge of just outside of Niamey in Niger, Africa. He kept close tabs on the mission, from which he was officially on temporary leave, and participated in making decisions that affected it. For a while that had been enough. Lately, though, he had begun to feel restless.

Shortly after the accident, Shay had made the decision to return to the mission in Africa with her children, and Don had assumed that the entire process of moving would take about a month, maybe less. A little more than a year had passed since she'd decided, and things were still not settled. At times he felt it might be better if he went on ahead of Shay and the children and let them follow when they were ready. But, no sooner did he think so than he tried to imagine life without them and couldn't bear the thought. It seemed he had lived his whole life for this time and these people. So much of what he had been looking for he had found in the simple life of a family. And they weren't even his family. Not yet.

"Hey! Good morning! You coming over for breakfast?"

Don saw Shay's arm poking out of a window, waving at him. He waved back and threw her a kiss. "I'll be right over."

"Good, because we're having scrambled eggs, and you're cooking."

He laughed. At the rate Shay cooked he really should have the kitchen paraphernalia moved over to his side of the duplex, he thought. "I'll be right there."

To outsiders they must have seemed a strange assortment of individuals, if they were grouped together. Don's skin was as "white as paste," Shay was fond of saying when she felt like teasing him. Hers was the color of milk chocolate, her mother having been mulatto and her father white. The children, both of whom she had adopted, were as dark as coffee beans. It just went to show you, Don often thought, that skin color does not a family make. In fact, their little multiracial group reminded him of the inclusiveness of God's family. Red and yellow, black and white, all are precious in His sight.

Marcus, the eldest, was nearly seventeen. When Don opened the door and stepped with relief into the air-conditioning of Shay's half of the duplex, Marcus was hunched over a schoolbook, looking up now and then to scribble industriously in a notebook. "He forgot to do his homework last night," Shay explained when she saw Don glance at Marcus.

"I did my homework," five-year-old Madina said, tugging on Don's sleeve. "Want to see? Look, I made all my letters and my numbers, and I even read a story to Mommy."

Don looked over the papers and made positive sounds while trying to catch Shay's arm and plant a kiss on her cheek. She was packing lunches and danced away from him playfully. "None of that before breakfast," she teased. "Come on, we're famished. Work your magic at the stove and feed us."

"I'll help," Madina volunteered. It was a good thing one female in the house wasn't afraid of the kitchen, Don thought with some amusement.

"Sure, Peanut, you can help." He got out the mixing bowl and handed her the eggs one at a time. With extreme seriousness she cracked each one on the edge and then fished out the shells, which invariably ended up in the bowl right along with the eggs. "Good job," Don said. "Now it's my turn. I'll whisk them. You watch, OK?"

Soon the eggs were cooking as Madina looked on with considerable pride of accomplishment. She wielded the spatula like a scepter and beamed at Don with pleasure. He smiled back. Her big brown eyes were nearly black, and they sparkled. Her forehead was broad, and her features, though she was only five, were sharp and angular. Good bone structure, Don thought. She seemed wise beyond her years and had always displayed an almost shocking maturity for a child.

Though he hardly ever thought about it, for some reason this day he had a clear picture of the day she was born. He could clearly recall the filthy hut where her mother had lain, her life's blood draining away. He remembered her desperate grip on his hand, her eyes burning with only one desire, to bring her child into the world as she exited. He and a mission nurse, Toby O'Connell, had struggled valiantly to fight off death, but in the end they had only succeeded in delaying it. The mother had died, leaving Madina, the squalling baby daughter. And she was unwanted by her father, Bossou. Unwanted by everyone except Shay.

"Look, Daddy." Madina broke into his thoughts and then stopped, looking uncertain. She glanced from him to Shay and back again. It was an awkward moment, but it wasn't the first time she had called him Daddy.

"What, Peanut?" Don asked smoothly, trying to distract her attention from the embarrassing moment while at the same time deciding with determination that he had waited a decent length of time to propose marriage by anyone's standards. Shay's children were starting to think of him as a father figure. Her husband, Nwibe, had been dead for more than a year. Don had waited long enough for propriety's sake to ask her to marry him now, he thought. Surely she wanted that. He was over here making scrambled eggs, wasn't he? Surely it was high time to get married and make them a legal family.

His heart skipped a beat as he sneaked a glance at Shay, but her face was unreadable, buried in his newspaper. Maybe she had missed the whole exchange. Still, he felt strongly that it was time and decided that he would talk to her as soon as Marcus left for school and Madina was occupied with *Sesame Street*.

"I think they're burning," Madina said, wrinkling her nose and waving the spatula over the eggs.

"Whoops, I think you're right," Don said, snatching the skillet from the stove and dumping the eggs out into a serving bowl. "Breakfast," he announced cheerfully.

"Great! I'm starved!" Shay put the paper aside and gave him a bright smile. Sniffing suspiciously, she heaped eggs onto her plate but said nothing about the scorched parts. "Great job, Muppet," she praised Madina.

Don busied himself making toast, but his mind was jumping ahead to the conversation he planned to have with Shay. *"Shay,"* he would say, *"you stop my heart. I've never known anyone like you. You complete me."* No, too corny, and it probably only worked in the movies anyway. No, better to go with something practical. *"Shay, we've been seeing each other for close to a year now, and I think it's time we got married, shared expenses, and gave the children a solid family."* No, no, that was a bit too practical. Women like romance, after all, especially in a marriage proposal.

He carried the toast to the table and absent-mindedly placed a basket of potatoes next to them.

"Don?"

"Yeah?"

"What are the potatoes for?"

He stared at the table, but it took a few seconds to register. "Oh, sorry, I meant to put out oranges." He knew she was snickering at him, but he didn't look at her. He could not believe how nervous he was all of a sudden. He couldn't remember the last time he felt so nervous.

Marcus slammed his book shut and jumped up from the table. "I'd better get going or I'll miss the bus."

Don saw the last bastion between him and bachelorhood disappearing, and he grabbed Marcus's hand like a drowning man. "I'll drive you."

They stared at him.

"No, that's OK." Marcus disengaged his arm gently. "Really, I like to ride the bus."

"But you haven't eaten." Don was desperate.

"I'm not hungry." Marcus gave his mother a quick kiss, and then he was gone. Madina meandered through her breakfast, picking at everything like a little bird. Shay ate methodically, looking at Don thoughtfully now and then as if she was wondering if perhaps he had contracted some sort of brain fever. Don ate woodenly, not even tasting the food.

This is stupid, he berated himself. *I love this woman. I love these kids. We're practically a family now, and I love it.* He felt like a bride getting cold feet seconds before beginning her walk down the aisle. He knew his fears were unreasonable. Change had always frightened him. "God," he prayed, "*I want what You want for my life, really, I do. But let me tell You what I want. I know this isn't news to You, but I want to marry this woman. If she is Your plan for my life, give me some backbone here. Cast out these fears of mine. They have no place in my heart. Fill it with love for Shay and the children so that it's overflowing. They deserve that much and more. Thanks, amen.*"

Merck had been having a rough day. Rough century really. He hadn't properly enjoyed himself since Don Germaine had realized God was not to blame in the tragedies he'd lived through in Rwanda as the doctor of a mission there. For Merck, the only bright spot in his recent past had been the brief period when Don was so sick with an infectious disease in Rwanda that he nearly died. It was a miracle that he had lived. Merck cursed his rotten luck.

The entire year he'd been stuck in the United States watching Don get dopey and lovesick was so disgusting that Merck could hardly see the point in getting up each day. Clearly, he was of no use until the lovesickness wore off and reality set in, so the few brief moments when Don began to question himself, his dedication, and his love for Shay had been the most sublime Merck had felt for, literally, ages.

At the start of Don's prayer Merck had shaken him hard. "What do you think you're doing?" he hissed. "You are right. Marriage would limit your freedom. These kids would limit your freedom. Keep things as they are. Better yet, break it off for awhile. Explore other options. After all, you've been so tied down here for so long you really don't know what . . . who . . . is out there. You're young. OK—well, not a spring chicken maybe, but you've got lots of years ahead of you. Why saddle yourself with this lot?

"And look at that woman! She's a girl, really. She's too young for you. Sure, she doesn't mind the difference in your ages right now, but she will. You'll be old and gray soon enough, and then she'll be embarrassed to be seen with you. Maybe she'll even leave you for a younger man someday. Who knows? In this day and age anything could happen.

"And what makes you think she really loves you anyway? You're convenient, that's what you are. You cook; you run errands. You're like a glorified, unpaid babysitter. Yeah, that's what you are. She doesn't love you. Has she said as much? Even once? OK, the time you guys sat in lawn chairs and watched the stars does not count. She was just feeling sentimental. She hasn't said it since, has she? Has she?"

Don was looking miserable, and Merck knew he was getting through at least a little. Julian moved in and placed an arm around his charge's shoulders. "Be not afraid, neither be discouraged nor disheartened. You know this woman; your heart knows her. She would not trifle with your affections. To her they are rock solid, and she relies on you. She trusts you not to break her heart and to take your relationship to the next level when you are ready. Her heart is tender and her spirit fragile. Do not hurt her with indecision or distance. Love is not a passing feeling; it is a conscious decision."

Don's shoulders straightened a little. Determination lit his eyes, and he almost smiled. He cleared his throat, and Shay looked up at him expectantly. "Madina? Isn't it time for Big Bird?"

"And Elmo!" squealed Madina. She put down the fork and spoon she had been playing with and ran into the living room. Soon Don heard the familiar strains of the *Sesame Street* song. He cleared his throat again.

"Well?" Shay had an amused look on her face.

"Well, what?" He knew he sounded defensive, but he wanted to do this right.

"You've been twitching like you have a rash or something. What's on your mind? Out with it. I'm sure you'll feel much better. Go ahead. I'm listening."

Don groaned inwardly. What a way to start a marriage proposal. A rash . . . really, the woman had no shame. "I haven't got a rash," he declared.

"So, what have you got? Have you heard something about the mission you don't want to tell me?" She looked suddenly sober. "Is that it?"

"No, I haven't heard anything out of the ordinary. It's just that, well, I was wondering, that is, I think maybe it's time that you, I mean, we, were, you know, married." There, he'd said it. He winced. What a way to say it. He inhaled deeply and got down on one knee, ignoring the stricken look on her face.

"Shay Judalon Beauregard Okeke, I love you with all my heart. Would you do me the great honor of agreeing to become my wife?"

His knee was beginning to throb before she finally gave a strangled cry and threw herself into his arms. Don really did wonder if perhaps he hadn't given the gap in their ages quite enough consideration as his knees protested at the strain and he toppled over onto the kitchen floor, Shay on top of him, hugging him and kissing his face over and over.

"I love you, you crazy man! What took you so long? I thought you were never going to ask me."

"Shay?"

"Yes, darling?"

"I think I've sprained my knee."

"What are you two doing down there?" Madina's voice asked. "Can I play too?" She stood looking down at them, puzzled.

Shay rolled off, still laughing, and helped Don get to his feet. He rubbed his knee ruefully. "You OK?" she asked.

"Yeah, nothing hurt but my pride, I guess. You sure you want to marry someone as old and decrepit as I am?"

"You're only as old as you feel. Besides, who says I'm not marrying you for your money?"

Don laughed out loud. "I should have known you'd have your eyes set on the fifty-three bucks I've managed to stash in my savings account. I demand a prenuptial agreement."

"Oh, pooh, you can keep your money," Shay teased. "Just give me all your love and I'll be happy forever."

"You're easy to please."

"Are you done wrestling? 'Cause I want to play."

"Madina," Shay said, pulling the little girl into her arms. "How would you like to have a new daddy?"

"No." The little girl set her mouth in a stubborn line. "I don't want a new daddy. I want him." She pointed a chubby finger at Don's chest. "I want him to be my daddy."

Shay drilled her finger into Madina's tummy, and the little girl squealed with delight. "He's the one I had in mind too. I think I'll marry him. What do you think?"

"Yea!"

Later, over iced tea, Don said it. "What do you think about going back?" He didn't even mean to, but the words just popped out of his mouth.

They both knew he meant going back to the mission in Niger. Shay didn't answer for a moment. "You haven't changed your mind, have you?" It was something he'd considered but not for very long. She had always seemed to want to be there. He thought she felt the same way he did about the place.

"No," she said quietly. Then with a resigned sigh she said, "No, I haven't changed my mind. I have so many great memories of Africa. But then I have so many horrible ones too. It's just something I'll have to get over, I guess. I've really been fighting it. I want to go back, but I'm scared at the same time."

"You don't have to be scared." Don took her hand and found her fingers cold. "Don't you think it will be different now? We'll be married. Won't things seem different to you?"

She shrugged a shoulder. "I hope so, because I know how much it means to you . . . and to the children too. I had such dreams when I went there. It almost seems a lifetime away. I feel . . . older, much older."

"Oh, you are older. I saw a gray hair on your head the other day."

She socked him in the arm, and he pretended to fall over. "I guess what I'm really afraid of is burning all my bridges, you know? What if we sell everything here, move back, and I hate it? What if I can't cut it over there anymore? We'd be stuck there, or we'd have to completely start over if we came back."

He thought it over for a minute and then said, "I think we ought to pray about this. Clearly you're not committed to the idea. But I am committed to you. Let's pray about it and see what God has to say, shall we?"

He was rewarded by one of her dazzling smiles. "You first."

Don took her hands and bowed his head. "Lord, thank You first for Shay. Thank You for her tender heart and her love. Help me to deserve her love. I will be grateful to You every day for her. We want to know Your will. Show us, Lord. Should we stay here or go back to Africa? We trust You to show us Your heart on this matter. And if You should want us to go back we ask You to remove the fear that Shay has about leaving. Please help the children to accept whatever decision we make. In the name of Jesus who saves us. Amen."

When Shay looked up there were tears in her eyes. "I love you," she said.

"I love you back."

Billie Jo Raynard stood in nearly the exact middle of her home with a mop in one hand and a bucket of dirty water in the other. From where she stood it was possible to survey a good amount of her house and admire the work she'd just accomplished. The floors shone and the whole house smelled of pine. She breathed deeply and enjoyed the feeling of cleanliness and accomplishment. *Too bad there was no one to see it before it got dirty again,* she mused ruefully.

She had just emptied the bucket and stowed it with the mop in the hall closet when a sharp rap on the door startled her. A glance at her watch confirmed that the children wouldn't be home from school for another hour. *Who could be at the door?*

She peered through the living-room window to see who was on the front step before opening the door and was surprised at the sight of her mother-in-law's car in the driveway. *What was Helen doing there?* It was unlike her to drop by for an unscheduled visit. She wasn't the type to socialize without a reason. Warily, Billie Jo opened the door.

"Why, Helen, what a nice surprise," she said, hoping her voice sounded sincere. A surprise it was; it was anything but nice.

Helen sniffed haughtily. "Are you going to let me in?"

Billie Jo stepped aside and hid a smile behind her hand. She pretended to tuck a loose hair behind her ear. She tried to smile but knew it looked as phony as it felt. Relations had never been good with her mother-in-law, but it seemed that lately they had taken a turn for the worse.

"What brings you here?" Billie Jo finally asked.

Helen stared at her blankly. "That's what I'd like to know."

Taken aback, Billie Jo blinked rapidly, hunting in her memory, trying to remember if she'd invited Helen and then forgotten. She came up with nothing and stood there feeling stupid, with her mouth hanging slackly as she tried to think of something to say. Before she had the chance, the door opened again and her husband, Jimmy, bounded into the house.

He gave his mother a peck on the cheek and slipped his arm around his wife's waist. Billie Jo wasn't a tall woman, and she stood up straighter to fit into her husband's awkward embrace. "Sorry I'm late, girls," Jimmy said with a radiant smile it was hard not to catch.

"Jimmy, what, I don't understand . . ." Billie Jo felt as though she'd stepped into her own personal Twilight Zone. "What's goin' on?"

"For once, I agree," Helen said. "I don't understand either. Why did you ask me to meet you here? Please clear up this mystery at once. I don't like wasting my time in this fashion."

Jimmy grinned from one to the other. "I got some great news."

Billie Jo's eyes flicked from Jimmy's face to Helen's. *Great news for whom?* Suddenly her mouth felt dry and her palms wet. She had a vague idea it was supposed to be the other way around. "Jimmy," she pleaded. Something dreadful was about to happen, she just knew it.

"I got me a new job," Jimmy supplied finally. "I got me a great new job."

Nog, who had grown perhaps not wiser, but more tenacious as time passed, hadn't been handed an opportunity like this for quite some time. He could hardly restrain himself. He wanted to see the fireworks, but at the same time he was enjoying the suspense. "He got a job! That's not all he got. Wait till you hear this one! You're going to love it!"

"Is that all?" asked Helen. Relief suffused her face. "Well, it's about time. Those imbeciles down at that plant you work at didn't know what they had in you. Now they do. It took them long enough. Congratulations, Jimmy, but you could have just phoned." Helen made a move as if she intended to leave, but Jimmy grabbed her arm.

"Mom, that's not all." He beamed. "You ain't asked me what the job was."

Helen's face arranged itself into patient lines as though she was dealing with a particularly tedious child. "What is the new job, Jimmy?"

"I'm going to be a partner in a carpentry business."

Helen and Billie Jo stared at him. He worked for a company that made canning jars. He had worked there for several years, since the logging accident that nearly claimed his life.

"Wha—"

"Where?" Helen guessed the truth first. "Where is it?" Her voice was very, very cold.

"In Vermont," Jimmy answered. For the first time since he'd entered the house Billie Jo saw the insecurity creep into his eyes. His show of bravado faltered. "I got this friend, Zeb Turner, you remember Zeb Turner? We was school buddies way back. His wife's got relatives in Vermont, and he moved up there. We kept in touch, you know, Christmas cards and the like, but the other day I ran into his ma at the plant. She works there now. She said he had his own carpentry business in Vermont and being there was a building boom going on, he needed help.

"Well, today Zeb called me up at work and offered me the partnership. Said it would be just like old times and was real glad I took him up on his offer. Seems he's been in a bad way up there, not being able to get any good help. He wants me to start as soon as possible."

"Isn't that a corker?" Nog cried jubilantly. "Moving!" To Billie Jo he said, "You're moving, and your husband never even told you!" Then he turned to Helen. "Give it to him! Let him have it!"

Helen's face had lost all color. "Vermont? Do you know where that is, Jimmy?"

Jimmy topped six feet by several inches, but under his mother's scornful gaze he wilted into a shame-faced little boy. "Up north, I guess."

"That's right. Up north. Way up north. Do you know how cold it gets in Vermont in the winter? It's nothing but mountains on top of more mountains . . . that's why they call it the Green Mountain State. Why, they have more cows than people in Vermont! Now, you just call Zeb back and tell him thank you, but no thank you.

You have a fine job where you are and plenty of security. Eventually you'll even have a pension and you'll be able to retire comfortably." Helen reached out her hand and took hold of the doorknob.

"I'm going to work with Zeb." The way Jimmy said it left little doubt about what he was going to do. "That is . . ." he shot Billie Jo a glance that was half supplication and half defiance. "That is, unless you don't like the idea, darlin'."

Billie Jo struggled against the feeling that none of this was real. Moving and all that it meant was more than her brain could comprehend on such short notice. Two implications shouted at her. The first was that finally Helen would be forced to recede to the background of their marriage. For the first time in their married lives they would be completely on their own. The second was that everything she knew and loved, everything familiar would be left behind. Billie Jo would not have been one of the pioneers, of that she was certain. But still, there existed in her being a streak of adventurousness. Ignoring the status-quo part of her nature, she listened to the adventure-seeking side and grinned at her husband.

"Tell him you think it's a lousy idea!" Nog urged. "No, no, don't smile. It's a terrible idea. What about your kids? You'll have to rip them out of school, away from their friends. What about you? What about your friends? What about this place? This house? Jimmy built this house. You've lived in this area all your life. You don't want to drag your family across the country. Even to get away from her." He jerked his head toward Helen. "I know she's a pain, but admit it. You wouldn't have moved to get away from her. Why would you do it now just because he wants to?"

"I think it's a great idea." Although she said it with as much enthusiasm as she could muster, she knew it would take some time before she could really get behind those words. Panicked thoughts were going through her head, and fear clutched at her heart, but she didn't own up to them.

Helen looked capable of murder. Glaring at her son, she began to shriek insanely while waving her fists at him. "If you think for one minute I'm going to let you move up to that god-forsaken wilderness with my only two grandchildren you are sadly mistaken. I'll talk to your father. We'll write you out of our will. You won't get a penny! I mean it!"

Billie Jo was trembling with nerves by the time Helen left, slamming the door behind her. She sat with Jimmy on the couch while he apologized for springing the news on her. "I guess I got so excited about it myself I forgot not everyone would be happy about it." He stared thoughtfully at the ceiling for a minute. "You know, when Zeb called me and we talked about that job, I wanted it so much I never even stopped to think about what you might want. I guess I'd like to know now."

Billie Jo smiled. "Well, it sure was some shock. But I like the idea. I don't have nothing against moving, I guess. The kids will be some disappointed about leaving their friends . . . come to think on it, so will I. But there are new friends. The important thing, I think, is that you'll be doing something you love. I know you ain't been happy at that canning factory. It was good, steady money, and I'm proud you stuck it out. This doesn't sound all that risky to me. But there was something I was wondering."

"What's that?" Jimmy stroked her hair.

"Where we gonna live?"

"Well, now, that's the interestin' part," Jimmy said, lighting up from inside. "Zeb knows this great old fixer-upper he said we can get for a song. The bank is foreclosing and selling it for whatever they can get out of it."

"You mean we're gonna buy a house we ain't never seen?" Billie Jo was incredulous. She couldn't have been more surprised if he had said they were going to live on the moon. "What if we hate it? How much fixin' up are we gonna have to do anyway? When are you gonna have time to fix up the house if you're working all day?"

"What did I tell you? He has no idea what he's doing. This idea is crazy." Nog ranted until he was foaming at the mouth. "He's not thinking ahead, planning with the security of his family in mind. He's jumping in head first with no thought for the future. He doesn't care about you and the children. All he cares about is himself and what's best for him."

Jimmy held up his hands to fend off her questions. "Relax, darlin'! Zeb emailed me a picture of the house." He fished in his pocket and pulled out a blurry photo printed on computer paper. All Billie Jo could make out was that the house had two stories and was built in the Victorian style with a wrap-around porch and gingerbread detail work, most of which appeared to be there. If it was half as nice as the picture it would be breathtaking, a much nicer house than she had ever expected to live in. A mansion, almost.

"It's pretty," she said hesitantly. "What kind of fixin' does it need?"

"Zeb said it's mainly cosmetic. Want to know the really good part? He thinks we can get this for about $50,000. Can you believe that? We'll actually have some money left over after we sell this place."

Billie Jo was afraid to let herself hope that there was a possibility they might have some real savings. They knew people who claimed to live from hand-to-mouth, but for as long as she could remember her family had always lived that way quite literally. Jimmy cashed his check on the way home from work on payday, and when he got home and handed it over she went out immediately to buy groceries. Whatever was left was split up among the many bills that always seemed to be on hand. Frequently someone had to wait to be paid. Occasionally they even received threats to cut off service, and on rare occasions those threats were carried out. Billie Jo could think of times in the past couple of years when she'd had to do without basic necessities like a telephone and once, during the winter, no electricity for a week, because they hadn't had the money to pay their bill.

Just the thought of having several thousand dollars in the bank to "fall back on" was so tempting, she wanted to pack up that very minute. "You really think we'll have money left over?" she asked skeptically.

"You do the math. If we can get the house for $50,000 and we sell ours for $80,000, which is what the town appraised it for, shouldn't we have $30,000 left over? Wouldn't that be a chunk of change?" Jimmy asked dreamily.

"How soon will we have to leave?" Billie Jo asked. She expected the answer to come in terms of months.

"Two weeks."

"Do what? We can't move in two weeks! We'd be pushing it to be out of here in two months!"

"Be that as it may," Jimmy said, unconsciously copying a favorite saying of his father's, "I put in my notice today, and Zeb expects me on the job two weeks from Monday."

"I'd better start packing then," Billie Jo said dully. As stress squeezed her from every side she realized there was no way she was going to be able to do this alone.

"You need never be alone," Jewel said. The angel supported her through the news but had not been given the opportunity for input. He moved in quickly when he saw a chance to encourage and strengthen Billie Jo. "The Master will walk every step of this way with you. He longs to love you lavishly. Don't settle for seconds . . . ask Him for everything you need."

"Everything you need except what you really want," Nog sneered. "You won't get stability by tearing your family out by the roots and flinging them up north. No good will come of this. Mark my words. You'll see."

Billie Jo's spiritual "ears" were closely attuned to God's voice, and she homed in on what the angel was saying, ignoring the demon.

"Lord," she muttered as she went to the basement to look for packing boxes, "I got no strength for this. Not now. I'm not even used to the idea. I want to do what's best for my family, but I'm so scared. Help me through this. Give me the strength to do what needs to be done so that we can move out in two weeks."

Suddenly an idea came to her. "And if it's Your will, Lord, help our house to sell before we move, 'cause I don't think we can move if our house don't sell." She doubted Jimmy had given that much thought.

Nog crowded close to Billie Jo. "Sure, you may be ditching Helen, but is it really worth it to go live in a house you've never seen, in a place you know nothing about, and, worse, have never wanted to know anything about? Come on, admit it. The only reason you're the least bit excited about the thought of moving is to get away from the old bat. Admit it."

Billie Jo squirmed uncomfortably. She had to admit, the only reason she was excited about moving at all was that she could get away from Helen. Otherwise she would be perfectly content to stay right where she was. Aside from Helen, there was no real reason to move at all. Except for Jimmy's job, of course.

She didn't really envy him, working at a job he didn't like. Lately she'd begun to think about getting a part-time job during the hours when the children were in school. If she made enough money it might give Jimmy the opportunity to look for the kind of work he enjoyed. It was a moot point now, however.

Two weeks. It didn't seem possible that they would be moved out in two weeks and living in some strange place. As she collected boxes she couldn't help wondering what kind of place Vermont was.

CHAPTER

Cindi waited three days before she broke down and called her brother Don. While the phone rang on the other end she winced, feeling stupid about being so compulsive and a bit anxious too, in case something was wrong that he just didn't want to tell her. She thought that being blessed with an active imagination was great when it was time to play with Esther, but it could also be a curse.

"Hello?"

"Don! I thought I was going to get the answering machine."

"Hey, sis! What's up?"

"I don't know. You tell me. Marc said you called a couple days ago. Did you want anything special?"

"No. Yes. No." His voice started to rise with excitement. "Not then, just calling to see how you were getting on. But I have some big news now."

Cindi waited. She knew it. He was going back to Africa. And she'd hardly seen him since he'd been home. She felt like crying.

"I'm getting married!"

It took a few moments for this to sink into Cindi's mind, and his voice began to sound worried. "Sis? Are you still there? I said I'm getting married."

"Married?" Cindi finally managed. She was so relieved that she nearly laughed. "To Shay?"

"Of course to Shay! I'm not likely to find anyone else who will take me," he joked. "Not in my lifetime. Yes, we're getting married. Will you come?"

"Come? Of course we'll come. When is the happy day?"

"We're not sure. It depends."

Here it comes, she thought. "Depends on what?"

"On whether or not we go back to Africa. We're praying about it right now. I want to go back, you know that. It's the only place I've ever felt like I belonged. But Shay has some reservations, naturally."

Naturally, thought Cindi. A shudder passed through her as she recalled the gruesome tales about the Marburg epidemic that had claimed the life of Shay's husband, Nwibe, and others at the mission, and nearly killed Don as well. "When do you expect you might know something more definite?"

Don laughed, and Cindi felt some of the tension go out of her. After all, he was getting married. This was a good thing. She was happy for him. And if he was going to move back to Africa, well, that was where he felt a calling. "We might know sooner if you put us on your prayer list."

"I'll do that," Cindi promised. "Hey, do you think we could get to spend some time with you, Shay, and the kids before you leave?"

"What makes you so sure we're leaving?"

"I'm not, but in either case we haven't seen much of you . . . both . . . since you came back. It would be nice to visit for awhile. Can you come here? Or should we go there? I'm not sure I could promise Marc would come, but Esther and I would. What do you think?"

"Why don't you let me talk to Shay, and I'll let you know if she's got a preference. How's that? And don't forget to put us on A Wing and a Prayer."

"I won't," Cindi promised.

Later, as she typed their request into the main body of her email, she couldn't help wishing it was something she didn't have to pray for. "I know they'd be doing a great work for You, Lord," she prayed under her breath. "But couldn't they do a great work for You closer to home?"

Her thoughts were interrupted by an instant message that appeared on the screen. "Now what?" she muttered grumpily.

"Are you still out there?" It was Jared.

"I'm here. How are you doing?" she typed.

"Same old, same old," came his reply.

"We must have gotten disconnected the other day. I waited for you. What happened?"

"I've been having computer problems. I lost my connection and then my computer froze up and I had to reboot it. When I got back on you were gone."

"Sorry about that," she typed, drumming her fingers on the keyboard. She really didn't have time for the chit-chat. She had phone calls to make and errands to run. She'd had a long, hard morning home-schooling Esther, who was now amusing herself nicely. But it was bound to wear off soon. *"Did you need something?"*

The answer was a long time in coming, and when it did come it wrenched Cindi's heart. *"I need a friend."*

She sat for a few minutes, her hands poised over the keys, not knowing what to say. We all need friends? I'm here? You can count on me? Nothing sounded right. Finally she typed hesitantly, *"I thought I was your friend."*

"I'm sorry . . . I didn't mean to discount your friendship. I'm just so fed up with the Internet. It doesn't allow for real friendship, does it? I mean, how well do we really know each other?"

Well, he had a point there. Though Cindi was fond of saying she had many friends, it alarmed her sometimes how many of them were Internet acquaintances. He was right. Email and instant messaging didn't allow for a great deal of intimacy, or if it did, it was usually the wrong kind. The frequent complaint was that it was so easy—you just dashed off a response and thought better of it later.

"I know what you mean," she typed fervently. *"I know exactly what you mean. People don't take enough time for each other anymore. They don't really care enough."*

"I agree," he wrote. *"So, can we meet?"*

Meet? Cindi felt her heart constrict in her chest. Never had she contemplated that in a thousand years. She had merely been sympathizing. Then a thought occurred to her. This was the Internet, after all. Jared could live anywhere in the United States, or the world, for that matter. Chances were remote that he lived within driving distance. *"I don't know,"* she typed. *"I don't think it's a good idea."* Well, she didn't, she thought as she hastily sent the message.

"Get a grip!" Ogel snapped. It had taken him days to set this connection up again, and so far everything was going smoothly. Now it looked as though Cindi was going to back out when the rubber hit the road. "You just said people don't care anymore. Or was that just talk? Do you really care? Or are you just a fair-weather Christian?"

"Cindi, you are doing the right thing," Shania urged. "You don't know this man. Advise him to get counseling with his pastor. This is not a good situation. Your intentions are good, but this is not a situation you will be able to control. It is best to flee from it."

"What couldn't be good about it?" Jared typed. Cindi could almost hear the annoyance in the words. *"Don't you trust me?"*

Bingo! You got it, Cindi thought. *"I don't really know you, do I?"* she typed, wishing she could just end the connection. This conversation was giving her a headache. And she felt vaguely guilty and hoped no one would walk in on her.

"That's the point, isn't it? Look, I'll meet you in a public place. If I'm so awful you can just walk away. No strings. Come on, please. I really could use someone to talk to."

"Why don't you talk to your pastor?" Cindi typed, grasping at straws.

"I tried. He tells me to snap out of it. He lost his wife about ten years ago, but now he's happily remarried. I'll never get remarried. I'll never be that happy again."

"You're probably nowhere near me," Cindi typed desperately. Little warning bells were going off in her mind. Pastor Willis, *her* pastor, had lost his wife about ten years earlier and was remarried, to a lovely woman Cindi knew well. But, it just *couldn't* be!

Granted, Pastor Willis shepherded four churches within a fifty-mile radius, so it was possible Jared attended a different church but still had the same pastor. Still . . . it just *couldn't* be! It was too much of a coincidence.

"Coincidence nothing!" Ogel cackled, highly pleased with himself. "I planned this, and I left nothing to chance. Coincidence has nothing to do with anything. I'm in charge here." He puffed up a little at the thought of his own importance.

"I've got nothing to do, and I love long drives. Where are you located?"

"Near Chattanooga." It wasn't a lie. She was *near* Chattanooga.

"So am I!" came the excited reply.

Afterward, she could never be sure exactly how she had agreed to meet him. She just knew, with an increasingly sinking feeling, that she had. They were to meet at the end of the week at a little café they both knew. Russell had asked to take Esther for the afternoon, so she actually had some free time. She had planned to use it catching up on A Wing and a Prayer.

"I'll still be catching up on it," she said aloud. "I'll just be catching up on it in person." But, no matter how she looked at it, she still felt uncomfortable. "I can always cancel," she assured herself. "I'll pray about it, and if I still don't feel good about it I'll just cancel the next time I hear from him. He's bound to get in touch before then, and if he doesn't I have his email, so I'll just write and tell him I've changed my mind."

Feeling better, Cindi went to find Esther so they could get ready to leave. She'd wasted enough time. Her chores weren't going to do themselves. Before she knew it, it would be time to make supper and Marc would be home. "I'm late, I'm late," she sang like the White Rabbit.

"Cancel, Cindi, don't meet him," Shania urged. "Cancel now. Don't wait. The longer you delay, the less apt you will be to cancel at all. Do it now."

"It won't hurt at all to wait." Ogel was as pleased as punch with himself. His plan had worked out marvelously. All he had to do now was make sure that Cindi showed up when she was supposed to. There was no doubt in his mind that Jared would.

The man was desperate. Ogel had seen to that. No one in his life understood him at all. But Cindi would. Ogel was sure Cindi would. He was going to stack the deck on that score presently.

He was aware of a foul presence even fouler than his own, before he registered that another demon was beside him. It was Rafe. The two were acquainted, though they hadn't worked together in some time.

"You've done an admirable job," Rafe commended him. Ogel inclined his head, accepting the praise modestly. "But, you can leave this part of the operation to me now."

Ogel bristled. He didn't like being usurped. This whole situation had been his brainchild, and he wanted to be able to take all the credit when it succeeded, as it surely would. Besides, he reported only to Sparn. "What right do you have to barge in here and take over?" he demanded. "This operation is under the sole direction of Commander Sparn."

"It was. Now it's under my direction," Rafe rejoined smoothly. "Cindi is my charge."

"You don't seem to take your responsibility very seriously," Ogel sneered. "I've been around for days working on this project. Where have you been?"

"I've been in meetings. Secret meetings," he emphasized. "With Sparn. He's agreed that I should be the one working on this situation. You can step aside."

"I think not."

Ogel fully intended to hold his ground, but without warning Rafe seemed to swell in size and towered over him and Ogel jumped back, startled. A dagger raked the air where Ogel had seconds before been standing. Spittle foamed at the corners of Rafe's mouth, and there was an evil look in his eyes that Ogel had the sense to respect. He vanished without further comment. After all, Jared would need lots of looking after too. He had plenty to keep him occupied.

Shania followed Cindi as she rounded up Esther and got the little girl ready to leave. She sensed Cindi's troubled thoughts, but despite her pleas, could not convince Cindi to cancel the meeting. Praying fervently, she waited.

Prayer Warriors: the Final Chapter

Before he rejoined Jared, Ogel made one stop. He found Marc Trahan hunched over a stack of documents on his desk. Phone calls had kept him tied up all day—Ogel had seen to that as well. Now Marc tried to concentrate on the work in front of him as a deep weariness pervaded his body. He wanted like anything to go home and go to bed, but his work wouldn't do itself. Instead, he stood and stretched.

"Call her," Ogel suggested. "She won't mind if you're late. She knows you've got a lot to do. Besides, you're doing this for her. If you make enough extra money she'll be able to have the things she wants. It's all for her. She should appreciate your sacrifice enough to cut you some slack about working late."

Marc sighed. Then he reached yet again for the phone. "Cindi? It's me. I'm going to be a bit late tonight. I have a pile of papers to work on. I'm sorry. I'll be there as soon as I can. Give Essie a kiss for me."

His mission completed, Ogel went to find Jared. He didn't see Marc, twenty minutes later, lay his head down on his desk and fall fast asleep for forty-five minutes. If he had, he would have been even more satisfied with his day's work.

Cindi was sitting in a kitchen chair having a cup of tea when Marc finally came home. "I'm sorry," he mumbled. His eyes were bloodshot and his hair flattened at one side. His tie was askew and his suit rumpled. "Took longer than I expected. I'm going to bed." She stared at his back as he dragged up the stairs. Watching him, she felt tears prick the backs of her eyes, and the bridge of her nose stung.

Why was he pushing himself like this lately? For the last week he had hardly known she existed. Esther only saw him in the morning before he went to work, and that had never been Marc's prime time, even when he wasn't exhausted.

"He doesn't like you anymore," Rafe said. "You bore him. Work is more interesting than you. The people at work are more interesting too. They have real lives, not the sorry excuse for a life that you have. They actually leave their houses in the morning, and they read the newspapers. They make interesting conversation."

Was Marc bored with her? Cindi wondered. *Was he sick of hearing of nothing but Esther's achievements and her plans for Ethel's house? Was she driving him away from home?* The thought caught her in the solar plexus, and she winced. Then she got mad. Really, really mad.

Well, he's not exactly the most thrilling company either, she said to herself. *Either he's falling asleep at the table, conked out in front of the TV, or gassing endlessly with clients on the phone. Home is the place he comes for food and a clean bed. If Essie and I disappeared he probably wouldn't even notice.* At this thought she burst into tears.

"You said it, sister," Rafe hooted. "That's exactly what I've been telling you."

"Cindi, do not indulge negative thoughts," Shania pleaded. "Turn your concerns over to the Master. He will conform your thoughts into righteous thoughts that honor your husband and do not cause you harm. 'And do not be conformed to this world, but be transformed by the renewing of your mind, that you may prove what is that good and acceptable and perfect will of God.' "

But, for the first time in a long while, Cindi did not heed the angel's advice. She continued to cry, and her mind was a whirlwind of self-indulgence. She dredged up every fault of Marc's that she could, and by the time she dried her eyes she was convinced that she was very poorly done by indeed.

They called her Crazy Carol. Only a few of the older social workers knew that her real name was Carol Bennington. She'd been in the system so long that even the few who knew it never thought about it anymore. She was just Crazy Carol to everyone. Years earlier, as a rebellious teenager, she had fried her brain on drugs. You name it and she had tried it, and tried it once too often was the general consensus.

They attempted to get her into housing with supervision. They attempted to get her on medication. They attempted to get her into therapy. Nothing worked. She evaded the supervision and skipped out of the house, disappearing for months before turning up nearby.

The medication was mostly so they could feel useful. There wasn't anything that could truly help her condition. You couldn't manufacture brain cells. But it made her more co-operative. At least that's how the people in charge of such things viewed doping her up so that she was unable to take care of herself. But, Carol didn't want the medication. She palmed the pills and disappeared for so long, they gave up hunting for her.

The therapy was useless, or so the therapist had declared. Carol's attention span wasn't long enough to allow for discussion of any significant point. Before they could make progress, even really get grounded in a subject, she was off on another thought. And unfortunately, even her deepest thoughts didn't scratch the surface of reality.

Carol was a conundrum to them all, but no one knew what to do about her dog. The few times they had maneuvered her into managed care, the dog had been sent directly to the humane society. Everyone thought that would have been the end of it, but the unbelievably skinny monstrosity, something of a cross between an Irish wolfhound and a bouvier des Flandres (the vet guessed), was as good an escape artist as its mistress.

The first time it had bitten the handler and run off before they even got it checked in. The second time it stayed a week and then overpowered a kindly teenage volunteer who was trying to take it for a walk to get a little exercise. The unfortunate girl was dragged ten yards before she had the good sense to let go of the leash. Considering the dog was nearly as tall as she was, everyone agreed she was lucky to escape with some scrapes and bruises.

Very infrequently Carol and Come Here, her dog, would show up at a shelter. This usually happened when Carol was sick or they were especially hungry. This time Carol wasn't sick. Come Here was dying.

"Now . . . Carol," a shelter worker said, biting her tongue at the last instant to prevent the "Crazy" part from slipping out. "You know dogs aren't allowed at the shelter."

"Gotta get help, gotta get help, gotta, gotta," Carol sang back in her odd singsong voice. She stank terribly and was thinner than anyone remembered seeing her in the past. There was very little black left in her wild hair. A ski hat was clamped firmly onto her head, leaving long snarled hanks sticking out beneath, twisting off every which way. She was wearing every piece of clothing she owned, no matter how tattered, and some of the pieces were incredibly tattered. They flapped around her as she waved her arms, like the clothes of a scarecrow.

"What do you need, Carol?" the shelter worker asked gently.

"Come Here, Come Here, Come Here," sang Carol. The old dog raised its head at the sound of its name, but it stayed in a crouch by her feet, looking uncomfortable.

"Come here? Oh, is that your dog's name? Come Here? Is there something wrong with your dog, Carol?"

"Gotta get help, gotta get help, gotta, gotta," Carol muttered in reply.

"What's going on?" Jesse Redcloud was the supervisor on duty that evening. He was summoned by some frantic hand signals from the frustrated worker.

"I have no idea," said the worker. "I think there might be something wrong with the dog. I can't tell if she knows he can't be here or what. And if he's sick, I don't know what to do."

Jesse knelt down beside the dog and stroked its head. He'd had a lot of experience with these two. In fact, it was getting to know Carol that had gotten him interested in volunteering at the shelter a year earlier. "How are you, Come Here? You're not looking so good, old man. Has he been like this long, Carol?"

Carol looked down and nodded, tears in her eyes. "Long time, long time, good friend."

Jesse straightened. "Go ahead and check her in."

"But, what about the dog?" the worker protested.

"I'll take care of the dog." He turned to Carol. "Carol, I'm going to take Come Here to Doctor Gregory. You remember Doctor Gregory? He'll tell us if anything is wrong. OK?"

Carols' fingers tightened over the frayed string that was the only collar Come Here wore. "Going away, going away forever. We been friends too long. Goodbye, old friend." She knelt down by the dog and hugged it hard around the neck. The dog patiently endured her embrace, and Jesse had to brush away a tear. Carol seemed to sense what he himself expected. Come Here wouldn't be returning from the vet's.

Hours later, Jesse found Carol kneeling on top of her bedding in her room. In his hands was the frayed string that had been around Come Here's neck. "I'm sorry, Carol," he said, genuinely meaning it. "Doctor Gregory said it was a massive tumor. Come Here's kidneys had shut down. He was dying already. Doctor Gregory said he was suffering and the kindest thing we could do was to put him down immediately. He'll take care of burying him. There's a nice pet cemetery behind the vet clinic, you know. I asked him to put up a memorial. I'll bring you there in a couple days so you can see where he's buried. OK?"

He reached out and took one of Carol's tiny hands. It felt like the claw of a bird. "I'm truly sorry, Carol. Let me know if I can do anything."

Carol's jet-black eyes didn't betray her soul. One couldn't look into them to see what she was thinking. But they glittered with unshed tears, and Jesse was sure that Carol had understood what he'd said. Carol reached out and took the string, rubbing her fingers over it in a way that suggested she had done the same thing many times while its wearer had been alive.

No one, least of all Jesse, was surprised the next morning to find Carol gone. Her bed had not been slept in, and there was no other trace that she'd been there. Her solitary figure could be seen, tramping the roads, clothes flapping around her. She seemed incomplete and very, very vulnerable.

Toby O'Connell rubbed a gritty forearm across her gritty forehead and groaned. The sun was sinking rapidly in the west, and still there was no sign of Davy. He had flown Ray Vargas to the outposts hours earlier to service some of the clinics. They should have been back by now, no matter what the patient load. Davy knew that under no circumstances should he fly after dark, and he wouldn't stay overnight at one of the clinics unless it was a dire emergency.

Toby wasn't sure if she ought to be worried that there had been an emergency or that they were having trouble with the ultralight plane again. The flimsy little aircraft had been very unreliable lately. Davy, sick of patching it up, had made noises about getting a real bush plane. Together, they had just about enough money to buy one as long as Davy assembled it.

The decision would be easier, Toby sighed to herself, if she and Davy were married. He'd been making a lot of noises about that lately too. It had been about a year since he'd dropped back into her life. But, the trauma of their plane crash, which had left Davy without a memory, and the consequences of that—Davy's leaving her, the divorce, and her flight to Africa ending up here at the mission—had taken their toll. Toby herself had been on the brink of committing to another relationship when Davy showed up again, claiming to remember her and their previous life. Breaking off the other relationship had been hard. That it had been with her supervisor, Don Germaine, had made it very uncomfortable.

Don hadn't been back since he walked out. She heard, through Dorsey, the project coordinator at Operation C.A.R.E., the agency that ran the mission, that Don was doing well. Apparently, he was still helping Shay out with the kids. Toby had long since stopped wondering if there wasn't something more to that. She knew Don pretty well, and not very much would keep him from coming back to the mission. Except love.

She was glad for him, if that was the case. Both he and Shay had been through a lot. They would be good for each other. Occasionally she had a twinge of guilty conscience, or was it regret? But their interest in each other had been so brief that even the memory of it seemed more like a dream than something that had actually happened.

Toby tapped her watch impatiently. It was definitely getting dark now, and she was going to pass worry and grind into real panic soon. If Davy was just messing around and taking his time she was going to give him a good talking to. She focused on these thoughts. It was easier than imagining Davy and Ron mangled amid the ruins of the ultralight somewhere between her and the clinic. She and Davy had both survived their last plane crash, but she knew that was something that happened by the grace of God and once in a lifetime. Davy had used up his chances.

Just as she was about to turn to go inside, she heard the faint buzzing, like the drone of a very large insect. The darkness had deepened enough so that she couldn't make out the shape of the little plane. "Akueke! Get me a flashlight!" Toby bellowed, racing into the kitchen. The startled cook threw her the flashlight, a large utility type that they kept on the counter to cope with the frequent power outages.

Toby knew the lights of the compound would provide some markers for Davy to bring the plane in, but he wouldn't be able to figure out where the runway was. They had never equipped it with light of any kind. They had never needed it before.

She sprinted for the little dirt runway with a speed she didn't know she possessed. The droning had become louder, but she still couldn't see the little plane. She stood at the beginning of the runway, marking where he should begin his decent and began waving the flashlight in wide arcs above her head.

The droning seemed to go on forever before she made out the shape of the little plane, coming in low. The wings dipped in a wobble, Davy's trademark maneuver to show her that he had spotted her. She stood her ground even when the plane got close enough that she could see Davy angrily waving her out of the way. When she was sure he could really see the runway she threw herself flat on the ground, and the ultralight buzzed over her, touching the ground softly and bouncing a few times, before rolling to a gentle stop.

"Are you crazy?" Davy screamed, jumping down from the ultralight, followed more gingerly by a visibly shaken Ray Vargas. "You could have been killed!"

"*You* could have been killed!" Toby screamed back at him as she threw herself into his arms. "You scared me! Don't do that again!"

"You either," Davy murmured into her hair. He kissed her for a long time, and she forgot being worried.

"All right, you two, cut it out," a voice complained. "Can't a guy get any sympathy around here? I could have been killed too, you know."

Toby pulled away from Davy and faced Ray Vargas. "Go get your own sympathy," she teased. "But you'll have to go looking for it. I haven't seen Julia for a couple of hours."

"You mean she wasn't worried about me?" Ray whined jokingly.

"Oh, I'm sure she was," Toby said. "She just hides it better than I do."

"Yeah, yeah, I'm going to find my wife and get a little consolation." He moved off toward the compound, still looking a bit weak in the knees.

"You really shouldn't have done that, you know," Toby said, wrapping her arms around Davy's waist. "What if I hadn't heard you guys coming and come out with the flashlight?"

"I could see," Davy protested. "Really, not great, of course, but enough to land."

"A few minutes later and you wouldn't have been able to see your hand in front of your face, Davy, and you know it. Now, what happened? Why were you guys so late?"

Davy sighed. "Engine trouble, what else? By the time I got it fixed I knew it was really too late, but Ray and I decided we'd rather try to get back than to stay. There's something going on back at the clinics that I don't like, Toby."

"What kind of something?" They had started to amble toward the mission compound. Toby stopped and turned to Davy, searching his face. "Not another outbreak?"

"No, no, nothing like that," Davy said. "It's not an illness, not of the body anyway. It's more a feeling, really, a feeling of unrest or ingratitude or hostility or something. Whenever we go out there, I feel unwanted."

Toby snorted. "Oh, come on! How can you say that? People

line up for treatment. We're never lacking for patients. They want us; they have to. Without us, where would they be? Some of them are so sick they'd die. Are you telling me they hate us for making them well?"

Davy shook his head. "No, not that." He shrugged. "Maybe it's nothing. I just feel like they resent us, or maybe that they're scared of us. But you're right. Whatever it is, if it's anything at all, it doesn't stop them from coming."

If Davy had been able to see the cluster of demons around them at that very minute, he would have shaken with terror. The feeling, far from being in his imagination, was something they had been working on, under the supervision of Sparn and Lucien, for months. Only recently had they felt like they had begun to make enough headway to hope that things might be turning around.

They cackled and danced around Toby and Davy. Soon, soon their work would be rewarded. Soon the mission would fail. Lucien felt sure of it as he strode into their midst. But he wasn't about to let them feel it yet. "Break it up," he said brusquely. "Do you see any reason to celebrate here? No . . . someone didn't keep them out long enough. I want to know who is responsible."

Heads dropped and eyes slanted to the side. None of them would look directly at him. He swelled up considerably and they tensed, waiting for the barrage of abuse he was prepared to hurl at them. Before he let it rip, Festus, who seemed to sense that any scapegoat was better than no scapegoat at all, shoved a fellow demon out of line so hard he collided with Lucien.

Lucien's eyes narrowed as he looked at the unfortunate, who knew better than to even attempt to defend himself. No one in particular was responsible for letting Davy and Ray leave too early. It had just happened. Davy had been too quick to fix the engine, their subsequent attempts to stall the little craft in flight had failed, and they were unable to make the sun set any faster. Now, however, there was someone on whom to pin the blame. The demon froze, preparing to take the brunt of Lucien's anger.

Lucien pushed him away and, straightening up, he squinted at him along the bridge of his considerable nose. He was inordinately pleased to have found someone to fill a difficult position. "You, eh? And what's your name? I don't remember seeing you here before."

"Sarl, sir."

"Well, Sarl, I have a job for you."

Sarl gulped and tried to sidle back into the group, like a zebra trying to blend into the herd, to escape selection. "Yes, sir?"

Lucien rubbed his bony hands together. He certainly had a job. It was a nasty job with a high probability of failure, and if this miserable creature failed there would be someone to blame. "Come here, Sarl."

The demon slunk forward, accepting Lucien's arm around his shoulders, no doubt fervently wishing he could disappear or that Lucien had exploded and raked them with profanity instead. Anything would surely be preferable to being given a chance to mess up solo on a colossal scale. He was bright enough to realize that, should he fail, what was coming was infinitely worse than what he had temporarily avoided.

"This is what I want you to do . . ."

If Festus hoped to learn what Lucien's plan was, he was sorely disappointed, for the great leader moved beyond their hearing range to give directions to the hapless Sarl where he couldn't be overheard. Festus heaved a disgruntled sigh. Still, he was bound to find out sooner or later. In the meantime, he would just keep doing his job and trying to stay out of Lucien's way.

CHAPTER

When Deniece Daignault burst into Shay's house, the entire neighborhood could hear her. "Girl, where are you? Tell me everything! What did he say?"

Shay laughed and hugged her oldest friend. "When I called and said to come over when you got a chance, I didn't mean you should leave work early and break all land speed records to get here."

Deniece smoothed her hair back and adjusted her smart, peacock-blue suit. "Oh, I know, I know, but when you said 'proposed' I thought, Finally! And I just had to hear the details right away. In person," she elaborated.

"Want some sweet tea?" Shay asked.

"No, girl! I want details—give me details!"

Shay knew it was no use to put her off any longer. Deniece could be a bulldog when it came to the things she wanted. She poured two glasses of sweet tea anyway and sat down at the kitchen table to relate the whole story to her. To her credit, Deniece kept a mostly straight face, even through the part when Shay knocked Don over onto the floor. By the time Shay finished talking, Deniece had a sappy smile on her face. "Well, girl," she said with admiration. "Well, now. He doesn't have much finesse, I have to say, but, girl, that was a righteous proposal. I especially like the part about 'I love you with all my heart.' So sweet."

Shay grinned happily. "It *was* pretty sweet. Of course," she shifted uncomfortably, "the part I hate to have to tell you is that we're talking and praying about moving back."

Deniece groaned and swatted her on the arm. "I should have known we couldn't celebrate without a little sorrow." She sighed. "I was beginning to hope you'd changed your mind altogether. I thought you'd move back right away, but when you stayed I got my hopes up."

"I'm sorry," Shay said. "It's my fault we've stayed so long. I have been afraid to go back. You know, I never even put it into words before. Now, I don't know. I'm almost excited at the thought. The children miss it. America just isn't the same, though there are some things they'll miss." She laughed, thinking of Madina and her love of ice cream, and Marcus, who had developed an attraction to a television channel that was all about dogs. His highest hope was to have his own dog.

Deniece gave her a quick hug. "I'll miss you, girlfriend. It won't be the same here without you. There is one thing you could do for me before you go."

"What makes you so sure I'm going to go?" Shay asked archly.

Deniece rolled her eyes. "Oh, you'll go."

Shay giggled. "What do you want me to do for you?"

"You know the prayer walk I've been talking about?" For months Deniece's church had been planning a prayer walk through the French Quarter of New Orleans. "I want you to come with me."

Shay stiffened. A prayer walk was one thing, but through the French Quarter? Just being in the Quarter gave her the shivers. There was an almost palpable feeling of evil there. It wasn't the sight of Goths or even the voodoo paraphernalia displayed in shop windows. It was something more. Something you could feel. It almost pulsated through the air.

"Oh, I don't know, Deniece . . ."

"Come on, girl!" Deniece pleaded. "You said anything. Do this with me. Do this one last thing with me." She straightened up and fixed Shay with a fierce gaze. "Do I ask much? No. Am I a demanding person? No. Do you want to let your best friend walk through the French Quarter praying her heart out without you?"

"No," Shay answered for her, grinning in spite of herself.

" 'Greater is He who is in me than he who is in the world,' " Deniece quoted to her.

"Amen," Shay agreed.

Deniece would have been impressed if she could have seen how a blade of light flashed out of her mouth like a sword when she quoted the Word of God. Demons scattered in all directions, cursing and twisting out of the way. The angels in the room crowded in closer. The blade of the sword passed right through them without harm. From the outskirts of the room the demons shouted negative thoughts.

"You'll never change anything in the French Quarter," one yelled.

"If those people wanted to change, they would change without your help," another asserted.

"A prayer walk is a useless exercise," one taunted. "You'll never get anywhere walking around praying. Don't you see that? It takes a special kind of stupid to think you can change anything by walking around praying. Prayer is for sissies."

Howling with rage, they kept on edging ever closer. Even the sight of Shay and Deniece on their knees didn't stop them. But, every time either woman quoted Scripture they danced quickly away to avoid the sharp blade of light. Angels arrived by the hundreds and began to crowd the demons out of the room. Their voices grew weaker and weaker. Finally, the one who was in charge decided it was time to do something. He disappeared, hoping to find reinforcements nearby. Otherwise this would be one skirmish they would lose for sure.

Gaius moved in close to Shay. Though her lips moved in sync with Deniece's and she parroted the same sentiments as her friend, Gaius knew her heart wasn't in it. She didn't really want to go on the prayer walk. But there was a very good reason she should go, and Gaius knew that simply by being willing to be made willing Shay was putting herself in the Master's will and so would receive His blessing in her life. Her heart could be changed. The Master specialized in changing hearts, as long as someone was willing to receive a heart change.

"Every trial, every sacrifice, every suffering you endure, every blessing you enjoy, all these things make you the person the Master is molding," Gaius whispered. Shay tipped her head in his direction as if she were listening to his words, rather than feeling his thoughts. *"Each experience, no matter how mundane or scary or exciting it seems to you, has intrinsic and eternal value, if you'll but look at it with a teachable heart. You do not know what you may learn from the prayer walk. You have given the Master permission to teach you. That is what is most important. Remain open to His leading and you will never go wrong."*

This thought evidently pleased Shay because she smiled, and Gaius, who knew her well, saw the tension go out of her shoulders. She visibly relaxed, and he gave her an involuntary hug. *"I love you, little sister. God give you peace."*

"You know," she remarked to Deniece, "I think I'm looking forward to this prayer walk of yours after all."

Deniece laughed and gave her a kiss on the cheek. "It's not my prayer walk, girlfriend. It's His." She pointed one sleek, polished nail heavenwards. "I did it once before, you know."

"Did what?"

"A prayer walk."

"In the French Quarter?" Shay was aghast.

"No, no, around my neighborhood." Deniece's neighborhood wasn't too much safer or less evil in Shay's eyes than the Quarter was. "Now, listen, I'm going to take you to Les Histoires on Friday afternoon. We'll have crème brûlée and croissants. Then we'll take a little stroll around and just gather some first impressions, shall we? I've wanted to go poke around the Quarter for a while anyway. Are you game?"

Shay giggled. She hadn't felt this giddy since they were in the first grade making great plans for intrigues on the playground during recess. "OK, OK, but I have to make sure Don can watch Madina. I'm not bringing her there. But I'll meet you. I haven't had a good croissant in ages."

After Deniece was gone, Shay puttered around the kitchen for a while. As she picked up the glasses and plates they had used she thought about how much she would miss Deniece when they moved back to Africa. Suddenly she stopped short. Even she was beginning to do it, to think as though the decision had already been made.

"You trying to tell me something, Lord?" she asked out loud. Shaking her head, she wiped down the countertops and wondered if maybe it was the answer she'd been looking for.

Billie Jo was packing when the phone call came. She almost let the machine pick up, but she was afraid it might be the school calling about the children, so she left the box she was packing and raced for the phone. "Hello?" she managed a bit breathlessly.

"Is this Mrs. Raynard?" an unfamiliar voice asked.

"Yes, it is." Billie Jo picked bits of tape off her fingers, hoping this wasn't another telemarketer.

"My name is Christine Ager. My husband and I were driving down your road this past weekend, and we noticed the For Sale sign on your lawn. We're interested in looking at your house. Would that be possible?"

"Yes, ma'am," Billie Jo said, nearly holding her breath. They'd only just pounded the sign into the ground. It seemed awfully early to have anyone calling about it. She set up a time for Christine and her husband to come by and then replaced the phone. A thousand thoughts went through her head, all of them things that had to be accomplished before the Agers' visit.

When she told Jimmy about the call later that evening he was even more surprised than she had been. "Wonder when they saw the sign?" he asked. "I only put it out Saturday night, and it was prit near dark by then. Must have been sometime on Sunday." He scratched his head. "Funny thing 'bout that is, I don't remember anyone goin' by on Sunday." They lived at the end of a dirt road, so it was hard to miss any of the traffic, what little of it there was.

Billie Jo shrugged. It wasn't nearly as important to her when they saw the sign as it was that the house be in decent condition when they saw it. "Jimmy, they're coming tomorrow night. We got to clear a path through these boxes or there won't be anything for them to see."

Together they lifted and carried boxes, maneuvering them into large, precarious stacks. Dallas and Cassidy made secret hideaways in the nooks and crannies between and used them for secret club-houses where they wrote coded messages to each other. For the most part the children were excited about the move. Dallas was most concerned about losing friends. Cassidy had suffered a falling out with one of her girlfriends and subsequently endured the wrath of the girl's friends. She'd had a tough time over it and almost thought it would be a relief to start over somewhere new.

"Do you think the girls in Vermont will be nice?" she had asked Billie Jo one day after school as she sat up to the counter slicing an apple to have as a snack.

"I'm sure they're like girls everywhere, honey. There's bound to be some nice ones and some not so nice ones."

"I wonder if the nice ones will like me." Cassidy lapsed into silence for a little while and then asked abruptly, "Mom, do you think it would help to pray about it?"

Billie Jo's head snapped up. "What? About making friends?"

Cassidy's head shook a little. "No, not to make a friend, exactly, but to make a friend who loves Jesus and wants to follow Him."

Billie Jo swallowed hard. Never having been a popular girl in school herself, she felt her daughter's social problems even keener than Cassidy did. But her daughter wasn't as worried about being popular in her new school as she was concerned that she find a friend who loved her Lord. That just beat all.

"Sure, honey, we can pray for that."

They had bowed their heads right there in the kitchen over a pile of boxes, and ever since, Billie Jo couldn't pass a packing box without misting up. At least she didn't have to worry about losing any friends, she reflected wryly. She didn't have any left to lose. Her best friend, Leah, had moved away six months earlier. They still kept in touch on the computer and the phone and occasionally by mail. The rest of her friends had drifted away.

"Lord, do You think You can find me a friend up there in Vermont?" she asked under her breath as she loaded Dallas's baseball collection into a box. "I sure could use one right about now."

Jewel smiled at Billie Jo, but the smile was melancholy, and several of the angels around him thought it remarkable. No one asked him about it though, not when they saw the golden tears slipping down his smooth cheeks. Not one had enough courage to find out what could make him cry.

Cindi Trahan was feeling desperate. She had tried to email Jared to cancel their meeting. By Wednesday she'd become convinced it was not a good thing to do, but when she tried to cancel, she received no reply. Now she didn't know what to do. Had he received the message and simply not answered? Had he not received the message? She didn't want to be rude and leave him waiting for her. It wasn't her style. He'd been hurt enough already.

By Friday she had resigned herself to the fact that she'd have to make the trip into Chattanooga and meet him just to tell him that she wasn't going to meet him. It seemed a senseless waste of time and a confrontation she'd much rather avoid, but she couldn't see any way around it. She had no contact information for him besides his email address. She hadn't been able to find a listing for him in the phone book and didn't even know where he lived. And when she thought about those facts she nearly talked herself out of meeting him at all.

But I can't do that, she reminded herself again in the car as she drove slowly and carefully to the little café where they'd agreed to meet. *It would be rude, and I'm not rude.* She winced. *I just wish I were a little more sensible sometimes.*

The scenery was lost on her. The green of the grass, the smell of honeysuckle, even the blue sky filled with picture-postcard fluffy clouds—none of it made an impression on her. It was cool for the season in Tennessee, and she drove with the window down, not even enjoying the feeling of the wind blowing her hair. She'd left Esther with Russell amid severe pangs of conscience, and they hadn't subsided at all.

"Aw, the little brat can do without you for a few hours," Ogel assured her as he rode shotgun by her side in the car. "I've worked long and hard on this scheme. I intend to reap a handsome reward for your disloyalty. Go faster already," he muttered impatiently.

Ogel's day had been very busy. He had already managed to get Jared out the door, talking him through his last- minute nerves. Now here he was, holding Cindi's hand. Rafe, despite all his threats, was nowhere to be found. Ogel suspected that, like most demons in positions of authority, he was sure of success and content to sit back and soak up the glory while others did the actual work.

"Go back," Shania urged. "There are other ways to help this man. The potential for danger is too great."

"Shut up!" Ogel screamed. He swiped at the angel with a clenched fist, hoping to deliver a good smack. "Don't make me get ugly."

The angel paid him no heed, but she stayed out of range of his flying fist too. "She's not listening to you anyway," he mocked. "Save your breath. It'll be the only thing you save today."

Cindi, to her surprise, felt angry. She didn't know who she was angry with, herself, for agreeing to meet him, or Jared, for pressing her. Maybe it was a little bit of both. She pulled up in front of the café and was dismayed to find that the parking lot was nearly deserted. She parked as close to the door as she could. "In case I need to make a quick getaway," she said and laughed nervously to herself.

Checking her hair once more in the mirror and then kicking herself mentally for caring what it looked like in the first place, she got out of the car, slamming the door harder than was absolutely necessary. Gravel crunched under her feet as she made her way across the parking lot. Mentally, she rehearsed what she was going to say. *"I'm sorry, Jared, I tried to reach you. I'm not comfortable with this. I can't stay. Please forgive me."* She said it over and over in her head to be sure she wouldn't trip on the words when they came out of her mouth.

The café looked very urban, with signs for all the latest designer coffees and banks of fancy pastries behind glass. Cindi didn't give them more than a glance. Her eyes swept the interior. A pair of strangely dressed teenagers was playing chess at one table. An elderly woman was eating a pastry and drinking something hot at another. The only other occupied table held a single man. He stared at her intently.

He stood up as she came to the table, and she could see that he was not overly tall, but couldn't be described as short; he was muscular but not stocky. He had dark brown hair shaved in a crew cut, frank blue eyes, and a lopsided grin that was charming. His face was weathered, as if he spent a lot of time outdoors, but it was a pleasant, open face. He offered his hand almost apologetically.

"Are you Cindi?"

His grip was solid, and he shook her hand briefly before releasing it. She found herself dropping into a chair opposite him, somewhat deflated, trying to remember exactly what it was she had intended to say. "Yes," she said finally, almost stuttering, "yes, I'm Cindi . . . Jared?"

He nodded, and they both laughed a little stiffly. Cindi had no idea what exactly she'd been expecting—maybe a smooth-looking hustler. But whatever image she had tricked up in her mind, it wasn't the reality of Jared. He looked for all the world like a big, grown-up boy.

"Not so bad, now that you see him in the flesh, is he?" Ogel chortled. *"Not the least bit scary either. In fact, I'd almost say he looked like any responsible, upright citizen, wouldn't you?"*

"His looks have nothing to do with anything," Shania whispered urgently. *"This is all wrong. Cindi, I implore you to leave immediately. The longer you tarry, the harder it will be."*

He was watching her expectantly. "Go ahead, you first," he urged.

Cindi laughed outright. "Well, I was just going to say that I came here only to tell you I couldn't come. I tried to email you but you didn't respond."

His face fell. "I'm sorry. My computer crashed for good the other day, and I haven't been able to get it working since. I think I'm going to have to break down and buy a new one." He searched her face. "You were going to cancel?"

Cindi swallowed hard and felt sympathy course through her. "Yes, well, I got nervous, and I thought this wasn't such a good idea." Her voice trailed off weakly. Now that she was actually there, it seemed to be nothing improper at all.

Jared grinned sheepishly. "I can't say I haven't had second thoughts myself."

"Really?" Somehow, his admission made her relax inside.

He licked his lips. "This isn't exactly easy for me. I'm not a great people person. After Krissy died I realized that I didn't even have any real friends. They were all *her* friends, and after she was gone there was no one." Jared ran a hand through his short hair, bristling it so that it stood even more on end. "The guys on the force were really good to me, ya know? But, I couldn't concentrate at work, and finally my chief told me to take some time off."

"So . . . you were let go? That's not right!" She was indignant for him.

"Not let go, exactly. I'm on a leave of absence. But, let's face it, in my line of work it's life and death. None of the guys wanted me responsible for their lives. The chief made a good call, even if it pains me to say it. Work was about the only thing that helped to take my mind off my problems. But if I can't keep my mind off my problems I won't have any work. I don't know what I'll do."

"What kind of work are you in?"

Before he could answer a waitress in black boot-cut pants and a starched white shirt interrupted them. Her hair was pulled back in a severe bun. She held a pad of paper in one hand with a pencil poised over it. She stared over the top of a pair of heavy, black retro glasses and down the length of her nose at them. "What can I get you?"

Cindi looked to Jared for support. She hadn't even intended on staying, to say nothing about actually ordering something. She was completely at a loss. Jared, however, commanded the situation smoothly. "Bring us a couple Lime Rickeys, please."

"Right. Anything to eat?"

Jared raised one eyebrow, but Cindi shook her head imperceptibly. "No, that'll be all. Thanks."

When she'd gone, Cindi leaned towards him and hissed, "What on earth is a Lime Rickey?"

"It's an Italian soda. You'll love it, trust me."

"So," she asked again, "what is it that you do for work?"

"I'm a dive instructor and special response diver on the police force." He was so matter-of-fact about it that it took a few minutes for the full impact to hit her.

"You mean, you're one of those guys who goes searching for, uh, bodies?" She couldn't think of a more tactful way to put it.

"Yes, that's part of what I do. We also do underwater crime scene processing and photography and video in addition to search and recovery. Does that bother you?"

Cindi swallowed hard and shook her head. "No, no, of course not. It's just that I had no idea you were a police officer." The truth was, and she would never admit it to him, she felt much safer. Jared was a police officer. Now her earlier panicked imaginings that she might have to call on the police to protect her from him seemed so ludicrous that she could have laughed and was only saved by the arrival of their sodas.

She swallowed hard and nearly choked on the bubbles. Jared sipped his soda and watched her. She waited, but he didn't say anything. "What?" she asked finally.

He grinned his lopsided grin. It didn't quite make it up to his eyes and erase the sadness that haunted them, but it broke the ice. "Nothing, it's nothing. Only, you're not at all how I imagined you."

"Oh? Well, you're not exactly what sprang to mind either," she said with a giggle. "I expected some tall, bookish type, maybe with dark hair, a mysterious air, and a family title buried in his background. A marquis perhaps, or a count. I knew a count once. The Count of Peregrine. He was a very bouncy, bald bank manager."

"Nah, the only title I'm ever likely to have is that of the loneliest man in the world." He arranged his face in careful lines, guarded, but at the same time Cindi could see the pain etched on every line. "Not very attractive, is it?" he asked ruefully. "Krissy, my wife, used to say that I had too much optimism. And when she got sick I was just so sure that she would get well. I even had her believing it. I'm not sure I hadn't half convinced the doctors too.

"But optimism isn't enough to cure cancer. I know medical science can't prove me out, but I'm positive that believing she'd get well gained her some time. I think she would have died sooner if she hadn't believed that." He stopped to dash his hand across his eyes. "I miss her. I guess I'll always miss her. What really frightens me is that Krissy believed in God. I know she'll be in heaven someday. And I won't be."

"Of course you will!" Cindi exclaimed involuntarily. She was deeply touched by Jared's suffering and wished she could do something, anything, to relieve it.

"No, you don't understand. I made a deal with God. I told Him that if He didn't make her live, I wouldn't believe in Him anymore. What good is a God who would let someone as sweet as Krissy die? Like *that*?" His voice grew angry, and they drew a few curious stares from other patrons. Cindi could see he was holding himself strongly in check and that the effort appeared to be a strain. "It is unspeakably painful to watch someone die of pancreatic cancer. You just can't imagine."

Cindi reached across the table and took his hand. "Jared, listen to me. God loved Krissy very much. Just because He allowed her to die does not mean that He doesn't exist. God isn't responsible for the evil in this world. Satan is."

Jared jerked his hand from her grasp. "Look, I know you believe that, but I just can't see it anymore. Can you understand that?"

Cindi nodded. "Yes, I can understand that. But I don't agree with you."

"You don't have to," Jared allowed. "You weren't there. You don't know how it was."

"You're right," Cindi admitted. "I don't. I wasn't there. But, Jared, I am a home health nurse. I have had terminal patients before. I'm not a stranger to sickness. Neither do I believe that God causes people to get sick or snatches our loved ones away from us on a whim. The God I know cares for us and has a much greater plan than life here on this old earth for each one of us."

Jared stood up suddenly. "I'm sorry. Maybe this was a mistake. I thought I needed to talk to someone, but I think I'm going to lose it. I'm sorry, I'm sorry . . ." Before Cindi could open her mouth, he flung some money onto the table and stormed out of the café. He was in his car and peeling out of the parking lot before she could recover her senses enough to stand up on shaking legs. She sat back down quickly.

"Dear God," she breathed, "please be with Jared right now. Help him to see a clear picture of You. Wipe away the distortions. Reveal Yourself to him."

Jared had paid no attention to Ogel's curses and threats, and now the demon ranted to no one in particular. "I worked like a dog to get you this gig, and look what you did! She'll hate you now. And if nothing else, she'll be terrified of you. What a pathetic display! I've never seen anything so pitiful in my life. What kind of a man are you?" His tirade carried on long after Cindi left, subdued and saddened.

Cindi drove carefully home, blinded by tears and aching for the pain of a man she barely knew.

CHAPTER 4

Shay shivered as she walked down the side of Jackson Park to get to Les Histoires café. Some small boys were posing as statues for money, and when she didn't drop anything in the hat they cursed her. She was still shaken up from passing the gauntlet of donkey carriages whose drivers tried to hustle her and insulted her when she refused a ride. Merchants, some painting, some telling fortunes, some selling souvenirs, tried to catch her eye, but she kept her gaze riveted on the sidewalk. No matter how many times she had come to the Quarter there were some parts of it she'd never get used to.

Outside Les Histoires a crowd had gathered, and Shay slowed her steps, approaching cautiously. A man dressed in clothes that could have been salvaged from a vaudeville show was holding an animal that had once been alive but was now stuffed and fashioned into a marionette. The crowd was laughing at something the man was saying, but Shay couldn't hear him. She tried to skirt the crowd to reach the door, and as she did she noticed another man edging closer to her. She didn't know if he was with the performer, but something in his eyes made her panic and she bolted for the door, wrenching it open and throwing herself inside. When she looked out again he was watching her through the large plate-glass windows of the café.

"Shay! Over here!" Deniece was waving her over. "What's wrong, girlfriend? You look like you've seen a ghost."

"There's no such thing as ghosts," Shay said automatically. "Just manifestations of Satan, and I think I saw lots of those. This place creeps me out." She set her purse down at her feet, leaned against the table, and tried to calm down.

Deniece looked around. "What's creepy about here? Did the croissants spook you?"

"No, it's that guy out there." She pointed out the window. The same man was keeping an eye on her.

Deniece sobered up quickly. "What happened?"

Shay told her the story as they ordered. "It seems to get rougher here each time I come. I can't walk down the street without guys hitting on me. It's like they feel it's their duty."

Deniece sighed. "I know. I don't feel altogether safe here any-more either. So many of these people, like him out there," she jerked her head towards the window where the man was still keep-ing one eye on Shay, "are lost. That's why it's so important to lay down Scripture here. God is the only One who can cut through this darkness."

Shay sipped her tea and nodded. "You're right. You know I'm scared to do this prayer walk, but I think it's important. Don agrees with me, but he says when we do it he wants to come. Marcus can look after Madina while we go." She laughed. "I had a hard enough time getting him to let me come alone today, and before I was two blocks away I wished I hadn't argued so hard. I would have felt a lot better if he'd been with me."

After they had finished eating, Shay glanced out the window, looking for the man who had followed her. He seemed to be gone, but it was hard to tell since the crowd was still milling around outside the door. "Do you think it's safe?"

"Safe as it's going to be," Deniece said. "Let's go."

Linking arms they made their way out of the café and headed out the door, turning right. Shay was holding her breath and praying. Every muscle in her body felt tense as she forced her-self along. Before they had gone ten paces they heard a voice behind them.

"Ladies!"

"Oh no," Shay heard Deniece say under her breath. "Dear Lord, please keep us safe!"

"Ladies! Ladies!"

Shay felt herself stiffen, waiting for the strong hand on the shoulder that she was sure was coming. "Keep walking," she hissed.

"Ladies!"

The voice didn't seem to be getting any closer. A sudden whir of tires startled Shay as a man on a bike passed them. "Hey, yo, there's a man back there with a purse," he said.

Shay reached for where her purse should be hanging and found nothing. "My purse!" She whirled around. A man in red tennis shoes was holding her purse out to her and looking rather exasperated. He was one of the waiters. "I'm sorry," she called. "You found my purse; thank you so much!"

"You left it under the table," he said, looking at her curiously. *Probably wondering if she was deaf,* Shay mused ruefully.

"Thank you so much! So much!" She took the purse from him, and he returned her smile, a bit hesitantly, showing bright gold teeth.

"You're welcome. Guess you didn't hear me calling you."

"Thank you," Shay said again, too embarrassed to tell him what they had thought.

When she got back to Deniece her knees were shaking, and she had to walk slowly. "I was praying so hard," Deniece said. "I thought he was coming after us for sure."

"Me too," Shay said. She rifled through her purse quickly. "It's all here."

"God was watching over you, girl."

"I know. Imagine if we hadn't turned around."

They passed the Beauregard-Keyes house and kept on walking, even though they were headed out of the Quarter. It was as if by unspoken agreement they had decided to avoid the crowded commercial district. They didn't pass many stores, but there was plenty of architecture to admire. Shay had a feeling Deniece was waiting for her to say something so finally she said it.

"I don't know if I can go through with it."

Deniece stopped in front of the entrance to Le Richelieu hotel and turned to face her directly. "Are you talking about the prayer walk? Why?"

Shay shifted from one foot to the other. She stepped aside to let a customer into the hotel. They regarded her curiously, and she lowered her voice self-consciously. "I'm just not sure I can do it, that's all. I'm scared, if you want to know the truth."

Deniece snorted. "No, lie to me, girlfriend," she said facetiously. "Of course I want to know the truth. But I want to tell you something too. It wasn't Satan that won today, was it?"

Shay shook her head. "No. No, it wasn't."

"No, that's right. It wasn't. Because Satan has already lost this battle. The victory belongs to God, and He isn't afraid of Satan and his little minions. The French Quarter doesn't scare God, Shay. And it shouldn't scare us either. We got a greater force inside us than anything this old Quarter can throw at us. And you'd do well to remember that, considering where you're going."

Shay felt the tears in her eyes. Deniece was right, of course, and she couldn't figure out what she'd ever do without her friend by her side. Shay realized that she relied on Deniece much more than the other girl knew. She'd known since the accident that she'd allowed fear to grow in her heart. Before the accident she had been fearless. After the accident she'd been paralyzed with fear. She expected it to go away, dissolve, disappear. But it hadn't happened. She was still afraid, astonishingly, desperately afraid.

Her close brush with death had made her so aware of her fragile hold on life that she was terrified of losing it. It wasn't that she was scared to die. Maybe a little frightened of the actual physical process, the pain of it, but not of being dead. No, what she was afraid of was letting people down. And she didn't want to miss out on life. She wanted to see her children get married. She wanted to enjoy the love she'd found with Don.

"Don't listen to her!" Jezeel warned. "She's on a crusade, that one. She doesn't know what she's talking about. There are dark forces at work here. You'd be well advised to remember that.

We are many, and we are strong. Do you really want to put your faith in Someone you can't even see? If your God is so powerful, how come He didn't save your baby? You could be next."

"Little sister, abandon this fear you harbor," Gaius's voice was urgent. "Give it to the Master. He will vanquish it for you. He is so much stronger than all your fears."

"You're right," Shay admitted. "I've got to let this go. That's all."

Impulsively Deniece hugged her. "Lord, I thank You for my friend. I claim her in Your name. Cast out her fear and fill her with Your perfect love. Help her be strong and to claim Your promises boldly. In the name of Jesus who saved us all, amen."

Shouts went up as angels came from far and near to surround the two women. Demons struggled to get out of their path and beat a hasty retreat at the same time. They watched with disgust from a safe distance. The light was blinding, and they shielded their faces.

They remembered that light from their long-ago days in heaven. At that time it had been warm, bathing them in comfort and love. Now it stung their eyes and twisted inside them. They could not face it so they hid in the dark places. They would wait until it was safe to come out once more.

Toby O'Connell thought, not for the first time, that she would be much happier if Don Germaine would quit messing around on leave and get back to the mission and make her life easier. She wasn't cut out for leadership; she realized that now. She could be fiercely opinionated at times, and some people would even say bossy, but that wasn't the same thing at all. It was much harder to make assignments and run things and keep an eye on people to be sure they were doing what they were supposed to be doing than to know how they should be doing it. She longed for the simple freedom of following orders, as contradictory as that might seem.

"Toby?" It was Julia Vargas. She was a capable girl, and Toby knew what a sacrifice it was for her to stay in Africa. She had once confessed to Toby, "It's not at all what I expected. I didn't know we had to sift the bugs out of the flour before we could make our bread. I have a problem with bugs, and not just all the ones I'm allergic to."

Toby pasted a smile on her face and turned to face Julia, but found she was totally unprepared for the shock. Julia was covered in blood. Davy supported her on one side and Toby rushed to prop her up on the other. "Julia! What on earth happened?"

"We went out to take care of one of the outpost clinics, that's what happened to her," Davy said, his voice trembling with emotion. "I left her for a few minutes to do some work on the ultralight, and a man came into the clinic swinging a club and shouting something about death to the white devils. He beat her up pretty good.

"When I heard her scream I came running, but by then it was too late. He dropped the club when he saw me and ran off. I didn't even get a good look at him. We left right away; I didn't know what else to do. She's going to be all right, isn't she?"

Julia's lips quivered as she tried to smile. She winced. "I think he might have cracked some ribs, and I know my lip is split. And my head is throbbing."

"Come on, let's get her to the surgery," Toby said. "I'll have to examine her, and if her ribs are broken they'll need to be taped." The final diagnosis was that Julia had three cracked ribs, some bruises, a split lip, and a laceration on her scalp that had caused most of the blood and was deep enough to require stitches.

"I can't believe anyone we've helped would have done this to her," Ray said as he sat by his wife's bed and held her hand. Julia looked fragile and forlorn as she lay among the white sheets. Akueke had insisted on fresh sheets and had clucked to herself as she made up the bed, her lip pursed down into an uncharacteristic frown.

Davy shook his head. "I don't know. Maybe it isn't someone who has been treated, but I still feel something is wrong out there. It just doesn't feel right, like we're not welcome anymore."

Toby eyed him thoughtfully. "And now you think you've got proof for your suspicions?"

"What do you think?" Davy asked, tipping his head toward Julia. "Isn't that proof enough?"

"Julia, what did the man say to you? Do you remember?"

Julia's brow furrowed in concentration. "He came into the clinic while I was bandaging a woman's arm. She had a sprain. I asked him to take his place in line, but he said something in French. I *think* he said something about death. The word *mort,* that means death in French, doesn't it?" She sighed. "I wish my French was better."

Toby's French wasn't much better than Julia's, but she recognized *mort.*

"Then he called me a *diable blanc,*" Julia continued. "That's 'white devil,' I think, and started hitting me." She turned her face toward Toby. "Do you think he meant to kill me?"

Toby hesitated. She put her hand softly on Julia's arm. "I honestly don't know. It would be pure speculation on my part. But I think from now on you should stick close to home. Davy and I will see to the outpost clinics."

Davy looked as though he was going to blow a gasket, but she silenced him with a fierce look that Julia and Ray didn't intercept. "We'd better be letting you get some rest," Toby said. "You're safe now, Julia. Try and sleep."

In the hall, Davy grabbed her by the arm and yanked her along until they were completely out of earshot. "What was that all about back there?" he said with a furious jerk of his head back in the direction they had come. "What do you mean, 'Davy and I will take care of the outpost clinics'?"

Toby rolled her eyes at him. "Come on, Davy. Don't tell me that spooked you?"

"Spooked me? It scared the snot out of me! There's no way you'll get me to bring you out there. Not for a long time." He glared at her. "And that's final."

Toby shrugged. "If you say so, but I really think it would be safer with two people. I was kind of depending on your protection. But if you are afraid to come with me, I'll go alone."

If the situation hadn't been so dire, Toby would have laughed at the stunned expression on Davy's face. "You can't mean that!" He took her by the shoulders and gave her a little shake. "Toby, listen to me. I can't bear the thought of some goon playing the marimba on your head with a club. I have thanked God over and over since this afternoon that He spared Julia. If I hadn't gotten there when I did, who knows what might have happened. Maybe that guy *would* have killed her. He was serious enough, I know that."

Toby released herself gently from his grasp. "Davy, I'm not looking to get killed. But the reason we're here is to help these people. How can we help them if we let the first madman scare us off? Won't Satan have won if we do that? What's the point of being here if we scare so easily?"

Davy had that stubborn look on his face that she knew meant a long, knock-down, drag-out fight. "You're not going."

"Not right now." Toby tried to keep her voice light. There was no sense in provoking him.

"You're not going," Davy repeated mulishly.

"Davy, we're tired. We've had a long, frightening day. Let's sleep on this, shall we?" She smiled at him and even worked up enough nerve to reach up on tiptoes and give him a kiss. His cheek was dirty and rough with stubble. Up close she noticed lines on his face that seemed to have appeared overnight.

She wrapped her arms around him and laid her head on his chest. She could feel his resolve in every rigid muscle, but with a groan he relaxed and crushed her against him. His fingers tangled in her hair, and he held her so tightly she could hardly breathe.

"I'm scared," he whispered. "I haven't been this scared since I realized our plane was going down. I didn't think I could be this scared ever again."

"God will protect us," Toby said, knowing He could, wondering if He would.

"Where was God today, huh?" Davy asked.

"Julia's alive, isn't she?" Toby reminded him. "That's where God was today. He was busy making sure you got there in time to save her from any further harm."

Davy's embrace tightened. "I want to save you from any harm at all. How am I going to do that?"

"With God's help, Davy, with God's help." Arm in arm they meandered to the kitchen for some warm goat's milk before making their way to their separate rooms. Toby couldn't help wishing that she didn't have to go to bed alone that night. Despite her brave words, she was scared inside. She wasn't sure she'd be able, when push came to shove, to follow through without Davy. She just didn't think she had it in her.

Outside the compound a very different meeting was taking place. It was nothing like the quiet, supportive rallying around Julia's bedside. Sparn had taken a personal interest in the attack at the outpost clinic, expecting great results, and he had been sorely disappointed. There had been blood but not death. He would be satisfied with nothing less than death.

Lucien knew that in part it was his own fault, but it was too late to correct now. He should have taken matters into his own hands rather than leave such an important task to inferiors. He had given the job to Sarl, thinking this attack would pave the way for others. What he didn't realize was that Sparn would think it was *the attack. Now he had to come up with something better. And quick.*

"I want the one responsible for this travesty," Sparn snarled.

Lucien thought fast. He could let Sarl take the fall. That was what he planned to do in any case, but that was before Sparn become so interested in the proceedings. Now he decided to turn the demon's error to their advantage instead. "My lord," he said smoothly, flattering Sparn with the title though he nearly choked on it, "this was just a little demonstration. We were merely warming up, toying with them, as a cat toys with a mouse it intends to destroy."

Lucien could see he'd have to talk pretty fast to convince Sparn the day had been anything but the worst kind of blunder. "We want them to fear us."

"But you put them on their guard," Sparn growled doubtfully.

"Surely not," Lucien protested. "You know the weakness of the woman called Toby. She relies too much on her own strength. But she is no match for us." He rubbed his hands together gleefully. "You'll see, my lord Sparn. The next time she ventures out of the clinic she will expect something bad to befall her, but we will wait. We will wait until she feels safe again. That is when we will strike.

"She is in charge here. There is no stubborn doctor to contend with. We will kill this woman, and the rest will go home. We have scared the others enough. Have you not noticed?" he said, spreading his arms wide around him. "There has been a subtle change here. Prayer cover has diminished. You see there are fewer angels to contend with?"

It was true, and Lucien knew that Sparn would immediately recognize that it was the result of Sparn's brilliant work with the new prayer warrior in the United States. Sparn's own minions had occupied her mind with other things, and her prayers had faltered. If she continued on her present course, soon they would dry up altogether.

A slow, evil smile crossed Sparn's lips, and Lucien knew he was imagining in great detail what he envisioned as the end of the mission. Finally they would be free of this thorn in their side. And if Lucien should happen to get a promotion to anywhere but this dustbowl, it would all be worth it.

Don was fixing supper for Shay and the children when the fax came in from Operation C.A.R.E. He didn't stop to read it until they were finished eating and Marcus was clearing the table. Madina brought the flimsy piece of paper to him.

He fully expected that it would be a field report listing the number of people treated and what they had been treated for. Possibly there would be a list of supplies needed. So when he read the actual curt message, it took a few minutes before he grasped what the fax said. He sat for so long staring at it numbly that Shay finally noticed and came to read it over his shoulder.

"Don, thought you should know that Julia Vargas was attacked today at an outpost clinic. We need to talk about security. Call me as soon as possible. Dorsey," she read aloud and then said, "That's awful! Poor Julia. I wish he said how she was doing." She put a hand on Don's shoulder and squeezed sympathetically.

"I'd better go call him," he said. Getting the whole story from Dorsey didn't help much. He had few details to share. But one thing he said shook Don up. In the field notes Davy had written a brief comment about the atmosphere at the outposts being somewhat frigid, whatever that meant. Dorsey didn't really know, and he hadn't been able to reach the mission either. Some of their equipment was down. They had managed to send the fax and that was all. Subsequent faxes requesting information had not been answered.

"I should be there," Don said. In his heart he felt it strongly.

Dorsey sighed heavily. "Look, I didn't tell you this to guilt you into going back. Your furlough is long overdue. What I need to know from you is what you think about security measures."

"Security measures? What are you going to do? Get them some flying German Shepherds?"

"People, Don, I mean people."

"Technicals?" he asked, using the slang word they had for security personnel. "How are they going to help? Do you have any who can fly? Because that's what you'd need. That rattletrap they fly around to those outpost clinics only holds two people, and I'm being generous with that statement. One person in that thing seems like too many. How do you expect them to take along a technical?"

Dorsey sounded exasperated. "I don't know, Don, that's why I'm asking you. What do you think we should do?"

Don ran a hand through his thick curly hair. "I don't know, I don't know. I can hardly think, I'm so upset. Why don't you give me some time to see if I can come up with a solution. I'll call you back."

Shay came into the library, where he sat cradling the phone against his shoulder though he had ended the call. She rubbed his shoulders. "I think it's time to go back," she said softly.

Don was instantly flooded with such a sense of relief that he nearly cried. "Do you mean that?"

"Yes, I do. I've been feeling that God is telling me we should. What do you feel?"

He knew she was only asking to be polite. He had been itching to get back since the day he left. As far as he was concerned, God had told him years ago to go to Africa and had never changed his marching orders. "I think we should, yes. God sure hasn't told me we shouldn't."

"When do you want to leave?"

"How quick can you pack?"

She shook him playfully. "Don't you want to get married first?"

Married! Yes, there was that. "I guess we should, huh?"

"Don Germaine," she cried in mock surprise, "don't tell me you've changed your mind already!"

He grabbed her hands and pulled her around to sit on his lap. "No, I haven't changed my mind, woman. Let's get married tonight."

"What? You *are* crazy!" She laughed happily.

"Yeah, but you knew that when you agreed to marry me. Why can't it be tonight?" He felt a little dizzy, but held his ground. He was perfectly prepared to get married that very evening. At least, he was pretty sure of it.

"But what about my dress? What about Deniece? She has to be my maid of honor. I promised her."

"I like your cream-colored dress, and I'll call Deniece right now." He made a move to dial the phone, but she stopped him. Her eyes were serious as she looked at him, and he found he couldn't look away.

"I'll marry you tonight. I'll marry you anytime you say. But

I want to know. Are you really sure you want to do this?"

Don took her face in his hands and pulled it close to his. Her lips were soft, and she smelled of jasmine. "Yes, I want to marry you. Tonight. This very minute. As soon as possible."

"And you're not just doing this so we can rush off to Africa?"

He laughed. "No, my dear. We could rush off to Africa anyway. But you want to get married here, remember?"

She smiled. "Right. OK, call Deniece."

He was pretty sure Shay could hear Deniece's shriek of happiness even though she'd already gone into the next room to change.

It was nothing even remotely close to the scream Deniece let out when she burst in the front door twenty minutes later. She was wearing a smart royal-blue silk suit and the most adorable hat Don had seen on anyone besides Jackie Kennedy. A large, billowy garment bag was draped over one arm, and she swept into the room like a cruise ship setting sail.

"Where is she?"

Don pointed, and Deniece disappeared into the bedroom, where Shay claimed she was trying to do something with her hair. It looked perfect to Don already, but all he got for saying so was a look that could melt steel.

He was glad that Deniece had arrived. He was a bundle of nerves and hardly knew what to do with himself, so he decided to try and dress Madina in something fancy. He'd been surprised how quickly Marcus had gotten dressed into his only suit. He sat, shiny as a new penny, at the kitchen table. Madina was another matter.

The little girl eyed him doubtfully as he went through her closet trying to locate an appropriate dress. "I don't like dresses," she told him flatly. "I want to wear jeans."

"No, no, honey, this is a special occasion. You need to get all dressed up pretty for Mommy. She'll be so proud of you."

She held out stubbornly. "I want to wear jeans."

Don decided to ignore her and concentrate on more pressing matters. He held up two dresses. Either would be suitable, but it would take a smarter man than he to figure out which would be better. Finally, he decided on the cream lace. It was a fancy little thing and looked wedding-ish.

It took three tries to get it on straight. While she glowered at him, he regarded her legs quizzically. There seemed to be something missing. Yes, shoes! That was it.

"Mommy always puts my tights on," Madina insisted accusingly as he tried to wiggle her feet into her dress shoes.

Don felt like smacking his forehead. "Of course! Tights!"

By the time she was dressed, and still none too happy about it, sweat was dripping down Don's face. "Marcus, I need to go next door and take a shower and get dressed. Would you keep an eye on Madina for me? Oh, and the pastor should be here soon. If your mom isn't out of the bedroom yet with Aunt Deniece, could you let him in? Maybe you could offer him something to drink."

Marcus was proud to bear this responsibility, and Don staggered out of the door, across the lawn, and into his own side of the duplex. The first thing he did was to crash to his knees and pray. "Dear God, I'm terrified. This is a big step we're taking here. But I feel that we have Your blessing. Please bless Shay and me. Keep us close to You. Guide us and be that voice in our ears telling us to go to the right or to the left. And help me to stay calm."

The blinding flash of angels congregating around his hunched form startled the demons that had moved in to torment him with more doubt. "You're making a big mistake!" they shrieked. "You'll regret this! You're acting too hastily. Think of all the women out there you've yet to meet. Don't do this."

Merck was especially desperate, but no matter how loud he shouted, Don wasn't listening to him. He cursed mightily as he looked at the tousled head, bent in prayer. "I'll make you pay for this!" he shrieked. "Marry in haste and repent in leisure. You'll repent all right, when I get through with you."

Julian fanned his wings gently and laid his hand on Don's head. Instantly he felt Don relax as he imparted peace from the throne of the Master. "You have made a wise choice," he said. "The Master is pleased with this union. You are two

*people who know what is ahead of you. No marriage is per-
fect, but both you and Shay know that life isn't always smooth.
You have both weathered your share of difficulty and will carry
these lessons into your marriage. As long as you always remember on whom to rely for strength you may falter, but you
will never fail."*

Don stood up and headed for the shower. He felt remark-
ably calm now. By the time he had spruced up and was heading back to the other side of the duplex he realized that he
was unconsciously humming the hymn "It Is Well With My
Soul." "How appropriate," he murmured, opening the door to
utter chaos.

"What's going on?" he asked Marcus as he slipped in and
tried to stay out of the way. Men he had never seen before were
setting up an arbor and an electric keyboard in the living room.
More men, dressed in long white coats with little patches that
said, "Camellia Catering" were laying out hors d'oeuvres on
the kitchen table, now spread with a pristine starched white
tablecloth.

"Who are these people, and where did they come from?" he
hissed to Marcus.

Marcus shrugged. "Aunty Deniece came out a while ago and
said if anyone came to the door to open it and let them in. So I
did." He raised his palms up in surrender. "And they just kept
coming."

Efforts to get word from the inner sanctum proved fruitless.
Deniece came to the door briefly, scolded him for interrupting
them, and then disappeared amid the sound of giggles. He stood
there flustered for a few minutes then returned to the living room,
where he found even more people, this time burdened with
armloads of flowers. There were lilies on every surface, perfuming
the air with such a smell that Don thought heaven must smell
something like that.

The pastor arrived, and then everything was a blur. Most of the
unfamiliar people disappeared except for a couple placed discreetly
behind the table to serve refreshments. The lights were turned
off, and what seemed like hundreds of candles were lit. The room

suddenly looked spectacular. Don was startled to realize that there were a couple of people present that he actually knew. They looked hastily pulled together, but they were there.

That Deniece, he chuckled. It was as though she had pulled the wedding out of a hat. He stopped chuckling the moment he saw Shay. She stepped timidly out of the bedroom like a vision floating on a cloud of ivory satin and lace. She smiled weakly at him, and he could see she was scared.

That, he later realized, was when it stopped being at all frightening to him. He stepped forward and tucked her hand into the crook of his arm to lead her down the "aisle" to the arbor as a musician played a muted version of "Here Comes the Bride" on the electric keyboard.

Deniece was at Shay's other side, and she looked him over critically, nodding with approval at how he had cleaned up. She fussed with Shay's veil and held her flowers at the appropriate times and, he could see, fought to keep the tears out of her eyes.

It was all over before he knew it. The vows had been said, and he had a vague recollection of saying them. The thing he remembered most was the look of complete trust in Shay's eyes. He said a fervent prayer that he would always be worthy of it. And then they were married. The keyboard player threw himself into a resounding chorus of something joyful, and the few people attending came up to give their congratulations.

Madina hovered near Shay, and Marcus stood proudly by Don's side. He had been touched to be asked to be Don's best man, and he was taking the job seriously. The guests raved about the food, but Don barely tasted it, he was so keyed up. It wasn't until everyone but Deniece had gone home that he realized something very important.

"We're not going to have a honeymoon!"

Shay looked stricken. "What? Oh! You're right. How could we have forgotten that?"

"Girlfriend, you'd forget your head if it wasn't attached to your body. Don't worry. Aunty Deniece is staying with the kids tonight. You all just mosey on over to Don's place for the night. Tomorrow we'll see what we can do about getting the two of you away for a little R&R without the kids." She gave them a parental glare. "There's only so much I can do on such short notice."

Don laughed. "You are a marvel," he said heartily.

Deniece sniffed good-naturedly. "Yeah, well, you aren't so bad yourself. You take good care of this woman, understand?"

Don looked into Shay's eyes and felt tears prick the back of his own. "I will," he replied, his voice husky with emotion. "I will."

"OK, you kids, get out of here!" Deniece commanded, shooing them out of the house. Giggling like children they raced hand in hand to the other side of the house, feeling as if they had gone around the world.

"Wait!" Don commanded. He pulled Shay to a stop.

"What? Did you forget something?"

"Almost." Quickly he scooped her up into his arms to carry her over the threshold. "I love you, Mrs. Dr. Germaine."

She laughed wildly. "I love you too, Mr. Dr. Germaine."

Crazy Carol hunkered down closer to the small fire by the riverbank. She hadn't made the fire. A young man with disdainful eyes and a swarthy look had started it. The smell of his breakfast cooking had brought her clambering down the riverbank to see if he had anything to share.

"Get on outta here, old woman," he had said, waving her off. But Carol was persistent. She was hungry, and hunger made her desperate. She'd spent the last few days sleeping under a bridge and hadn't eaten for two of them.

"Awful hungry, hungry, hungry," she sang. "Care to share? Share to care?"

"Aw, get on outta here," he said again, moving over and shielding his meal from her sight.

"Not nice," she scolded. "Share to care." The smell of the food was overpowering. Suddenly she pushed him aside and lunged toward the fire. In one swift movement she didn't look capable of, she had knocked his stew pot off the fire and onto the riverbank where some of the contents spilled onto the ground. Like an animal she threw herself into the dirt beside it, scooping up handfuls of stew and dirt and shoving them into her mouth.

"What are you doing?" the man cried. "Are you crazy?"

Carol shrilled, "Crazy! Crazy! Crazy!"

Disgusted, he picked up the pot and pulled it closer, keeping a wary eye on Carol. "If you're that hungry you should at least eat like a civilized human being," he told her, scraping some of the stew out of the pot and into a clean-enough looking bowl. "Here."

Carol wiped her mouth with the back of her arm, smearing dirt and stew across her face. Her mouth cracked into a crooked grin as she reached out and took the bowl. He offered her a spoon too, but she refused it, scooping the hot stew with her fingers and shoveling it into her mouth. He watched her with an air of disgust and disbelief as he ladled his own portion and ate it slowly.

They didn't need the fire for warmth, but Carol crouched close to it anyway when she had finished eating. She reached out her fingers with their ragged, dirty nails. Years of homelessness and neglect were written on those hands. They told their own story.

"Hey, ain't you got a big dog?" the man said suddenly, looking over his shoulder nervously as if he expected Come Here to materialize out of thin air. "Yeah, I seen you with a big brute of a dog. Where's he at?"

Carol cocked her head at him in the peculiar way she had. "Come Here!" she hollered. "Come Here!"

The man scrambled to his feet, kicking sand into the fire to put it out. "Shut up!" he hissed. "Shut up!" His hand jerked back to deliver a blow to Carol's grinning face when something stopped him. Instead, he grabbed his things and clambered up the steep incline toward the road, throwing fearful looks up and down the riverbank as he went.

Saiph stood as a powerful barrier between Carol and the re-treating man. Preventing him from harming Carol had proved easy. He hadn't really wanted to harm her but reacted from fear. She was delighted to see that his heart had not become completely hardened. So many in reduced circumstances allowed the evil one to manipulate their hearts.

Several angels followed the man, shielding him from the demons who also trailed in his wake. Saiph knew that somewhere people prayed for this man. She also prayed for him to bury his pride and go to these people who cared about him. They could help him get back on his feet again.

She turned her attention back to Carol, who was picking through the ashes of the fire, looking for anything that might be edible. She was muttering to herself. Her face was nearly as black as the ashes before she gave up and began to wander down the riverbank. The odd-shaped birthmark beneath her eye that made her look as though she had a shiner did nothing to remedy the disreputable look she had.

Still, it wasn't her looks that bothered the angel. It was the empty spot by her side. Carol had been on her own for a long time before Come Here came along. But she was older now and, to the angel, seemed much more fragile than she ever had. It was a worry.

"She's not going to last, you know," Balor observed. "You've got every right to worry about her." His words were honey-smooth, filled with compassion and care, but Saiph wasn't fooled. The demon cared nothing for Carol.

"Get thee behind me," she said forcefully. "I want no part with you."

His cackling rang in her ears long after he had departed, and she hurried to catch up with Carol. More than anything she needed protection right now, and Saiph was there to provide it.

Billie Jo found that when the whirlwind of moving was all over she was as dazed as though she'd been through a brief war. Everything had happened so fast. Their house had sold to rich people seeking a vacation residence and closed within a week, something the loan officer said she had never seen before. Members of their church took up a collection to help them with moving expenses, and they ended up with enough money to hire two moving vans.

Billie Jo, with white knuckles and tight lips, had driven one while Jimmy had driven the other. Even Helen and James had stayed away until the very last minute. The scene with them was something they could all have done without. Billie Jo had seldom seen her father-in-law so upset and knew that it gave Helen a certain sense of satisfaction to have worked him up into such a state. It was a validation of her own feelings.

"Do you see what you're doing to your father?" she had demanded smugly. "He hasn't eaten a bite in days; I'm quite sure he's lost weight." She was always nagging James to lose weight, but she didn't mention that now. "He doesn't sleep at night. Why, I've had to sleep in the guest room just to get a wink of sleep at night myself. And it's hardly a wink at that, I'm so upset myself."

Jimmy had looked sorry, but there was also something new in his bearing that Billie Jo had never seen in him before. It was a quality of resolve. "I'm real sorry, Dad," he'd said. "But I just gotta do this. It's the best thing for my family. It's not like we won't see each other no more. We'll come down and visit. We'll be here for Christmas, and that ain't so far off."

"Christmas!" Helen had scoffed. "Christmas! Ha! You do that, Jimmy. You come for Christmas and visit us at the cemetery. Because if you leave, that's where you'll put us!"

The visit had deteriorated from there. Before Helen and James left, the kids were both crying, Jimmy was angry, and Billie Jo had a splitting headache. The only possible saving grace was that it had been the last time they'd seen Jimmy's parents since then. Now they were safe in Vermont, and Billie Jo felt a sense of elation and freedom she had never known in her married life.

She pulled up behind Jimmy's van and parked. The surroundings seemed to settle, and the quiet sounded loud after she cut the engine. "I think we're here," she told Cassidy, who looked up from the book she'd been reading.

"We're here?" Cass opened the door and jumped to the ground. Billie Jo followed slowly. The ground felt strangely still after three days of driving. She stretched, anxious to move around the vans and see the house for the first time, and also afraid to. What kind of people bought a house sight unseen?

Jimmy wasn't about to let her acclimate slowly though. He bounded around the back of his van and grabbed her hands. "Come on, darlin'! Let's go see our house!"

It was huge. That was her first impression. It was two stories high and built in the shape of an L. The realtor had explained to Zeb that the main structure was a farmhouse and that sometime in the early 1900s someone had added the rest. Up close Billie Jo could see that the gingerbread detailing that had come through as fuzzy perfection in the fax was in reality very chipped, with large sections missing altogether.

They walked up onto the porch but stopped when they saw the gaping holes in the floorboards. "Guess I'll have to reinforce those," Jimmy said with a nervous laugh. "Come on, we'll go around to the side door."

The stairs on the side were not much better, but they made their way up and into the house. The kitchen was so primitive that Billie Jo wondered how anyone could rightly describe it as a kitchen. There were no cabinets, no refrigerator, and no stove. Instead, rickety shelving hung on the walls, and one greatly stained sink sagged sadly away from the wall. The best feature of the room was the beautiful hardwood floorboards.

To the right, stairs went up to the second floor. They ignored them for the time being and pressed on into the house. There was a long, narrow pantry on the left that Billie Jo thought had possibilities. The doors of the cabinets in that room were of stunning leaded glass. She felt her spirits rise a little.

A big airy room lay beyond that. Sunshine filled it from the bank of windows and French door that comprised an entire wall.

She could see them eating breakfast there bathed in sunlight and felt her heart soaring. Maybe this place was going to be all right after all. Although it was laid out unconventionally, in the final analysis Billie Jo and Jimmy were both pleased with it aesthetically.

Structurally, it was a different story.

Jimmy's face was grim later when they sat down on some packing boxes that the kids had hauled in. "It's going to need a new foundation, a new chimney, and new shingles for the roof. We gotta replace all the wiring and blow insulation into the walls. And I'm not sure yet, but I think the overlays in the cellar might have to be replaced."

"Mom?" Dallas yelled.

"What?" Billie Jo hollered back impatiently. Her mind was still reeling from the implications of what Jimmy had said.

"We got no water," Dallas informed them.

"That's no problem," Jimmy told his son. "I ain't turned on the water main yet." He got up to do it, but when he returned there was still no water. "I think we're going to need a new pump too."

Billie Jo felt like crying.

"You go right ahead and let it all out," Nog *said with false sincerity. "What did I tell you? Didn't I say this was a bad idea? What were you thinking? What a mess. I don't envy you."*

"Do not jump to conclusions," Jewel *urged. "You are making many assumptions ahead of the facts. Be patient, little sister. God will take care of your needs. Trust Him."*

"Ha! Yeah, look what a great job He's done already!" Nog *scoffed. "He'll take care of your needs . . . as long as you don't have any! Just wait until winter comes and you don't have money for insulation. Then we'll see how warm your Master keeps you."*

"Mom?" It was Cassidy this time.

"What?" She felt totally defeated. What on earth were they going to do?

"There's a whole bunch of old stuff in the barn out back."

"Great," Billie Jo grumped. "More stuff to haul to the dump." The rooms in the house were full of trash that would have to be cleaned out before they could even unpack.

Cassidy didn't pick up on her mother's sarcasm. "Yeah, there's an old sleigh back there, a couple of them I think, and a big old tool chest and some furniture. There's some dressers back there that maybe me and Dallas could use since we left ours back home."

"Yeah, honey, that's real nice. But right now we got bigger problems," Jimmy said. He pulled out a crumpled piece of paper from his jeans, an old receipt for snacks they'd bought on the trip, and smoothed it out on top of the packing box. "OK, figuring high, this here is how much we're gonna need to fix this place up."

"You mean to fix everything that has got to be fixed, the necessities, not the cosmetic stuff, right?" Billie Jo asked. She was wondering how long it would be before they could afford the things she wanted, like paint, new boards to fix the porch floor, and material for curtains.

"Yeah, just the necessary stuff. It will be, oh . . ." His pencil scribbled hastily across the paper, adding a line of figures. "It's gonna be about $35,000."

Billie Jo groaned. Her head sank onto her arms on top of the packing crate, and she fought hard not to cry. There went all the money they had counted on saving. They were back where they started, or where they had left off, she supposed. They were, once again, penniless.

Jimmy laid a hand on her arm and squeezed sympathetically. "It's gonna be all right, darlin'," he said. "Really. It won't be no time at all before we're ahead. You'll see."

His optimism, so unlike him, perked up Billie Jo. If Jimmy could be positive, she guessed, she could too. "Right." She drew in a ragged breath and began issuing orders. "Dallas, you start helping your dad haul the boxes in from the vans. Don't bring in anything too heavy, mind, just bring the ones you can lift. Cass, you help me sort them in here. We'll sort them by rooms, but stack them all here in the living room until we get the rooms cleaned out. Then we'll move them into the rooms where they belong." By that time, she hoped, they'd have some idea what to do with them.

It was a bit like camping, she mused later. They had cooked a meager supper on the barbecue and now were stretched out in sleeping bags on the floor of the kitchen, the only clean room in the house. Billie Jo was proud of that room. It was worthless as kitchens went, but it was sparklingly clean. Jimmy had fixed the old sink so that even though they couldn't get any water out of it, it no longer sagged away from the wall. He had a few days before he had to report for work, and he promised her that she'd have some proper kitchen cupboards before he did.

Her muscles ached from the heavy work. She had never known a body could do so much work in one day and accomplish so little. She wouldn't even let herself think about the other rooms and what possible occupants they had. She studiously ignored the sounds of scuttling above. One thing at a time, she reminded herself. In the dark of the room, Jimmy reached over and took her hand.

"What are you thinkin'?" he asked.

"Nothing much," she replied. "Just thinking about what I need to get done tomorrow, that's all. There's a powerful lot of work to do here, even before you start all that remodeling work."

Suddenly she giggled, and the harder she tried to stop, the more she giggled. "What?" Jimmy finally asked. "What's so bloomin' funny?"

"I was just thinkin'," Billie Jo said when she could manage to draw a breath, "I was just thinkin' how glad I am your mother can't see us right now. We'd never live it down, that's certain!"

Jimmy chuckled. "You got that straight. It's a good thing we don't got a phone either. At least we don't have to tell her how it really is. I think I'd be strongly tempted to lie about it."

Billie Jo squeezed his hand. "It'll be better soon. I think we was just expectin' too much." She was silent for a minute then added, "All the same, when I see Zeb Turner he'd better have his running shoes on."

"I don't expect I know what he was thinkin' either," Jimmy admitted. "Anybody with half an eye could see this place needs a lot of work. Maybe he figured we'd have enough left over because the selling price was so cheap that we wouldn't have any trouble coming up with some cash to fix up the parts that need fixin'."

Billie Jo stared up into the darkness for a while. "Jimmy?" she finally asked. "Do you think Zeb even looked at the house?"

Jimmy sighed. "I don't know, darlin', I plumb don't know. He said he did, but that don't mean much, I guess. I forget sometimes that I ain't seen Zeb for years. We was close once, and I would have trusted him with my life in them days. But maybe things has changed. I don't know. Guess that's what I get for uprooting my family and dragging them clear across the country. I should've checked it out better."

Billie Jo patted his hand. "It's OK. Everything'll turn out all right, like you said. We're just tired now. We should get some sleep. Tomorrow will be a long, dirty day."

At the time it was a mercy that she had no idea how long and dirty it would turn out to be. In fact, had she known, Billie Jo was pretty sure she would have just rolled over the next morning when the sun streaked in the windows and never gotten out of bed.

Shay and Don were holding hands, waiting outside Les Histoires café with a handful of other people. Although it was early in the morning the heat was so intense they were all dripping wet. Deniece was the next person to arrive. She hustled down the street.

Shay was amused to see that her friend was as fashionably dressed as if she were going to work. She was wearing a silk suit the color of a latté with sling-back heels. Her hair was knotted up in a simple and elegant way. As she approached, Shay was enveloped in the fragrance of her signature scent, *L'Interdit,* an expensive Givenchy number. Trust Deniece to spruce up for a prayer walk around the Quarter. Shay looked down at her own linen dress, already crumpled from the heat, and stifled a giggle.

"Hey, girlfriend," Deniece said breathlessly. "Did I miss anything?"

"No, we're still waiting for a few other people. We're supposed to start halfway down the back of Jackson Square where someone has a prayer booth. I didn't know that, did you?"

"What? That someone has a prayer booth? I'd heard about it, but never seen it. I guess quite a few people stop and pray with whoever is manning the booth."

Don nudged Shay. "That woman over there just said she gave her heart to the Lord at that prayer booth. That's why she's here today."

"Wow. Funny how you can never tell what's going to have an impact." Shay looked unconsciously toward the door of Les Histoires, which had been the cause of an impact on her own life just recently.

As they moved en masse toward the prayer booth the sun was bathing the street in a rosy light. They stopped in front of the prayer booth. The young woman who was there to pray with passersby joined their circle, and the pastor began to pray.

"Lord, we invite You to walk with us today. Send Your Spirit before us with truth and with power. Break the forces of darkness and drive the evil one away. As we speak Your holy Scripture, lay down ribbons of truth. Let Your words convict the hearts of all those who walk through them. You said Your Word would not return to You void. Help us to sow Your Word where it will do the most good. Guide us and direct us, we pray. In the name of Jesus Your Son who saved us for all eternity. Amen."

A hearty "Amen" answered him. The young woman at the booth wished them Godspeed and said she'd be praying for them. The group began to move down the sidewalk in the direction of Magazine Street. As they walked, each person in the group prayed

Scripture. Some were audible, but most prayed silently with their lips moving. Shay and Don and Deniece held hands, walking abreast down the sidewalk. Shay prayed every powerful scripture that came to mind, and when she ran out she started all over again.

Shay believed that there was a spiritual world. She believed that the forces of good and evil battled for the souls of every human being. But she had never consciously fought against the forces of evil before. She had often reacted to their effects, battling the bad things in her life that could have destroyed her if she had not held on to God. She wondered exactly what that spiritual world was making of their prayer walk. She dearly wished she could see if it made any kind of difference, but she firmly believed that it must, whether she could see its effects or not.

The effects Shay could not see were raging all around her. Demons were boiling around the French Quarter like oily smoke, pouring down the streets, from the windows, off fire escapes. There were screaming, shrieking legions of them, filthy misshapen things with ratty wings and hideous faces twisted from centuries of embracing evil. Their eyes, as they watched the angels coming in with the puny group of human beings, were filled with more than suspicion. Their eyes were filled with hatred and fear.

"The host of heaven!" they wailed.

One demon whose eyes blazed with something more than fear pulled apart from the throng. Anger twisted his distorted features. "They are few!" He roared. "We will send them back where they came from."

The others worked themselves up with venomous shouts before pouring down upon the helpless people and their small angel guard. As they approached, the human beings broke a circle and began to walk. Howling, the demons fell upon them, wrestling with the angels and trying to reach the people. Before they had made any headway a strange thing happened. Though none of the human beings was armed, suddenly glittering swords flashed from their mouths, slashing at the de-

mons. Wherever the swords struck they laid down paths of light, like ribbons—the light of truth. It shone so brightly that it burned the eyes of the demons, and they were forced to look away.

Some became entangled in the ribbons as they tried to avoid the swords and they screamed terribly when the ribbons cut them as much as the swords had. Screeching, they withdrew, consoling each other and cursing the human beings whom they raged against but were unable to attack. As they watched, people who were moving about the city began to walk through the ribbons, which they could not see. When they did, the ribbons passed through them.

Years of observing human reaction to various situations, thoughts, and stimuli had given the demons the ability to read the human mind. They could not hear the actual thoughts, but they came as close to that as was possible without hearing the words as they passed through a human being's mind. This ability let them see how the ribbons of truth affected the people.

One woman began to think of her estranged daughter and made a decision to call her and try to patch things up. A man cursed the truth the ribbon of light had brought him and retreated even further into his own inner darkness. A young woman passing through one ribbon questioned her lifestyle. The demons could see that the truth would set her free from the chains they had placed all around her.

As people came into contact with the ribbons of truth they only reacted in one of two ways. They either accepted the light or they rejected it. As the demons realized this they began to congregate around those who had rejected the light or questioned it. Upon these poor beings they heaped doubts and criticisms, trying to destroy the hope the light imparted.

The ribbons did not disappear once they had been laid down either. They continued to stand, as though they would hold until the Judgment Day. Great waves of people were affected by them as the day progressed, long after the prayer walk had ended and everyone involved had returned home, feeling hopeful but tired.

The demons cursed and hid from the light and were careful not to touch it. It appeared as a living thing that shimmered and glowed with the white light of intense heat.

In the darkness of the Quarter, one small grid was criss-crossed with this light. And at every intersection stood a bright and brilliant angel with a gleaming sword. The darkness boiled around but not through it, and the darkness mourned its loss greatly.

Shay and Don held hands as they walked to their car, and Shay noticed that the men who glanced at her did not follow their glance with rude words. She felt infused with a sense of accomplishment from the walk, though she had seen nothing visibly accomplished, and that was a bit of a letdown. She had fancifully expected to see angels and demons swashbuckling around with swords like pirates, which, when she thought about it, was probably kind of silly.

CHAPTER 5

Cindi spent a miserable week agonizing over Jared in her thoughts and in prayer. *"Dear God, what did I do wrong?"* she asked herself over and over. She felt the heavy weight of responsibility. If she had only done or said something differently, maybe the Holy Spirit would have been able to work in Jared's heart and help him to see that God was not to blame, that God, in fact, was hurting more over the loss of Jared's wife than even Jared did.

"You did nothing wrong," Shania reminded her gently. "The most you are expected to do is to plant the seeds. The Holy Spirit will water them. You cannot make an apple tree grow any more than you can make a spiritual seed grow. That is not your job.

"But you must turn him over to the Master. You are walking on the wrong path and walking away from the Master. Your compassion is admirable but misplaced in this situation. It will only cause you harm. Break away from this relationship while there is time, before it crosses a line."

Rafe snorted. "You can't do anything right. You're just a stupid human being. God doesn't want you to be responsible for anything. Let it go already. You'll get another chance to save the world, or Jared's corner of it anyway. I'll never understand people. They're so egotistical, so completely caught up with them-

selves, that they think the universe revolves around them and that they can single-handedly save the world. Your Savior came in vain," he chuckled. *"He could have just stayed up in heaven for all these people care. They don't rely on Him. They pray to Him and then they go out and do as they please anyway. What a waste."*

Shania ignored his speech. She knew he didn't believe what he was saying anyway. He just hoped Cindi would. If he could discourage her she would stop caring about what happened to other people. She'd become as self-centered as he hoped. But this was a dangerous game they played. As much as Shania wanted Cindi to be sensitive to others, she was sure that where Jared walked there was danger. She didn't know exactly what the demons had planned, but she was sure it wasn't holy. It wasn't God's best intentions for Cindi.

"You have done all you can. If he contacts you again, urge him to seek professional help. Refer him to another pastor if his will not listen to him." *The angel knew her voice was being heard, but only time would tell if Cindi would ask God for the strength to heed it.*

Cindi picked up the schoolbooks from the kitchen table. Esther had gone outside to play as soon as they had finished their home school session. After she had neatened the kitchen area and placed all the books back into the milk crates where they were stored, she walked idly into the living room.

Now was as good a time as any to work on A Wing and a Prayer, she supposed. She pulled up the email and began cutting and pasting without much interest. In a vague, far-off corner of her mind she hoped that Jared might send her an instant message. She worked slowly, but there was no incoming message. She was just about to turn off the computer when it finally flashed. At the same time the phone rang.

She pulled up the message and picked up the phone. "Hello?" she said while her eyes scanned the message. *"Are you out there?"* it read.

"Sis? It's Don! I've got some big news. Are you sitting down?"

He sounded as if he was charged with electricity. "What's happened?" Her blood ran hot and cold, the message on the screen in front of her temporarily forgotten.

"Shay and I are married!"

In spite of the miles between them, she felt as though he had punched her in the stomach. Tears welled up in her eyes, but she tried to keep her voice light and happy. "Married? But why? We were all going to come down. What happened?"

"I know. I'm sorry, Sis. We just decided so fast. We were married right here at the house, though Shay's friend Deniece whipped up a lot of extras. It was really pretty nice. I wish . . . I wish you could have been here."

"Yeah," she said wistfully, biting her lip to keep from breaking down. "Yeah, me too."

"Look, I can't talk long. I've got to call the travel agent and book us some tickets."

For a second her heart soared. "Are you coming here?"

The long pause answered her question before he did. "No, I'm sorry, there won't be time. We have to get back to the mission right away."

Cindi felt an uncharacteristic surge of anger toward the mission, Shay, and Africa in general. "What's the big rush?"

"There have been some . . . developments . . . that Shay and I don't feel comfortable ignoring any longer. They need us out there. You know how it is, Sis. I really shouldn't have stayed away so long."

"When are you leaving?" she asked dully.

"At the end of the week."

"So we won't get to see you at all?"

"Not before we leave, I'm afraid. But, next time, for sure."

She sniffed. "Take care, Don. I'll keep you on the prayer list."

"Thanks, Sis. I love you."

"I love you too."

She sat holding the droning phone in her hand until a sharp beep from the computer reminded her that Jared was waiting for her.

"Are you still out there?" The cursor seemed to blink impatiently.

Cindi dashed her hand across her eyes and began to type furiously. *"Yes, I'm here. Are you OK?"*

"Yes, I'm fine. Just really embarrassed. I made such a scene the other day. I apologize. I'll understand if you never want to speak to me again."

"Of course not," she typed. *"Don't be silly."*

"I've been thinking about what you said. I still don't agree with you, but do you think we can still be friends?"

Shania leaned in close. "Tell him he should get counseling. Tell him you can't be friends. It won't work. He needs someone too much."

"Jesus was friends with sinners," Rafe sneered. "Aren't you supposed to follow Jesus? What are you scared of?"

Cindi realized her heart was pounding in her chest. Conflicting thoughts passed through her mind. She didn't know what to do. While she felt hesitation at becoming involved with this man, the sense of being desperately needed appealed to her vanity and was overwhelming. She didn't *want* to ignore it. There was an opportunity before she began to type when she could have asked for help, but Cindi didn't take it. Instead, she followed her feelings.

"Of course we can be friends," she assured him, heart fluttering as she typed the words.

"Will you meet me again? I promise to behave this time. :^)"

It was the smiley face that got to her. All her fears melted at the sight of it. *"Sure. When?"*

They set up a date at the same café. She was just logging off when Esther bounded into the house. "Mommy? There you are! Will you swing me now? What are you doing?"

She peered over Cindi's shoulder and for a reason she didn't really understand, Cindi felt vaguely guilty. She was glad Jared had gone. Smiling brightly, she switched off the computer monitor and said, "I'd love to swing you. Let's go."

Outside the heat was nearly intolerable, but she forced herself to stay and swing Esther far longer than she normally did. In a way it felt like penance. While her arms mechanically pushed Esther's swing her mind flipped through her cookbooks, wondering what she could make for Marc that night that he would really love. Being extra nice to her family proved that everything was all right. Didn't it?

The balance between demons and angels around Cindi had shifted, and Shania gravely observed it. The demons had the most influence now. They were closer to Cindi, and while she didn't realize it, it was their voices she was listening to. They, who had once been angels of light, could be so persuasive, sound so reasonable, and had convinced her to rely on her feelings rather than her intellect. While she was held in the grip of her feelings it would be difficult to persuade her of her error. Yes, as Shania saw the Mona-Lisa smile on Cindi's lips she knew it would be very difficult indeed.

"Davy! Davy!" Toby held the telegram in a viselike grip as she ran out of the clinic and toward the mission compound. "Davy! Don and Shay are coming back! They're coming back!"

She found Davy poring over airplane manuals in the kitchen. Akueke had made him a sandwich, and he was polishing it off absently. When he looked up she saw shock and possibly a little fear on his handsome face. Then he latched on to a key thought. "They're coming back together?"

"Of course, silly! They're married."

"Married? Married! How wonderful!" His face lit up, but Toby overlooked it. "They should be here by Sunday. We've got a lot to do before then."

"What do you mean?" Davy protested. "Things look fine around here."

"I don't mean here," Toby said impatiently. "I mean the out-post clinics. I'd like them to look their best. Don was never very crazy about them as it was. You've got to bring me out there to-day."

Davy set his jaw firmly. "No."

"Davy," Toby said with forced patience. "We've talked about this before. What happened to Julia was a fluke. Besides, you'll be with me. You can protect me." She flashed him a winning smile that she didn't feel in the least. It didn't do much. "Unless you want me to go without you," she persisted stubbornly. "I'd rather not, but if you force me I will do it." She licked her lips nervously and waited.

"OK." Davy didn't look up. He studied the table in front of him. "You win. When do you want to leave?"

Toby wasn't sure if she was happy or scared stiff. "How about right now? I can be packed up in fifteen minutes."

"I'll meet you out at the ultralight." Davy shuffled his paperwork together and left.

"Right . . . then . . ." There didn't seem to be anything left to say. She went to her room and started throwing stuff into a bag. Bug dope. Sunglasses. A hat with mosquito netting. Her portable first-aid kit. Her eyes took in the room. It was still as stark as the day she'd moved in. She had accumulated a few more possessions, but her room had never felt as though it belonged to her. It was more a place to crash at the end of a long day.

For no reason she could think of, she remembered the way Shay had fixed up her own room, so bright and cheerful. How different they were. She searched her heart but could only feel happy at their news. It wasn't as if she hadn't been able to see it coming anyway. Driven men like Don Germaine didn't suddenly abandon their calling to hang out and baby-sit for sick friends, no matter how engaging they were.

For the first time she realized that it was really over between her and Don. Whatever had existed there, whatever potential they'd had for a relationship, had gone. There was nothing left in its place, not even regret. She was perfectly happy for Don and Shay, and she was also perfectly happy where she was.

Her course was set. She realized that now. She and Davy would get remarried. She'd known that for a while now too. She just hadn't felt the need to tell him. Things had been going so well. She was half afraid to spoil it. Maybe she should tell him. It might improve his mood.

Thinking happy thoughts and whistling a little tune, she made her way out of the mission compound, blinking up into the glare of the sun. She almost skipped on her way to the ultralight. When she rounded the corner of the clinic she stopped, dumbfounded. For a second she simply felt confused, thinking Davy must have moved the little plane. Then suspicion began to grow, and she wheeled around.

She burst into the clinic and found Julia and Ray inside. Julia was propped up on a stool, sterilizing equipment in the ancient autoclave. Ray was treating patients. "Hey, guys, have you seen Davy?"

Ray looked up. He had very chiseled features, large dark eyes, thick black eyebrows, and olive skin. Toby often thought he must have an Italian or French heritage. "He left. Said he had to check on the clinics. I told him he wasn't leaving himself enough time, but he told me not to worry about it."

Toby just stared at him as though she'd lost her mind. "He didn't take anyone with him?"

Ray shrugged. "No. But I wouldn't expect him back tonight if I were you. I know how he hates to stay overnight out there, but he had an overnight bag with him. I don't think he planned to come back tonight. I didn't ask though, so maybe he will."

Toby didn't think she could be more shocked if someone dashed her with a bucket of ice water. "Oh. OK."

She wandered back out and sat on the stoop, not knowing quite what else to do. It was beyond belief that Davy had tricked her. He had betrayed her, in fact. The more she thought about it the madder she got. How dare he? But beneath the anger was the cold hand of fear. What if something happened to him? It would be all her fault for pushing him there in the first place.

It was only because he didn't want her to get hurt that he had taken off without her. She could have shaken him until his teeth rattled for that. On the other hand it was very touching. But then, look what a perilous position he'd put himself in. There was no way to even contact him. She was going to have to live with this cold dread until he came back safley.

And as soon as he did, she'd wring his neck.

Billie Jo straightened up and stretched the kinks out of her back. She felt as though she'd been on her knees scrubbing this floor for years instead of hours. She didn't even want to know what had made it so filthy. Whatever it was had left the tiles so covered with grime that until she'd scrubbed off all the layers she hadn't even known it was tile. The part of the floor already scrubbed was a beautiful honey-colored tile that was quite impressive. As she reached the edges of the room, Billie Jo was beginning to suspect that there was a border made of tile too and she was just about to uncover it. It made the chore slightly less tedious, but only slightly. Right now she'd trade a beautiful tile floor for one made of plastic if it were clean.

"How are you doin', darlin'?" Jimmy asked. He had his tool belt on and was going around the house making whatever repairs he could.

"Getting there," Billie Jo said. "Sure am tired though. What are the kids doin'?"

"I think they're out poking around in that barn out back. They're pretty interested in it. I think Dallas is hoping I'll build him a clubhouse."

"Jimmy?"

"Yeah, darlin'?"

"Where we gonna go to church this weekend?" It was something she'd thought about a lot but hadn't dared to ask. Right after the accident Jimmy had been very interested in spiritual things. As time went on he fell into old patterns. A lot of the time he didn't even go to church with them. "What do I need that for?" he'd ask. "I got too much stuff to do to be sittin' around in a church of a weekend."

She knew it bothered the children that he didn't go to church with them. Dallas seemed to feel it particularly. Occasionally he said or did something to make her think that eventually he'd rebel against church himself. Cassidy was mostly quiet on the subject, but Billie Jo knew a lot went on in her head on the days Jimmy stayed home.

"I don't guess I know. I've got too much to do here to go to church even if we did find one."

"The children and I are going," Billie Jo said with quiet resolve. "I don't care how much I got goin' on."

"It's not the same for you, though, is it?" Jimmy asked, measuring the opening of a door that was missing a molding strip. "I got to start work soon, but you'll be here with all the time in the world to clean this place."

Billie Jo swallowed hard. His remark stung. She knew he didn't mean to, but often his comments about how she didn't work hurt. For so many years she had been busy with the children and hadn't had the energy to work outside the home. After the children started school she'd spent a lot of time catching up and even some, yes, resting and relaxing.

She had a lot of hobbies and was an energetic fixer-upper. The things she did saved them money. But at times like these she couldn't help thinking that Jimmy thought she ought to be more industrious and get a "real" job. Convincing him of the worthiness of being a housekeeper was beyond her.

"Yeah, I guess. Suppose they have listings in the phone book. Or maybe I can call down to the town clerk or something."

"Suit yourself."

Which is exactly what she did, because she knew that if she waited for him to change his mind she'd never get to go to church. That weekend when they headed out to church for the first time in their new town, Dallas and Cassidy exchanged looks but otherwise said nothing. Billie Jo was more scared than she would admit to anyone.

The church was small, and she felt the curious stares of many well-meaning pairs of eyes. The half-smile on her face felt strained, and she avoided actual eye contact with nearly everyone. It wasn't until they were filing out that someone greeted her.

A sweet-faced woman Billie Jo guessed to be about her own age approached her. "Hello," she said smiling warmly. "My name is Greta Garbeaux."

Billie Jo swallowed a hysterical laugh so that it came out sounding like a snort. "Do what?"

Apparently it was an old joke. "Awful, isn't it?" the woman sighed. "My mother was a fierce Greta Garbo fan, and she also had a sense of humor. I'm just thankful our last name wasn't Marx. I don't fancy myself answering to Groucho!

"In fact," she confided, "when I got married I never changed it because it would have broken my mother's heart." Greta slipped her arm through Billie Jo's and it felt natural, like they'd been best friends forever. "I just call Greta Garbo the 'other' Greta." She laughed. "You're new here . . . it's hard not to notice newcomers." Again that blazing smile that made her whole face light up. "Where are you from?"

"Tennessee," Billie Jo said. "A place called Ooltewah." Cassidy and Dallas were clinging to her as they made their way slowly down the aisle. The minister was shaking hands with everyone as they passed him. Most everyone stopped and said a few words. Billie Jo had been so keyed up she'd barely heard the sermon, so she had no idea what to say about it.

"Down South," Greta was saying. "I don't know anyone down there, but I've heard it's nice. My relatives all come from here in Vermont and some from Quebec."

"Quebec? Ain't that in Canada? Is that near here?" Billie Jo asked absently.

"Sure, we're only a few minutes from the Canadian border." Greta sounded puzzled. "Didn't you know that?"

"We moved up kind of fast," Billie Jo said by way of explanation. "I don't recollect I even saw a map of the place. Not except the one Jimmy had that we used to drive here. But I didn't notice about Canada."

"Jimmy . . . is he your husband?"

"Yes, he's not here 'cause, well, he's just not here. I don't rightly know why. He just didn't want to come. But he may come sometime."

"That's nice. We'll look forward to meeting him." They were getting closer to the preacher, and Greta released Billie Jo's arm so she could shake hands with him. "Pastor Richards, this is . . . I'm so sorry! I don't know your name!" She blushed furiously.

"Billie Jo Raynard, pastor. So nice to meet you. These here are my kids, Cassidy and Dallas."

He had soft hazel eyes that crinkled in the corners when he smiled. "I'm glad you could all join us. I do hope you'll come again."

"Oh, yes, sir. We'll be here every week now that we got settled a bit. My husband, that is, Jimmy, he might even come with us sometimes."

Pastor Richards released her hand. "That would be great. I'll look forward to that."

When they were outside, Greta shaded her eyes against the glare of the sun. "I'd like to invite you back home for dinner," she said.

Billie Jo felt her stomach tighten. The thought of going home with this nice stranger was too much for her. "I'm sorry, maybe another time? Jimmy's expectin' us, and we don't have a phone in yet, so I couldn't even call him to tell him why we were late. You understand." It was more a statement than a question because whether or not Greta understood, Billie Jo was not going home with her that afternoon.

"Of course I understand! Some other time, after you're more settled maybe?"

"Sure, that would be fine." Billie Jo was infused with relief.

"We'll see you next week?"

"Next week."

She wasn't going to tell Jimmy about this, no sir. He was even shyer than she was. If he knew there was even the remotest chance he'd be invited to the house of someone he didn't even know she wouldn't be able to pull him past the church doors. No, she'd just keep her mouth shut. After she made some friends she could introduce them all gradually.

"Don't wait too long, little one," Jewel urged. *"You will need strong Christian friends very soon. Do not delay."*

Shay thought that if just one more thing went wrong she was going to sit down and refuse to get up again. Three times security officials had riffled through everything in her suitcases. They were nice about it, but by the third time she folded her unmentionables she was about ready to drop her suitcase in the nearest trash bin and start over when she got to Africa. On top of that, Madina was fighting a bad cold, and she knew that the hours ahead of them on the plane, where the air was dry, were going to make her worse. Not to mention the effect that confinement with a sick child on an airplane would have on her sanity.

When Don lost the tickets she knew that things could get worse yet. "What do you mean, you lost the tickets?" she asked. "You just had them."

"I don't know. They were in that black pouch I carry. I don't know what we're going to do. It's not just the tickets. All our passports are in there, and about $1,000 in cash." His face was whiter than his shirt. She'd never seen him so unraveled.

Marcus picked up on the crisis quickly. "What is happening?" His voice shook with concern and his big, dark eyes were pools of India ink.

Shay put her arm around him and gave him a squeeze. "We're having a little trouble. Can you pray for us?"

Marcus nodded and obediently dropped his head and began to pray.

"Don't do it, kid," Gorn hissed. Defeat and despair radiated from him like poison. He moved in as close as he dared. "Don't pray. There's no use. You'll never find something that valuable in a place like this. There are a million con artists out there. Everyone is out to get you. They'll rob you blind. If you want to find that pouch you should look in the garbage cans and maybe you'll find the pouch. The rest of the stuff that was in there, that's history."

The boy didn't look up but continued to pray. The demon be-came annoyed. "Look! Look! Boy!" He moved in close to Ayala, who was protecting the pouch. He pulled a shining sword from the sheath by his side. "Look, boy, see how useless prayer is?"

With a mighty lunge he struck at the angel, who parried swiftly. He attacked again, moving with blinding speed and trying to catch her off guard. His thrusts were aggressive, and she was forced to yield some ground.

"I can do all things through Christ who gives me strength," Marcus said suddenly and out loud, his head still bowed, his eyes still closed. A blinding flash issued from his mouth, arching toward Gorn and catching him on the side of his sword arm. With a howl of pain Gorn gripped his arm and turned to face Marcus, eyes blazing fiercely.

"You fool! You'll regret that!" He withdrew but kept a watchful eye on the proceedings from a safe distance.

Shay was no longer paying attention to Marcus, and she didn't hear him say anything. To Don, she said, "Why don't we go report the loss to a security officer?"

He nodded, his eyes not focused on her or anything in particular. He seemed to be tracing the path of his black pouch, trying to remember where he'd seen it last. "Yeah, I guess. No! Wait." He grabbed her arm. "We should go through the stuff again before we get security involved."

"OK," she agreed. Together they wheeled their carry-on luggage over to a bank of seats at one of the airport gates. Slowly, methodically, they pulled out everything, checked it over, and slid their hands into every crease and behind every lining. There was nothing. When they were finished they looked at each other with mutual dread. Marcus sat a few seats down from them, his hands covering his face, lips moving soundlessly.

"Let's go," Don said, sighing with resignation. "Come on, Marcus."

Ayala had her hand over the black pouch that belonged to Don Germaine. He had left it near the public phones where he'd taken his phone card out of it so Shay could make a phone call. Many people had come to use the phone since Don walked away from it, but Ayala's hand covered it and they saw nothing. She had been standing sentinel over the pouch from the moment Marcus had begun to pray.

As the family began to cross in front of the phones she looked for some way to make them notice the pouch. She lifted her hand from it and blew softly against Don's face, but he was too preoccupied to notice. Next she reached down and jammed the wheels of Shay's luggage. The party ground to a frustrated halt.

"Oh, great, just what I need," Shay muttered. There was exasperation in her voice; Ayala could hear it. "Don, can you fix this?" She looked around for some place to lean her duffle bag so she could maneuver the suitcase into position for him. As she did, Ayala saw her eyes light on the black pouch. When recognition hit, her mouth dropped open.

"Don, look," she said, pointing.

At the same time, Gorn had succeeded in interesting a gentleman of questionable morals in the pouch. Airports were this guy's beat. Increased security had really put a damper on his profits. He had no idea what was in that black pouch he had just noticed, but he intended to find out. He pushed past Shay and before she realized what was happening, he grabbed the pouch, slipped it inside his coat and walked swiftly off.

"Hey! Hey! He stole my purse!" Shay shrieked. A few curious people looked, but no one did anything except for Don who sprinted after him.

"Stop that guy!" he roared. Security was on top of them before they made it twenty-five yards.

Gorn cursed as angels surrounded the security officers in force. Knowing he'd been beaten, he slunk off. Next time . . . there was always a next time.

"Officer, officer, that man is my husband," Shay was screaming as she dragged Madina behind her. The little girl, who was bewildered, now started to cry. "He stole my purse!"

A burly security guard intercepted her. "Ma'am? Your husband stole your purse?"

Shay's laugh bordered on the hysteric. "No, no, that man is my husband," she said, pointing to Don, who was being detained. "And that man stole my purse . . . well, not my purse exactly, it was my husband's pouch. All our money and passports are in there."

"I see." He took her arm, and she accompanied him meekly, trailing Madina and Marcus, who was goggle-eyed at all the excitement.

It was two hours before everything was straightened out to the satisfaction of all parties concerned, with the exception of the thief who was carted off to jail. Shay had to repack her suitcase for the fifth time that day and didn't even bother to fold anything. They had missed their flight, but another had been booked. They'd be waiting for another hour in the airport, but then, God willing, they'd be on their way.

"Mama?" Marcus asked timidly. "I prayed really hard, and we found Dad's pouch. Do you think it was because I prayed?"

Shay put her arms around her son and hugged him hard. "I sure do. I sure do."

Cindi woke up with the same angry feeling she'd gone to bed with. She stared at the ceiling in the darkness and listened to Marc's deep, even breathing beside her. She could just see his tousled black hair poking out from under the sheets. They hadn't been getting along lately, and she turned onto her side so she couldn't see him anymore.

She wasn't sure exactly what was wrong. There had been a series of misunderstandings and small irritations that hadn't really been resolved. And then he was gone so much. They hadn't really talked about anything for weeks, unless you counted requests to pass the milk, which Cindi didn't. She frowned. All of that was the basic foundation. It was certainly what had led to the big blow-out they'd had the night before over Esther's schooling.

Cindi wanted to keep doing home school, but Marc thought they should send Esther to a local Christian school so Cindi could pursue some of her other interests, the most important being to get

Ethel Bennington's house turned into a community shelter. She had looked into it for about six months following Ethel's death, but there were so many obstacles in the way and she was so busy with everything else, that she had dropped the ball.

Cindi plumped her pillow and stared out the window by her bed, watching the landscape brighten in the early morning light as the sun began to rise. The softly rolling hills outside were lush and green and the scent of honeysuckle hung heavy on the morning air.

Marc doesn't understand anything, she thought sullenly. Esther was more important to her than anything, more important certainly than what became of Ethel's home. What was worse was his bull-headedness. Why couldn't he just accept that she was doing what she wanted to be doing? Why was he pushing her to do something about Ethel's house? Ethel's house could wait. Esther's education couldn't. She was growing up fast enough as it was.

Another thing that annoyed her was the amount of time he was spending with other people lately for work. It had gotten so bad that she was beginning to feel like a single parent. Even when he was home he was on the phone most of the time, talking to clients and schmoozing. She wouldn't tell him so, but she privately thought he was feeling guilty about all the extra pressure he was putting on her and trying to come up with a solution to help her out. But it was the wrong solution.

Gently she got out of bed so as not to disturb Marc. She was meeting Jared later, and there were some things she needed to do so she could be on time for their meeting. They were going to the same café, though privately Cindi thought that was a mistake. She was afraid of another scene.

She'd fought with herself over and over in the last few days, questioning her own motives, but truly thought that it was Christian charity that motivated her. No matter how many ways she looked at it, she didn't see it in any other light. She sincerely wanted Jared to see that God loved him and was not punishing him with Krissy's death. Her own hand in it was of no consequence, she believed. She was simply a vehicle to deliver the message of

God's love and forgiveness. That she was an increasingly emotionally needy vehicle didn't register in her thinking.

It was a great relief to her when Marc was finally out of the
house. The chill that surrounded them was evident even to Esther,
who was unusually quiet, observing them with wide eyes. After he
had gone she asked timidly, "Is Daddy mad at me?"

Cindi swooped down and crushed the little girl in an embrace.
"No, honey! He's not mad at you. Daddy and I are having a dis-
agreement, that's all. It's nothing for you to worry about. I'm sure
it will all blow over soon enough."

*"Liar, liar," Rafe said with an evil smile. "It won't be over
soon and you know it. This could drag on for a long time. In
fact, if it gets bad enough maybe you'll get divorced over it.
Lots of people get divorced over issues they can't even remember later. Ask them where it all started and half the time they
can't remember. How often was it something like this, a bunch
of simple little arguments that built on each other? But, no
matter. If you get divorced at least you have someone all lined
up to replace Marc."*

*"What are you saying?" shrieked Ogel. "Are you trying to spoil
everything? Do you know what pains I've gone through to keep
that information from her?" Cindi had an introspective look on
her face and a deep frown was creasing the corners of her mouth.
"This woman won't respond to thoughts like these the way we
want her to. If she suspects that her present course of action will
lead to divorce she'll stop it immediately. Don't even suggest such
a thing to her."*

*Rafe snarled. "What do you know about it? You haven't been
around long enough to know how to handle her. Stick to your
own side of the fence and make the grass as green as possible."*

*"But, I . . ." Ogel didn't get to finish what he started to say. Rafe
made a threatening movement toward him and he vanished.*

*Shania moved in close to Cindi. "Cancel this meeting, Cindi,"
she urged. "Do not go. Nothing good will come of it."*

*"Shut up!" Rafe commanded, and because Cindi was listen-
ing to him more than the angel, lately, Shania was forced to back
off. There were tears in her beautiful eyes, and she never stopped*

entreating Cindi to cancel the meeting, but her voice was so weak that all Cindi heard was a faint echo, which she guiltily ignored.

This time Jared had their sodas ordered and waiting for her when she arrived, breathless and somewhat late. "Thanks." Cindi flashed him a nervous smile as she sat down. "You didn't have to do that."

"I know." His eyes seemed even bluer today, she thought, and his tan deeper. "I thought I'd save us the interruptions."

"Oh." She sipped quietly at her soda. "So, what have you been up to lately?" It was a lame opener, but now that she was actually here she felt a knot of tension in her stomach.

"I've been diving, mostly," he responded. "Just to keep my skills up. Found some neat things though. A few days ago I found part of a cannonball."

"That's . . . interesting."

He leaned forward, reached across the table and took both of her hands in his. The movement was so sudden that Cindi nearly started out of her chair. He mistook her action for an attempted retreat. "No, please, let me say something before you go." Conflicting emotions crossed his face. She read regret and sadness and anger and something that bordered on terror. "I am so sorry for the way I behaved last time. Really, I don't know how you can forgive me.

"I've thought of nothing else for the last week. It was so stupid. You were only trying to help me. And maybe I need that kind of help. I don't know. But I know I need you. You're the only person I feel like talking to. Everyone else shuts me out or shuts me up. I need to talk to someone. I need . . . " His voice broke for a minute, and she was afraid he wasn't going to be able to go on. "I need to talk to someone about Krissy."

Cindi swallowed the lump in her throat. All of a sudden she felt vital and needed. She felt as though she was where she was supposed to be. She relaxed into her chair and returned his grip, holding on to his hands as though they were the lifeline between which all his words must pass. "Then talk. Tell me about Krissy."

Two hours and two sodas later Cindi felt as though she and the late Krissy had been the best of friends. Through Jared's stories the mysterious Krissy had come alive. He didn't idolize her, making her memory more than the woman had been. She had her faults, and he talked about those too. Mostly what came through was how much they had loved each other. Their love was strong enough to work things out when the going got tough.

"Do you know, she nearly left me once," he confided. "I was pretty awful to her when we were first married. Everything else was more important to me than she was, and she knew it. She put up with me for about five years, and then I knew she was going to split. But when I realized what I was going to lose, I changed instead." He laughed a little. "She said the man I turned out to be was even better than the man she thought I was in the first place. I guess that's a compliment, huh?"

"Yeah," Cindi smiled dreamily. "I guess it is. A great one."

Jared looked at her steadily. "I hope I don't sound improper or anything, but I really think you're a terrific person. Your husband is lucky to have someone like you. Honest, I mean it. Thank you for being such a great friend."

Cindi blushed and tried to think of something to say, but only managed to stammer, "Thanks," which sounded inadequate. She glanced at her watch. "Oh, no, I've got to get back. Esther was only supposed to stay at her friend Ashley's for two hours. I'll be late by the time I get there."

Jared stood up. "I'll walk out with you," he said.

They walked companionably to her car. "Well, I've got to get going," she said again. She started to open the car door, but he stopped her, drawing her towards him and giving her a quick hug. Embarrassed and slightly angry, Cindi got into the car without another word. She was seething as she pulled out of the parking lot. In the rearview mirror she could see Jared standing in the parking lot waving after her.

"Why did he do that?" she asked aloud. "Why did he have to go and do that? He ruined everything." Though what constituted "everything" she wasn't exactly sure. Maybe, she mused, the hug made her see him in a different light, and it wasn't one she liked.

CHAPTER

It smelled bad in the alley where Crazy Carol had spent the night, but she barely noticed. What she did notice, though she didn't pay much attention to it, was the strange man she'd seen lately, sleeping not ten yards away in a cardboard box.

Carol was familiar with the concept of a person's space, so she kept her distance. Still, it bothered her a little that he was so close. Everyone knew this was her alley. It had been for so long that she'd forgotten when she had started sleeping there. But Carol wasn't the type to try to bully him out. Instead she ignored him and hoped he would go away.

Generally she didn't pass judgment on the people she came into contact with. She didn't really have the mental capacity to entertain such thoughts, but she did register feelings at a more primal level. She instinctively trusted or distrusted people. This man she didn't trust. It wasn't anything he had done. It wasn't even the way he looked. His long, matted, graying hair was no better or worse looking then her own and only slightly shorter. His tattered clothes were no more holey than hers. It wasn't even anything he'd said. Carol distrusted him on a far deeper level.

She picked up her few things as early as possible and made her way to the park, where she sat on the bench and let the early morning sun seep into her. She turned her face up to the sky and enjoyed the warmth, though she was probably the only one who appreciated it on such a hot day. Unconsciously she reached down to pet Come Here's shaggy head. Her hand landed on air, and she was painfully reminded that her old friend was gone.

A smartly dressed woman was making her way purposefully down the sidewalk with a little girl in tow. The youngster stared fixedly at Carol. Hesitantly she smiled and raised her hand in a sort of wave. "Hi," she offered.

Carol didn't respond, and the woman gave the little girl a startled look. She took in Carol's disreputable state and the interest the girl was showing. "Esther," she hissed, "it's not polite to stare."

"I'm not staring," the girl replied defensively. "I was saying hello. That's the lady from the church."

The woman lowered her voice, but Carol's hearing was quite acute. "You are mistaken. That woman does not attend our church."

"She does," the girl insisted. "Sometimes. She usually has a big dog."

The woman looked uncertain for a minute, but her pace slowed. She glanced at Carol, though pretended to be looking at something beyond her. Her eyebrows knit together as she tried to remember something, but she was not quite able to grasp it. Finally she shook her head, sending her black hair tumbling about her shoulders. "Come on, Essie, we're going to be late."

Their footsteps echoed down the sidewalk. The little girl looked back and gave Carol a big smile, and then they were gone. Carol sat for a long time on the park bench, even after the sun ceased to be warming and became brutal instead. She dozed off, her head drooping down on her chest, her mouth hanging open.

She had strange and terrible dreams, but she was accustomed to them. They were a result of the drug overdosing, and she'd had them for so long she had forgotten what normal dreams were like. As the day wore on she dozed and dreamed, and she didn't notice the strange man from the alley watching her.

"He's dangerous," Saiph said.

"I know." It was Reissa who was checking in on Ethel Bennington's daughter. "Her mother's prayers kept her safe while

she was alive, but now . . . " *Her voice trailed off. "The Master says it is time."*

"That's right," Balor chuckled. "We win this one. The old prayer warrior won't have her daughter in heaven anyway. Score one for us."

The angel was thoughtful. When she spoke, her words were not meant to refute the demon, whom she barely acknowledged, but to give comfort to the angel who would soon know the pain of loss once again. "Thus says the Lord: Even the captives of the mighty shall be taken away, and the prey of the terrible be delivered; for I will contend with him who contends with you, and I will save your children." She put her arm around Saiph as the demon backed off snarling. "Only the Master knows what is in her heart. We must trust His wisdom."

Carol woke up and stared around her for a few minutes, disoriented and groggy. Finally she pushed herself stiffly from the bench and began to stagger down the sidewalk. Her stomach told her that it was time to find something to eat, and she was pretty sure where she could get some decent leftovers. She didn't notice the dark shadow that followed her at a distance, nor would she have been particularly concerned if she had.

Everyone at the mission knew better than to interact with Toby in the mornings. "I don't do mornings," she would growl. And she really didn't. She might have been awake and moving around, but her brain didn't really function until sometime after ten o'clock. The morning after Davy disappeared, however, she was the first one at the breakfast table, though not to eat and primarily because she'd fallen asleep there the night before, praying and anxious.

Julia's hand on her shoulder had woken her early. "Toby? Ray and I want to pray with you. We've been praying in our room, but we thought it would be nice for all of us to pray together."

"Yeah, that's a good idea," Toby mumbled thickly. She felt sick from lack of sleep. Sitting up straighter, she held out her hands. Ray took one and Julia the other. They all bowed their heads.

"Lord, we give You Davy O'Connell," Julia's soft voice said. "We ask You to keep him safe in Your care. Protect him from harm, and give him a safe journey back to us at the mission. Give us Your peace as we wait and help us to trust You in every circumstance. In the name of Jesus, who saves us for eternity, we pray, amen."

Light surrounded them as angels moved in, forming a hedge around the trio and Akueke who had come in during the prayer and joined them. A group of demons stood off to one side, not interfering, just looking uncomfortable in the presence of so many of the angelic host.

Lileah knew that Davy was in no real danger from them. They had no plans to harm him yet. In a sense, she supposed, these human beings were praying for nothing, but then, not for nothing. After all, prayer was the way they placed themselves in the Master's will. Their prayers put them where they needed to be; they didn't change God. Thinking about prayer in this way made her gladder than ever that she could speak with the Master face to face.

Akueke was the first to hear it. She looked up, a frown on her wise and solemn face. "He is coming," she said shortly.

With a half-strangled cry, Toby fled the kitchen, racing for the runway. Julia and Ray followed her to the door and then dropped back and let her go ahead. *He's back. He's safe. He's back. He's safe* was the litany that ran through Toby's head as she ran, stumbled, righted herself, and ran on.

Davy brought the little craft down gently and hopped out almost before it had stopped moving. He held up his hands defensively. "I know what you're going to say, but there wasn't any way I was going to risk you going out there before I had a chance to assess the situation. I know you're going to yell at me, so go ahead. Get it out of your system."

Toby didn't embrace him so much as she collided with him and threw her arms around his neck. "You crazy fool! What did you go and do that for? It wasn't safe! Anything could have happened. I've been worried sick."

Davy looked as though he couldn't believe his luck. "Wait, you mean you're not mad?"

"Mad? Mad? Of course I'm mad." She pummeled her fists against his chest. "I've been up half the night praying for you. I haven't eaten. You worried us all. Of course I'm mad," she said again. "I'd have to be mad to be in love with you."

Davy cupped her face in his hands. "I love you. Or I wouldn't have gone without you." His eyes searched hers. "You know that, don't you?"

"Yeah, sure. But that only works once, you know."

"I know. It's OK though, because things seem pretty quiet back there. People were nice to me and seemed genuinely happy I was there, even though I couldn't do much for them. I straightened out some stuff, fixed some structural damage caused by windstorms or vandalism, it was hard to tell which sometimes." He bent down to kiss her gently. "I just couldn't let you go. You understand that, don't you? I couldn't lose you again."

Toby felt tears sting her eyes, and she had to swallow past a lump in her throat. "You won't be losing me any time soon. Davy. I want to get married."

His eyes widened incredulously. "What? When?"

"I don't know, today, tomorrow, whenever we can."

"You're sure about this? It's not just because I scared you?"

"No, it's not that. I've known for a while, just wanted to be sure."

"And it doesn't have anything to do with that other guy getting married?"

She laughed at him. He always referred to Don as "that other guy." "No, it doesn't. You aren't trying to get out of this, are you?"

"Get out of it? I've been trying to get back into it for so long that some of the natives call me a French name that means 'the man who flies the plane so he can marry the nurse,' only I can't pronounce it. Let's go." He grabbed her hand and began to tow her toward the ultralight.

"Where are we going?" Toby protested.

"Where you said. To get married. Get in and buckle up; this is going to be the ride of your life."

"But you don't even know where to go," she hollered over the roar of the buzzing engine.

"I'm sure there's someone who can marry us in Niamey," he shouted back. "Wahabi will know."

"Yippee!" she shrieked, feeling wild and adventurous and completely free for the first time in years.

Don was anxious to stop and see Wahabi. It was more than just the urge to see the face of a friend after their grueling trip. He knew that Wahabi would have a good feel about what was going on at the mission and could tell him what to expect. The only thing that worried him was how the man would feel about the fact that he and Shay were married. It wasn't so long ago that Shay had been Wahabi's sister-in-law.

They arrived in Niamey exhausted and out of sorts. Wahabi's anxious face was the first they saw, rushing up to them as he did, exclaiming over the children and helping with the baggage. The tall African had not changed in the year they had been gone. His bearing was still as regal as ever, and his manners faultless. His gallantry still seemed out of place.

"Madame, it is good to see you again," he said, stooping his tall frame to bestow a kiss on Shay's flushed cheek. "The children have sprouted like weeds after a rainstorm." He indicated Marcus. "Especially this one. He grows more like his father every day."

At the mention of Nwibe, Shay flinched. Don knew she was afraid of the emotions she would have to confront at the mission where her husband had died. But she smiled bravely. "He sure does. And that American food didn't seem to slow him down."

They all laughed at that and Marcus began to tell his uncle about the things he had experienced in America and which of them he liked best. At the same time, Madina got over her initial shyness and began to compete for Wahabi's attention as well. Don was amused watching Wahabi trying to keep up with both conversations at once, but even that didn't seem to fluster him.

Inside the Tokoulakoye, Wahabi's bar, it was darker but not much cooler. Wahabi offered them all some of the warm cola he kept around for special occasions. Don declined, but Shay and the kids each wanted one. Don waited impatiently for them to be settled so he could draw Wahabi off to one side and speak with him alone. Finally he pulled Wahabi away.

"Fill me in," Don urged. "What's been going on here? Dorsey's reports seem pretty sanitized to me. When I left, the place was deserted because of the outbreak. I understand it's better populated now, but do people really trust us again?"

The tall African regarded him solemnly for a few moments before he spoke. "I have not been there much. It is still too painful for me, you understand?" Don nodded. "But I know the things I hear in my bar. There are some so desperate, it is true, that they go to the mission; they have nowhere else to go. The risk does not seem so great. They face death by one means or another.

"There are others who are becoming restless. They do not trust the people at the mission. They have a name for them, '*diables blanc,*' white devils," he elaborated. "They say you carry the disease like animals and they want all of you to leave." Wahabi looked thoughtful for a moment. "I have seen the fear on the faces of these men, and I know they are very serious. I think it would be a mistake to take them lightly." His eyes dropped. "You will find that Toby O'Connell does not share my views."

Don nodded. Remembering Toby, he understood. The fearless O'Connell. No, she'd not take some local "blowhards" seriously. He could almost hear her voice as if she were standing there talking to them: "They don't mean it," she'd say. "You know that. They're just letting off steam. Are we going to let them scare us or what?" He smiled. It would be good to work with her again, despite the fact that they always got along like oil and water.

"Thanks, Wahabi. I appreciate the heads-up." They rejoined the family just as Jean-Robert arrived to transport them to the mission in his jeep. "Hello Jean-Robert! It's good to see you again, my friend," Don greeted him.

"Big family?" Jean-Robert said, his wide grin displaying the lack of most of his teeth. "Last time I see you, got no big family. Fast work, huh?"

Don laughed heartily and squeezed Shay. "Yeah, we work fast."

She poked him in the ribs. "Liar. It took you forever to finally marry me!"

The bumpy ride in the jeep was nearly as unpleasant as Don remembered it to be. Every time they were jolted, Madina let out a squeal. It was time Jean-Robert looked into getting some new shocks, Don thought, gritting his teeth and holding on to the door handle.

Finally the mission appeared. As they drove up, a small crowd gathered around. He recognized Toby and Davy right away, and an Italian nurse who had spent some time with them. He couldn't remember her name. There were a couple of other Americans; they must be Ray and Julia Vargas. They had arrived shortly before he'd left the year before. But where were all the native staff? Where were all the children?

The jeep stopped with a flourish, covering everyone waiting with a layer of fine dust. Jean-Robert made a big show of helping them all out of the jeep and stacking their baggage in a teetering pile beside the jeep. Don paid him, and he roared off, waving and grinning. Don turned to face everyone.

Toby went for Shay, hugging her as both of them talked at once. Davy and Don faced each other uncertainly until Davy finally stuck his hand out. "Hey, glad to have you back."

"It's good to be back," Don agreed, shaking Davy's hand briefly. He wasn't sure what else to say.

"We've got some place cleared out for all of you," Davy continued. "Here, let me help you with those bags." He started picking up luggage.

Don felt that having something to do was a mercy. Now he was back in his element. He just wished he didn't feel so much like the outsider.

Ray Vargas grabbed the leftover luggage, and the guys made their way into the mission compound. Before they could start down the hallway they were stopped by the purposeful figure of Akueke, who hustled over to Don, making a high-pitched noise he could only guess was a squeal of excitement.

"Dr. Germaine, they tell me you come, but I did not believe them until I could see you with my own eyes. Welcome back, sir."

Don leaned over to kiss the old woman's wrinkled cheeks. "Thank you, Akueke. We're glad to be back too."

Don learned that Shay and Nwibe's old room, where Nwibe had died, had been turned into a storeroom. His own old room was vacant and was still his. It felt strange to go in there. He hadn't realized how much he'd left behind, but he had no doubt that Shay would soon decorate it to suit her tastes.

The children each had a room on either side of his and Shay's, which was convenient, but he had a feeling Madina would be sleeping with them until she got used to the place. She'd come down with a cold on the way over and had been unusually clingy because of it and wasn't sleeping well at all.

The guys deposited the suitcases in the rooms and then they milled in the hallway, not quite knowing what else to do. "Should we leave you to unpack?" Davy asked uncertainly.

"No, no, I'll let Shay do that. If I do it she'll just go behind me and redo it anyway."

"I heard that!"

Don grinned sheepishly. "Well, it's true." He turned to Davy and Ray. "I want to see the clinic. Let's leave them to it."

"That's male-speak for let the women do the dirty work," Toby said, and all the girls burst out laughing.

Outside, striding across the compound toward the clinic, Don felt his sense of purpose and belonging returning to him. He was back. He was in charge.

And then he was shocked. There were no patients in the clinic. He looked around. "Where is everybody?"

"Well, you know, it's a funny thing. They come and they go, but they don't like to stay over."

"But the field reports I read . . . " Don tried to put everything together.

"Sure, we treat them. But, most of the time they leave directly after. Of course, Toby can't do any operations, so they're usually moving on their own. For anything really serious that requires a doctor's care, they go up to Our Lady of Mercy Mission Hospital, where Flory's from."

Flory! That was the Italian girl's name. He remembered now. He'd trained her on a few procedures before he left. "Do you think more people will make use of the mission services now that there is a doctor on staff?"

Davy shrugged. "I don't know."

"I do," Ray Vargas said, speaking up for the first time. "They use what we have now. I don't see why they wouldn't take advantage of additional services."

"Our Lady doesn't have the bad associations with the outbreak that we do," Davy argued. "Why wouldn't they just keep going there?"

"They might. But some of these people die on the way just because the journey is too long. If there is a doctor nearer I believe they will come here, despite what they think about the outbreak."

"What do they think about it?" Don asked.

"They think we caused it, from what we can gather."

Ray nodded in agreement. "My wife was attacked, but I guess you heard about that."

"Yes. I'm sorry it happened. Has there been any more violence? Dorsey was talking about getting technicals out here."

Davy shook his head. "It wouldn't help. It would just escalate the violence. I don't mind telling you that I've had a really bad feeling about the clinics. Toby calls it my 'boogeyman' feeling. I get bad vibes from the people at the outposts mostly. The last time I went out, a few days ago, everything seemed OK. It's the kind of thing I don't trust though."

"Fair enough. Maybe you could fly me out first thing tomorrow so I can make an assessment. Then we'll go from there."

"You're the boss." Davy flashed his easy, charming grin, and Don found himself able to return it.

It was great to be back.

CHAPTER 7

Billie Jo sat nervously waiting at her freshly scrubbed kitchen table. Any minute now Greta Garbeaux would drive up for a visit. After two weeks of having Greta invite her home and Billie Jo refusing, she'd finally bitten the bullet and invited Greta to come to her house one afternoon. She could explain the difficulties of her life without the children eavesdropping on every word. Cassidy and Dallas were still at school and would be there until around 3:30 unless the bus was late. Billie Jo had discovered that the buses could be early or late and you just had to wait for them.

She heard the crunch of Greta's tires just as she was trying to decide if she should start the kettle for tea or wait until Greta arrived. "Phew," she murmured to herself. "There's one less decision to make."

She didn't know exactly why this visit had her so unnerved. Certainly it was difficult inviting anyone to the house when it looked so rough. They'd barricaded the porch door so no one would try to go in by that entrance, but it made the place look deserted. And then there were the remnants of old-fashioned wallpaper peeling off the walls. They'd pulled down all the trailing pieces, but the rest had stuck fast, and Billie Jo hadn't had time to finish the job properly so it was still on the walls in odd, ragged strips. It looked hideous, she thought.

The rest of the house had cleaned up fairly well, and though she didn't have nice furniture, most of it was serviceable and some was even "antique," or at least old and quaint. Billie Jo was fond of decorating magazines, and she would have classified her house as country/primitive, though not nearly finished. Hard as it was to reveal the house in its present condition, what was worse, she figured, was being completely honest with a near total stranger.

Billie Jo hadn't had a real, true friend since Leah had moved. And except for Cindi Trahan, she hadn't really even had any casual friends. After the mothers' prayer group they'd been in had split up, shortly after Ethel Bennington's death, the women had gotten wrapped up in their own lives, and Billie Jo had simply slipped away unnoticed. Once or twice she had contacted Cindi and they'd gone on a picnic, but Cindi had her own life and was very busy. It never seemed to work out, somehow.

Billie Jo had felt drawn to Greta from the moment they'd met. In their quick snatches of conversation she'd discovered that they had a lot of interests in common. But there was something else that drew her to Greta. Billie Jo considered herself a good Christian. She had devotions every morning. She prayed throughout the day. She helped others and went to church every week. In Greta's life she sensed something more. She sensed a connection with God, a rapport, that she didn't have and more than anything she wanted that.

She walked over to the kitchen door, mentally cataloging everything she noticed on the way that she should have fixed before Greta's arrival. It was hard for her to let go of her pride, but she made a conscious effort to do it, knowing she'd never enjoy the coming visit if she was obsessed about how her house appeared.

"Hello!" Greta's voice projected into the kitchen. Billie Jo could make her out beyond the screen door. She carried something bulky in her hands.

"Hey there!" Billie Jo said, opening the door for her friend. "You found us all right then?"

"No problem at all. You know, I used to drive by this place all the time and wish it were occupied. It's my dream home. You know, one of those abandoned old places that you long to fix up just how you like."

Billie Jo smiled. "I guess I can see that. We had a place like that down in Tennessee that I'd drive by all the time and just itch to fix it up. Never thought I'd end up with a house to fix up though 'cause Jimmy is a builder, and he never wanted to buy a place before. He always said he'd build any house we lived in." She laughed shortly. "Course, the way this place is falling down around our ears, he'll practically have to rebuild it before he's through."

Greta held out her burden. It was a large package wrapped in bright pink tissue paper. "I brought you a housewarming present."

"Do what?" Billie Jo exclaimed, taking the package and feeling both embarrassed and pleased. Gingerly she unwrapped the tissue paper to reveal a gallon of Vermont maple syrup. "I'll be," she exclaimed. "I've never had real syrup. Jimmy cooks pancakes every Sunday morning, but we always had the fake stuff before. Thank you so much, I'm that pleased!" She was too. Not only had Greta given her a thoughtful gift but Jimmy would warm up to her friend sight unseen.

"Sit down. I'll make us some tea. You like tea, don't you?" Billie Jo set the maple syrup on the counter and hurried to fill the kettle.

"I love tea," Greta said. "Anything herbal that you have is fine."

"I got blackberry. How's that?"

"Fine, fine." Greta was looking around her with interest. "I always wanted to see the inside of this house. I really like what you've done with it."

"It's not done by a long shot," Billie Jo groaned.

"No," Greta agreed. "But half the fun is in the planning and tackling of the project once you know just what's perfect for it. I have to live in a space for a while before I know just what I want to do with it."

"You know," Billie Jo said thoughtfully, "I agree with that, but I never thought of it that way before. I was always in a hurry to get it done." She looked around with new eyes, seeing everything in a completely different light. It was a work in progress, not an unfinished project. She found that just that slight change in her outlook lifted a weight off her shoulders.

She brought the tea back in her two best teacups. They weren't matched, but she'd learned that that was what they called "shabby chic," so she was almost proud of the presentation.

"What beautiful cups," Greta murmured. "Don't you love finding little orphans like these and pairing them with other pieces?"

Billie Jo nodded, though she'd never given it conscious thought before. The new ideas swirling in her head were almost overpowering. Listening to Greta was like getting an attitude adjustment. She'd noticed that since the move she'd been depressed, what with the constant mess of the house, the stress of making sure everything was done that needed to be done, and the lack of funds for the repairs. She'd let the negatives outweigh the positives. She leaned in toward Greta, ready to share confidences with this extraordinary woman. "The reason I asked you to come is 'cause I wanted to explain my situation some when the kids weren't around."

Greta nodded, her expression open, her brown eyes alert and interested. Her blonde hair curled at the ends, making her look more than ever like the old-time film star she'd been named after. "I understand completely."

"You see, it's like this. My husband, Jimmy, he's a good man. He's been through an awful lot. He was close to God for a while, but now he's not." She paused and considered how to phrase her words. "It's not that he isn't interested in God, or doesn't love Him. It's just that he lets life get in the way of serving God and following Him. That's why he hasn't been to church. I don't like to bring it up in front of the kids. It's not that they don't know, of course. They're smart as whips, and they notice everything.

"It's just that I don't want to bring a lot of attention to it in front of them." She sighed. "And maybe I hope that if I don't make a big deal out of it that it will change eventually. I don't know. I ain't got that far in my thinking. I just wanted you to know, so that, well, so you wouldn't think I wasn't interested in being your friend. It's just that it's hard for me to leave Jimmy. I go to church without him because I have to, but I like to come back home and spend the rest of the day with him. That's why I ain't accepted your invitation to go home with you for lunch. It's not 'cause I don't want to."

" 'I wish I were supernaturally strong so I could put right everything that is wrong,' " Greta sighed wistfully.

Billie Jo looked at her puzzled. "Do what?"

Greta laughed. "I'm sorry. I was quoting the real Greta Garbo. Not that I don't have the same wish." She reached across the table and squeezed one of Billie Jo's hands. "I feel that I've been putting you in a stressful situation, and I apologize." She waved aside Billie Jo's protestations. "No, no, I know I didn't do it on purpose, but I've caused you discomfort and I'm sorry for that, however unintentional it was."

She sipped her tea thoughtfully for a moment. "I understand about your husband. Maybe you've noticed that my husband isn't ever at church?"

Billie Jo was ashamed to realize that she'd been so preoccupied with her own life and problems that not only had she not noticed the absence of Greta's husband, but she hadn't even wondered if Greta *had* a husband. "I, uh, no. I guess I've not met him?"

Greta laughed. Her laugh tinkled like little brass bells "No. And I'm sorry you won't. He was a lovely man. He died three years ago of leukemia. But he was never what you would call a practicing Christian.

"He was one of the nicest fellows you'd meet. He'd stop to help people stranded on the side of the road. He'd give his lunch to children at the school where he taught if they came without one. He sent a lot of money to people we knew in Bangladesh because they had, literally, nothing.

"But he never went to church. He was upset by some of the people there who didn't practice what they preached, so to speak." Greta took a sip of her tea. "I only saw him read the Bible occasionally, and as far as I know he never had any regular devotions. I know he loved God and did what he believed God wanted him to do. So you see, I get very nervous when people judge whether or not someone is a Christian. There's a lot you can tell by their actions, of course, but there are some things that are between only that person and God.

"I wouldn't presume to judge Jimmy's spiritual condition by the fact that he doesn't go to church. Though I doubt everyone there would be so inclined. Still, you see now why I understand your situation?"

Billie Jo nodded. Two things struck her powerfully. The first was the relief of being understood and not judged. The second was the singular revelation that Jimmy might indeed have a relationship with God that she, in her humanity, didn't understand. She deeply regretted judging her own husband in the way that Greta was determined not to do herself. And she was particularly upset at having done so considering that she, of all people, should have been the most forgiving and understanding.

"You never know too," Greta said suddenly, "when God is just waiting for someone who hasn't made a complete commitment to Him. You see that sometimes. Some people who weren't what we'd call obvious Christians become more committed to God during hard times. When my husband, Nathan, was dying, before he got too bad, I know he spent a lot of time reading his Bible and praying. He didn't do either much before his illness, and I always thought it was because he didn't care to. But during his illness it never seemed so much like he found God, as he grew closer to Him in a different way than he had while he was well."

"I know what you mean," Billie Jo said excitedly. "Jimmy was in an accident awhile back and he got lots closer to God afterwards. But," she added in a subdued voice, "it didn't last. Leastways that's what I've thought till now. Considering what you said, I ain't so sure anymore. I guess I'm not the one to judge, huh?"

Greta smiled. " 'For man looks at the outward appearance, but the Lord looks at the heart,' " she quoted. She smiled brightly, and Billie Jo felt her facial muscles responding with a grin of her own. Being around Greta was like a tonic.

"So, will you show me around? I'm dying to see what the old place is like."

Billie Jo would rather have had her teeth drilled, but to please Greta she led her on a tour of the house. She felt like introducing each new room with a preface of how much it was going to cost to fix it up. Something like, "And this here's the living room. It will take $2,000 to fix the floors and the electrical wiring." Instead she bit her tongue and accepted Greta's praise for her cleverness in decorating.

After the tour Greta was pretty bent on leaving, and Billie Jo, who happened to glance at her watch and realize the children would be home soon, reluctantly agreed that she had some things to accomplish before they arrived. Greta gave her a big hug. "Thank you so much for inviting me. Next time you'll come to my house?"

"If I can walk there," Billie Jo agreed. "We've only got the one vehicle, and Jimmy takes it to work. We thought we'd get another after we moved, but things is tight right now so we can't."

"I'll pick you up, how's that?" Greta asked.

"If it's no trouble."

"No trouble at all. See you this weekend!"

When she had gone Billie Jo thought it was like a light had been extinguished somehow. Greta glowed from the inside out. "Thank You for giving me a friend, Lord." Before she could say more, the yellow school bus lurched to a stop in front of the house, letting off Cassidy and Dallas. Billie Jo hurried to find them a snack and settled down to listen to a recounting of all they'd done that day. It was one of her most important hours of the day. The second was when Jimmy came home, though that one was trickier. The children were always in high spirits. Jimmy could be either excited about his new job or depressed about their finances, depending on which he'd been dwelling on that day.

As she was making supper later when he came in, she could see immediately that today it had been the latter. "How was work?" she asked cheerfully.

"Fine." Jimmy's voice implied that it had been anything but fine. He crashed down into a chair at the table and sat there looking morose.

"Something wrong?" Billie Jo knew exactly what was wrong.

"Same as usual," Jimmy muttered. "Been working in my mind how to pay for all the stuff needs doing around here. Wish we had enough extra to hire someone to do some of it. I tell you, I'm so tired when I get done working I don't wanna think about lifting my hammer again at night."

Billie Jo had known, before they even moved, that things would be like this. Besides Jimmy's attitude, she had to struggle against her own, which tempted her to say, "I told you so" every time he brought up the subject. The problem was that she never had any solutions to offer him. She couldn't do the work because she didn't know how. He couldn't do the work because he was exhausted. And they couldn't hire someone because it was too expensive.

"Do you want to pray about it?" she asked hopefully. She'd been praying on her own, but so far they hadn't prayed together.

"Nah. I been praying about it, and it ain't done no good so far. Seems like a waste of breath."

Billie Jo felt let down, but she tried not to let it show. "Maybe some other time."

"Where's the kids?"

"Out playing in that old barn. Seems to keep them occupied a lot. Guess it's a good thing we got it with the place."

"Yeah. Might as well play in it all they can. Someday I'll be wanting to knock it down, I reckon."

Billie Jo, who had plans to convert the old barn into a gardening shed, and maybe even a greenhouse, said nothing. There was no sense getting into an argument about it. They didn't have enough money to put in a garden, let alone make a gardening shed. They'd spent every penny they had on the repairs they'd made so far, and it hardly made a dent, though she tried to remain grateful for the things they did have. Like water. At least she didn't have to haul it to the house anymore. After a week of that she'd been ready to go back to Tennessee.

The phone rang, and Billie Jo and Jimmy stared at it. It was the first time it had rung since they'd installed it two days before. Finally Jimmy answered it. Though he didn't say anything specific to make her think so, Billie Jo was pretty sure it was his mother. She grimaced. A phone was one thing she could have done without.

As she popped the casserole into the oven and mixed up some juice in a pitcher, she half followed the conversation between Jimmy and Helen. Apparently his mother wanted something that

Jimmy wasn't going to give her, but Billie Jo couldn't figure out what it was. From the look on Jimmy's face she guessed the conversation wasn't going well, because his only contribution was a series of grunts and the word "no" repeated over and over. Finally he blew his top.

"Look, Ma, the kids can't spend the summer with you and that's final. They gotta make new friends here. We ain't been here that long. Give them time to settle in. We'll be back soon for a visit. Or you could come up here."

"Please Lord," Billie Jo begged silently. *"Don't let them come here! We haven't even settled in yet."* She could just imagine Helen's criticism of the house in its present state. She heard Helen's barrage of anger on the telephone from across the kitchen. No, it didn't sound like they would be coming to Vermont any time soon. Billie Jo hid a smile.

Jimmy rubbed his temples after he got off the phone. "I wish she'd quit pestering me. She's been calling me at work, and it's starting to get to Zeb. She cornered him the other day on the phone and wanted to know, did he think any kind of good son would act like I act toward her? Then she chewed him out for taking me away from my roots. I got enough problems. I can't be dealing with this." His face was grim.

"I might as well tell you now. The money they usually give us for swimming lessons and such for the summer . . . well, we won't be seeing it this summer."

Billie Jo had figured as much. Since the move, Dallas had celebrated a birthday without presents from Helen and James, who usually showered him with gifts besides giving him a substantial amount of money that they put in the bank for him. Jimmy's birthday was next, and Billie Jo was interested to see if he received the same treatment. Helen's passive-aggressive tactics seemed to know no bounds.

"It's OK," she said and didn't add that she had expected as much, although she was thinking it. "We'll make out."

"How?" Jimmy demanded, his frustration barely held in check. "This place is eating our money faster than we can make it. Already we're plumb broke, and I don't get paid for another week.

How are we gonna make out? You got a stash of money some-where I don't know about?"

"No," Billie Jo said quietly. Her eyes filled with tears. She hated it when he got so angry.

"Well, then, how? You gonna get a job finally?"

"That's right, you slug!" Nog chortled. He'd been waiting for his opportunity.

Billie Jo felt her eyes sting with tears, and she didn't bother to answer. She fled to their room, threw herself on the bed, and cried stormily. "Why is this happening to us, God?" she sobbed. "You trying to punish us for something we done? Seemed like You were leading us here. Why have You abandoned us now?"

" ' "I will never leave you nor forsake you," ' " Jewel quoted, laying a sympathetic hand on Billie Jo's shoulder. "The Master hasn't forsaken you, though in your despair it may seem so. You only have to look and you will see His many blessings."

The angel paused, reflecting. So often human beings sabotaged the Master's efforts to strengthen them. They railed against the slightest trial, simply getting through it, not learning anything. And when a harder trial came they went to pieces. Jewel felt a sense of urgency for Billie Jo. He had a good idea what kinds of trials were ahead of her, and right then she was so busy with the mundane problems of life that she couldn't see anything beyond her little day-to-day crises. If she didn't begin to pay attention to her life and where she was headed, it could prove very difficult for her to get through the coming days.

"You have the unlimited power of heaven at your disposal," he reminded her. "Use the Master's power to defeat the enemy and drive him away."

"She doesn't want to drive us away," Nog said matter-of-factly. "She likes having us around. Some people are perverse like that. They like chaos. All these problems with the house and now her husband are all great because she misses Helen." He looked at the angel, sizing him up. "You don't believe me, but it's true. She misses that upheaval in her life. You took that away from her. Now she's looking for some other crisis to take the place of Helen."

"Pray. Pray," Jewel urged.

Nog grinned, displaying rotten teeth. "She won't. I'm telling you. She likes this, even though she doesn't realize it."

Billie Jo heard the wooden floorboards creak under Jimmy's weight and as she expected he sat down beside her on the bed and pulled her into his arms. "I'm sorry, darlin'. I know you do plenty of work around here. It's just I'm so scared about . . . well, about lots of things. We need money to do stuff, to make this place livable, and I can't make it all. Some of the things that need to be done can't wait, but we don't have the money to do them. It weighs on me heavy, being the sole provider. I'm sorry I took it out on you."

Billie Jo buried her face in his work shirt and inhaled deeply of woodchips and the outdoors. "I know. I'm scared too. It's OK. It'll be OK."

She wondered dully if she should get a job. Jimmy might be sorry for his angry outburst, but she knew that didn't change how he felt. She had a tremendous sense of guilt over it. After all, she was only cleaning and keeping up the house during the day. She didn't have any great purpose or project, though she would have liked to start volunteering around the community when they were more settled. Maybe she should think about it more. Maybe Jimmy was right.

CHAPTER

Cindi was scrubbing down the kitchen table when the phone rang. A pasta dinner was simmering on the stove, and Esther was playing with her Lego blocks on the floor of the dining room.

"I'll get it!" Esther said eagerly, jumping up and neatly vaulting over her Lego building. "Hello, this is the Trahan residence."

Cindi swelled with pride. *Bravo, Esther,* she thought.

"It's for you, Mommy." Esther held the phone out to her. "It's some man, but it's not Daddy."

"Oh?" Cindi took the phone. "Hello?"

"What would you say if I told you that I'm falling in love with you?"

Jared! Cindi felt a wild kind of terror at the way her treacherous heart leapt at the words. "I'd say you have the wrong number," she said, trying to keep her voice level but hearing it shake just the same. "Where *did* you get my number, by the way?"

"I looked it up. It's not a secret, is it?"

"No, but why are you calling me?"

He sounded hurt. "I wanted to talk to you. I have some good news. They're letting me come back to work on probation. My leave of absence was up, and the chief called me to see how I was feeling. I told him I feel a lot better thanks to a good friend of mine. I had to take some tests, and I can't do any diving yet, just

134

deskwork, but it's something. I was so happy I just had to tell someone. I'm sorry if I bothered you."

Cindi fought to keep her voice casual. Esther was listening to every word. "No, no, it was just so unexpected, that's all. I'm so happy for you. I'm . . . I'm glad you called." It wasn't strictly a lie. It was nice to hear his voice, but she wasn't sure how she felt about him calling her. She hadn't seen him since the episode at the café. They'd emailed a bit but nothing had been said. She wondered if she should mention it or not. In the end she decided it was probably nothing, and it would be best not to draw attention to it at all.

"What have you been up to today?" Jared was asking her.

"Not much, just home school and working on my email. Oh, I almost forgot. I do have some news. I started checking around today about starting the homeless shelter I was telling you about, and I think I made some progress." She didn't add that the strain of trying to fit that in around home schooling and her other chores had nearly driven her to the brink of insanity. Marc thought she couldn't do both, but she was going to show him.

"I'm friends with a guy who is a supervisor at a local homeless shelter run by the state. He's interested in running the one I'd like to start. It won't be strictly a homeless shelter because there are already a couple of those. It'll be combined with a soup kitchen and a food shelf, and we'll help people find jobs and get permanent housing." She stopped, feeling a bit breathless at the idea. It was hard to believe that her dream might come true after all. "It'll be a center where the community can rally around people who find themselves homeless and help them back on their feet instead of ostracizing them. What do you think?"

"I think you're wonderful," Jared said sincerely. "I do. You've got all this enthusiasm and you just infect the people around you with it. I'd volunteer. In fact, I do. I volunteer. Put me to work."

Cindi knew she was blushing furiously. "It's just an idea right now. But we'll need lots of help. I'll put you on the list."

Later she wondered how it would be to have Jared around, working with him, not snatching minutes here and there for some hurried conversation. But as soon as the idea popped into her head she dismissed it guiltily. Jared was just like any other friend. *He is a friend,* she reminded herself. *Only a friend.*

"*That's what you think,*" *Rafe said.* "*You humans are so short-sighted. Can't see the forest for the trees, can't see the attraction for the friendship. If this guy is such a terrific friend, why haven't you told anyone about him? Why don't you admit it; you like him. You like him even more than you will admit to yourself.*

"*It's OK. You wouldn't be the first one to ditch your husband for someone who cared more about you. And at least this guy cares. Your husband is never around. If he were, maybe you wouldn't have come this far. It's his fault really. If he were around more and took an interest in you, this guy would be old news. You'd never have given him the time of day. But your husband doesn't really care, does he? All he cares about anymore is his work.*

"*Why would you want to be with someone who doesn't love you? Why not get out? Take your chances with Jared. He loved his wife. You know that. And he's attracted to you; you can see that without half trying. What would you really lose, after all? Think about it.*"

Shania, tears slipping down her cheeks, called to Cindi to pray for guidance and to ignore what the demon said, but her voice was so soft in Cindi's ears that it was like an unintelligible whisper. Instead, Cindi seemed to be listening to the demon. Shania dispatched angels, one on a special assignment and the other to suggest to Marc Trahan that he should pick up some flowers on the way home and remind his wife how much he loved her. She was dismayed to learn that the latter failed in his mission. Hoping the other would be successful, Shania kept up her vigil by Cindi's side, praying that something she said would get through.

Crazy Carol was dreaming. But this dream was different. Aside from all the bright lights flashing and strange, disturbing images, there was the smothering feeling of something heavy on top of her, crushing her. She groaned and thrashed in her sleep. The night before she had found shelter beneath a tree on the riverbank. In her dream, it was Come Here, not dead, but being playful, wrestling with her. In the next instant she was no longer asleep.

She blinked her small eyes and became aware of her surroundings. A large man was leaning over her, digging through her pockets, cursing under his breath because she had so many of them. He was not aware that she had woken up, and Carol lay very still, not wanting him to know. Her survival instinct was very strong, and when she reacted it was calculated to achieve the most damage.

With a strength born of self-preservation, she drove her elbows into the man's side. His exhalation was half pain, half surprise, and he turned to Carol and grabbed her wrists. "Don't move," he commanded.

Carol was not listening. Bringing her knees up, she drove them into the man's side, catching him unaware and knocking him off balance. Before he could recover, she rolled away from him with more agility than she looked capable of. She scooted out of his reach and in another moment would have been on her way up the riverbank toward the road, but he was faster than she was, and he collided with her knees. She went down like a bowling pin, falling flat on her face. Her hands reached out, fingers clawing the ground for purchase, trying to pull away from the man.

Saiph stood a distance away, not trying to help, only calling out to Carol in a soft voice to be brave. Tears streamed down her face, and Reissa stood by, giving her courage to watch something that should never have been allowed to happen. In the new earth it would never happen, Reissa assured her, and Saiph clung to that knowledge. She didn't know how the Master could stand the evil that humankind was capable of.

Balor was in his glory. He and some other demons were urging the man to greater heights of evil. The man caught the impression of their frenzied pitch.

He picked up a large stone that was lying nearby and with a malicious smile drove it into Carol's skull. She dropped onto the dirt and lay still. Looking furtively around, the man finished his examination of her pockets. Then he threw the rock into the river nearby.

The only evidence left of his crime was Carol's body, which he dragged down to the river's edge. First he loaded her pockets with rocks. Groaning with the weight of her and the burden of the rocks, he maneuvered as far out into the river as he could before letting go. The current was swift in that area, and it carried Carol's body down into a small but powerful whirlpool, and it did not surface. Smiling with satisfaction, the man made his way back onto shore. Later he would go into town. Sometime someone would likely find the old broad, but by that time he'd be long gone. And with no murder weapon, the investigation of the murder of a homeless woman would be one of those things that slipped through the cracks of justice.

For Don, it was almost as if he'd never left. The year of absence melted as though it had never been. After the first few uncomfortable weeks of settling back in and everyone establishing a pecking order, they were back in business. Except that there was still not much business to get back to.

The clinic was always open, and now there were more than enough people to man it, as well as the outpost clinics. Flory, who had been in residence while Don and Shay were away, had returned to Our Lady of Mercy Mission Hospital. Davy had begun making regular trips to the outpost clinics, and there was a smattering of work there, though so far no danger signs. Everything else seemed to have ground to a standstill. The school Shay had started was gone. The native families who had lived at the mission compound were gone, dispersed and not returned. It was clear to Don that their first order of business was to come up with a plan of action. They couldn't go on hanging around and hoping.

They had the meeting in the kitchen where it was ever so slightly cooler. Julia and Ray opened a package of cookies Julia's father had included in the last care package, and everyone gratefully munched stale cookies and looked expectantly at Don.

"OK," he said, remembering how much he hated meetings before the word was even out of his mouth, "I've been thinking." He held up his hands defensively. "Now, I'm not criticizing anyone, OK? I know I haven't been around, and you guys have done a fantastic job without much to build on. But I'm looking around and I'm seeing a mission outpost that is barely holding its own in patients and doing no witnessing at all. Let's discuss this. I want ideas. What can we do to make this place a vibrant clinic and mission?"

He was greeted by silence and thought that before it broke he'd be forced to say something more. Julia saved him. She looked around the table shyly before she spoke.

"I think we should get the school started again."

"We have no kids," Davy pointed out.

"You didn't, but you do now," Shay countered. "Even if ours are the only ones, they will need to go to school. Maybe if we go ahead and start school and put out the word that it's open, people will start to come. After all, we can't expect to just place an order and have it filled. Things are going to move slowly; I don't think we can expect anything else."

Don nodded. "Yes, but they should move."

Toby bristled. "Are you saying we haven't been doing enough around here?"

"No, absolutely not. I said that already." He sighed in exasperation. "I just want us to put our heads together and think of some ways to make this place a little more worthwhile. Otherwise we might as well pack our bags and move on." He paused a moment to collect his thoughts and prayed that they would come out of his mouth the way he intended them to.

"We've been gone awhile, I know. But maybe that gives us better perspective. Ever since Ethel died it seems as though God's protective hand has been removed from this place and it's been suffering. I think we need to claim some Bible promises here and make a stand for God. These are His children, and we are His servants. We're here to do His will and serve these people to the best of our ability in whatever ways we can. If that isn't God's will then we are in the wrong place and we should move on."

Silence met his speech and he sweated, waiting for someone to say something. Finally Akueke spoke. She lifted her scrawny arms in the air and said, " 'Hallelujah! Glory be to God! Thus I will magnify Myself and sanctify Myself, and I will be known in the eyes of many nations. Then they shall know that I am the Lord.' "

Don's eyes twinkled. "Thank you, Akueke. Do we have another?"

" 'The Lord is near to all who call upon Him, to all who call upon Him in truth,' " quoted Ray Vargas, giving his wife a nudge. "Go on, honey. Tell them the promise God gave you this morning."

Julia's voice was soft, but her words reached every heart present. " 'Be in pain, and labor to bring forth, O daughter of Zion, like a woman in birth pangs. For now you shall go forth from the city, you shall dwell in the field, and you shall go even to Babylon. There you shall be delivered; there the Lord will redeem you from the hands of your enemies.' "

Don swallowed hard. "I think we should pray."

Angels swarmed in force to form a living wall of light around the people gathered at the table, whose heads were bowed in prayer. Demons had skittered away at the first words of Scripture, keeping well out of the reach of the sharp swords. They milled uncomfortably, powerless to stop the revival that appeared to be beginning. If they had seen it coming they would have moved away altogether, but they were unprepared, lulled by inactivity.

The human beings heard nothing, saw nothing. The angels suddenly grew even brighter and a whistling, like the sound of a wind soughing through tree branches was heard. That was the only warning they had before the Spirit of God descended on the room and settled like a soft blanket over those gathered. Demons, blinded and scorched by the Presence, tumbled out of the way, flinging their companions aside to make way. There was a mad scramble and unearthly shrieks. Even Lucien, who had been in attendance and equally unprepared, was caught off guard. As they huddled en masse, licking their wounds and regrouping skittishly, he regarded the light beaming from the building with a feeling of deep disquiet. This was not good. This was definitely not good.

Billie Jo had a strong urge to call Cindi Trahan. Which, she told herself, was the silliest thing she'd ever heard. She hadn't talked to Cindi in at least six months. In fact, the last time she'd talked to her was to discuss a baby shower they were throwing for a mutual friend. She'd been civil, friendly even, but they hadn't been in touch since. If Cindi wanted to talk to her, Billie Jo reasoned, wouldn't she have called?

Well, no, she thought finally. Cindi would have no way of knowing that she had moved and wouldn't even know where to start looking for her phone number. The impression came again, stronger this time, to call Cindi. She spent the morning fighting it, telling herself she was being ridiculous. Around lunch time, as she cobbled together something to eat, she decided that, in fact, it made a lot of sense to call Cindi. They had history. She could talk to her about the possibility of getting a job, and Cindi could give her opinion without any bias, which she suspected Greta of harboring. Greta had strong opinions on whether or not she ought to work. She was forcefully against it.

"You'd never have any time to do anything with me," she'd said. Which was true, and as far as it went, Billie Jo agreed. But that could not be her prime consideration in making a decision. She'd miss spending so much time with Greta, surely, but the reasons she thought she ought to work went beyond her own personal preferences anyway. No, Greta's opinion was too biased.

"Call Cindi," Jewel urged again. Ever since the messenger had arrived from Shania he had been putting the thought to call Cindi in Billie Jo's head. She'd resisted it until now, but he sensed that she was considering the idea. "Make the call. You two need each other right now."

"She can't help you," Nog roared, trying to drown the angel out. He, too, could sense she was about to make the decision to call, and it was the last thing he wanted. He was having enough

trouble keeping her away from new friends. If she had a support system, it made his job that much harder.

Billie Jo finally decided to make the call, but even then it took her another hour to locate her address book, and she almost gave up. She finally found it in a box with some kitchen stuff she hadn't gotten to. She had no recollection of putting it there.

"It's almost as if someone don't want me to call," Billie Jo mumbled under her breath. She took the address book to the table and sat down with the phone. It rang on the other end and she waited, a little nervous because it had been so long.

"Hello?" She recognized Cindi's voice immediately.

"Cindi? It's Billie Jo. Billie Jo Raynard," she added, just in case.

"Billie Jo? How are you? Someone told me the other day that you had moved. I was so sorry to hear that! We didn't even have a chance to give you a going-away party."

"Aw, there wasn't no call for that, but thanks for thinking of it just the same." She hesitated. "I was wondering if you had a few minutes to talk."

"Um, sure, I'd love to. Just let me check on Essie. OK, she's fine. I wasn't sure if she'd gone outside. What's on your mind?"

"Remember how we used to talk about our husbands and how they wanted us to get jobs?" Cindi emitted a snort, and Billie Jo knew she remembered their talks very well. "Well, Jimmy's after me again, and I don't know what to do. I really wanted to talk to someone about it, get some advice, like, but there wasn't anyone to ask. Then I remembered how we used to talk about it, and I thought I'd give you a call and see what you thought." She heaved a sigh and then said, "Truthfully, I kept getting the feeling that I should call you. It's been real strange."

Cindi was silent for a moment. Then she said, "Really? That's so odd, because I wanted to talk to someone too, and I couldn't think of a soul, but I think now you're the person I should talk to. But let's consider your problem first."

"The kids are in school all day," Billie Jo explained. "Jimmy thinks I ought to get a job. The problem is that I like what I'm doing. It takes all my energy to clean up around here, but I have my free time. I go to the library, and I been walking a lot. Those are the things I'd give up if I got a job. There's just no way I could do both."

"That's a tough one," Cindi admitted. "I don't know what to tell you. Can you get by financially?"

"No," Billie Jo replied dully. "Not the way we'd like. This place needs a lot more repairs than we planned on."

"I'll tell you what. I'll put it on the prayer list, and we'll see how God answers. How's that? Maybe there's a compromise we aren't seeing or something."

"Thanks, I'd appreciate that," Billie Jo said, greatly relieved. "What did you want to talk to me about?"

"Well . . . " Cindi hesitated. "Have you ever had any male friends?"

Billie Jo thought for a while. "Not really. I mean, I had some cousins away back that were friends, but we were young. Then there was this guy I met in the library back home. He was sort of a friend, but we only saw each other at the library."

"Do you remember Rainman from the prayer list?"

"Sure. He lost his wife to cancer. Seems like he was real sure God was going to heal her too. It was real sad."

"Yeah, well, I've met him a few times and we've gotten to be friends. The problem is that I think he might have feelings for me."

"Oooh," Billie Jo said ominously. "That's a tough situation right there. He's in a bad spot just losing his wife like that. People like that they do strange things sometimes. I had a cousin whose wife was gone a lot and he met a woman on the Internet. Ended up leaving his wife for this woman. They got married and everything, but now they're divorced. I think he'd a' been better off telling his wife how he felt so lonely and maybe she woulda stayed home more."

"So, you think we shouldn't be friends?"

"I think it's a dangerous game being friends with a man who just lost his wife," Billie Jo said bluntly. "I'm sorry to sound so cold, but that's the truth. And if you're thinkin' he might have feelings for you it's better to break it off before it gets any worse."

"But," Cindi sounded desperate, "he's blaming God for his wife's death, and I'm trying to help him see that it isn't God's fault."

"I hate to say this, but it don't matter how good your intentions are. It's just not a good mix, is all. The way I figure it, God can defend Himself without our help, don't you think?"

"Yeah, I guess." Cindi sounded unconvinced.

"Let's just say if God's got a mind to defend Himself to this man, He's not going to use you to do it if it means more pain for Rainman, which it will. As it is, you won't get out of it without hurting him. You should do it as quick as you can. Prolonging it's just going to hurt him more." Billie Jo felt sure her advice was right. "I'll be praying for you though, 'cause that's going to be hard."

"Yes, it will," Cindi agreed. She sighed heavily. "You're right. I know you're right. It's just that, well, with Marc being gone so much lately and us not getting along very well, it's been nice to have Jar . . . that is, Rainman around. And I know that's wrong, but it's how I feel."

"It's hard sometimes, but we can't go by our feelings," Billie Jo said. " 'Specially when we got to do something that makes us feel awful or stop doing something that makes us feel good."

"Yeah." Cindi sounded defeated and close to tears. "You're right. I know you're right. Thank you for being honest with me. I've been telling myself everything is OK, that there's no problem, but in my heart I know there has been. I've even stopped praying." Her voice was a whisper. "I haven't told anyone that. I feel like such a hypocrite sending out A Wing and a Prayer when I can't even pray. At least now that I've confronted my problem I know what to do to get myself right with God again. Thanks." She chuckled. "It's kind of funny. You called me for advice, but I think you helped me more than I helped you."

"No, no," Billie Jo protested. "You helped me, really. Just being able to talk about it and not have someone telling me what to do helped."

Ogel was furious, and in a demon so lowly it was really a sight to behold. Even the normally condescending Rafe, who outranked him significantly, cowered a bit in the face of his rage.

"You blew it!" Ogel was screaming with an intensity that could split eardrums. "I told you not to push her and you pushed her.

Now she's going to send him packing and all the work I've done will be spoiled. I'm going to report you!" he threatened.

"Listen, you peon," Rafe countered, his shoulders hunching defensively, "don't you criticize me. I have the situation well in hand, and I suggest you go back to your little job and stay out of it."

"This is my job!" Ogel howled with frustration. "I'm the one who's been here. I'm the one putting in the hours while you're here and there at meetings. I'm the one who has been doing this job. You waltz in when you feel like it and mess things up. I demand you step down this instant and let me try to repair the damage you caused."

"I will not!" Rafe bellowed, losing what was left of his patience. His eyes narrowed to little slits, and he leaned toward the smaller demon so that Ogel, even in his anger, backed off. "You will leave. You will leave immediately and go back to your charge. I will take care of things on this end. You will not question me about my methods. Is that understood?"

Ogel struggled visibly for long moments but could not force a civil word between his lips. Finally, with a sound that could have shattered glass, he disappeared. Rafe was left smiling quietly to himself. He knew what he was doing, and he wouldn't be questioned.

CHAPTER

Shay knew something was wrong, but she couldn't put her finger on it. Things were certainly coming together for them all. She and Julia were planning and preparing to open a school. Don was doing surgery again, though not nearly the volume they were capable of when in full swing. Toby and Davy had taken on the outpost clinics with unrestrained zeal, and they were reporting growth there. Everyone was busy.

It wasn't so much in what they were doing or not doing as it was in the way they were relating. At first she had chalked it up to the restraint they all felt from the newness. She and Don had felt like outsiders at first. But that had worn away quickly. It wasn't long before the others treated them as though they had never left, and they were beginning to feel that way themselves. In the end, that didn't explain it.

Things seemed to be going well on the surface. If she'd been really thinking about it, Shay reflected later, she might have been able to figure it all out before things came to a head. As it was, she was still mulling it all over the day Toby and Davy made their big announcement.

It happened after dinner and everyone was sitting around the table shooting the breeze. Shay had forgotten the fun of these sorts of talks. Even Madina's patter didn't dull the excitement of real ongoing grown-up discussion. Shay reveled in it. She was just warming up to her topic about the impact of mission schools when Davy cleared his throat and half stood. Toby glanced at him self-consciously, and anyone with half an eye could see they were preparing to make a big announcement.

"Ahem, may I have your attention, please?" Davy said. He knocked his spoon against the side of his tin cup. "Toby and I have some very important news we'd like to share with all of you. I hope you'll be as excited about it as we are."

Shay couldn't help herself. She just blurted it out before she could think. "You're pregnant!"

Davy, with remarkable composure, said, "No. I'm not. But it was a good guess." Over the howling that followed they hardly heard what he said next. "Toby and I have pooled our resources, called in some debts, begged and borrowed, and we are purchasing for the use of the mission a real, honest-to-goodness airplane so that we can expand the outpost clinics." His face was positively aglow as he described the plane. "It's a Cessna 208, used, of course. But this baby is the bomb! It can carry some major loads, up to 3,000 pounds, but it only needs a short airstrip, maybe 1,200 to 1,800 feet."

Lucien was pleased. It had been a real struggle to restrain himself these past few weeks. Everything in him screamed that they must put a stop to the growth now. It shouldn't even have been happening. He'd been meeting with Rafe, who assured him that the pesky woman who had been providing prayer cover for the mission since the old Prayer Warrior died had been dealt with. Rafe himself, so he claimed, had put an obstacle between her and God. Her prayers were going nowhere.

As usual, Lucien mused, it was often better to rely on yourself than any outside help. He was thankful now that he had not gone ahead with the plans to destroy some of the mission personnel but had waited. His instincts had been right. It had been better to hold off.

From the moment the doctor and his new wife had returned to the mission, Lucien had sensed that there would be problems. He could feel the tension between them all as though it were a tangible thing, a screen that separated them. At first he had not been able to discern what that screen was made from, but the longer he waited, the more he understood.

They were divided.

The two couples most in charge were in discord. And as Lucien knew, as every spiritual being knew, there could be no growth where division existed. Even if there seemed to be growth in the beginning, as when the Holy Presence came, it was doomed to fail. The foundation was rotten. Sooner or later it would crumble, and then any growth would vanish with it.

Still, it had been hard to watch the growth without doing anything to stop it. It had been particularly hard because Sparn was watching him impatiently, and Lucien sensed that he would not wait much longer, no matter what happened. But this, this was the moment he had been waiting for. The events that happened next would be decisive. Now, when they went ahead with plans to kill some of the mission members it would be a delivering of the coup de grâce. Lucien determined that he would do it himself. It was the only way to ensure the success of the move and that he would receive all the credit. He hoped it would be Toby. Then, basking in glory, he would be reassigned, hopefully to somewhere worthy of his capabilities.

"Sarl," Lucien hissed, bringing himself back to the task at hand. "We need everyone who is available. This situation is volatile. Get me more troops. Now!"

Sarl scurried off to do Lucien's bidding, his face a mixture of glee and fear. Lately he had been hanging around a great deal, and Lucien was becoming suspicious of his motives. He was glad to have the demon out of the way. Until others arrived, he was going to handle this situation himself.

The laughter died off abruptly, and a strained tension filled the empty space. Eyes shifted all around the table, but in the end they came to rest on Don. Each person wondered how he would react. It had been a long time since Shay had seen him in one of his "moods." She'd almost forgotten the particular shade of livid he got when he was really mad. But he was getting it now, and she braced herself for what was coming.

"What do you mean by 'expanding the outposts'? We haven't exactly discussed that, have we?" His voice was barely in control. Julia and Ray began to shuttle their chairs back, hoping to beat a hasty retreat, but Don stopped them. "No, don't go anywhere. This is as much your business as it is ours. You work here too. You have some say. What do you think about this? Are you in favor of expanding the outpost clinics?"

His gray eyes were dull, the color of lead, and a nerve in his cheek twitched. Shay found his hand under the table and gave it a squeeze, hoping to give him some support and maybe bring him back to himself. But his grip on her fingers was so strong she yanked them away. He wasn't looking at her, barely was aware she was in the room.

"I have some say too," she said a bit defensively.

He looked at her, and she wished he hadn't. He had the same look on his face that he used to have when she first met him. A kind of cold, detached hostility. "Yes? What do you have to say about it?"

"You're sorry you married him now, aren't you?" Lucien sneered. "Thought all this anger was past, did you? It hardly took anything to bring it right back to the surface. I guess that God of yours isn't so powerful after all, is He? If He was, your husband's anger would be gone, not just hidden, waiting to gush out of him again like a roaring river. Scares you, doesn't it?" Lucien knew he had tapped a nerve with his last remark. The fear in Shay's eyes confirmed it.

"I'm not in favor," she managed to squeak, avoiding Don's gaze as though he had turned into an eagle and she was a defenseless field mouse. "I think we've got plenty of work right here, and if we don't build up what we have, the outposts won't have the support they need. It's like putting the cart before the horse."

Don's smile was triumphant. "Precisely what I think."

"They're against you," Lucien warned, sidling closer to Davy and Toby. He felt the hostility emanating from them. They would not give up their dream without a fight. "They've been against you since they returned. They don't want you here anymore. You've outstayed your welcome. Can't you see? They're taking

over. Your help means nothing to them. They don't even appreciate how you hung in here and kept things going. Don't you think it's time to move on? Go somewhere you're wanted."

Davy and Toby, rather than passively submitting to this show of resistance, had dug in firmly and were going to be stubborn about it. "Well, we think that if we extend the outposts and build them up, they will support the mission." Davy was getting angry. "Listen here, we had to go out on a limb for this plane. The least you could do is be grateful and let us go ahead with our plans."

"I can't do that," Don replied sarcastically. "If you had asked me ahead of time I would have told you before you had gone to any trouble. The direction we take with this mission isn't at your sole discretion. It isn't mine either, but I have a lot more say in it than you do."

Reinforcements had arrived by this time, and the demons gathered around the table like buzzards flocking to carrion. They all took part, contributing to the division as they fed off the anger and frustration and fear. As these negative emotions increased they gained power and swarmed in a thick cloud around the table, creating oppression and fanning the flames of the worst emotions in an attempt to make the crack of division into a chasm that could not be breached.

Don and Davy were standing now, glaring across the table, inches apart. "We were doing just fine before you came back, and we'd be doing fine if you *hadn't* come back," Davy yelled. "You think you can just waltz in and out when it pleases you. Well, Toby and I have sunk everything we have into this place. We haven't been off gallivanting on vacation. We've been here. We've been doing the work. I think we should have some say in what happens with the place. And if we don't then maybe it's time we moved on."

"Can't you see what's happening?" Julia cried, leaping to her feet. "Satan is trying to destroy us all. It's so obvious."

"Yeah, guys, let's calm down a little, huh?" Ray pleaded. "This kind of thing isn't going to get us anywhere. Why don't we take some time and pray about it? We'll work through it. Maybe there's a compromise."

Demons howled as truth flashed from the couple. It made a bright circle in their midst, and as one they twisted away from it, knowing that if it touched them they would feel pain. Quickly they countered it, suggesting untruths to the human beings:

"Compromise is cowardice in disguise."

"Satan isn't trying to destroy this place, God is. He only brought you all out here to punish you."

"You're right; they're wrong. Stand your ground."

"Prayer won't change anything. None of you agree. Pack up and go home."

"This isn't worth it. You're wasting your time out here, all of you. And think of what you're missing out on at home. Give up."

"There can be no compromise." Don ran his hands through his hair in agitation and made a mess of the already rumpled black and gray curls. "I'm telling you, it's not going to happen. Look, I'm sorry. I know this has been a sore point before. But expanding is not a wise choice for us right now. We need to concentrate on what we have. We have to build that up, regain people's trust, before we do any more expansion."

"We're getting the plane," Davy said flatly. Toby nodded firmly in agreement.

Don shrugged. "Maybe we can make some airstrips at the existing outposts that are more substantial than what we need for the ultralight so you can use the plane instead." Shay could tell he was forcing himself to make the concession, to be "big" about it. He hated planes. He had never fully supported the outposts.

"Maybe." Davy cut the word off sharply. "Or maybe we'll find another mission somewhere that could use a couple of bush pilots, one of whom is a nurse. I'm sure a lot of places could use a dedicated, energetic couple like that."

"Now you're talking!" Lucien whooped. The thought of Toby and Davy going to another mission didn't exactly thrill him, but he could deal with that decision later, if it was still necessary. When the dust settled it was quite probable that only one of them would be left alive. If it was Toby, it was still possible that he could convince her to go back home and begin her life over. Life hadn't been so bad back there.

"It's your decision," Don said tiredly. Shay wanted to wrap her arms around him. He was such a sweet man, like a teddy bear most of the time, but his people skills could use some work.

The group broke up soberly. No one suggested having prayer together, though they each returned to their own rooms to pray separately.

To Lucien it was simply a confirmation. They were cracking, and it was now only a matter of time. But, he also knew there was something else vital to the failure of the mission. And this he couldn't leave to chance. He had to see to it himself.

Cindi was pacing the kitchen. She felt uneasy and knew why. Ever since she'd spoken with Billie Jo she'd known in her heart that she should break off her friendship with Jared. The hard part was doing it. She felt like a murderer. She'd put it off for weeks, thinking that something would happen, that maybe the issue would resolve itself. Now she knew beyond a shadow of a doubt that Billie Jo was right. She knew what she had to do.

She waited until Esther was finished with school and watching the hour of television she was allowed for the day. That way she wouldn't be interrupted. She went into the bedroom. Palms sweating, she knelt down beside the telephone and prayed. "Dear Lord, help me to be strong and to do what is right. Help Jared to understand that I can't be his friend, not because I don't want to or because he's not worth my friendship, but because it isn't suitable under the circumstances. Help me to be strong when I end our friendship even if he resists. Continue to help me, even if he persists with 'change back' actions and words. Help me to remember that I'm doing the right thing and that I can't dictate how someone will respond to me. I can only do what I believe to be right. And I believe this to be the right thing. Thank You. In Jesus' name, amen."

Even as Shania covered Cindi with her wings and provided support, Ogel rushed to Jared. He had seen this coming. Rafe had gone too far. Ogel was livid with rage. There was only one chance now to salvage all his hard work. He must convince Jared to ignore Cindi's boundaries. If he could do that, all would not be lost. Eventually she might relent and continue their relationship, giving him more opportunities to present something inappropriate. But he had to keep the lines of communication open. She could not sever the relationship or his job would be intensely difficult. Not impossible, but harder than he liked to imagine.

He found Jared reviewing a case at work. It was a missing person, only a homeless person so there wasn't much activity. The investigation, such as it was, had pretty well died, and Jared was only going over the case because it was a slow day and he didn't have much else to do. When Cindi called he was in the middle of the woman's case history and actually finding it interesting. He even thought he remembered seeing the old woman a time or two tottering around the streets at the end of a leash attached to the biggest dog he'd ever laid eyes on.

Cindi waited for Jared to pick up the phone. For a few seconds she was afraid she was going to get his voice mail, and the mental anxiety of having to put off this emotionally charged discussion was making her stomach cramp. "Hello?" he shouted as he picked up the phone finally. "Hello? Hello?"

"Jared? It's Cindi."

"Oh hi! I thought I'd lost you. This stupid phone isn't working properly. They're changing over the system and there's a glitch somewhere. So, what a nice surprise! What's up, Beautiful?"

Cindi cringed at the bright, cheerful tone of his voice. After months of being down in the mouth and defensive, he was finally starting to warm up. He'd even told her he was going back to church and praying again. She felt awful as the words came tumbling out of her mouth. "Jared, I'm sorry, I hate to do this, but I feel that we need to step back from our friendship."

"What? Why?"

"To be honest, I'm not comfortable with it. I feel that it's unfair to Marc. And to you."

"I see. Is this because I have feelings for you?" came his cold reply.

"Uh, well, yeah," Cindi stammered. "Don't you think that's inappropriate?"

"So, does this mean you don't have feelings for me?"

Cindi twisted the phone cord miserably. "Yes, no, I don't know. I want to be your friend, if that's what you mean. I don't want to end our friendship. But it's just not right."

She could tell he was exasperated. "If you don't want to end our friendship then why do it? I don't think it's necessary. Why don't we just forget this conversation even happened? We'll just go on as before." There was a long agonized pause, during which Cindi thought her heart would stop. "I don't want to lose you, Cindi. If it means backing off I'll back off. I'll do whatever you want. Only, don't do this. Please don't do this."

Lucien could hardly believe what was happening when he showed up. He bowled Ogel over as the smaller demon ranted at Jared, promising him hell on earth if he didn't win back Cindi's trust. "Incompetent!" Lucien shrieked. "I knew I shouldn't have taken Rafe at his word. Where is he? Rafe! Rafe! Face me, you coward!"

Ogel was beside himself. First it was Rafe interfering, and now this. "Get out!" he cried, struggling to right himself. "This is my job, and I'm doing it. Get out or you'll ruin everything!"

An upstart telling him where to get off was beyond Lucien's ability to handle at the moment. Things were falling apart all over; this was a prime example. Lucien didn't have many opportunities to really do justice to his nasty streak, but he was about to make up for it. He pounced on the hapless Ogel, pinning him to the ground, his hands around the smaller demon's throat. Ogel struggled and thrashed, but Lucien was bigger and more powerful.

Lucien gave vent to all the frustration built up in him from the failures at the mission over the years, and the fear that things might not still turn out as he hoped. He loosed all the rage he felt at his circumstances; it came out in a flood of punishment directed at Ogel. He used every weapon at his disposal. At last he had spent his energy, and he staggered away from Ogel, feeling some relief from his impotent rage. Ogel barely stirred. Lucien

*knew it would be a while before he was getting around and be-
ing insubordinate again. Breathing heavily, Lucien turned his
attention, somewhat belatedly, toward Cindi.*

Cindi was sobbing so hard she could hardly get the words out.
"I'm sorry, Jared. I can't. I can't." She placed the phone back in its
cradle before Jared could say anything else. Almost immediately
it rang, and in a panic she covered it with a pillow. The muffled
ringing continued until the answering machine picked up. After
the greeting she heard cursing before the caller crashed the phone
down. It only made her cry harder.

"I didn't mean for this to happen," she sobbed into the pillow,
wishing she could pick up the phone and explain. But she knew
she couldn't hold out against his pleas. "I'm sorry, God. Please be
with Jared right now and help him. I know he's hurting as much
as I am."

Through the intense pain that nearly crippled her, Cindi was
vaguely aware of relief. There had always been an improper element in her relationship with Jared, and she had ignored it, hoping, as with most unpleasantness in life, that if she ignored it then
it would go away. But ignoring this had only made it worse. She
felt extremely guilty that Jared was suffering now. It was much
easier to bear her own pain, knowing she was ultimately responsible. Knowing that he was suffering because of her was agonizing.

After a half hour, during which Jared called and hung up twice,
Cindi pulled herself together, washed her face, and went into the
kitchen to make dinner. She stood at the kitchen counter chopping vegetables and ignoring the ring of the phone whenever it
sounded. She hoped with a little desperation that he wouldn't keep
it up too long.

*Lucien prowled the kitchen, but it was clear to him that things
were swinging the other way. There were now more angels than
demons crowded around, and it was plain to anyone watching
that Cindi was listening to them. As hard as he thought, he
couldn't come up with any further action on this end. There was
only one way he could think of to make Cindi pay attention to
Jared now, and that was for Jared to show up in the flesh and
demand that she reconsider.*

Lucien nudged Ogel with a toe. "Get up." He didn't care to waste words on a creature as useless as Ogel, but he needed the demon's help. Deep moaning was the only response he received. "Get up!" He kicked Ogel none too gently.

The demon groaned and rolled over, the effort about all he could manage. "I can't," he whispered, his voice slurred. "I can't."

"Can't? Or won't? Lazy creature." Lucien paced the floor in front of him. "The situation is desperate. She won't talk to him. The way I see it, we need to get him here. How can we do that?"

Ogel whimpered piteously. "This would never have happened if you hadn't interfered. I was doing just fine without your 'help.' Why couldn't you leave me alone to do my job? Why?"

Lucien gave up in disgust, planting his foot in the solar plexus of the demon. It knocked out all the wind that was left in him, and he collapsed helplessly. Lucien cursed. The situation here was hopeless. Instead of the triumph that would have clinched his victory at the mission, he faced returning under the very direst of circumstances. If the new Prayer Warrior was not out of commission, his chances of victory were slim indeed. He was right to have come and checked on the situation personally.

The best he could do was to charge Rafe to continue his efforts and return to the mission. Perhaps even with this defeat they would be able to close the mission simply on the strength of the division. And if not, well, someone would die. Someone must die.

Billie Jo plunged her hands in the warm dirt of the flower bed she'd just dug by the front step. As the house shaped up, so had the gardens. Summer vacation had ended the question of whether or not she should get a job, at least for the time being. There was no one to leave the children with so she couldn't very well go off and get hired somewhere. Jimmy wasn't happy about it, Billie Jo knew, but she was happy. She was desperately happy. She'd spent weeks with the children, and it had been wonderful.

They'd found a little recreation center not far from the house with a nice man-made pond for swimming. The children had taken swimming lessons all summer long and were swimming like fish. They were golden and healthy. They'd made some friends and really looked forward to each lazy day of sun and swimming. If it hadn't been for their ongoing financial problems Billie Jo would have felt as though life was practically perfect.

The bank was starting to become a problem. Collection officers had called, and they had gone from polite to demanding. Billie Jo knew it was only a matter of time before they began to take action. Jimmy was a bear at night, coming home and working on the house or taking odd jobs when he could to make a little extra money "to keep the wolf from the door," he said. Billie Jo felt guilty that she couldn't help out financially, but she thought she was doing the children more good by staying home. She'd been praying faithfully about the money situation, and God had given her peace about it. Not that she knew what He was going to do, but she felt sure that He would do something.

"Mom?" Cassidy plunked down in the dirt by her mother and wriggled her toes in the grass. "Can you help me? I want to get a trunk out of the barn and bring it up to my room. It's big, but I think the two of us can manage it. I thought it would be a great place to store my sheets and blankets."

Storage space in the old house was at a premium. One thing those old builders didn't believe in was closets. A couple of the rooms had been furnished with decent armoires, but in the rest Jimmy had been forced to put up temporary pegs for hanging clothes and shelves for things like sweaters and shoes.

"Sure, honey, I'll help you." Billie Jo stood up and dusted her hands on her pants. She'd be glad of a shower tonight. "I been wanting to take a look-see in that old barn since we moved in. Just never get around to it somehow. Let's go take a look."

By and large, Nog had been pretty happy with the way things were going. He'd worked hard to create some strife in Billie Jo's marriage, and that was going well. He would have liked to see her go to work and spend less time with her family, but he was making some progress laying a guilt trip on her about it, which was nearly as good. The one area he felt positively triumphant over was their debt.

He had a reason for being so proud of keeping them in dire financial straits. In fact, it was a minor masterpiece of clever deceit, and it was just possible that it was about to be destroyed in one fell swoop. "Keep out of the barn!" he yelled, running after Billie Jo and Cassidy, flapping his tattered wings ineffectually and making shooing motions with his arms as he attempted to block their path.

"You don't want to go in there. There are spiders and bats and probably mice with nasty diseases. Keep out of there."

"Call upon the Lord and He will answer you," Jewel whispered. "Go . . . go . . ."

"Aaaahh!" Nog made a stab at distraction, sending out a bat searching for an early meal, but Billie Jo didn't seem to notice it.

Billie Jo supposed that the barn behind the house had originally housed the horses for the sleighs and farm wagons, perhaps even the plows. Since the property had once been a working family farm, chances were the barn had held a few cows, a sheep or two, and some chickens as well as horses.

The property was situated on a small knoll, and behind the barn the land dropped away into rolling meadows. The sun had begun to yield to the embrace of the horizon, but before surrendering it turned the clouds into pink cotton candy. Billie Jo had loved Tennessee, but Vermont still took her breath away.

Cassidy pulled the creaking door open, and they stepped inside. She grabbed a flashlight off a little shelf by the door and clicked it on so they could see the interior clearly. "See, Mama, there's the buggies. I like that one the best." She pointed to a dilapidated barouche. "Sometimes Dallas and I have races. Pretend ones, of course," she added quickly.

Billie Jo followed her, stepping around old decaying harnesses and around milk buckets. "The trunk is in here." Cassidy moved ahead confidently. She and Dallas had spent lots of time in the old barn.

"See, I think this is where they put the milk." They were standing in what appeared to be a small milking room. An old milk tank took up most of the center of the tiny room. The once shiny stainless steel looked filthy, and the tank was filled to the top with old chicken feeders. "There's a little chicken coop over there, but it's really dirty," Cassidy said. "I think this was the tack room."

Another small room led off an area of the barn that held two box stalls. Faded old signs above the doors told the names of the long departed occupants. "Ginger" and "Fly" were the names Billie Jo made out. Attached to Fly's stall was a ratty piece of ribbon that had clearly been an award of some kind. Billie Jo imagined that Fly had been fast, maybe a trotter who won the ribbon at a county fair.

In a way it was sad seeing all the evidence of other lives and other times. But it was interesting too. Billie Jo wondered why she had never taken the time to look in the old barn. Maybe she would have, she mused, if she hadn't been so busy in the house, so occupied with her problems.

"Here it is," Cassidy was saying. Tucked in the corner was a huge chest. "It had this old horse blanket over it, and it's filled with old tools and junk, but we can clean that all out, can't we?"

Billie Jo lifted the lid. She didn't know much about tools. Still, the inside of the chest was remarkable. The top seemed to be made out of a reddish wood inlaid with marquetry done in a lighter wood that showed off the design. Obviously, it had been crafted by someone who cared about their workmanship. "Honey, you and I are never going to budge this. We're going to need your daddy."

At that moment they saw Jimmy's headlights slice through the chinks in the walls of the barn. "He's home!" Cassidy squealed. "I'll go get him."

Without Cassidy's flashlight Billie Jo had nothing to do but stand in the dim interior of the barn and wait. Large shapes were humped up around her, inky black against the sooty darkness. She could smell hay, musty with age, probably stored above her in a loft. The scurrying of many tiny feet made little rustling sounds above her head, and she wished Cassidy would reappear with Jimmy.

"Get out!" Nog hollered. "You don't want to be in here. This is not important. It's a waste of your time. Don't you have something more important to do? Jimmy is not going to be happy if

that kid drags him all the way out here to look at this worthless piece of garbage."

Billie Jo didn't move, but he could see she was listening uneasily to the rustlings overhead. "Mice," he said, chuckling. "Icky, creepy mice. They're coming to get you."

Billie Jo reached out and touched the surface of the chest. It was smooth and cool to her fingers. If they were going to be able to move it they'd need to remove all those old tools, she thought. They had no time and money now for hauling this stuff to the dump. It would have to stay in the barn.

Billie Jo wondered what Jimmy's mood would be like. He'd been surly for so long now, worrying over their financial problems, that it was getting to be a strain on their relationship. She couldn't remember the last time they'd laughed together. She half suspected that Jimmy felt she wasn't regarding their circumstances with the gravity they deserved. But she knew they were grave all right. It was just that she had prayed over them a great deal, and as worried as she was when she thought about them, she felt a deep peace that God would take care of them.

She'd talked about it with Greta one morning over a delicate jasmine tea that Greta had just received from a new tea company. As she couldn't wait to try it, she'd called and invited herself over for tea and a chat. At first, Greta's spontaneity and forwardness had made Billie Jo uncomfortable. She was apt to invite herself over, or invite Billie Jo over, without a moment's notice. Sometimes she would just show up without warning. After her first visit she didn't even bother to knock, just let herself in and started making tea or cleaning up the table or doing dishes without so much as a by-your-leave. Eventually, Billie Jo began to feel a certain satisfying sense of kinship with her. It was almost like having a sister, which Billie Jo didn't have and had desperately wanted.

This particular morning Billie Jo had been commiserating with Greta about how desperate she felt over their financial situation and how Jimmy wanted her to get a job. "I know how you feel," Greta had assured her, and then she had launched into a story about a time she'd gone through a similar situation when her husband was ill. "But you know," she had finished up, "at the time I was so upset that I couldn't concentrate properly and hadn't been as faithful with my devotions as usual. I guess I'd been so caught up in my heartache that I was having trouble reaching out for the help I needed. I remember finally going into my bedroom and dropping to my knees and begging God for a Band-Aid."

"A Band-Aid?" Billie Jo couldn't think what kind of Band-Aids God would have.

Greta had laughed a little, at herself apparently, because she had flushed a bit self-consciously too. "That was the only way I could think of to put it. But, yes, I asked Him for a Band-Aid. Then—and I'm not saying this is a great way to find out God's will, of course—I closed my eyes, opened my Bible, and stuck my finger on a page. And do you know what it said?"

Billie Jo remembered her skepticism. No doubt something totally irrelevant. She had shaken her head and taken a sip of her tea. It was almost ethereal, a taste that, had it been a smell, would have been the merest hint of jasmine blossoms.

"When I opened my eyes, my finger was pointing at a verse in Isaiah forty-three. I felt my heart sink. I guess I was hoping for Psalms; it's my favorite book. Anyway, when I read the text I nearly fell over. It said: ' "Fear not, for I have redeemed you; I have called you by your name; you are Mine. When you pass through the waters, I will be with you; and through the rivers, they shall not overflow you. When you walk through the fire, you shall not be burned, nor shall the flame scorch you." ' I remember I just started bawling. It was as though God had spoken directly to me, and I was pretty humbled."

After Greta had left that day Billie Jo had taken her own Bible to the kitchen table. She'd felt a bit foolish, but she had followed Greta's example, laying out her problem before the Lord and then opening her Bible. With a trembling finger she'd stabbed at her Bible. Peeking at the text, she was amazed to read, "I will lift up my eyes to the hills—from whence comes my help? My help comes from the Lord, who made heaven and earth.

"He will not allow your foot to be moved; He who keeps you will not slumber. Behold, He who keeps Israel shall neither slumber nor sleep. The Lord is your keeper; the Lord is your shade at your right hand. The sun shall not strike you by day, nor the moon by night.

"The Lord shall preserve you from all evil; He shall preserve your soul. The Lord shall preserve your going out and your coming in from this time forth, and even forevermore."

Billie Jo had been overcome with such a feeling of awe that she could hardly breathe. In an instant her worry about their finances was gone. She'd tried to show Jimmy when he came home from work that night, but he hadn't been too impressed. Still, she'd kept her faith, knowing that somehow God would work it out for them.

Cassidy's flashlight beam caught her square in the eyes, and she blinked like a deer caught in the headlights.

"Oops, sorry Mom," Cassidy said. "See, Dad? Can we move it do you think?"

Jimmy emerged from the darkness behind Cassidy. Billie Jo gave him a weak smile, but his eyes were on the tool chest. He reached out one hand and touched it, almost caressed it. Without hurry he opened the lid, tracing the patterns of the marquetry. One by one he opened the drawers, removed objects—planes, levels, chisels, and rules. He examined each carefully, sometimes taking the flashlight from Cassidy, who was becoming impatient.

"Well?" she burst out finally. "Can I have it for a blanket chest or not?"

Jimmy seemed to come to himself. "No, darlin', I'm afraid not."

"Why?" Cassidy's voice threatened to turn into a full-blown whine. "I found it. By rights it's mine. Nobody else cares about it." Finally curiosity got the best of her. "What are you gonna do with it?"

"Sell it."

Billie Jo caught Cassidy's eye, but she shrugged, not able to explain why the old chest was worth anything to anyone, except as a blanket chest.

"Darlin', this here chest is at least a hundred years old. If it wasn't so dark I could tell you more about it, but near as I can tell all these tools belonged to the man who made this chest. Some of these tools are worth a lot of money."

Billie Jo felt her heart skip in her chest. *Money?* "How many hundred, do you think?" she asked, trying to keep the excitement out of her voice. No sense getting her hopes up. Could be they weren't worth all that much.

Jimmy chuckled. "Hundreds? We're talking thousands!"

"Thousands?" Billie Jo and Cassidy gasped together.

"Many thousands," Jimmy murmured, stroking the smooth wood of the lid, a grin stretching his face wide. Suddenly he whooped and scooped up Billie Jo, taking her right off her feet. When he set her down again, he ruffled Cassidy's hair. "You done it, girl. You done it; this here's a gold mine. If we get as much money for these tools as I think we can, I'll buy you the nicest blanket chest you ever saw."

"Cool!" Cassidy said, beaming from one parent to the other. Things were definitely looking up.

Billie Jo was so infused with happiness that she didn't feel the slightest pang of apprehension or dismay when Helen called later that evening and asked if the kids could come for a visit before the end of summer vacation. She generously gave her assent when Jimmy asked her what she thought about it. The kids would be gone for a week, and Billie Jo and Jimmy planned the major projects they could get done while they were away. Still talking drowsily they slipped happily into a deep, satisfied sleep. Just before sleep completely overtook her, Billie Jo was conscious of a deep gratefulness, and she tried to formulate a prayer. But she fell asleep before the words made it past her lips.

Jewel watched his charge sorrowfully. He knew that she felt rich, richer than she had ever felt in her whole life. But only he knew how shallow these riches really were. They wouldn't mean anything in the approaching trial, and he prayed that Billie Jo would hold on to the real Treasure she had in her possession.

CHAPTER 10

Toby was fiddling with the engine of the new plane. It was a real beauty. As soon as Davy returned from a test flight on the ultralight she was sure he'd be at her side helping out. The two of them were never too far from their new toy these days. The situation at the compound was pretty grim lately, and it was much easier to avoid dealing with the others. Working on the plane provided a great excuse.

Despite the negative response they'd received they had decided to go ahead and get the plane. There had been no question in their minds about that. It was simply something they were going to do no matter what. The only real question was, would they be staying at the mission or was it time to move on?

Davy was all for moving on. Toby, on the other hand, felt conflicted about it. She felt a huge sense of responsibility toward the mission. In a way she'd found herself again at the mission. She'd started over there. It was a strong emotional attachment she was reluctant to break. She had put down roots, and (maybe it was a sign of advancing age, she told herself) she would really prefer to avoid starting all over again, at least for a while anyway.

Still, she and Davy were married now. She didn't have complete control over where she went and what she did. She had Davy and his needs to consider as well. She had convinced herself that Davy felt the way she did about the mission. But in her heart she knew it wasn't true. Davy could take the mission or leave it. He didn't feel the special pull she did toward it.

She sighed. Everything seemed so complicated now. It had taken a lot of emotional energy to build a new relationship with Davy, and she still felt a little emotionally raw about it. But as much as she wanted to stay put, she just wasn't sure she had it in her to repair all the ruptured relationships at the mission.

"What should we do, God?" she asked for what seemed the hundredth time. Her voice sounded small in the open space. "What do You want us to do?"

"I think we should talk," came a voice behind her.

For an instant Toby was thunderstruck. *God?* Then she grinned. *Davy!* She wheeled around. But it was Don who stood behind her, arms folded across his chest. "Talk about what?" she said, trying to keep the nervousness out of her voice. If there was one thing she would prefer to avoid, it was talking to Don. She wished the ground would open up and swallow her. Grimacing, she put a hand to her temples, trying to push the growing headache away. Inside, she felt the contents of her stomach revolt in response to the sudden stress of confrontation.

"This is beautiful," Lucien growled sarcastically. "The doctor and the nurse, together again. Say it ain't so." Here was a golden opportunity, a chance to bring everything to a head. It was now or never. "Feeling a little sick, are you?" he sneered. "That's nothing. Let's play." Turning to Don, he goaded, "You'll never get anywhere talking to her. She doesn't want to talk. She just wants to sulk. Like a little kid."

Don made an exasperated noise in the back of his throat. "Come on, I don't have time for childish games. You know perfectly well what I want to talk about."

"Fine, have it your way," Toby replied testily. "You want to talk, so talk."

"Look, this isn't how it's supposed to go," Don protested. Toby could hear the frustration in his voice. "I'm supposed to suggest we talk, and you're supposed to be nice and say that would be great, and then we're supposed to have a civilized conversation. We're *not* supposed to bite each other's heads off."

When Toby didn't offer a reply he continued. "We don't want you to leave. I don't want you to leave. We're all like family here. We've been through hard times, the hardest. We can't jeopardize all that because of a difference of opinion. Can we?" He waited and then repeated, "Can we?"

"Can we? Can we?" Lucien mocked. "It's all give, give, give, with this guy, isn't it? I wouldn't put up with that. Where does he think he gets off, traipsing in here and telling you what to do? Who does he think kept this place together while he was vacationing, anyway? The Easter Bunny?"

"So, what do you want?" Toby asked. What was he saying, that she and Davy should back down and cooperate to keep the peace? "We don't want to go either, but we feel pretty useless here, especially if our opinions aren't valued. We aren't greenhorns. We've been here for a while now. We should have some say."

"That's right! You should have some say. In fact, you should be running this place, that's what. You and Davy should be calling the shots. And he should be in the back seat for a change, taking orders from you."

"You can't have a say about this." Don was trying to be patient, but it was wearing thin already. Toby knew he'd blow shortly, and she braced herself. "There is no discussion on this one. The only question about the outposts is if they should be closed down temporarily. Especially after what happened to Julia. Expanding them isn't even part of the equation right now."

"Get ready! Any minute now!" Lucien chortled. He couldn't remember the last time he'd had so much fun. This was almost too easy. He'd had enough of bumbling subordinates. It was about time he took matters in his own hands. This felt right. This felt good.

"Davy and I think it should be."

"Well it's not!" He was nearly screaming and red in the face.

"Some apology this turned out to be," Toby remarked snidely.

"I'm not apologizing!" Don yelled. "I don't have anything to apologize for!"

"Pow!" Lucien pointed an imaginary gun at Toby. "One for the doc."

"You do now!" Toby screeched, flinging a handful of sand at him and forcing him to step aside. "Get out! I don't want to talk about this anymore. We're leaving. Are you happy? Now you won't have to worry about us anymore."

"Nice return by O'Connell." Lucien would have patted himself on the back if he hadn't been too sophisticated for such antics. That took care of that little problem. Now, it only remained to carry out the rest of his plan. After that, well, he was still too cautious to count his chickens, but he felt surer than ever that he was on his way out of this hole for good.

Don threw up his hands and stomped off in the direction of the clinic. Beyond him Toby could see Davy sauntering toward her. As the men passed each other they veered as if skirting a large mud puddle on opposite sides. If Toby hadn't been so upset she would have laughed. "And we call ourselves grown-ups?" she muttered beneath her breath.

"Hey, Babe, what's with old Thunderpuss? You two have words?"

As Toby related her conversation with Don to Davy she couldn't help wondering what would have happened if she had been more civil. Had she truly met him halfway? She'd been asking God what His will was, and then Don showed up. Maybe God was trying to tell her something. She shifted uneasily, hoping she was mistaken.

Davy put his arms around her, and she melted into his embrace. Being hugged by Davy had always been like returning to a safe haven. "Don't let him get to you, huh? We're adults. We can make a decision, the right decision, without interference from him or anyone else."

"I know; it's just that, well, what if he's right? What if we're wrong?"

Davy held her at arm's length and gave her a little shake. "Hey, hey, don't say that! He's got you rattled, Babe, that's all. He's un-

167

dermined your confidence. You know we've talked about this at length. We're going to do what we feel is best."

"Yeah, but what about what God wants? You know we haven't prayed about this like we should."

"So, what's stopping us?" Davy countered. "Let's pray. We can start right now."

He folded her against his chest again, their classic prayer position, and began to pray. "Dear Lord, thank You for bringing us here to this place to serve You. We love You, Lord, and we want to follow You. We come before You today as two sinful people who want to do what is right in Your sight. Help us to know if we're being headstrong in wanting to expand the outpost clinics. Should we stay here and stand firm for what we think is right? Or should we strike out after Your will and find a new place to serve You? You have said that You would show us the right road. You said, 'Your ears shall hear a word behind you, saying, "This is the way, walk in it," whenever you turn to the right hand or whenever you turn to the left.' Lord, today we claim that promise. Tell us the right way to go. We ask this in the name of Your precious Son, Jesus. Amen."

Toby felt tears in her eyes as she looked up. "Now what?"

Davy grinned. "Now we wait to see what God says. You OK, Babe? You seem, I don't know, a little off somehow."

"I don't know. I don't feel so good. It started after breakfast."

"Maybe you should go lie down," Davy suggested.

Toby placed her tools back into their compartments in the toolbox and snapped the lid shut. A nap sounded like a good idea to her. The sun felt unbearable on the backs of her eyes, and keeping them open much longer was more than she could bear thinking about. "Yeah, I think I will. But what about the clinics? We were supposed to go out and check on them today."

"Don't worry about that. I'm sure Shay will come with me just this once."

Cindi was preparing root vegetables to roast in the oven for dinner, with the radio on in the background. A news announcement caught her attention. She paused in mid-chop, her knife poised over a parsnip, her heart thumping in her throat.

"In other news, recent freak flooding has resulted in several auto fatalities. Among the deaths—three teenagers driving under the influence of alcohol who drove off a steep bank; and a local couple with their grandchildren who were returning home from a shopping excursion. Authorities say a tractor-trailer hydroplaned on the wet roads and flipped onto the couple's car, killing all four occupants. Names of the victims have not been released.

"Today the death toll rose to eight when a new fatality was discovered. The body of a homeless woman, missing for nearly two months, was located today, the victim of an apparent homicide. Lila Parker brings you our report."

A new voice cut in, and Cindi's knife resumed chopping. She wasn't sure what she had expected, but all the flooding, along with the damage it brought, had put her on edge. The thunderstorms alone had been horrific. She chopped efficiently, her movements comforting and familiar. She was on autopilot, and her attention drifted until she heard the announcer say, "The body of a homeless woman was discovered today in Hudson's Gorge. A jogger discovered the body floating amid debris stirred up by the recent flash flooding in the area. Lieutenant Jared Flynn was at the scene. Lieutenant?"

Cindi didn't have much time to consider the name before she heard Jared's familiar voice on the radio and felt a cold jolt of recognition. She hadn't spoken to him in weeks.

"All we're prepared to say right now is that we believe this death to be a homicide. The body has been positively identified as that of Carol Bennington, a local transient, who was reported missing by shelter authorities six weeks ago. The coroner believes the body to have been submerged for at least six weeks, possibly longer. Our dive crews will continue to investigate. We have nothing further to offer at this time."

"Thank you, Lieutenant. This is Lila Parker for WMAX in Chattanooga."

Cindi leaned forward and clicked the radio off with fingers that were so numb she barely felt the knob. She made her way to a chair and sank heavily into it, her head spinning. Pictures flashed through her mind like a slide show. Ethel, talking about her daughter Carol, who had run away. The picture, found among her possessions, of a young girl with a birthmark on her face. The old homeless woman Essie was so interested in, who had a similar birthmark on her face. Ethel's daughter. Found, after all this time. Found and lost again. Cindi wept bitterly.

It was in the memory of Ethel and Carol that Cindi had begun plans for the community center to benefit the area's homeless, never dreaming that Carol herself might benefit from such a place. Could a safe haven like that have saved her? Only someone in Jared's position might venture to say, but she certainly couldn't call and ask him.

"Call," Ogel wheedled. He'd been flitting between the two for weeks and hadn't been able to get either to back down from this stance of uncommunicativeness. Thanks to meddling from demons who should have known better, his plans had failed utterly. Not only had Cindi and Jared both admitted the unhealthiness of their relationship, but both had repented—hateful word—and were seeking God. Ogel felt so desperate from despair that he was capable of doing anything. "Call him. You know you miss him. Think of all the information he has! He was one of the ones who found her. Surely it couldn't hurt to call for some information. Just ask a few questions and hang up. How difficult is that?"

Cindi wondered where Jared might be at that very moment. Was he still at the crime scene? Was he back at the station filling out paperwork? Was he home? She had phone numbers—his cellular phone and his direct line at the station. Surely it couldn't hurt to call and ask him a few questions, things that might help her to feel better? The urge to call was so strong that she found herself standing without any recollection of how she came to be there. Immediately she dropped to her knees, bowed her head against the chair and cried, "Lord, help me know what to do!"

It took less time than a thought for Shania to arrive at heaven for the Master's instruction and return to Cindi's side to impart it. She unfurled her gracious wings and placed them protectively around Cindi's shoulders. In human beings, she knew, this felt like a warm and comforting presence, a blanket of peace. "Hold fast, child," she implored. "The Master is well pleased with you. Your actions are honorable and your work is good in the sight of the Lord. This time of testing will not be easy, but the Master gives you strength to overcome.

" 'Resist the devil and he shall flee from you,' " she quoted. A sword of fire leapt from her mouth, narrowly missing Ogel, who had tried to crowd in too close as he shouted temptations to be heard over the words of the angel. He howled in frustration but doggedly tried to weasel his way close enough to be heard.

"You know you want to talk to Jared. He's always willing to listen to you. He always cares about you and how you feel. Where's that husband of yours? Can you say the same thing about him?" Ogel knew he had hit one home.

Cindi winced, remembering how Jared always seemed to care about the least little problem she had, how he was so interested in her projects. Marc barely knew she had a project, and he wasn't supporting her at all. In fact, if anything, Marc was hostile about the time she spent at the community center.

"That's right," Ogel said, pressing his advantage. "Jared cares. He truly cares about you. Your husband cares more about his job than he does about you."

Shania leaned closer. "Marc is going through his own troubles. The best thing you can do for your husband is to love him unconditionally and pray for him. When the time is right, talk to him. He surely doesn't realize what you're going through."

Cindi felt peace settle over her, and all her muscles relaxed. God was with her in this thing. She knew it. "Thank You, Lord," she breathed.

"Mommy? What are you doing?"

Esther came in from outside where she had been playing and gave her mother a questioning look. Cindi got to her feet and smiled through her tears.

"I'm praying, Essie. There was something I had to talk to God about."

"But you always pray in your bedroom, in that chair by your bed, with your Bible on your lap."

"Most of the time when you see me, that's where I pray. But I talk to God all the time, and sometimes you don't even know. This time I needed to pray right away, so I prayed here."

"Oh." This seemed to satisfy her. "When is Daddy coming home?"

Cindi felt a pang of regret. "I don't know, Honey. He's been working late a lot, I know. Hopefully he'll be home before you go to bed tonight." Silently she prayed that it would be so. Marc had been gone so much lately that she hardly saw him, but Essie saw him even less than she did and missed him keenly.

"Why is Daddy working so much?"

Cindi sat down at a kitchen chair and pulled the little girl close to her. "Daddy has a lot of customers, and they all need to have his attention. He's got a very important job, and it's important that he talks to them. It's a tough time for all of us, Peanut. I know you miss your daddy." She stroked Esther's hair absently. Maybe she should talk to Marc about how much he was missed around home. Maybe he didn't actually know.

It was late by the time Marc's car pulled into the drive. His face was a study in exhaustion and the effects of stress. He threw off his suit jacket and collapsed into a kitchen chair without kissing her. Cindi sat down at the table opposite him, but before she could say anything his cell phone rang. Wearily he answered the call, his voice miraculously changing and becoming full of an energy she could plainly see he did not feel.

After fifteen minutes, during which Cindi did nothing but pray silently for guidance, he finally hung up.

At the rate angels began gathering, Ogel knew something was going down before he actually figured out what it was. "No, no!" he screeched. He was afraid, had a terrible feeling in his gut, that everything he had worked so hard for was about to become null and void. The pressure was too much. After all he had been through he reached the snapping point at last.

With an unearthly howl he pitched into the first angel he came to, swinging wildly, scrambling for purchase. Queer little yelps of pain squeezed out between his lips as he came into contact with the angels. Drawing his sword he attempted to clear a path to Cindi. He desperately needed an advantage and would take whatever was afforded him. The blade glanced off the shields of the angels and harmlessly whittled nothing but air.

He was simply no match for the stronger beings, and he was greatly outnumbered. But he pressed on until at last he could stand it no longer and backed off, cursing and panting. Limping, he made his way to the outskirts, where he assessed the situation. He needed back-up. In the next instant, he fled.

"Do you want something to eat?" she asked.

He shook his head. "No, thanks. I grabbed dinner with a client. I'm sorry. I should have called you. Where's Essie?"

"In bed. She was hoping to see you tonight."

His expression was pained.

"Marc?"

He sighed. And she knew that he knew what she was going to say. "Yes?"

"You know, we really miss you around here. You've been working so hard we don't see much of you, and when you do come home you're so tired . . ." Cindi's voice trailed off. "Do you really have to work so hard? Can't you cut back some?"

"Yes. No." Marc ran his hands through his hair in agitation. "I guess that all depends on what you want to do."

"What I want to do?" Cindi was mystified. "What do you mean?"

Marc sighed. "We've been through all this before. If you want to start that shelter—"

"Community center," Cindi corrected.

"Community center, shelter, mission, whatever it is." He waved impatiently. "You're not going to be able to keep up home schooling. It's one or the other, Cindi. You can't do both."

"He has no faith in you!" screamed Ogel, who had returned, emboldened by a contingent of demons who had joined him for the fight. For once he was in charge. They were following his lead. "Can't you see? You're weak."

"You don't have what it takes, that's what he means!" another howled.

"You're so stupid you can't do anything right!"

"Why can't I?" she demanded.

"Because . . ." He hesitated. "Because . . . I won't let you."

Cindi felt her chin drop. "What?"

"Ooh," Ogel chuckled. "Now it comes out. He's railroading you. You're just the weak little woman who needs to follow the orders of her man. Yeah, he's got you nailed."

"Remember, be submissive. The man is the head of the house. Yeah, like we believe that," another taunted.

Marc put his fists down on the table and leaned on his forearms. He looked into her eyes, and she could see him struggle to keep his composure. He wasn't angry, but he was having a difficult time expressing himself. His words, when they came, were like bullets, each one spit out between his teeth. "I . . . just . . . can't . . . watch you . . . drain yourself . . . that way."

"There's the line. The one that covers it all. You, you, you, that's what he says. But he's only thinking of himself. Don't be fooled," a demon warned.

The angels paid no attention to the demons. They circled the couple and laid protective hands upon them. From inside the circle the cries of the demons were weak, and neither Cindi nor Marc could hear them. They heard only the instruction of the angels and chose to follow their counsel.

"Look, Cindi, it takes a lot out of you to do home school. You said so yourself when you decided to quit home nursing. You said it was too much. I agreed with you. We decided that was best. I know it's been a struggle to keep up paying the bills with only my income. I'm doing the best I can. In fact, I'm wearing myself out doing the best I can.

"I know how much you want to run that community thing, but I can see where this is going, and I don't want to go there. It's bad enough with me being gone so much, but if you're gone all the time too, Esther would have to go to school and be left with sitters. You can't be dragging her to meetings and functions for this center. What kind of life will that be for her? I don't want that for either of you."

Marc's voice got quiet. "I know I'm failing you, but I just can't run any faster than I am now."

"Oh, Honey," Cindi said, tears welling up in her eyes. "You're not failing us! Not in the way you think. All we want is to see more of you around here. Is that why you've been working so much? For the money?"

"Why did you think I was working so much?" He sounded puzzled, as if it never occurred to him that there might be any other motive for working to excess.

"I don't know," Cindi said miserably.

"Tell him the truth," urged Shania.

"Honestly? I thought you were angry with me and didn't want to be around."

Marc didn't say anything. He stood up and came around to her chair, reached down and pulled her to her feet. Then he put his arms around her and held her for a long time. "I love you. I love you very much. I have been working so hard because I'm feeling overwhelmed with responsibility. When you started talking about putting so much time into the center and you weren't even going to get paid for it, I guess I did feel resentful. I just don't know what more I can do. I'm tired and I need to slow down."

Cindi held on to her husband as if she were drowning. After all the misunderstanding and lack of communication she felt as though he were pouring love into her. Finally she understood. Everything she had done to try to help the situation out of stubbornness had only made things worse. She had taken her eyes off her family and what was best for them. It was time to put things right.

The demons could see the end before it hit and they scattered, leaving Ogel to face his final humiliation alone. The angels offered suggestions to the couple, and one by one they were accepted and voiced. Ogel himself could finally stand it no longer. There was too much love in the room, and he fled before it as if it were fire.

"Marc, listen, I don't have to do this community center. Not in the way that I need you to be home more. I am the executor in

Ethel's will, but I can name someone else as the manager of the center. I don't have to work there at all. My part is finished when the paperwork has been dealt with.

"I'll continue to do home school with Essie, and we'll see what bills we can cut down. If we have to, I'll pick up a little part-time work somewhere. Maybe I can find a job that can include Essie, delivering meals to the elderly or something like that. It wouldn't pay much, but it should take the crunch off you."

Marc held her at arm's length and then pulled her close and kissed her. "I've missed you so much. I feel like I'm never home."

"You aren't ever home," she murmured, kissing him back.

"I'm home now."

"I'm glad you are."

CHAPTER
11

Billie Jo stared at the top of the table. A sound somewhere in the house broke through the fog in her brain, and she nearly jumped out of her skin. The children! Then it hit her again, as fresh as the day a kindly police officer had called to tell them the awful news. The children were dead.

Dead. Her children. In a car accident. Her children and her in-laws. In a bad storm a speeding tractor-trailer had hydroplaned on the wet road, flipping onto James and Helen's car, killing them all. As bad as she felt, she knew that Jimmy had to feel worse. They'd flown down for the funerals. Billie Jo had frankly been amazed at the outflow of community support. There was a huge impromptu memorial of flowers at the site of the accident. Billie Jo had a hazy memory of feeling overwhelmed with grief upon seeing the place where her children were crushed and awe at the support of people she did not even know who had never met her kids or her in-laws.

But life went on. Which was perhaps the cruelest part. *It shouldn't go on*, she told herself. *It should all stop. I should be able to lie down and die. I shouldn't have to go through the rest of my life with a hole in my heart. Life will never be normal again. It will never be pleasant, and above all it will never be happy.* Every day was a new torture. Simply getting out of bed was often too difficult, and she spent days on end simply cowering beneath the covers, her mind blank, escaping from the reality of it all.

Jimmy, on the other hand, though he was suffering as much as she, had taken a new direction. He'd begun going back to church. He read his Bible. He prayed. When he asked Billie Jo to go with him to services or to prayer meeting, she declined, saying she didn't feel up to going out in public yet. Still, Jimmy went. He seemed to find peace, if not comfort, in God. But, neither one of them had leaned on the other.

It seemed that there was a wall between them. A big, solid wall that Billie Jo did not have the strength or energy to break down. She knew it shouldn't be there. They should have been helping each other through the crisis. But the wall existed, as tangible as if it were built of bricks.

She traced a pattern in the worn wooden top of the table, wondering if with every mountain peak there came such a valley of shadow. They had just discovered the tool chest in the barn and sold it for enough money not only to cover their bills, but far above that. They had a comfortable nest egg put away. For the first time in their lives they had felt financially secure. As far as Billie Jo was concerned, their troubles were over. Jimmy had walked around looking ten years younger.

Billie Jo cringed to realize that she hadn't even felt a pang of misgiving when Helen asked for the children to come visit before the summer vacation was over. She had been so buoyed up by their financial windfall that she hadn't given it hardly any thought at all. It was only for a week. At the time she had almost welcomed the chance to really dig into some decorating projects while they were away.

"How could I have been so blind?" she asked aloud, jumping at the sound of her own voice. It sounded old and tired. She felt that she had aged a decade for every day that had passed since the accident. Surely she couldn't be only thirty-seven. Not when she felt two hundred years old at least.

"That's right," Nog told her with complacency. *"You should have known better. But you weren't thinking about your kids,*

were you? Too busy gloating over all that lovely cash." He rubbed his hands together, warming to his subject. "You who was always so suspicious of your poor dead mother-in-law, couldn't see past your bank account to be the slightest bit concerned about your own children whom you say were more important to you than anything else. Well, I guess we can all see what was most important to you after all, can't we?

"Of course," he said casually, "your God could have saved them anyway, couldn't He? That's what you thought, isn't it? But you don't think so anymore, do you? No, you don't think so anymore." He chuckled, an evil sound that made Billie Jo's skin crawl even though she couldn't hear it.

It was God she blamed. She knew that, even admitted it to Him when she went on a crying jag and demanded to know what she had done to deserve this, what her kids had done to deserve to die so young and full of promise. How could a loving God allow something like that? It was insane, that's what it was. She had no desire to worship a God who didn't play fair.

As if hearing it from a long, long distance, Billie Jo became aware that someone was knocking on the door. Not knocking, pounding was more like it. She shuffled across the kitchen floor and peered through the curtain, not really wanting to know, not wanting to talk to anyone, not even the mail carrier or UPS driver. Unbelievably, it was Greta.

Billie Jo groaned. She thought about just ignoring her to see if she'd go away, but she knew that Greta knew she was there and Greta wasn't a person you could put off. She unlocked the door slowly. Greta pushed her way in and stood sizing up Billie Jo with a quizzical expression on her face. "Since when did you start locking the door?" she asked.

"Greta, I really don't much feel like company at the moment. I hate to be rude, but would you mind?"

"Mind that you don't want company? Not at all. It's only to be expected. Would you like some tea?"

Billie Jo cursed. She hadn't cursed in years. "Greta, please leave me alone. I just want to be alone."

"Get out, can't you?" Nog snarled at the busybody surrounded

by angels. He was more afraid than he could say that they would ruin all his hard work.

"Listen to her; give her a chance," Jewel urged. *His heart was sore with concern over Billie Jo. More than anything he wished he could alleviate her pain, but he knew that nothing short of the Master's return would truly wipe out the pain of earth's darkness.*

Greta didn't hesitate. She continued to fill up the teapot and placed it on the stove. After she had turned on the burner she faced Billie Jo, her hands on her hips, her lips tight. "Look, Billie Jo, I know how you feel. Don't you think I know how you feel? I watched my husband, a man I loved more than anyone on the planet, die a slow and agonizing death. I fought with God about it. I blamed Him. And I don't want to see you making the same mistake I did. There's no sense in it. Not when I can prevent it."

"You can't prevent nothing," Billie Jo replied sullenly. "I'll think what I want to think; how can you stop me?"

"I can't stop you," said Greta matter-of-factly. "I can try to show you that you're wrong. You're blaming God right now, aren't you? But God didn't kill your children. A semi-truck killed your children."

"Stop!" Billie Jo screamed. "Stop! I don't want to hear it no more. You think it don't go round my head often enough?"

Greta laid a hand on Billie Jo's shoulder, but she shrugged it off and pulled away. "Go on home, won't you? I want to be alone. I don't want to talk about this no more. It's bad enough I got to live it."

"Leave!" *screamed Nog. "Get out! She doesn't want you here and neither do I!"*

Jewel watched sadly as Greta prayed. Angels crowded close. They knew something she was only slowly accepting. Billie Jo was not ready for consolation. Not yet. It would be better to leave her to her grief, pray for her, and return again. Often, at times like this, human beings tended to become offended and give up. But Jewel was pretty sure Greta was not going to give up.

Behind Greta the teapot whistled shrilly, but she made no move to take it off the stove. Her lips moved soundlessly, and her gaze was focused far away. Then, amazingly, she left. Billie Jo shut the door behind her with mixed feelings of relief and regret. Then she sat down at the table and bawled, knowing she had driven away her only friend.

Two days later Greta was back. This time the door was unlocked and she came right in. For a split second Billie Jo was fooled into thinking that maybe the accident had been only a terrible nightmare from which she had finally woken. Then it crashed against her consciousness again, wearing her down with its relentless grip of pain.

"Hello," Greta said brightly. "I brought you a casserole."

Billie Jo, humbled by her previous behavior, accepted it meekly. "Thank you." She put it in the refrigerator, and while her back was to Greta she said, "About the other day . . ."

"Please," Greta broke in. "Don't let's talk about it. You were upset, and I was too bold. I'm sorry. I shouldn't have intruded on your grief. I do have an awful habit of poking my nose in where it doesn't belong. We'll say no more about it."

"Oh Greta," Billie Jo wailed, turning and throwing her arms around Greta's neck, sobbing. "My babies, my babies . . ."

Greta pulled Billie Jo close and held on to her, smoothing her hair and patting her back and making soothing little noises. "I know, I know," she said. "There, there, it will be all right."

"It won't, it won't," sobbed Billie Jo. "It won't never be all right again. Not my whole life. I'll live with this ache forever. I just want to rip my heart out so it will stop hurting me. I can't take this, Greta, I can't take it. I want to die."

Greta led Billie Jo to the sofa and sat her down. Then she sat next to her and held her hand. "Billie Jo, now, this is all natural, what you're feeling. I felt the same way. I remember it like it happened yesterday. Seeing you suffer has brought it all back for me in the worst way. But I have to tell you that dying is not going to solve your problems.

"Where would Jimmy be if you died? Or me? Or your other friends? I know it's hard, but you have to face this grief and feel it and let it pass on by. If you don't let it in and come to grips with it, you'll never shake it. It'll poison everything. Come on now, I want to pray for you."

"No!" Billie Jo said forcefully. She looked up. Her eyes were red from weeping, but they snapped with fire. "No! I don't want to talk to God. It's all His fault my babies are gone. He could have prevented it. He didn't have to let it happen. If He's so powerful, why didn't He save them?"

"That's right!" Nog agreed. "If God is so big and so powerful, if He's got the whole world in His hands, I guess He could have prevented a little accident like this. What's the deal?" He regarded Greta with a confidence he was far from feeling.

There was something steely in this woman that frightened him. Billie Jo was easily swayed in her present condition, but this woman was another story. She had already faced her demons and prevailed. She was a formidable enemy, and he would be a fool not to treat her as such.

Greta paused for a moment of thought and then said, "When I was a girl I was a rebellious little thing. My mother told me it was better to learn from other people's mistakes, but I told her that I wanted to make my own mistakes. And I made plenty of them. My father left us when I was young, and to fill that void I had lots of boyfriends. Well, I got pregnant when I was just sixteen, not much more than a child myself.

"I lost the baby, but that's not the point. My mother warned me. I could have followed her advice. Instead I put myself up as the authority and followed my heart. The heart can be a treacherous thing."

"What's this got to do with my babies?" Billie Jo sniffed.

"Don't you see? When God made Adam and Eve He could have forced them to do what He wanted. But could you really love anyone who forced you to obey them? He had to let them choose. Which did they want to do? Follow Him or follow Satan? They picked Satan. Even then, God could have destroyed them and started all over again. But He didn't. Because He loved them He was forced to watch them walk away.

"We're reaping the harvest that they sowed. Sin has infected the whole earth. Satan is running things down here. The only hope we have is to follow Jesus and love Him enough to obey Him. That's our only hope. And that's not so that we can have a good life here. Maybe we will and maybe we won't. There are no guarantees in that department. It's a sinful world full of sinful people. But if we believe, if we hope, if we follow Jesus, there is a much better life coming. One that will make this one seem like a dusty memory.

"In that life, Billie Jo, you'll finish raising your children. And you won't have to worry about semi-trucks or drugs or school violence. There will be no death, random or otherwise. That is what you have to look forward to, Billie Jo. Lift up your eyes and look ahead. We can't stay here, in this mire of sadness and pain. We have to look ahead to what we know is coming. This old life is just a temporary thing. The life that is coming will last forever."

"Lies! All lies!" Nog bellowed angrily. "God didn't want Lucifer or anyone else to be like Him because He wanted all the glory for Himself. He threw my master out of heaven so He wouldn't have any competition. How fair is that? Lucifer was exiled to this planet, thrown this dirty little bone, to placate him. God created you all and then abandoned you to your fate. So, why do you stick up for Him? Why do you rely on Him? Why do you trust Him? How dare He judge any of us when He discarded us all?

"There isn't going to be any 'happily ever after' for any of you! Heaven is just a fantasy tricked up by religious leaders to keep people in line. There is no life that will last forever. You're all going to die, and since God doesn't want you you'll be dead forever. Forever!"

Jewel moved in close to Billie Jo, shielding her from the worst of Nog's tirade. He could sense a change in her heart. She was softening, and the demon's spewed poison could send her back into darkness, which was precisely what he wanted. Jewel knew that Nog had no hope so he couldn't bear to see others hopeful. Noxious fumes emanated from him, and Jewel protectively covered Billie Jo with his shimmering wings.

This enraged Nog, who reached over and drew his sword. He held it up menacingly and waved it at the angel. "Get away; she is mine."

"She is a daughter of the Most High God," Jewel calmly replied.

"I claim her for the kingdom of Prince Satan," Nog returned coldly. "Be gone. You have no business here. She has abandoned your Master."

When the angel ignored him, he flew into a rage and attacked, the sword seeking its target with more skill than Nog looked capable of. Jewel countered with his own sword, the steel of which was so bright the light alone nearly blinded the demon. The two fought skillfully and seemed evenly matched. Billie Jo's doubts had given the demon more power, and the angel was hard pressed to fight back against his foe.

Nog knew this would give him an advantage, and he pressed it mercilessly. He had not fought in hand-to-hand combat for some time, but he could feel his skill returning with each thrust of his sword. With a sudden twist, he gained the advantage of the angel and smiled wickedly, pointing his sword at his enemy's heart.

Billie Jo was silent, and Greta continued to pat her back reassuringly. "I just don't know if I can right now," she whispered.

"That's all right," Greta replied encouragingly. "You don't have to be ready right now. Just be willing to ask God to make you ready when the time is right."

Billie Jo nodded. "OK. Will you do that?"

Greta put her arm around Billie Jo's neck and bowed her head. "Our holy heavenly Father, we come before You today with thankful hearts. You have given us Your only Son to save us from our sins and the sins of others. You have given us hope in these dark days we're living through. You've given us a reason to go on and a destination to attain. Please be with us in our pain. I ask You to give my friend Billie Jo the strength to live and hope again. I ask You to soften the pain she is feeling and help her to rely on You through it, even if she can't see You right now.

"You said, 'Blessed are those who have not seen and yet have believed.' Help Billie Jo to believe even when her heart is hurting. Help her to see that You love her and Your heart is hurting for her too."

As Greta spoke the Word of God, swords of light flew out of her mouth, slashing Nog and stealing his triumphant moment. Wounded, he was forced to abandon Jewel before he could harm him further. He limped away, defeated and cursing.

"You are there and are ready and able to take all her burdens if she will only let You. Give her the strength to lay them down at Your feet when the time is right. We thank You and praise You for bringing her husband, Jimmy, closer to You through this difficult time. Please keep him close to You and keep him strong. We ask all this in the name of Jesus who died to save us. Amen."

As Greta finished praying, the demons, which had collected in hordes, cheering on Nog and filling the house with a fetid air, scattered to the four winds. Light, very bright and powerful, filled the house. Not a shadow existed. It bathed the two women, still bowed in prayer, in a warm glow. Angels followed this light. Filling the rooms of the house, crowding around the women, they lifted their hands and worshipped the Master. Their songs were an intricate harmony of pleasing sounds, their words full of praise. Jewel rose and joined them.

Billie Jo looked up at Greta and almost managed a smile. "Thank you for doing that. Will you stay with me for a while yet? I don't want to be alone just now."

"I'll stay as long as you want me to. How about some tea?"

As Greta popped off the couch and headed for the kitchen Billie Jo leaned back against the sofa. She felt an easing of the pain she had carried every moment since the accident. It was still there, but it was like seeing a light at the end of the tunnel. She had been trying to carry it all alone, and there was no need. God was willing to carry her burdens for her.

"Help me to let go," she breathed. Then she laid her head back on the couch and fell into the first restful sleep she'd had in days.

Shay watched Don as he returned to the mission compound after speaking with Toby. His face was chiseled into hard lines that she knew did not mean good things. He walked with his shoulders hunched over, as if trying to carry the weight of the world. Shay realized later that she should have read the signs and kept her mouth shut, but she had not figured out the best way to communicate with her husband yet, and so she plowed blindly ahead.

"What's wrong?" she asked innocently. She had an idea but wanted to give him the chance to air his grievances and talk through his feelings.

"Nothing's wrong," he snapped.

Shay knew something was wrong. She was pretty sure he'd had a fight with Toby about the sticky outpost clinic issue, so she bristled. "What's wrong?" she persisted, determined to get something out of him, even if it was only vague.

"I said nothing's wrong. Didn't you hear me the first time? Would you get off my back? As if I don't have enough problems without you pestering me." And he stalked off.

Shay felt tears well up in her eyes and she staggered back, propelled by the force of his anger. He had no call, she told herself, to speak to her like that. She was still trying to recover from Don's harshness when Davy approached her.

"Hey, Shay? Would you mind coming with me to do a check on the outpost clinics? Toby's not feeling well and she's gone to lie down for a while. I'd go by myself, but there are usually patients on a Wednesday, and I can't do much about them. I mean, I can pass out Band-Aids as good as the next guy, but if it requires more than that, they're out of luck."

Shay forced herself to smile at him. "Sure, Davy, I'll go with you. Just let me get a bag together." She packed a few things and then on an impulse, grabbed her father's jacket in case it was cold in the air.

When she was packing back in the States she had agonized over what to leave in storage, what to bring, and what to give away. One of the things she had decided to pack was her father's favorite suit jacket. It was frivolous, she knew, and Don had disapproved, but indulgently given no complaint. Shay rationalized bringing it because she'd worn it a few times as a light jacket with jeans. It was the one thing of her father's she had with her, and right now she wanted the comfort of having it, even if she didn't end up using it.

Before she left, Shay found Marcus and Madina, giving them both hugs and telling them how much she loved them and would miss them. She purposely avoided Don, though it gave her a pang to climb into the little plane without some sign of reconciliation between them. She knew he'd be sorry when he cooled off, but it was hard to wait until then.

They found the first outpost clinic strangely quiet. Davy secured the plane while Shay approached the clinic door and gave it a tug. A rough hand spun her around before she could get the door open.

"Hey!" she exclaimed, but the exclamation died in her throat. A man dressed in army fatigues grabbed her wrists and bound them in electrical tape. He had a black ski mask over his face. "Davy!" Shay screamed, but out of the corner of her eye she could see it was too late. Two men had wrestled Davy to the ground and were taping his wrists and ankles together.

Three men tackled the little ultralight, ripping out anything that wasn't screwed down and checking over the engine as if hunting for spare parts. They spoke to each other in French. Shay had grown up in Louisiana and the dialect was very different, but she was able to pick up the gist of their conversation, though she tried hard not to let on.

"Should we kill them now?" one was asking.

"No, not now. We will wait. We might be able to get some money for them first," another replied.

"It is too risky. They are Americans. This could be trouble."

"Americans are rich. After we get money and their promise to close the mission we will kill them. Then they won't come back here with their devil sickness. The others will go away. If they don't, we will have to kill them as well."

Shay felt herself go hot and cold. *Dear God*, she prayed, *please be with us. Help us to get out of this mess. Help us to trust You no matter what happens. And help us to be witnesses of Your love. And, God*, she added, *help me to be brave.*

Gaius, who had expected trouble from the moment he saw the state of affairs at the mission, rallied around Shay, protecting her from abuse by the kidnappers. One of them grabbed her by the elbow and steered her into the darkened shed; two others followed with Davy who struggled and tried to speak past the tape that was over his mouth.

By an oversight, Shay was only bound at the wrists. Whether the kidnappers trusted she wasn't going to resist or they had over-looked further restraint, she couldn't tell. They were left uncer-emoniously inside the clinic, a small hut made of corrugated iron with a dirt floor. Davy's eyes were wild as they regarded her above the gash of black tape that covered his mouth.

"It's OK," Shay whispered, sidling close to where they had dumped him in a corner. "God will take care of us. We just have to trust Him, OK? Pray."

She decided not to tell him what she had overheard. It would only make him worry more, and she wanted him strong in faith and in spirit. It was hard enough knowing herself what their prob-able fate would be. She sank down in the dirt beside Davy and closed her eyes, straining to hear the conversation of the men just on the other side of the thin wall. The words were muffled, inter-spersed now and again with a harsh laugh.

Shay felt her breathing speed up in panic and forced herself to stay calm. She inhaled slowly a few times and concentrated her attention on their surroundings. It had been a long time since she had visited one of the outpost clinics; she hadn't been in one since she had returned.

Around them everything was a shambles. It was clear the men who were holding them had done a thorough search before they had arrived. In fact, it appeared to Shay as though they might have waited there some time for them to arrive. The remains of meals were scattered on the primitive examination table, and garbage was strewn on the floor. Flies buzzed incessantly, lighting on her and Davy, who had a hard time shrugging them off. The stench of the place was overpowering. A few rolled-up blankets occupied one corner and what appeared to be personal belongings were heaped in another corner. The door appeared to be latched from the outside, but for all Shay knew it was only pushed closed. The kidnappers had no reason to believe she would dare to leave, and Davy was certainly unable.

Shay eased herself nearer to Davy, her bonds making it hard for her to maneuver. She could clearly see the question in Davy's eyes, but she purposely avoided it. "Are you OK?"

He nodded.

"Listen, I think they are going to hold us for ransom. We might be here a while. We've just got to hang tight and see what happens. If we get the chance to make a break for it, do you know how to get back from here? On foot?"

An eloquent shrug was his only answer.

"OK," she sighed. "We'll leave it in God's hands. In the meantime, let's pray."

Davy bowed his head and Shay bowed her own, praying as fervently as she knew how while keeping one ear attuned to the still muffled conversation she couldn't quite understand on the other side of the wall behind her.

Lucien was parading proudly among the kidnappers, clearly in his element. His plans were coming together in such a way that he had no doubt about their success. It had taken him no time at all to find willing participants in his schemes. The men he commanded were more obedient to his every desire than the demons he commanded. These men were so easily molded that it was almost hard for him to take pride in his accomplishment. But then, his plan was coming together so perfectly he didn't like to squabble about minor issues.

He had no doubt that these men would murder Davy and Shay in cold blood. He had seen them commit heinous crimes against people, had even instigated several of their attacks himself, and knew that they would not even think twice. Their big-

gest concern was to get the timing right. Lucien knew he would have to be on the ball to prevent either an escape or a rescue attempt by people at the mission. Either could conceivably result in bloodshed, but he wanted to make certain. There would be no unnecessary risks taken.

If Davy and Shay were murdered, two of the major players at the mission would be taken out in one fell swoop. Don and Toby would not be able to carry on. Their differences of opinion were too strong. Their personalities were incompatible. The death of Shay would leave Don the sole caregiver for two children, not a task he was in any way prepared to undertake. No, killing Davy and Shay would be as effective as throwing a bomb in the middle of the mission, not that Lucien hadn't considered a bomb. This was just more personal, in his opinion.

Lucien clasped his hands behind his back and stalked among the men as they plotted their next few days and struggled to operate their radio so they could send a ransom call. The one thing that concerned him was the marked presence of angels in the vicinity. So far as he knew, there was no reason there should be so many. Certainly the two in the shed were praying as if their lives depended on it. But that didn't account for it. Nor could it be accounted for by tallying up the people at the mission praying as they ought. The mission was divided by strife and struggling to stay afloat. No one there was praying enough to make a real difference.

There was something else going on, some other factor he hadn't taken into account. It weighed on his mind. He wanted to know every variable and have control over every possible factor. While it niggled at him he would have no peace. A squawking of the radio made him jump nervously. The kidnappers were ready to roll.

"This message is for the missionaries at Operation C.A.R.E.," the leader among the kidnappers barked into the radio. His accent made his words difficult to decipher. He repeated himself several times, demanding a response. Finally the radio crackled to life.

"This is Don Germaine, come in. Dorsey, is that you?"

"We have your nurse and your doctor," the kidnapper replied. "We will kill them if our demands are not met."

"Who is this?"

"That is not important. We demand that you close down your hospital immediately. You must leave and take your devil sickness with you. You are killing our people, and we will kill you. We start with these two."

"What two? What are you talking about?"

"If you do not close the hospital immediately we will kill your doctor and your nurse."

"Do you mean Davy and Shay? Let me speak to them."

"You have twelve hours. If the hospital is not deserted in twelve hours we will shoot them and then we will come for the rest of you. Do you understand?"

"Yes, yes, I understand. Please, let me talk to my wife. Please, I must . . ."

The kidnapper terminated the connection, and Don's anguished voice hung on the air for a few seconds. The men ranged about the plane. A few of them worked on starting a fire to warm up some water and cook a little dinner. One pulled out some cigarettes and another dug out a bottle of liquor, and they settled down to wait until their next communication.

Don Germaine stared at the radio. The static crackled monotonously, mocking him. A thousand thoughts raced through his head, the first of which was complete and total panic. In that split second he could clearly see that not a thing on earth mattered as much to him as getting Shay back safe and well. In that small window of clarity that always follows a catastrophe, his heart was laid bare and he recoiled at the truth he saw there.

All the problems that had clouded his daily life were of his own making. His headstrong attitude and need for control had very nearly torn the mission apart. And for what? Now that there was a very real threat to the mission, as opposed to only a perceived one, he could clearly see the difference and he was ashamed.

Foremost in his mind was the awful memory of Shay's face as he'd lit into her before she'd left. Hateful, ugly words might be the last she'd ever hear from him. This woman who meant more to him than the breath that whistled in and out of his lungs had for her last memory his anger and harsh words. Don was beyond mortification. He writhed in a mental agony that was almost physical in its intensity.

"That's right, you good-for-nothing heel," Merck crowed. "Look where all your self-centeredness got you. Happy now? It's too late for you, pal. Your wife will be killed and you'll have to live with that for the rest of your life. You couldn't wait to get out here, could you? I warned you to stay home, but no. You had to come back and be a do-gooder. Well, I hope you're happy. Your wife sure won't be. You think you saw some awful sights in Rwanda? Let me tell you, that's nothing to what your wife will look like when those guys get through with her."

"Pray, Don," Julian urged. "You need help. Ask for it."

"Oh, God, forgive me," Don cried, crashing to his knees. Some children, playing outside the window, stopped a moment and stared in at him, but he paid them no heed. "God, I've been so selfish and blind. It's not my job to control things. I've been rigid and unyielding and all to the detriment of Your work. Please forgive me my arrogance, my selfishness, and my pride.

"Keep Your hand over Shay and Davy. Keep them safe. Help us to know what to do. Please save them and the mission if it be Thy will. Amen."

Angels converged on Don, filling the room and spilling outside. Demons ran for cover. Merck stepped aside, watching, wondering, where had they all come from? Surely one simple prayer could not be that effective? "It's too late," he snapped. "No matter what you do, it's too late. They will die and you'll have no choice but to leave. If you are even left alive to make that decision."

Don pushed himself off his knees feeling as though he had aged two decades on the way down. Toby must be told. Then they could decide what to do. Don saw no alternative but to remove everyone from the mission until it was safe to return, if it ever was. As he hurried down the corridor to Toby's room a sudden thought froze him in place. The kidnappers seemed to be in total control of the situation. They had insinuated that they would come to the mission next if it wasn't cleared out. But how would they know? Did they have people stationed somewhere in the vicinity watching? Was everyone at the mission even now threatened by danger? Where were the children?

Don took the rest of the corridor at a gallop. He knocked briefly on Toby's door before throwing it wide. The room was dark, and Toby was stretched out on the bed. "What is it?" she moaned. "What are you doing?"

"Listen, I'm sorry, but you'll have to get up." Don sat down on the bed and took Toby's hand as she regarded him with suspicion. "Davy and Shay have been kidnapped. We have to evacuate the mission immediately. That is the kidnappers' demand. That's all they say they want. If we don't leave in the next twelve hours . . . they say they'll kill them."

"What? Who wants?" Toby cried, flailing her arms and legs in an attempt to sit upright. "What are you talking about?"

"Look, I'm sorry, but they could be watching us right now. I have to go find the children. We're in extreme danger. We must leave immediately. I need your help. Please get as many people as you can together in the kitchen area. I'll make an announcement, and we'll divide up into vehicles. It may take two trips, but we'll have to take everyone into Niamey for their protection. I'm sure Wahabi will help us out."

"Where's Davy?" Toby screamed. She struggled to get off the bed. "I want to see Davy right now!"

Don took her by the shoulders and forcibly restrained her. He struggled to keep his voice level. "Toby, listen. Davy's not here. He went to the outpost, remember? Shay is with him. They were kidnapped. We need to evacuate. Do you understand?"

Toby's eyes were wild, and she fought back tears. "Yes, I understand. Go for the children. I'll get everyone else."

Don found Marcus reading a story to Madina in the library, a ramshackle little room stuffed with books in boxes and teetering on makeshift bookcases. Sunlight shifted through the window, sending dust motes spiraling through the air. Don paused on the threshold, struck suddenly by how precious these two were to him. A lump caught in his throat as he realized that their family could be destroyed in the blink of an eye, and he chided himself because he of all people should know how quickly such a thing could happen. He, of all people, should have cherished every second. He, of all people, should have been more careful.

"Hey, kids." Don forced his voice to sound cheerful. He might have fooled Madina, but he knew Marcus sensed something was wrong immediately. Don scooped Madina up in his arms. "Guess what! We're going on a field trip into Niamey. How would you like to see Uncle Wahabi? I'll bet he's got some soda put away just for us. What do you say?"

"Is Mommy coming?" Madina asked.

"Not yet," Don answered smoothly. "She'll have to come out after she gets back. She's still at the clinics with Mr. O'Connell."

"She could be gone a long time," Marcus observed carefully.

"Yes. She could." Don refused to meet his stepson's eye. "Come on now. We have to hurry. The others are waiting for us. We're all going to go together. It'll be like a big party."

When they reached the kitchen a small crowd had assembled. It was clear to Don that Toby had apprised everyone of the situation as she understood it. The sight of Marcus, Madina, and the other children prevented anyone from asking the questions that were uppermost in their minds, and Don was vaguely grateful.

"Thank you all for coming," he said simply. "As you know, we're going to be taking a trip. I'd like to ask you to gather anything you consider irreplaceable and meet back here. Please don't take anything that isn't absolutely necessary. We need to leave as soon as possible. If we can get the old Land Rover to work we'll all be able to go in one trip.

"If not, we'll have to take turns. I'll ask those without young children to remain behind until the second trip, myself excluded, of course. I will go out in the last trip. Julia and Ray, would you please take my place and go with Marcus and Madina?

"We'll be going directly to Wahabi's home and regroup there. Now, Ray, if you'll come with me, let's see if we can get the old Land Rover moving. I have to ask the rest of you to go gather your things and come back here in no less than a half hour. Please remain inside and stay together. We'll be back."

Thrusting Madina into Julia's arms and instructing Marcus to stay with his sister, he plunged out the door with Ray at his heels. Before he could get far, Akueke stopped him. "Dr. Germaine," her shrill voice rang out.

"Akueke, please, go inside. It isn't safe for anyone to be outside," Don shooed the old woman back toward the doorway.

"It's not fair to them kids. They lost father, maybe mother, now another father? You go with them kids." Akueke clucked her tongue between her remaining teeth. "Not stay behind. Go."

Don winced. He knew she was right, but on the other hand, he was not about to run to safety while others were at risk. It simply wasn't in him. "Don't let's worry about this right now," he pleaded, pushing Akueke back toward the door. "It may not be necessary."

"What necessary is them kids having a father, that is what necessary," the old woman grumbled, moving slowly back indoors, casting a dark look behind her.

"She's right," Ray observed.

"Not you too," Don groaned. "I can't go and leave anyone behind. I just can't."

"The captain's got to go down with his ship, is that it?"

"Something like that. Listen, we're going to pray and be brilliant and fix this old Land Rover, and then we'll all be able to go, OK?"

Although they worked hard for two hours they could not get the engine to turn over, much less run. Grease-stained and weary, Don finally wadded up the rag he'd been using and threw it on the ground in disgust. "That's it, I guess. We can't waste any more time on this. We've only got ten hours left. Let's load up the other vehicle and send the first group on its way."

Sober faces greeted them in the kitchen. The few couples who had children with them, natives who had only recently arrived to fill places as nurses, filed out the door first, followed by Julia, leading Madina and Marcus. Akueke refused to budge. "If I go, you go. You go?"

"No," Don repeated. "I can't go now. But you must."

"No." Akueke's mouth set in stubborn lines. "I will wait."

Ray nudged Don. "She respects your decision. You're going to have to respect hers."

Don sighed. "OK, all right, you better get going yourself."

"I'm not going."

Don rolled his eyes. "Look, this is not a game. We've got to get as many people out of here as possible. This is not the time to be self-sacrificing. Get on the good Land Rover with your wife and move out. We need that vehicle back here pronto."

"Go, Ray," Toby broke in. "I'll stay with him and make sure he doesn't get into any trouble. Hurry. We don't want to be here any longer than we have to, and you're burning daylight."

Ray looked from one to the other. "I give up." He threw his hands up. "We'll pray for you every minute. Take care of each other." It was obvious he wanted to say more but was unable.

Don said his good-byes to Marcus and Madina and watched resolutely as the Land Rover carried them away. He waved until the vehicle was just a speck in the distance.

"Tell me exactly what they said." Toby gave him a look that said she would brook no nonsense and didn't care to be coddled. "Tell me straight."

"OK, but let's get out of the sun." He led the way back into the kitchen, telling her as they went, trying as hard as possible to use their exact words and inflections, trying not to read anything into what they'd said or play it down in any way. When he finished she was silent.

"Do you think they'll be killed?" she asked finally.

Don opened his mouth to say No as vehemently as he could, but then he stopped. Realistically he had to say their chances weren't good. "I don't know," he answered simply. "I think there is a good possibility, yes. I won't lie to you. But, then, the kidnappers don't have God on their side and we do. I think that we have to determine here and now to follow God and trust Him, no matter what happens."

He walked over to one of the kitchen chairs that had been over-turned in the evacuation. He set it upright and sat down heavily. "I think we have a choice. We can choose to follow God only if we get the outcome we want and expect. Or we can let God be God and follow Him no matter what outcome we get. Even if it ends up being the very worst outcome we can imagine.

"Already He's humbled me. I thought I was in charge here. I thought I was following Him. Now I can see that I was just follow-ing Don. It's a hard thing for me to admit. You and Davy had the right idea. Maybe you are a little too progressive. Certainly we can see now that we need to consider some safety issues, but you want to expand. God won't fit in this tiny little place I have for Him. He will go wherever we are willing to let Him lead us. I wouldn't admit that. I think I'm ready now.

"But I don't want to move on from here and put God into yet another box, the box of what I hope will happen. I mean, when I think about what's going on I want to say, I'll only follow you *if*. Then I remember Rwanda. That's what happened there. I can't be so quick to go back there."

"I'm not sure I can do it." Toby bit her lip, her face tortured.

"No. I can't either. I have to keep forcing my mind away from what might happen because I just can't handle it. That's why we have to ask God to help us. Are you willing to do that?"

Toby nodded. "I guess so. Yes. I can do that."

"Let's get everyone together and pray." Four people besides themselves had remained behind. Akueke was one; the other three were native teachers who had recently arrived to help with the new school.

Legions of angels filled the room, surrounding the people, ef-fectively blocking the demons from reaching anyone gathered in the humble kitchen. Only a few angels were present as a direct result of prayer by people at the mission who knew what was going on. Many more had come at the request of Cindi Trahan's Wing and a Prayer email prayer list.

Cindi had been impressed to spend extra time praying for her brother and his wife and family when they returned to the mission in Africa, even though she would have preferred he remain in the United States. She had mentioned her concern in the email list, and hundreds of people had begun to pray for extra guidance and protection for Don Germaine, his wife, Shay, and their adopted children. As the direct result of these petitions, hundreds of angels had come to the mission to help in whatever way they could.

As they arrived, the angels had battled demons of strife who were wreaking havoc among the missionaries. The kidnapping was just one more example to the angels of Satan's plan to destroy the mission and the people who had dedicated their lives to it. They had begun by encouraging the receptive people there to pray and ask for help. And they recited scriptures, which sent the demons scrambling for cover. Slowly, the people at the mission had responded to the wooing of the Holy Spirit.

Now, as they huddled on their knees in the middle of the cramped kitchen, angels surrounded them, giving them strength, offering encouragement, and carrying their prayers to the Master. Demons, gathering momentum, swirled around the edges, careful to stay out of reach of the angels, but clearly biding their time before making a full attack.

The group in the kitchen remained on their knees for nearly an hour, but when Don stood up, it seemed as if only a few moments had elapsed. They had submitted themselves to God's will, no matter what. Now it remained for them to do what was physically in their power.

CHAPTER 12

Cindi Trahan hadn't been back to Ethel's old house in months. When she opened the door it felt like a million years instead. Carpenters were working on the stairway. Some rooms had been turned into offices and others into a playroom, nursery, and even a library. The smell of new paint was in the air and busy people were going about their business. A few glanced at her, but most were too preoccupied.

"Cindi Trahan?" a bright voice asked.

Cindi turned to find a fresh-faced young man, with all the youthful eagerness and enthusiasm of a puppy bundled into an urbane and painfully professional exterior. "I'm Sean Buchanen, the center's assistant director. Mr. Redcloud told me you were coming today. In fact, he's in his office right now if you want to see him."

"Yes, I would. Thank you very much." Cindi hid a smile at the young man's effusive zeal as she followed him to Jesse's office. Jesse Redcloud rose to greet her with a warm smile.

"Hey, Cindi! I was hoping you'd get here before I had to leave. I've got some applications I'd like to get your opinion on. How have you been?"

"Fine, just fine, getting into home school. It's always an adjustment after summer vacation." Cindi looked around the office and took in the fresh paint, the modern bookshelves, and the second-hand office furniture. Though they hadn't had much of a budget, she thought they had managed to pull together a perfectly respectable community center.

Jesse's dark eyes followed her glance. "What do you think of the place?"

"It's nice," Cindi said, grinning. "Nicer than I expected even. You've done a remarkable job. I knew when they wanted a recommendation for the director there was no one more capable of pulling this off than you. And I was right."

Jesse's black eyes shone. "Considering my history, I think that's one of the nicest compliments I could ever receive."

Cindi laughed. "Well, you may have had a rocky start, but in the time I've known you I've watched God transform your life into a shining example of what someone can do in His service. I'm proud to know you, Jesse. I am."

"I appreciate that." Jesse's face was suffused with gratitude. He had certainly come a long way, from a broken home and through foster families, running away from the last one. He'd met Cindi shortly after he had been planning to rob her church until an encounter with angels had changed the course of his life. "Why don't I give you the grand tour?"

"I'd love that!" she exclaimed. "Thanks."

They had just finished with the upstairs rooms and Cindi was about to wrap up the small talk and leave when she heard a familiar voice. As she was turning toward it, trying to remember why it was so familiar, she placed it.

Earlier there had been a meeting, a none-too-pleasant meeting, Ogel recalled. Sparn had called it and even sent for Lucien, who had come with great reluctance, having been in the middle of something of vast importance in Africa. Rafe had been summoned as well. Though Sparn had surveyed the three of them with a countenance that brooked no objection, Lucien had slumped in the corner, his whole aspect conveying the message that it was beneath him to show up at all.

"Do you think you are above culpability in this matter?" Sparn toyed with his long dirty fingernails, and a malignant gleam shone

in his small, dark eyes. His sallow cheeks were hung with folds of skin as white as if he were touched by leprosy. He turned his nose, a thin blade long and hooked at the tip, toward Ogel because he dared make a sound of pleasure at Lucien's discomfort. "Yes? Have you something to say as well? Between the three of you, you have managed quite well to destroy all my careful plans."

Ogel sincerely doubted Sparn had spent much time concerned with this business, beyond approving Ogel's own plans, but it would never do to say as much. Sparn was looking for an example, and Ogel had no desire to become one.

"I need for this to happen," Lucien said sullenly. "There are far too many blasted angels at the mission. They will ruin all my plans. You two," he spared a jerk of his head for Rafe and Ogel, "have been playing cat-and-mouse games with this couple long enough. It is time to fish or cut bait as the humans say." Here he paused to sneer, his lips drawing back from fearful teeth, the grimace on his face horrible to behold.

"I am in the process of bringing death and destruction to the mission in Africa, the one she is praying for." Lucien pointed an accusing finger at Cindi. "Her prayers are interfering with my success. She must be stopped. I don't care what it takes. You have the elements you need most. Time is of the essence. You have squandered that most precious commodity in power struggles and mistakes." Lucien conveniently neglected to mention his own part in the power struggles, Ogel noted.

Lucien was not to escape blame so quickly. Sparn nodded thoughtfully. "Your own actions, as they have been related to me, do you no credit, Lucien." His eyes narrowed as he pinned the unfortunate demon beneath his gaze like a bug in a collection. "You would place the blame on your brothers, but you yourself deserve a fair share. It was your meddling that pushed matters to their present course. In your haste you did not listen to those in charge of the situation, and as a result you pushed this couple apart when we would have them illicitly together. What do you have to say for yourself?"

Lucien, to his credit, seemed to know when it would be bad politics to point a finger. "If I acted unwisely," he murmured diplomatically, "I did so with the very best of intentions." A demon would not go so far as to extend an apology. Taking responsibility for a failing of any kind was the sort of thing a Christian would do, but not a demon with any self- respect burning in his breast.

"I want you to remove yourself immediately and leave the rest of this operation in my hands. You are not to interfere any longer. Am I making myself clear?" Challenging Sparn in this kind of mood would take a braver demon than Lucien. He merely nodded his subservience and disappeared, presumably back to Africa to finish his own job.

Then Sparn turned his attention to Ogel and Rafe. "I should have known the two of you couldn't work together on this mission. There is entirely too much of self in both of you. An admirable quality most of the time, but your egos have proved disaster to us today. We are no closer to attaining our goal than we were months ago. In fact, we are much further from it. The advantage we gained has been taken from us all because the two of you cannot cooperate. What have you got to say for yourselves?" There was a malignance behind Sparn's eyes that made Ogel quake with fear.

"I was only trying to do my job, sir," he squeaked.

"Only trying to do my job, you mean," Rafe growled. He for one didn't seem to be cowed by Sparn's dark looks. "I was in charge, and you saw fit to disregard my authority. That is grounds for the most severe of punishments."

"Yes," Sparn agreed in a soft voice laced with pleasure. "The most severe of punishments. How true."

Ogel felt that his heart would surely fail him. Sweat poured from him, and his limbs seemed turned to water. He knew better than to ask for mercy, for mercy was the providence of heaven and never, never of their dark world. Mercy was weakness. He knew that whatever came, he must endure it.

"Rafe will take the punishment."

Rafe's back straightened with indignation, and his voice fairly crackled with anger. "What? But that's not fair!"

A slow, terrible smile played on the outskirts of Sparn's twisted, shriveled lips. "No, it's not fair is it? Not fair at all." He seemed *more pleased with this than the anticipation of torturing Rafe, though he was known to enjoy the pain he inflicted on others. "Ogel, consider yourself warned. You are to continue with this mission. And you are to see that it is completed. You are to bring the human beings into an adulterous relationship by whatever means you can. Or you will suffer the same punishment as your brother. Do you understand?"*

Ogel nodded wordlessly and tried not to listen to the impassioned pleading and outright screams of terror proceeding from Rafe as that worthy was dragged away. The cruel light in Sparn's eyes told him that it would not take much to find himself in the same predicament. Now he stood beside Jared, having positioned him for this one last hurrah. He had schooled him, through many sleepless nights, in what he must say and what he must do to win this woman. It was his one last chance, and he couldn't afford to blow it.

"Hi, Cindi." It was Jared. His eyes searched her face. "I'm here to sign up. I want to volunteer my services."

For the life of her, Cindi couldn't think of a single reply. Her mind was a perfect blank. She cast about frantically for some trivial topic, anything to fill the silence that was stretching out tightly between them.

Ogel sidled up to Cindi. "Confrontation can be hard, I know, but hear him out. You need to listen to what he has to tell you. There was a time when you were attracted to him. You could be again. Just listen to him."

Shania crowded in close, forcing the demon to scurry away. "Forget decorum, forget manners. Ask Jesse Redcloud for help. Now." Cindi wavered, and Ogel used her indecision to his advantage. Quickly he arranged a phone call for Jesse to get him out of the way.

Jesse Redcloud looked from one to the other, but before he could offer anything a young girl informed him that he had a call. "Cindi? I hate to be rude, but I'll leave you two to catch up. Stop by any time."

Mutely, Cindi nodded, watching Jesse's retreating back the way a drowning woman might watch a lifeboat slip away with the current. She turned uncomfortably back to Jared, wondering in a panicked way if there would be a scene. She hadn't talked to him since the conversation in which she'd told him they couldn't be friends.

"Jared, I . . ." she tried, but he interrupted her.

"Look, Cindi, I can see you don't want to talk to me, and I understand that. Just listen to what I have to say." He ran his hands through his hair in agitation and glanced around. "Can we step outside?"

"I'm not sure that's a good idea."

"Come on, Cindi. I'm not going to bite your head off. I just want to talk. Can you spare me five minutes?" Without waiting for a reply he took her elbow and steered her toward the door. Outside the humidity was oppressive, and Cindi longed to be back in the air conditioning. She turned warily to face Jared.

"Look, Cindi, I have tried to call you, but you won't pick up the phone. I think you owe it to me—to us—to hear me out."

"There is no us, Jared. That's what I'm trying to get through to you," Cindi interrupted desperately. "There is only you and me and a relationship that is getting out of hand. I can't do this anymore. I wanted to be friends with you; I thought I needed to be friends with you. But I was wrong. You don't want to be friends, and I don't have anything more than friendship to offer you. I'm sorry." She started to turn away, but he grabbed her arm angrily.

"Where are you going? I haven't said anything yet." He held himself stiffly, and Cindi felt anger billowing from him in waves. "If nothing else, you are going to listen to me, do you understand?"

Cindi bit back tears. His fingers had bruised her arm. She looked around for someone she could call to for help but couldn't see a soul. His grip lessened, and he leaned toward her, his expression apologetic, his eyes begging her to understand.

"I'm sorry. I didn't mean to hurt you." He took his hands off her and backed away slightly. "It seems like I'm always doing the wrong thing. I'm so messed up in my head I don't know what to say or do anymore."

When he looked up at her Cindi read the most intense anguish and pain she'd ever witnessed in the eyes of another human being. She nearly cried out with compassion, but checked herself sharply. This was not her fight. Silently she prayed for someone to come and help her out of this difficulty and for the words to say to this man that would preserve his dignity, but make the break between them final.

"No!" Ogel screamed. "You're not listening. Listen to the man. Hear him out. Is that so much to ask?"

Angels began to gather in droves, and Ogel was forced to flee, hurling curses as he moved farther and farther from where he could effect any difference in the proceedings. He could hear the angels relating promises to Jared, and he writhed in agony, powerless to argue. The specter of himself sharing in Rafe's fate rose up before him and filled him so full of desperation that he began to lash out at the angels closest to him in an attempt to gain back his precarious purchase on his charge.

The light was brighter than he remembered. From the dim recesses of his mind he recalled a softness that had bathed him in love and security. When he was an angel, the light from the Master had filled his life with brightness. Now, as an enemy to all that was good and honest and true, the light burned him with an intensity that was agony indescribable. Feeling wretched, he broke away from the angels and watched from his distant vantage point with increasing despair.

"Cindi, I never thought I'd say this to another woman after Krissy died, but I love you. I love you." He broke down and wept. "I need you in the worst way. I can't eat or sleep. I can't concentrate on my work. I'm worse off now than when I met you. Only now, it's not Krissy I miss; it's you.

"I hear your voice in my mind. And I talk to you. You're so kind. I can't believe that you really won't have anything to do with me. Please tell me it is all a misunderstanding." His whole aspect was imploring, beseeching her to refute her stand, begging her to back down and accept him in a way that was impossible for her to do.

Cindi felt her whole body tense for flight. In the back of her mind she mapped out routes to take the moment he lunged for her as she was sure he would. She didn't believe he was dangerous, but it was clear he was desperate and not thinking clearly.

"Jared, you know why we can't be friends. Please understand, it's nothing personal . . ."

"How can you say that? Of course, it's personal," he snapped. "What can be more personal than rejection? You are rejecting me."

"I am not rejecting you," Cindi returned, easing away from him. "I'm not. It's just that we can't be friends. You don't want to be friends. You want something more."

"More?" he echoed, as if considering the possibilities. "I only want you."

"But, Jared, I'm married," Cindi said emphatically.

"I know," he whispered, his voice cracking with emotion. "I'm not insensible to the obstacles. Give me more credit than that. But I thought if we were truly meant for each other it wouldn't be wrong for you to get a divorce. Would it?"

"The Bible says, 'What God has joined together let no man put asunder.' I don't think it gets much plainer than that. And you are assuming that I want to leave my husband, but I can assure you that I don't."

"Don't you love me, Cindi? I thought . . . sometimes I thought that you did. Then I wanted you to so much that I told myself you must. I just don't know what I'll do if you don't." He seemed bewildered, like a lost child. So much had happened to him in the last few months that Cindi wasn't surprised at his confusion. She was only sure, as she should have been all along, she realized in a tiny moment of absolute clarity, that she was not the one to deal with his problems.

"Jared, you need to talk to someone, get some counseling. I can recommend a good man. He's a youth pastor at my church. His name is Lyle Ryan, and he's been through some tough times himself. Let me give you his number." She fumbled in her purse for a scrap of paper and a pen. Down in the flotsam she found what she was looking for and scribbled the information quickly, handing it to him.

He took it, unwillingly, but obediently. "You think he can help me?" The question was plaintive, the question of a man at the bottom and grasping toward any shred of light at the end of a very long, dark tunnel.

"I think God can help you," Cindi replied with conviction. "Lyle Ryan knows Him, and I think he can help you come to know Him too."

"I'm sorry," he said, "sorry that I bothered you. I just had to know; I had to be certain there was no way. You're sure there's no way?" He heaved a resigned sigh but didn't wait for a response. With the steps of an old, old man he turned and made his way out to the parking lot, got in his car, and after a moment, drove slowly away, hunched miserably over the steering wheel. Cindi watched him until she could see the car no longer.

"Cindi?" The voice cut into her thoughts and made her start with surprise. Turning, she found Jesse Redcloud approaching with a sheaf of papers in his hand. "I didn't realize you were still here. I was looking for your friend. He didn't leave, did he? I got hung up and didn't have time to conduct his interview."

"He left," Cindi confirmed. "But I think he'll be back another time. I'd hang on to that application if I were you. When he's ready to complete it he'll be a volunteer worth having."

Jesse's eyebrows shot up with surprise. "Oh yeah? I'll do that then. Thanks."

"No problem," Cindi said lightly. "Well, I guess I'd better be getting back myself. I'll stop by again soon," she promised. Jesse lifted his hand in a cursory wave, and she turned and hurried down the walkway to her parked car.

Davy lay on his side and tried not to think about the knot of earth that had worked its way into his muscles or the flies that landed with soft annoyance, tickling every inch of bare skin. Slowly the dusty daylight seeped out of the hut, but sleep eluded him. In the blackness of the hut he could see nothing, though he heard Shay's steady breathing. She was lying on her side with her back to him. She was pressed against him, for reassurance, he supposed, and he was grateful for the contact.

Hours before, their captors had removed their bonds and locked the door of the hut. Then they had gone, disappeared it seemed, into the vast foliage. In the hut was only one bucket of water, the quality of which was dubious at best. A very stale loaf of bread was on the ground beside it. Bugs wriggled in its depths, and it remained untouched. They weren't that hungry . . . yet.

At some point during the night one of the kidnappers returned. Davy woke from a troubled sleep startled to find that he had dozed off. He could hear someone banging around outside, and by looking through the gaping slats between the corrugated iron of the hut's walls he could see one of the kidnappers start a small fire and cook something. The smell of it made his stomach cry with hunger.

He spent some time crouched close to the wall, eye to the gap, wondering why this man alone had returned. Had he been sent back as a guard? Why leave at all then? Where were the others? Were they coming back too? How soon? Questions buzzed his head like planes circling a landing strip. Shay had not woken up, and he did not wake her. If she could sleep he would not disturb her. Let her rest while she could. Who knew what was in store for them.

Dawn was lightening the sky when the kidnapper outside became weary and rolled up in a blanket beneath a shelter they had constructed of tree branches and tarps. Surely he could not be expecting his fellows soon or he would not risk getting caught sleeping. Davy jumped up and paced the floor in agitation. If only they had some way of escaping! He castigated himself mentally. Why had they not tried to dig out while they had the chance? Now they would surely be heard if they tried anything.

Or would they?

Jes had been trying to get through to Davy for hours, but he was so busy worrying about his situation that he had not paid attention to the voice of the angel. "Quickly, Davy, you must escape from this place. There is no doubt that these men mean to kill you even if they get what they want. You must dig your way out."

Outside, an army of angels surrounded the sleeping guard, keeping the host of demons who were accompanying him at bay. They shielded him in such a way that he slept as the dead. No sound could penetrate his consciousness. But they knew what Davy did not. The other men would be back soon. Time was running out.

Davy picked up a scrap of twisted metal, one of the many objects cluttering the floor of the hut. He dropped it and watched the figure wrapped in the blanket. Nothing. Tentatively he struck the metal on the wall and watched keenly for a reaction. Nothing. He struck harder. Still nothing. He scratched the surface of the hard-packed dirt but received no response at all from the sleeping figure outside.

Quickly he fell to his knees by Shay's side and shook her with barely contained excitement. He felt electrified with hope. "Shay!" he hissed. "Wake up! Quickly!"

She rolled toward him, waking instantly. "What is it?"

"There's only one guard out there, and he's asleep." Davy kept his voice barely audible, his lips almost brushing her ear. "I made some noise, but he's dead to the world. I think we can dig our way out while the others are gone, but it will take two of us. You go watch while I dig."

Jezeel, who found himself blocked from warning the guard outside the door, began to prey on Shay's apprehensions. "Don't do it. It'll be worse for you if they come back suddenly and find you've tried to escape. There is no way you can cover up a hole that size. They'll know what you've done, and they'll punish you for it. They may even kill you for it."

Shay bit her lower lip and stared at Davy with mute appeal. He felt a surge of irritation. "Come on. What are you waiting for?" he hissed.

"What if they come back and see what we've been doing?"

"Look, I don't know what their intentions are. I can't understand a word they speak. But, I know one thing. I know determination when I see it. And I see plenty of it. Whatever it is they want, we're the pawns. When they're done with us we'll be done for. I'm sure of it."

"This is your chance," urged Gaius. "Take it, little sister. They are coming. There is no time to waste. Trust the Master. He has promised that when you come to a fork in the road He will speak in your ear. Can you hear Him, little sister? Take your chance and live."

Shay nodded and crawled over to take position by the crack in the iron wall. While she huddled there, Davy went to the area of the hut that was exactly opposite the door and bent to dig into the dirt. It was so hard packed that the work was more like scratching and chiseling with the piece of waste metal than digging. In moments Davy was drenched with sweat. He wiped valiantly as it poured off into his eyes, stinging and clouding his vision.

"This is useless," Jezeel taunted, stalking around the narrow confines of the hut. "It's stupid. It's preposterous. You don't have a chance in a million anyway. Do you really want to spend your last minutes on earth trying to dig out like a coward? Wouldn't you rather face those guys with your head up and take what's coming to you?"

Davy slowed down, dragging his sleeve across his brow. The faint light of defeat glimmered in his eyes. Then he took a deep breath and began digging again. Jezeel never knew what hit him, but suddenly he found himself flying through the air and landed with his back against a tree outside in a most undignified position. Having been occupied inside the hut he hadn't noticed the changes taking place outside.

Great battalions of angels surrounded the sleeping kidnapper, and Jezeel knew that he slept deeply. Swirling around the angels were demons hurling abuse and picking fights. Small skirmishes had broken out around the perimeter, but the angel guard was so strong that the outcome was not in question. Jezeel knew at a glance that the demons who streamed in, though, were the vanguard of a much, much larger force. And judging from the rate at which they were arriving, the main contingent of demons was not far behind.

He tried to force his way back into the hut but found it so crowded with angels that it was impossible for him to get even a toe in the door. Enraged, he joined the others circling the angels, taking out his aggression on any being that moved into his path.

The dirt scraped away so slowly that Davy had to struggle with himself not to give up. It seemed hopeless. Then suddenly Shay elbowed her way in next to him and began to dig alongside. "What are you doing?" he hissed.

"The same as you."

"What about the guard?"

"Sleeping."

"What if he wakes up?"

"What if he does?" There was a determined set to her lips that Davy had seen before. She was scared but resolved. "What are they going to do? Kill us deader?"

Davy nearly smiled. She was built of sterner stuff than he was. He grunted. They made the hole as shallow as they possibly could, knowing that to get out they would have to wriggle and trust God. When the tunnel began to open up on the other side of the iron wall they took turns, spelling each other as they tired of lying in the cramped space and digging.

Each scraping motion deposited dirt into the tunnel behind the digger. Whoever was not digging tried to help remove this extra dirt as quickly as possible in between periodic checks to make sure nothing had changed outside. Once, when Davy was in the hole, Shay had been unable to remove the dirt he dug fast enough and he'd become trapped in the hole, wedged between the sharp edge of the wall and the dirt below. He had almost started to panic, but forced himself to remain calm. Shortly after that he broke through on the other side.

"Do you think you could squeeze through now?" he asked Shay.

"I'll try." Between her own efforts to pull herself through and

Davy's energetic, almost frantic pushing that resulted in a painful abrasion along her back as the wall scraped it raw, Shay managed to squirm and wiggle her way through the hole.

"I'm out," she panted, turning to stop him before he could follow her. "We'll have to make it a little bigger or you won't make it."

"I can do it," Davy objected. "I'm coming through. Help me."

"Davy, wait . . ."

But he couldn't wait. Their captors could barge through the door and stop him at any moment. He threw himself into the hollow they'd made. Dirt filled his nose and eyes, but he ceased caring. He wriggled and contorted his body, straining for the other side of the wall, but it was no use. He was stuck. The wall pinned him down effectively. He couldn't go back, and he couldn't go forward.

"Davy," Shay's voice was a frightened whisper.

"Go!" he said angrily. "Go hide! Now!"

"Go," Jezeel commanded, pointing a long finger to the woods, only steps away. "Save yourself. Leave him to his fate. You don't owe him anything."

"No!" Her eyes blazed with anger to match his. "Not without you!"

Frantically she dug, sometimes striking his side with the metal, in an effort to free him. Davy shut his eyes and tried not to think about the sharp pains when she nicked him, tried not to think about what would happen if she failed. Finally she tossed the metal and used her hands to dig beneath him, pinching him, but moving enough earth that he felt himself shift. "I'm loose, I'm loose!"

She grabbed his wrists and pulled as he angled his hips and squirmed. Inch by inch he was released and his body slid through the hole. "Run!" he told her, grabbing her hand and staggering to his feet. In a crouch he made for the dense brush beyond the hut, not even daring to look behind. He did not want to know what might be after them now.

As silently as possible, they disappeared among the thorn trees and moved quickly along, watching their footing and trying to put as much distance as they could between themselves and the kidnappers. Davy had no idea where they were going. And he had no idea where they should try to go. Anything, even death by slow degrees in the grasslands, was preferable to any way the kidnappers might decide to torture and kill them. That was the only thing he was certain of.

"Where are we going?" Shay managed to gasp breathlessly.

"Away, anywhere."

"But do you know where you're going? Are we headed for help?"

"We're headed away from them." He made a vague gesture back the way they had come.

Shay tugged on his hand, slowing him down. "You don't know where we're going? You don't know how to get us back on land?"

Davy yanked her, possibly harder than was strictly necessary, to get her moving again. "I have a general idea, yes, but do I know how far and how long? No. This is *not* the direction we should be going, I can tell you that. But we have to circle around."

Shay thought that circling around seemed too fraught with danger, but she had the presence of mind not to say so to Davy. He spoke again. "I'm doing the best I can, OK? It looks different from the air. It's simpler. I think we want to stay as far from the beaten paths as possible and avoid any main routes when we come around on the other side. Chances are those goons will be coming back along well-traveled routes."

Many hours later, as night was falling fast, Davy had to admit that he was hopelessly lost. He didn't know if they were near the outpost clinic where they had started or miles away from it. He wasn't sure if they were moving north, south, east, or west. The only thing he knew was that he was bone tired, more tired than he had ever been in his life. The stars above him swam dizzily, and he couldn't make sense of their position. Even his hunger pains paled before his body's screaming need to rest.

"We're going to stop here for tonight. There is no sense trying to move in this darkness. We need to rest up so we can get an early start tomorrow. I'm sure it will all look different in the morning."

"We're lost, aren't we?"

No sense deceiving her. "Yes. We're lost."

"We're going to make it out of this."

He was touched by her strong faith. He tried to smooth out the ground beneath them, moving twigs and bits of branches. The earth was warm and smelled of dry grass. "Yes," he replied finally, with as much conviction as he could. "Yes, we'll make it out of this."

"When we do, there are a lot of things we all need to talk about."

"You mean the mission? The plane?" He didn't really need to ask. It had been on his mind as well. It seemed so stupid, under the circumstances, to know that the entire mission, their friendships, their very lives, had nearly been destroyed because of their own stubborn pride.

When the future is distilled to its very essence, the way theirs was at this moment, momentous matters like the ones that had consumed their lives recently assumed their actual proportions. Davy was ashamed to admit that if only they were rescued or found their way out of this awful place, he would gladly fly his plane wherever and whenever God wanted him to do so. He would be thankful just to draw breath. He wouldn't waste it arguing about flying in the first place.

All his old prejudices fell away, chiseled off by terror and hope combined. If Don Germaine materialized right there in the grassland at that very moment, Davy felt himself capable of hugging him as though he were a long-lost brother. And Toby . . . he missed her with an intense ache.

"We've all behaved very badly," Shay said, bringing his thoughts back. "We have not acted as Christ would want us to. It's sad. We've wasted so much time and effort. And now this." She was quiet for a moment.

"I—I didn't tell you this, but they said they were going to kill us."

He thought this over and nodded. "I think I knew."

"But you didn't say anything."

He shrugged. "What was there to say? It was only a hunch anyway. They seemed pretty serious to me."

"They were. Look, I know we've got enough to worry about right now, but there was something else. They said something about if they couldn't close the mission they'd kill whoever was there. They wanted money too. They think we're rich."

Davy laughed without humor. "We are rich, just not the way they think we are. What do you think? Will Don get everyone out of there or will he try to stand the attackers off?"

Her voice was soft and uncertain in the darkness. "I don't know. I want to say he'll evacuate everyone, but it would be a guess and probably not a very good one. I imagine he'll evacuate most of them, but he'll stay behind. That's just how he is."

"And Toby will stay with him," Davy said, voicing the thought that was in both of their minds.

"You'd know better than I would," Shay said lightly, but Davy knew she agreed with him.

He groaned. "As if this isn't bad enough. Do you think that's where those goons were heading when they left us?"

"I don't know where else they might feel like hiking to for no particular reason."

"OK, OK." Davy clutched his hair, trying to force his brain to work by sheer willpower. He felt as though he were wading through mental pea soup. "There's nothing we can do about this right now, so we should try not to worry about it. We need some sleep so we're fresh in the morning. There's going to be a lot of walking to do."

"I disagree."

"You think we're going to fly?" Davy countered archly.

"No, I think there is *something we can do about Don and Toby and the others right now. We can pray."*

Davy was immediately humbled. "You're right." He bowed his head, and in a few moments Shay's voice came through the night, and with it, a powerful presence they both felt. Instantly he felt protected. No matter what happened, God was in control of it all.

"Dear God, please be with everyone at the mission. Help them to all get away safely. We pray especially for Don, my children, and Toby. Keep them all safe. Confuse the plans of the terrorists, Lord. We trust You to defeat our enemies and to help us walk in Your ways.

"We acknowledge that we have sinned before You, Lord, and been presumptuous. We are sorry for our pride and ask You to forgive us. Show us all how to work together without strife and further Your work here among these people. Please send angels to watch over us and in the morning show us how to get home. Amen."

Davy didn't bother to open his eyes; he simply slumped down on the ground and fell deeply asleep. In his dream he saw angels, hundreds of them, lighting up the underbrush around them. They stood in a ring, towering higher than any human being. He smiled in his sleep and dreamt on.

A wall of angels surrounded the pair, who, without knowing it, was sleeping just steps away from the main trail leading back to the outpost clinic. The angels acted as a shield when, a few hours later, a group of armed men made their way down the path, passing within yards of Davy and Shay. Any noise, premonition of proximity, or scent of their quarry would have alerted any of the men instantly, but they walked on. Not even the howling of the demons or their cursing and threats were enough to penetrate the thickly grouped angels and endanger the sleeping missionaries.

Jes cloaked Davy with one shimmering wing. He'd been through a lot, and Jes couldn't help comparing his reactions now to what they would have been a few short years before. Human beings, he knew, had difficulty seeing how they grew in grace, but angels could see it clearly, as though it were measured out by inches rather than subtle character changes reflecting how the Master was working in their lives.

Davy would probably consider himself a failure. He had allowed a spirit of pride to rule his thinking in the matter of the plane. But now that it was obvious to him, he was convicted of his sin; he was repentant, not rebellious. The Master desired a contrite heart, and Davy had one. It was as simple, and as complex, as that.

From down the path he heard the tramping of feet and the curses of men who were ruled only by the demons' whims. They were controlled in every action by their weakness in withstanding the demons' suggestions. Like a horse with a bit in its mouth, they were ridden by their evil desires, galloping their way toward destruction.

Jes shuddered to think at how easy it was for demons to sway a human spirit that was not made strong by the power of the Holy Spirit. On their own, human beings could not prevail, though he knew it did not stop many of them from trying. A great sadness welled up in his heart as he considered these lost sheep of the Master.

Jes settled down for a long wait. Darkness would not prevail this night. His job was to make sure that Davy received a good night's rest so he would be ready to face the challenges of the next day. There would be many challenges.

CHAPTER 13

Christmas was coming. Billie Jo could feel it as though it were bundled into weights hung around her neck. There were moments when she found herself actually looking forward, with a *frisson* of excitement, to the holiday season. In those moments she felt intense shame and hated herself. How could she enjoy anything now that the children were gone? This question went through her mind constantly, like the snatches of Christmas songs she caught herself humming under her breath.

"You need to stop beating yourself up for living," Greta observed one day, when Billie Jo had shared the agony she was experiencing with the advent of the holiday season. " 'Anyone who has a continuous smile on his face conceals a toughness that is almost frightening.' The other Greta said that. But it works both ways, my dear. You can't go through the rest of your life feeling guilty that you are alive and your children aren't. It won't help them one particle, and it'll hurt you plenty."

Billie Jo didn't know how to live any other way. Even Jimmy seemed to have a peace that she did not yet possess. Slowly, as she cracked eggs for a frittata and her hands moved deftly tossing a salad to go with it, her mind reached ever so tentatively toward the idea that she could be happy again. Was it possible that she could ever rejoice in the strains of the *Messiah* or walk a country road or pet a dog or experience any one of a hundred pleasures without feeling every second that she was betraying Cassidy and Dallas because they could not be there to share it with her?

The very idea was repulsive. How could she enjoy anything when her children lay in the cold ground of Tennessee, in a graveyard so far from her home that she couldn't even go there to lay flowers beside the gravestones? A thousand times a day she thought of something they had never done, and now would never do. There were dozens of things she desperately wanted to share with them. If only she could have them back, even for an hour, even if it was only to say Goodbye, to tell them one last time how much she loved them. She yearned to hold them one final time. Sometimes she thought that if she could only do that she would be satisfied. But she knew, deep down, that her heart was greedier than that, and no amount of time would be enough to spend with her children.

"I want to think that I could be happy if I could have only a few hours with them," she confided to Jimmy that night as they lay side by side in bed, staring into the darkness, unable to sleep. "But I know that I'd want more. I'd never be satisfied with such a short amount of time. I couldn't ever have enough of them. Not in a thousand lifetimes."

"This is how the Master feels about all of you, Billie Jo," Jewel insisted, excited at how close she was to an important truth. "He can't stand to be separated from you in this darkness. This short time you are alive on earth is not nearly enough time for Him to be with you. He wants to spend eternity with you."

"Sure, that's what He says," spat Nog, who was feeling pretty smug about how well he was handling Billie Jo's torment. It was true that he'd lost the first round, but Billie Jo couldn't seem to drag herself out of the spiritual slumps, and she resisted spiritual help from her so-called Master. She'd start to rally for a while, but Nog was always able to beat her back down.

If only her meddling friend would stay away, everything would be perfect. He wasn't even concerned about the husband "getting religion" because nine times out of ten it was only tempo-

rary. Once the fix wore off, Jimmy Raynard would be as hopeless as his wife was now. Just look at what happened last time, Nog thought. He could wait for that. What he didn't want was some busybody angel putting any more ideas into her head.

"That's why God makes it so hard for you to follow Him, because He wants you with Him forever," he sneered sarcastically. "If you ask me He's stacking the deck against all of you."

"The way I see it," came Jimmy's deep voice from the dark. "God knows all about how we feel. He made us, didn't He? He had to watch His Son die too."

"But His Son rose again," Billie Jo said bitterly.

"So will ours."

"What do you mean? This ain't Bible times. People don't get raised from the dead nowadays."

"Don't the Bible say the 'dead in Christ will rise again'? Our kids ain't dead forever. Not if they were believers. I'm more ashamed than I can admit that I didn't help you bring them to church and learn to know our Savior. But I'm mighty thankful you did. Cassidy and Dallas, they was good kids. They knew Jesus, and some day Jesus is gonna come back and they'll rise again and go live in heaven."

Billie Jo fought back tears.

Jimmy's voice was quiet but strong with conviction. "I don't know about you, but I intend to be there to see that and apologize to them kids about how I failed them as a daddy when they was my responsibility. I pray for you, darlin', I pray for you all the time. I want us to be a family together again in heaven."

Billie Jo rolled over and buried her face in Jimmy's chest, sobbing as though her heart would break. She knew it couldn't because it was already broken. "I want my children," Billie Jo wailed.

"I know, I know, hush, darlin'," Jimmy soothed, caressing her hair and holding her in his strong embrace. "We'll have them back someday. We'll have them in heaven, and won't that be a sight, raising them there? Think on it. We won't ever have to worry about none of the problems we have here. They'll never have to go without no more. But the best of it is we'll always be together."

Nog felt the smallest tremor, as if the ground was shaking slightly beneath his feet. A dump truck passing close by a house might make the same sort of rumble. This tremor was in the spiritual fabric that he moved through and not a physical sensation at all. He knew what it meant and cried out with fear and anger as he scrambled to get out of the way.

The angels who had been following close to Jimmy Raynard since the accident raised their noble heads and gazed into a distance only they could see, their eyes alive with anticipation and happiness. Nog was just able to shield his eyes and pull himself out of range before a luminous light filled the entire room with a soft soughing sound, like wind through pine branches on a clear spring day, carrying a promise of renewal.

It was the Holy Spirit, that great interferer, Nog thought stormily as he watched, shielding his eyes to avoid the brightest beams. He could see Billie Jo still crying, could tell she was praying silently. After studying human beings for so many centuries, he could always tell. He grimaced. She was inviting that deceiver into her heart, Nog could just tell. He couldn't read her thoughts, could not hear the actual words of her prayer, but knew, still, that she was turning her heart over to His keeping again.

Just that quickly he was on the losing end again. He'd done everything he could and failed. It was a painful knowledge. Not because it was over. No, it was far from over. He had hundreds of ways to defeat her that she couldn't even dream of. It was never over with people until they were dead. No, it was just that life, for him, was so much pleasanter when lived with doubt, strife, envy, jealousy, intolerance, and a host of others as constant companions.

A Christian life, the kind that Billie Jo and Jimmy would be living now, irritated him. He would again be subjected to the close proximity of angels and the nauseating presence of the Holy Spirit, which he found to be beyond endurance. He would get his jabs in, gain his victories, but until they were under his influence again life would be uncomfortable at best and intolerable at worst.

Billie Jo allowed herself to sink into Jimmy's embrace as she cried until she could cry no longer. When her harsh sobs had faded, she began to reach out in prayer. She believed what Jimmy said; she had always known it. But in her pain she'd let go of God and hadn't allowed Him to minister to her deepest needs. She knew that with Job she had to say, "Though He slay me, yet will I trust Him."

I trust You, God, Billie Jo thought. *I'm sorry I've been so stubborn. Show me how to live without my kids. Show me how to live for You again.*

She hadn't expected to feel anything special. She'd prayed the same prayer a few times in her life when she'd gotten off track and never felt the sudden comforting blanket of peace that settled over her this time. She let out an audible sigh as she felt it slide over her, lifting the overwhelming sense of loss she felt. It was as though strong reassuring arms were holding her and she never wanted them to let go.

"Maybe," Jimmy said, interrupting the experience, "maybe someday we'll have another child?"

Billie Jo stiffened. It was hard to think about having more children.

"Not to take their place, mind," he supplied quickly. "No other children could ever take their place, just like they couldn't have done before, if we'd had other children when they was alive. But, someday, maybe we'll want children in the house, when the pain lets up some."

"Do what?"

Billie Jo fought the urge to scream that she never wanted another child. She couldn't bear to love that much again and lose someone so precious. But before her thoughts could even completely take shape a sense of longing for a child stole over her, taking her breath away. "Maybe," she conceded finally. And though she couldn't see him, she knew that Jimmy Raynard was smiling in the darkness.

"What's so funny?" she demanded.

"Nothing," he replied innocently.

"What are you smiling for then?"

"No reason. Only, making babies takes time."

"Yeah?"

"Sometimes lots of time. I was thinking maybe we could practice some?"

Billie Jo felt her husband roll toward her in the dark. He cupped her face in his big hands and kissed her gently. She knew then that something had shifted inside. The old terrible grief had been softened by the Spirit of God, and she was able to let Jimmy love her again. Their lives would never be the same, but for the first time since the accident she could look ahead without turning away. She could look ahead with hope.

The next day she was sitting at the kitchen table with a mug of peppermint tea, looking over her shopping list, when Greta bounced in the door. She wore an outrageous oversized red-and-white striped sweater that put Billie Jo in mind immediately of a candy cane. She had a Russian fur hat on that dwarfed her head and felted mittens that she seemed to have trouble keeping on her hands. Her jeans were tucked into a pair of large and serious looking snow boots with wicked looking faux fur trim.

"Well? What are you waiting for?" she demanded.

Billie Jo felt her jaw drop. "W-what do you mean?"

Greta rolled her eyes. "We're going to get our Christmas trees, silly. Get dressed."

"Did I know this?" Billie Jo asked, fiddling with her papers and stalling for time. Although she was feeling better she still felt emotionally fragile. This might not be the best time to go hunting for a Christmas tree. As well, she couldn't remember Greta mentioning anything about it.

"I'm sure I told you," Greta said in the vague way that Billie Jo recognized as meaning that it was something Greta herself had planned on, but not necessarily something she had bothered to tell Billie Jo. This sort of thing had happened a number of times in their relationship. Mostly it was only slightly annoying, but Billie Jo found that this time her feelings bordered on resentment. Why couldn't Greta have asked her to go looking for a Christmas tree instead of making an assumption that she wanted to go in the first place?

"Look here," Billie Jo began, and then she caught sight of Greta's face. It was crumpling up and tears were forming and spilling down her cheeks. "What on the green earth is wrong?" she asked, jumping up to put her arms around Greta's neck.

"I'm sorry," Greta blubbered. "I thought I'd told you. I have to go today. It's tradition. Nathan and I always got our tree exactly two weeks before Christmas. I can't go alone. Don't make me go alone."

Billie Jo stifled her own resistance to the idea. "Of course I won't let you go alone," she said, patting Greta on the back. "Santa would be liable to think you was a giant candy cane in that git-up and take you home to decorate the North Pole," she added wryly.

Greta snorted with laughter and reached for a tissue to blow her nose. "Thank you, Billie Jo. I'm good at picking trees. I'll find us real good ones. I even brought two sleds so we can haul them home."

Billie Jo got suspicious at the last remark. "Just where are we going that we have to haul trees home on a sled? Can't you buy one on any corner?"

"But those are already cut!" Greta was indignant. "They've been cut since Thanksgiving. They'll shed needles all over your floor in days."

"So, where are we getting these trees?"

"From the woods."

"Whose woods?"

"Why, yours. You have plenty."

"You mean to tell me we're gonna truck out into the woods ourselves and haul a couple Christmas trees home on sleds?"

"Now you're catching the spirit!" Greta cried, hugging her enthusiastically.

"And who's going to cut them down?" Billie Jo demanded.

"Oh, I never handle the saw," Greta insisted. "Nathan always did that part. Besides," she continued brightly, "didn't you tell me once you are an old hand at lumbering?"

"I've cut firewood," Billie Jo said, not seeing how it pertained exactly to cutting down Christmas trees.

"Well, there you go." Clearly it settled everything in Greta's mind. "You'll man the saw. I brought the folding one Nathan always used. I'm sure you'll have no trouble."

Billie Jo was sure of no such thing, but she hauled on her winter things and together they trooped out the back door toward the woods, dragging two bright plastic sleds behind them. "It's time's like these I wish I had me a horse," Billie Jo muttered under her breath.

"What was that?" Greta tramped on, seemingly oblivious to the raging cold (Billie Jo estimated it had to be fifty below at least) and not the slightest bit deterred by the banks of snow they were forced to bushwhack through. Once they reached the woods the going was somewhat better except where they hit pockets of snow that reached to their hips. When either one broke through, the other had to pull her out.

"We'll be lucky we don't break a leg," Billie Jo gasped. To her surprise she noticed that she felt good, self-sufficient, like an old-time woman pioneer. The cold was not nearly so noticeable now that she'd gotten her blood moving and her cheeks felt flushed with a cozy glow.

Greta paid no attention to her but studied every conifer they passed with a critical eye. Most she disdained for being too full on one side and too skimpy on the other. "What you want is a nice uniform tree," she instructed, "unless it's going up against a wall or window. Not too tall either. Blue spruce is the best, in my opinion, but a good balsam can be pretty too. Now, white pine," she sniffed condescendingly, "is a pain. Some people like those long needles, but every time I fall for that my ornaments slide off onto the floor and I'm forever picking them up. Now I stick with the short-needle trees."

Billie Jo could feel sweat trickling down the middle of her back. Her lungs were seared with the cold. She figured she'd settle for anything green soon. "How about that one?" she cried, pointing to a decent-looking tree that looked as though it would fit nicely in the living room.

Greta sized it up. "Not bad. I think you could do better if you wanted to look longer, but you could do worse. Shall we cut it down?"

"Yes, yes. Let's." Billie Jo struggled with the collapsible saw.

"I'll hold and you—no, not that way. You have to unscrew that little thingy part and put it in the doohickey. Yes, that's it. Now screw it back in and see? It's a saw. Clever, isn't it?" She grasped the trunk with both mittened hands and turned her face to avoid getting struck in the face with branches.

Billie Jo took a deep breath and plunged beneath the tree, wincing as branches slapped her cheeks and brushed close to her eyes. She stuck the saw down in the direction of the trunk, which she could not actually see, while trying to avoid getting scratched, and began to saw as best she could.

"That's it!" Greta called encouragingly from her position steadying the tree. It swayed as Billie Jo came close to reaching the other side of the trunk. "You've got it!" The trunk waggled precariously and then crashed down beside Billie Jo on the snow.

"One down." Greta had a satisfied look in her eye, like a hunter after a kill. "We'll leave it here with the sled and come back for it."

As it turned out they didn't have far to go. Greta found her "perfect" tree just yards beyond the site of Billie Jo's. They managed to hack it down too without incident and loaded it on the sled, strapped down with baling twine, for the journey home. Billie Jo's was packed up as well with little trouble, and soon they were headed back through the drifts of snow, heaving with tired arms on the strings of the sleds that cut into their hands.

Billie Jo longed for her warm kitchen and another mug of steaming hot peppermint tea with a candy cane stirrer. She glanced at Greta, groaning as she struggled through the snow in her silly sweater and started to laugh. She laughed so hard she had to stop and hold her sides.

Greta stopped and plopped down in the snow, rubbing her palms ruefully. "What's so funny?"

"Y-your s-sweater," Billie Jo howled.

Greta, fortunately, didn't take offense. "I know. My *mémère* knitted it for me, and I've always worn it going to get the Christmas tree. Nathan always laughed at me too, but it's as traditional as the day to get the tree. Now, come on. I'm parched, and I would absolutely murder for a mug of tea."

By the time they made it back to Billie Jo's house and found some baling twine to secure Greta's tree to her car, putting a blanket down on the hood first, they were both wet clear through and getting chilly.

"I'll boil some water for tea," Billie Jo said, reaching chilly fingers for the teapot. "But, this ain't goin' to be enough to heat us up. Go right up and take a shower. I'll loan you some things to wear. Otherwise you'll catch your death."

Greta's teeth were chattering so she didn't take the time to object and simply made her way up the stairs. In a few minutes Billie Jo heard the water running and saw steam begin to float down the stairs. Then she heard the door close and knew Greta was immersed in the scalding shower.

She put some scones she'd baked that morning on the table and found two candy canes for stirrers while the water heated on the stove. By the time the teapot whistled the drumming of the water in the shower upstairs had stopped. Greta appeared, wrapped in Billie Jo's terry cloth robe and toweling her hair. "I didn't know what to put on. My things are soaked."

"I'll find something for you. Hold on." Billie Jo put a mug of hot tea in her hands as she went upstairs to find some clothes that Greta could wear home. She rummaged around, pulling out her best pair of flannel-lined jeans, an old cable-knit sweater, and a pair of thick woolen socks.

"I'll put the clothes on the chair in here," she called down the stairs. "I'm going to jump into the shower before I freeze."

The hot water felt wonderful. The heat penetrated her skin and made the coldest parts feel tingly and new. It was like coming alive after having been buried in the snow. Billie Jo had found it difficult to adjust to the cold temperatures in Vermont but had come to enjoy the contrast. You could get really cold but just as easily warm up, and you appreciated the warmth so much more after being frozen near to death.

By the time Billie Jo made her way back into the bedroom wrapped in Jimmy's flannel robe the stack of clothes had disappeared. Greta had dressed and gone downstairs. Billie Jo struggled into another pair of jeans and a sweater. She raided Jimmy's drawer for some woolen socks because her own sock drawer was empty. Pulling a comb through her long, straight dark hair, she eased the tangles away. It would dry nicely by the fire downstairs. It was much too cold upstairs to hang around longer than necessary.

Greta was curled up on the sofa watching the fire in the fireplace crackling cheerily. Her hands were wrapped around her mug, eking out as much warmth as she could. She sucked on the end of the candy cane, which had melted in the hot tea until the stripes were all gone. Billie Jo settled herself gingerly beside her friend, taking care not to spill her own tea.

"I love winter," Greta said dreamily. "Don't you?"

"I guess. This is really my first. I mean, we have winter down in Tennessee, but it ain't this cold. There's not so much snow either. Leastwise not this long. It comes and goes. Mostly goes."

"Snow is nice. Especially for Christmas. It wouldn't really be Christmas without a proper snow."

Billie Jo considered the white expanse of lawn outside the living room windows. "It's hard for me to realize Christmas is coming." She was silent for a moment, sipping her tea. "How was it? Your first Christmas?"

"Without Nathan?" Greta leaned back and closed her eyes. "My first Christmas without Nathan was a nightmare, to be honest. But that had a lot to do with me. I shut people out, even my own family. I wouldn't let anyone help me. That first year I did go get the tree by myself. My friends and family thought I was crazy. They couldn't understand why I had to have one.

"But it was our thing, you know? We'd go get the tree and decorate it that night. Then we'd pop popcorn over the fire and watch *It's a Wonderful Life* and fall asleep in sleeping bags right next to the fire. It was really a special time." Her voice cracked. It was a minute before she could go on. "I wouldn't let anyone come over, and I didn't go out. I just sat there and brooded. So, you see, I know what you're going through. I wanted to spare you the pain of what I went through."

"Don't you think we each gotta go through it for ourselves?"

"No." Greta shook her head so that her wet blonde hair swung vigorously. "No, I don't. Because there are some things you're better off learning from the sad example of others. There are plenty of mistakes to make in the world. If you can't learn from those of others, well, then, I guess you're destined for a whole lot more pain than you need to experience."

"I suppose," Billie Jo agreed. "But it's hard to let other people in when you're grieving. There's some things that are that private. Outsiders just don't understand. Do you know a woman at the church told me that I ought to be thankful my kids are dead because now I don't have to worry about them getting into trouble later on or leaving the church? Some people just say things that make the pain worse."

"I know." Greta sighed. "You're right. I guess the trick is in knowing who you can trust to let in and then letting them help you."

"You can help her," Jewel suggested to Billie Jo. "Reaching out to others in pain always helps to bear our own. Give her the kind of Christmas she remembers."

"Don't do it," Nog warned. "You've got enough of your own business to take care of. You can't bring back the past. It's dead and gone, just like your kids."

Billie Jo studied Greta's profile thoughtfully. Tears sprang into her eyes. Maybe there was nothing she could do this Christmas to make things easier for herself or Jimmy, but there was something she could do for Greta. "Hey, what say I go home with you and help you put up that tree? Then we can do what you said, pop popcorn and watch that movie, what did you say it was?"

Greta turned incredulous eyes on Billie Jo. "You mean *It's a Wonderful Life?*"

"Yeah, that, and I'll bring my sleeping bag and we'll camp out on the floor. Just like you remember. You want to?"

"Jimmy won't mind?"

"Not for one night, no. He'll be fine. He's been so tuckered out lately he'll probably go to bed early."

"It would mean a lot to me," Greta admitted. "It's been a long time, three years. I know it's just a silly tradition, but it's special to me."

"Let me just give Jimmy a call at work and let him know where I'll be. Then I'll fix him a plate he can heat up when he gets home."

"Oh, don't do that," Greta interrupted with a glimmer of her old bossiness. "Tell him to come join us for dinner at my house. I've had a stew simmering all day in the crock pot, and it'll be far more than we can eat."

"OK." Billie Jo went to the phone to call her husband. As it rang on the other end she stared out the window and noticed a small Christmas miracle. It was snowing.

Almost ten hours had passed from the time the kidnappers radioed the first time. The only working Land Rover had departed the mission nearly eight hours before and should have been back already to pick up those who remained at the mission. The four weary native workers slumbered on mattresses on the kitchen floor. Akueke snored loudly. Toby was slumped in a chair at the table, her head in her arms. Don sat, tense and watchful, in a chair by the door.

He'd been watching outside for some time. A cloud of dust had caught his attention some time earlier. There was movement, but it did not alter position. Whoever was out there was content to remain on the perimeter. That eliminated the possibility that it was Ray returning with the Land Rover to pick them up.

Don had come to the conclusion that for whatever reason the Land Rover would be returning late, if it returned at all. Something had happened. Given the age and delicate condition of their vehicles, something mechanical had gone afoul, he thought. He just hoped that it had happened after the first party had arrived safely in Niamey. The possibility that they were broken down somewhere on the way to their destination didn't bear thinking about.

"Wha's goin' on?" Toby mumbled in her sleep. "I did not. It's in the drawer."

"Toby?"

"What?" She started, and her eyes, which had the blank stare of a sleepwalker, focused slowly. She rubbed her palms over her face. "What? What is it?" She got up from the chair and went to stand by him. "I fell asleep," she told him unnecessarily.

"I know. Look, what do you see out there?"

"Sand."

"Over there. See that spot? Can you make it out?"

She squinted. "My eyes aren't that great, but it looks like a few people walking around, maybe a temporary shelter of some kind. Who are they?"

"That's what I want to know."

"How long have they been there?"

He shrugged. "I don't know. A couple hours maybe. At first I thought it was Ray coming back for us, but they parked themselves there and haven't moved since. I think probably they're watching us."

"Do you think they know we're in here?"

"Hard to tell. Yes. I guess so. Otherwise they would come right in, wouldn't they?"

As if by prearrangement, the radio hissed to life. "Come in," a harsh voice said. It was hardly a greeting. More like a command.

Don hesitated before picking up the handset. Would it be better if they thought the place was deserted? But then, they seemed to know it wasn't. "Yes," he said, trying to keep his voice steady.

The accent of the person at the other end was thick and his words were difficult to decipher. "Why do you stay there? We had an agreement."

"I know. I'm sorry. We had a problem. We couldn't leave."

"You must leave now."

Don wanted to tell this man that he fervently wished he could leave, but it was impossible. "I know." It was the only thing to say. "We will leave as soon as we can."

"Now!" the voice barked. The radio crackled and went dead.

"Hello? Hello?" Don jiggled the connections, but the radio was dead.

"It's probably the battery," Toby said wearily. "What do we do now?"

"I don't know. What can we do? We can't fly with the ultralight gone and your plane not operational yet. I don't know any other way out of here, do you?"

"Not alive," Toby rejoined ruefully.

While they were talking, Akueke woke up and got unsteadily to her feet. "Getting water," she said as she went out the door. It crossed Don's mind to stop her, but being preoccupied with their problems the moment passed and the old woman stepped outside.

Immediately there was a rifle shot and dust kicked up at Akueke's feet. She screamed in terror and staggered backwards, nearly falling. Don leaped to his feet, reaching out the open door to grab her, and pulled her back to the safety of the room. She clutched at him, sobbing hysterically.

"What that?" she demanded, supplementing her broken English with streams of French.

"Don't go outside anymore," Don said forcefully. The close call had rattled him. He couldn't imagine what he would have done if Akueke had been shot. It was much too close a shave. Now he knew beyond a shadow of a doubt what fate awaited them. The only question was, how long could they hold out? There were only six of them, and they had no weapons of any kind.

It was impossible to guess how many terrorists waited outside or the strength of their arms. Obviously they had at least one high-powered rifle. Now it was simply a matter of playing cat-and-mouse. They would see how many they could pick off and then take their chances storming the place to take out the rest of them.

"What are we going to do?" Toby asked tensely. "We're no match for them."

"You got that right," Don muttered. "But God is. He's still on our side, remember? We've got to pray. God fought a lot of battles for the Israelites, and they were often outnumbered. There were even times when they didn't fight at all. God fought for them. We'll have to trust Him to fight for us."

"Fight for us?" Toby sounded doubtful. "Would He really do that?"

"Why not?"

"Well, this isn't like Old Testament times, you know. I mean, has God fought any battles lately?"

"Sister," Don said with feeling, "God's fighting a battle right now against Satan wherever he shows up. Whenever you take a stand against evil, God is right there by your side. He's by our side right now. I'm willing to bet that He knows how we can defeat our enemy out there. And I want to know how too. So, let's ask Him."

"OK," Toby said, somewhat skeptically.

"You do it."

"Me?"

"Yes, because you are having trouble believing God will help us. So, you ask Him."

Toby's jaw jutted at a stubborn angle. "It's not that I think He can't," she said defensively, "it's that I'm not sure He will."

"Ask Him. Akueke, join us."

The trembling old woman joined hands with them, and they bowed their heads. Toby cleared her throat. "Heavenly Father, I ask You to be with us here in this place. Also be with those who left for Niamey and with Davy and Shay wherever they are. Keep them safe.

"I ask for Your protection, God, on those of us here. There are evil men out there who want to kill us. We have no way to leave. But we know You are stronger than those men and that You can save us from a much mightier force than the one out there. Please give us wisdom. Show us what to do.

"No matter what happens to us, or to those we love, please help us to keep our faith and trust in You. Help us to accept Your will. Keep us strong for You. Thank You for hearing us. Amen."

A soft chorus of "amens" greeted the end of her prayer.

Lucien waited with the men and a gang of demons at the perimeter of the compound. They had arrived sometime in the night and set up here. Throughout the journey more men had joined up with them, until there were about thirty men preparing to take orders.

Lucien watched the mission with keen eyes, missing nothing. He fought back a growing impatience. Angels formed a thick barrier, but he was confident they would turn tail and run when the time came. The biggest problem he had at the moment was convincing the leader that there were no hidden forces behind the solid walls of the mission. At the most there could be only ten people in there. They were outnumbered at least three to one.

This leader, no matter how bloodthirsty, was in no hurry to put himself or his men in jeopardy. He was methodical to a fault. After the abortive attempt to make contact and ascertain numbers, he divided up his group and spread them out around the compound at a good enough distance to prevent them being picked off by sharpshooters, assuming there was such a thing at the mission, but close enough so that they could move in quickly and be within range to take down anything that moved.

"Wimp," Lucien goaded. The leader calmly smoked a cigarette and studied the stillness of the mission.

"Something is not right," he muttered to the man who stood next to him. Only this man, his friend for years, was trusted with confidences. "Why do they stay? Do they not care for these people we will kill?"

"Maybe they protect something," his friend suggested. "Maybe they protect their American money, hidden in there. Tell them to put the money outside and we will not hurt them. Once we have the money we can send the men in to kill them all."

"I do not know. The man said they could not leave. Why can they not leave?"

"It is money," the man beside him persisted stubbornly. "They cannot leave the money there. It is greed."

The leader nodded sagely. "It might be greed. But I have a bad feeling about this situation."

"Forget your feelings," Lucien snapped. "I'm all the feelings you need. This isn't about money. It's about revenge. Now get in there and stop thinking so much. I'll do all the thinking that needs to be done. Understand?"

"Move some men around to the back side. We will try to flush them out."

A contingent of ten men moved into place opposite the mission, but rather than give a signal, the leader continued to stare at the mission, lying like a smoky smudge against the sepia tones of the desert. Something bothered him. Something was not as it seemed. Indecision plagued him. Anxiety gnawed in his belly.

"Move, you worthless excuse for a man!" Lucien roared. He had handpicked this man for his leadership skills and his ruthlessness. It was impossible that he now hesitated on the brink of victory. Seconds could prove disastrous, and still he waited. "Move! Kill them all!"

He used every persuasive mental strategy to shake the man out of his lethargy. He knew he was getting through to him because the man grasped his abdomen and winced. His ulcer was acting up under the pressure. Still he did nothing.

Inside the mission, angels, coming and going from the court of heaven, returned with their orders. They formed protective hedges around the small group of people in the mission. Julian placed a strong hand on Don's shoulder and spoke earnestly. "You have a weapon in the mission more powerful than guns. You have the weapon of germs, which was devised by their master, but which you can use against them. If they thought there was an outbreak at the mission, causing you to remain behind, those men would not be able to stand against their own fear. They would be defeated by their own weapons and scatter to the winds."

As Don stood up, something occurred to him. With a sharp gasp he looked intensely at Toby. "Where are the biohazard suits?"

"What on earth does it matter?"

"Where are they?"

"There are some in the clinic, of course, but we put most of them in one of the back rooms along with that massive container of supplies Dorsey sent after the last outbreak, you know, just in case. But I don't see how this matters. There aren't any guns or anything in there, unless they packed flares or something." She looked at him keenly. "Is that what you're after? Flares to scare them or send up a distress signal?"

"No, nothing like that. We can't fight them that way. But if those guys out there thought we were having an outbreak, do you think they'd come anywhere near this place?"

Toby caught on quickly. "No way! That's brilliant!"

Don grinned. "I told you God had ways of fighting we knew nothing about. Come on, let's get the suits."

They found the biohazard suits packed in boxes. There were far more than they needed. Don pulled out two. They hurriedly struggled into them. He could see fear in Toby's eyes. "What's wrong?"

"This is creeping me out," she said quietly. "I can't help thinking about the last time I put one of these on."

Don stopped for a minute and reached for her hand. "We could fail, you know. We have to go out there, and they could shoot us anyway and ask questions later. But I don't have any other ideas, and I sincerely believe this one came from God because we asked for it."

He took a deep breath. "Before we go out there I have something to say to you. I realize now that I was wrong. I came back here swinging with both fists, ready to establish myself as the leader again. I had a chip on my shoulder; I can see that now.

"I'm sorry I didn't listen to you and Davy. I'm sorry I didn't hear you out. I didn't value your input and, I'm ashamed to say this, but I was afraid of losing control of the mission. I was afraid it would grow beyond my ability to control it, and I didn't want to lose any of my control.

"I was wrong, and I'm sorry. I hope you'll forgive me."

Toby squeezed his hand. Behind the mask he could see tears in her eyes. "Yes, I forgive you. And I'm sorry about my attitude. I could have been a lot more understanding and loving."

"Me too." He released her hand, and they finished suiting up in silence.

"Do you think they'll shoot us?" she asked as they headed out the door of the small room to return to the kitchen.

"I don't know."

"Can I have a minute here before we go out?"

He turned and looked at her. Tension made harsh lines on her face. Fear made her eyes bright. He nodded, hoping that his feelings weren't so transparent. "Sure, take a minute. I'll wait in the kitchen."

As he made his way out he wondered if he should take a few minutes too. After all, these could be his last minutes on earth. There were so many things he wanted to say and do. Of them all, one floated to the surface of his thoughts. He took a detour to the room he shared with Shay. Taking a sheet of her scented stationery, the kind she reserved for writing long, chatty letters home to Deniece, he sat down awkwardly and pulled off one glove so he could write.

He had to apologize to Shay and tell her and the kids how much he loved them, just in case. It was imperative that he make some attempt at amends. He wrote for a few minutes and signed the letter with a flourish. Placing it in an envelope, he propped it up on the dilapidated piece of furniture that served as her dresser. If she made it back and he didn't, he was sure she would find it.

Toby was already in the kitchen when he arrived. "I figured you were taking your own minute," she said.

"I was. Are we ready?"

"Yeah, only, how are they going to know it's an outbreak? There isn't anything to show them except us in these suits."

"I thought of that. We're going to need a volunteer."

"Me. I do it." Akueke could be stubborn and this moment, Don noted, was no exception. The old woman set her jaw and dared him to challenge her. He knew he had to make some noises of protest but didn't expect her to back down.

"Akueke, why not let someone younger—"

"You call me old?" she spat. "You are only old as you feel. Besides, I have a full life. These ones are young. I should be the one. I do it."

Don shrugged in exasperation. "OK, you do it."

"What I do?" she asked, inflated a little by winning her case so easily.

"You have to pretend to be dead."

"I can do," she said eagerly.

"We'll carry you away from the compound and put you down on the ground. Then we'll start digging a grave if they stick around long enough to watch more than that. I doubt we'll finish it before they are gone."

Akueke lay down on the ground, face up, and raised her arms to Toby. "Let us go."

Toby grasped Akueke's arms, and Don took her ankles. He tried to be gentle as they lifted her and, staggering, made their way outside. When he stepped out into the relentless sunshine he stiffened involuntarily, waiting for the bullet that would find him and end his life. Nothing happened. "Keep going," he hissed at Toby who was moving slowly, and trying to look around. "Ignore them. Pretend they aren't there."

They walked a hundred yards from the mission. "You go to the clinic for some shovels," Don instructed Toby. "I'll stay here with Akueke."

It seemed ages before she returned, dragging the shovels on the ground behind her. "It's so hot in this suit, I'm going to roast if they don't shoot me," she gasped.

"Don't talk. Dig."

The ground was hard from the lack of rain. The shovel hit with force and bounced back. "This is going to take forever."

"You got something more important to do?" Don felt sweat beading up on his forehead and winced as it dripped into his eyes. He tried to see what the kidnappers were doing without seeming obvious. Then he caught some movement on the periphery of his vision and turned his head to see what it was.

Unbelievably, ten men were approaching, guns held at the ready. It was their faces that really arrested his attention. They looked terrified, as if they had seen a glimpse of hell. *Arrêt! Arrêt!* They waved their guns but did not come closer.

"Death!" Don yelled, pointing at Akueke's motionless body. "Death *ici!*" He hoped he'd remembered the right French word for "here" and that they would understand.

They seemed to catch on because they broke and ran, bumping into each other, shoving for position. One was even knocked to the ground and trampled in their haste to get away. Don straightened, leaning on his shovel, and watched them, amazed.

When they reached the others, panic ensued. Fights broke out and gun shots rang out. "Get down; get down! They'll shoot us by accident."

He threw himself across Akueke and lifted his head only high enough to watch what was happening. The dust kicked up in the chaos made it difficult to see if their ruse had worked as well as they hoped. Only time could tell now.

"It's a trick! There is no outbreak, no disease," Lucien screamed, furious at the weakness the men displayed. "Are you children to be tricked like this? Kill them! Shoot them all! They brought disease with them, and now they hope to trick you with it."

"It is disease, disease," a man shrieked, his voice high and keening as if he could already see his own death.

"No," their leader cautioned. "Do not be so hasty. They could be bluffing."

"It is no bluff," one man raged. "I saw with my own eyes. An old woman was taken. We must go quickly before we are next." He ripped part of his shirt off and used it to cover his mouth, afraid the very air could infect him. "I have seen this before. I will not die this way."

"I am going," another yelled. "Who is with me?"

It seemed they all were. The leader raised his gun and pointed it at the nearest man. "No one leaves."

But they were like spooked cattle. Their eyes rolled back in their heads. Their bodies quivered. Breaking, they scrambled away from the madman who would expose them to such a gruesome death. Without flinching the leader pulled the trigger, and the man he was aiming at dropped. The others did not stop but continued to sprint away, preferring death by a bullet in the back to death by a dreadful disease.

In frustrated rage the leader shot several more of his men before they could escape. "What will we do?" his friend asked.

"What will we do? What will we do? Nothing!" Angrily the leader strode back and forth, looking from the fleeing men to the distant, suited figures still digging beside a body. "I will not go anywhere near that place. Will you?"

"What if it is an outbreak?"

"Precisely. What if it is? We cannot tell unless we approach, but to approach could mean death. And those we could send are now disappeared." He waved his gun in the direction of the men who had deserted them. "You will not go, and I will not go. Our only choice is to go back and kill the other two. We will hope that these die as well and that they do not send more after. This place will be a monument to their failure, and in time maybe I can forget ours."

"You cannot let them beat you like this," Lucien urged. "Go and see. That is no dead body. This is a trick, only you are too stupid to see it. I chose you," he raged, "because you were the most ruthless man I could find, and you have failed me."

The leader grasped his abdomen, his face twisting in agony. "What is wrong?"

"It is nothing."

His friend seemed puzzled. "Are you hurt?"

"I said," panted the leader, pointing his gun at his friend's startled face and deliberately pulling the trigger, "it is nothing."

Lucien staggered away from the scene of his defeat dazed and drained. He had done everything in his power to destroy the mission, and he had failed. The missionaries would return, and everything would go on as before. Nothing had gone as he had planned. Then he stopped, a sudden thought popping into his head.

There was still the chance that those who remained behind could be bribed with the lives of those they had captured. Surely the destruction of those two would force the mission to close. The doctor and the nurse could not continue if their spouses were dead. Yes, Lucien mused, it was vital that Davy O'Connell and Shay Germaine die as soon as possible.

"Come on, you worthless excuse for a man," Lucien growled. "We have work to do."

When the dust finally settled, Don scanned the horizon for any sign of the men who had been waiting. He could see a few bodies on the ground, but there was no one standing. He stopped his half-hearted efforts at digging. "Toby, I think they're gone."

She straightened up and rested on her shovel handle. "They are? Praise God!"

"Let's take a walk over to be sure."

"Oh, absolutely." There was sarcasm in her voice. "Let's just take a little hike over and see if there's anyone left who wants to shoot us. Are you nuts?"

"No, but as much as I hate to say this, even if the rest of the bad guys are gone, the ones who are down could need our help."

"We're going to help them?"

"Well, we're not going to leave fellow human beings to suffer and die of gunshot wounds," he said stoically. "I don't care if they were going to kill us. Love your neighbor as yourself, remember?"

"Let me get my bag." She sounded resigned, but Don knew that no matter what she said, she would never leave anyone to suffer. Not even the men who would have killed them all in cold blood.

They examined all the men they found who had been shot but could find no one alive. The only other evidence that anyone had been around was the torn-up earth. Even now those marks were being erased by a wind that had sprung up.

"Come on, let's go back inside. We've got some prayers of thanks to offer." As they trudged back to the mission compound Don felt as though, in spite of the biohazard suit, he could almost have flown back. "Praise God!" he yelled suddenly with a wild laugh. "Praise God!"

Toby giggled and joined him. "Praise God!"

CHAPTER 14

Shay woke and felt stiff all over. She rolled onto her hands and knees and gingerly pushed herself into a sitting position. The sun was barely creeping over the horizon. Davy was curled into a little ball. She shook him gently.

"Davy? Davy, wake up."

He sat up quickly, eyes red, chin grizzly with two days' growth of beard. "Did you hear something?"

"No, but it's time to get moving. The sun is coming up."

He nodded and stood up shakily. "I could do with some grub."

"Me too." Shay had been trying to ignore the stabbing pain in her abdomen for the last few hours. "Not much use thinking about it though. We should go, shouldn't we?"

Davy surveyed the landscape, made note of the position of the sun, and set out at a fast clip. He hadn't gone fifteen yards when he dropped to his knees. "Look at this."

Shay had never heard him sound like that before. She dropped quickly, thinking that he had seen someone coming after them. "What?" she hissed, her heart hammering in her chest.

Davy pointed to tracks in the dirt of a well-worn trail. "We slept right next to the trail last night. These are fresh. These guys practically walked over us sometime during the night."

As the full implication of what he was saying broke on Shay's weary mind she felt cold all over. "You mean if we'd camped a little closer to the path they might have found us?"

"They might have found us anyway. See how close we were?" Davy looked grim. "There were angels watching us last night, that's for sure."

"Yeah," Shay breathed. "There must have been."

"Come on. We don't have any time to waste."

Shay knew he was worried about the direction the tracks were coming from. If these men were the ones who had kidnapped them, it could only mean one thing. They were returning from the mission. "Wait," she called to Davy as he plunged into the grass, off the trail. "Why don't we follow the trail? It goes back to the mission."

"Because," Davy called back over his shoulder, "we don't want to run the risk of meeting any who might be straggling. We'll head in that direction though."

"Oh, OK," Shay replied without certainty. Her thoughts turned to the mission. "Please, God," she murmured under her breath as she set out after Davy's retreating form, "please let them be safe. Please protect them as You've protected us."

It was hours before Davy stopped so they could have a breather. Shay mopped the back of her neck with a scrap of cloth she had ripped off her shirt. "How much farther do you think it is?"

Davy avoided her eyes and she knew before he said it that they were lost again. "I honestly don't know where we are," he confessed.

"But—but, you seemed so confident. Why have we been tramping around here if you don't know where we're going?"

Davy threw up his hands in exasperation. "I don't know what else to do, do you? I can navigate by the stars, but unfortunately they only come out at night when we can't travel. I'm doing the best I can."

"I know. I'm sorry. I'm just so tired. I don't know how much farther I can go." Shay sat down and slumped over, burying her head in her arms. Maybe they would never get out of this. Maybe the best they could expect was eluding the kidnappers. Even if that was the only result of escaping, she thought she could be happy. But her heart ached to see Don and the children again. And then, there was something she had not told him, something that would be lost if she died here in the middle of nowhere.

"We have to get back," she said softly, but with conviction. "We need to pray about it."

"I've been praying," Davy argued. "But you're right. Let's pray again."

Shay bowed her head. "Dear God, please help us. Please help us to get back to the mission, and please keep everyone there safe."

Her head was swimming, and she found she couldn't concentrate. She looked up for a moment to get her bearings, and what she saw made her sure that the lack of sleep and thirst were causing a hallucination. A familiar-looking African man stood looking down at her, a bag hanging at his side. She hadn't heard him approach, and he stood quietly, making no sound at all, but a grin was spread all over his face. He bent down and took her hand, shaking it vigorously. Surely this could not be a hallucination.

"What—?" Davy sputtered, apparently sharing her hallucination. "Where did he come from?"

The man answered in fluent French, but in the dialect Shay found hard to decipher. Years before, she hadn't understood a word he said. Now, having trained her ear, she pulled from his heavy patois what could turn into a long, detailed greeting and the story of how he came to be in the vicinity and his surprise at finding them.

"Davy," Shay said, not taking her eyes from the man's face. She nodded and smiled at the man, though she realized she must look a fright, not wanting to interrupt him. "This man is Madina's father, Bossou."

"Your Madina?" Davy was incredulous. "How can that be?"

"It just is," Shay said, talking under her breath and making the appropriate noises so Bossou would think she was engrossed in his story. "He knows where the mission is."

"So, where is it already?"

"Be patient." But patience was not going to help after all. As Shay tried to concentrate on what Bossou was saying she began to see little gray spots in front of her eyes and heard a familiar buzzing in her ears. With horror she realized that she was about to faint for the second time in her life.

When she woke up, her head was pounding and she found herself cradled in Davy's arms. His face was white, his lips pinched in concentration. He was holding a canister of water near her mouth, and his voice was saying, "Wake up, wake up." It sounded far away. He slapped her face lightly.

She blocked his hand weakly. "Stop that." After a few minutes she was able to sit up as he supported her, and she drank from the canister Davy had received from Bossou. Then she looked around in fear, hoping Bossou hadn't taken off. He was standing behind Davy, regarding her solemnly.

"You are with child," he said slowly in French.

Shay managed to smile. "How do you know that?"

His face took on an aloof, superior look that made her want to laugh despite the dire circumstances. "I have much experience, many wives. But they know better than to carry on in this manner."

Shay was sure they did, but she didn't say anything. Bossou was notorious for keeping many wives and treating them like cattle. "Bossou, we need to get to the clinic right away. Can you help us?"

"Certainly, certainly," he replied with a wave of dismissal. "There is much time, as I was saying before."

"No," Shay interrupted. "There is not much time. People need us, you see. Madina needs me. Do you remember Madina? She's a darling little girl now, not a baby. It's very important that I get back to see her at the clinic right away. If you could help us get there as soon as possible we would appreciate it so much." She had a sudden inspiration. "We would appreciate it with a *cadeau.*"

"What are you saying to him?" Davy demanded. "I feel like the odd man out here."

"I told him we'd give him a gift if he brought us to the clinic," Shay managed to explain in an aside to Davy.

Bossou considered her thoughtfully. "That is not necessary, of course. But, if it would please you I would be happy to accept a small *cadeau.*"

"Then you'll bring us?"

"Certainly, certainly." He stood up gracefully, in a way that reminded Shay sharply of Nwibe, her first husband who had died at the mission in the Marburg virus outbreak. She pushed the thought from her head, determined not to start thinking about painful things. She had enough to think about at the moment.

"*It's hard, isn't it,*" Jezeel observed laconically. "*Death is all around you. Your first husband died here. You lost his child. Your children and your second husband could be dead already. Soon you could be dead and another unborn baby with you. Why don't you just give up? No matter what you do or where you go, death follows and waits for you. You can't escape it.*"

"*Death is but a brief sleep,*" Gaius said. "*So brief will it be for you that you will not even feel it passing. It is the hope of the future, which the Master has given you, that should be the object of your thoughts. Do not dwell on the sorrow of death, for death passes quickly. The future, which will be everlasting, is infinitely more important.*"

"The future is important," Shay said suddenly.

"What?" Davy was hard on her heels as they followed Bossou in what he claimed was a "short path" to the clinic.

"Did I say that out loud?" Shay felt a flash of embarrassment. "I didn't mean to. I was just wondering if we'd get out of this alive and what we'll find at the clinic. I guess I was feeling discouraged. I've seen too much death. I don't want to see more."

"So that's why the future is important?" Clearly Davy was puzzled at this logic.

"No, the future, you know, heaven and eternal life. That is what's important. I was just reminding myself. Only I didn't mean to do it out loud."

"I'm glad you did. Right about now I could use some encouragement. I've been so busy trying to keep us alive and get us back that I've pushed Toby out of my mind. I haven't wanted to face what will happen if she's, you know, if they've been killed. I still don't want to think about it, but I'll try to remember that the here and now isn't all there is. We've got a hope for the future. Whatever happens, whatever we find when we get there, we have to remember that."

"You want to know what's important? You want to know how long you'll gush about 'heaven' and 'eternal life'?" Jezeel sneered. "I'll show you." With a sudden lunge she pushed Shay.

Shay stumbled on a root and went down hard on one knee. She felt a "pop" and pain shot up the length of her leg. She screamed and clutched the knee, breathing deeply, hoping it would subside.

"What is it? What's wrong? Did you twist it?" Davy knelt down beside her and tried to examine her knee through the tear in her jeans. "You're not bleeding or anything, just a little scraped up. Did you hit a rock or something?"

"I don't know," Shay moaned, rocking with pain. "I felt it pop when I went down."

"Aw, man," Davy said miserably. "I think you might have snapped a ligament or something. I tore the anterior cruciate ligament in my knee playing high school football, so I know what that feels like. Here, we've got to cut your jeans some more because if that's what it is, that baby's gonna swell up."

Bossou, who had halted when Shay fell, watched the proceedings with skepticism. "What are you doing?" he asked Shay.

She tried to explain as best she could through gritted teeth and suppressed whimpering as Davy slit the leg of her jeans.

"But now you cannot walk," Bossou protested. "How will you come with us to the clinic?"

"What's that guy saying?" Davy muttered.

Suddenly, overwhelmed with fatigue, hunger, pain and worry, Shay burst into tears. As she sobbed she was aware of the two men watching her. A little voice in her head soothed her with reassuring words. *"There, there, you're just tired. Have a good cry. You'll feel better after."* Perhaps it was the long-ago voice of her mother, remembered from childhood? Or maybe it was her father.

Shay sucked in great gulps of air in an attempt to regain control of herself. "I'm sorry," she blubbered. "I just can't help it."

Davy looked helplessly from Shay to Bossou, probably thinking that the man had caused her collapse. When neither was forthcoming with information he pulled Shay into his arms and patted her back. "It's OK, it'll be OK. We're not going to leave you here. Did he say we'd leave you?"

"No," Shay managed to sob. "But you should. Who knows how far it is to the clinic from here, and I can't walk."

"I'll carry you."

"I'm t-too h-heavy."

"Shay," Davy said, somewhat testily. "I may not look like superman, but I'm perfectly capable of helping you. And if you think for one minute I'm just going to leave you here you are sadly mistaken."

Shay felt small and weak and vulnerable and contrite. "I just meant that . . ."

"Forget it." Davy got to his feet and put out his hands. "See if you can stand up."

Using her good leg she levered into a standing position. The leg of her jeans flapped alongside the injured knee, which, true to Davy's prediction, was swelling up alarmingly.

"Can you put any weight on it at all?"

Shay tested it, putting her foot down on the path and immediately drawing it back with a muffled yelp. "No. Nothing."

"Put your arm around my shoulder. See if you can walk if you lean on me. If not I'll just carry you."

Shay put her arm around Davy's neck and limped along, putting as little pressure on the injured leg as possible. Even so, every step was agony. She pursed her lips together with determination and ignored it as much as possible. She would not be carried unless there was no other alternative. She wouldn't be a burden.

In this slow, painstaking manner they made their way down the path. Bossou, for his part, made no complaint. Only with long, silent looks did he express his disapproval. It would be far better, he told Shay in stern French, if she stayed behind. Someone could always come back for her, should they care to. Davy interpreted this comment despite the language barrier. He muttered, "You're not staying here," as she limped along beside him. "No way."

Darkness was beginning to creep up, twilight making shadows where there had been none. Every slight movement in the periphery of her vision made Shay uneasy. This journey was taking forever. Just when she thought she might collapse on the path Bossou turned to them with a broad grin. "The clinic," he announced.

Limping into the clearing Shay was dismayed to see that Bossou had not brought them to the mission clinic, but the outpost clinic, the very place they had so recently escaped from. Fear clutched her heart, and she gripped Davy so hard he cried out. "We've got to get out of here," she whispered hoarsely.

"Wait. Something is different. Sit here. I want to look around."

Bossou was examining the surroundings with interest and a little caution. He spoke rapidly in French, but Shay's brain was so overloaded the words were a tangle and she could only understand a phrase now and then. She sat tensely, torn between agony over the pain in her knee and fear that they would be discovered and recaptured. "Dear God," she prayed out loud keeping her eyes wide open for any sign of danger, "please keep us safe. You helped us escape from here once; don't let us be caught again now that we are so close to getting away. Please be with everyone at the mission and keep them safe as well. Send Your angels to watch over us and fight for us because we are helpless, Lord, without You."

Davy hurried over, clearly excited. "I don't know what happened here, but we've got to get out. I think we're safe enough for now, but I don't want to hang around. Remember the guy who was guarding us? The one who fell asleep? Well, someone came back here and shot him while he was sleeping. They tore up the clinic and did some damage to the ultralight, but I took a quick look at the engine and I think I can get it working well enough to get us out of here."

"You mean we can fly out of here? Now?"

"Not this second, but very soon, yes. We've got to hurry though. It will be dark soon, and we can't fly in the dark."

Shay felt like weeping with joy and then realized that she was.

"Come on. I want to get you over near the ultralight where I can keep an eye on you. What's he doing anyway?" Davy jerked his thumb over his shoulder toward Bossou, who had stationed himself, like a sentinel, near the door of the clinic.

"I don't know. Take me to him, please."

Bossou's dark face was inscrutable. He appeared as though he could remain where he was indefinitely if need be.

"Bossou? Thank you so much for helping us." Shay could not think of words strong enough to really express her appreciation. And then she realized, the promised gift, that's what he was waiting for. But what did they have that would interest him? It came to her suddenly. Her father's suit jacket was still under the seat of the ultralight unless the kidnappers had taken it. If it was still there it would be the perfect *cadeau* for Bossou. It would lend him distinction, and she knew it would please him.

"Davy, is my jacket still rolled up under my seat?" Davy rummaged inside the ultralight and came up with the jacket, a little crumpled but safe and sound. Shay shook it and snapped out the wrinkles. She felt a lump in her throat as she offered the jacket to Bossou.

"This belonged to my father," she said quietly. "It was his favorite. He died some time ago, and I kept this. I always thought my son might like to have it some day. But I want you to have it. Without you we would surely have died. I can never thank you enough for all you've done for us."

Bossou took the jacket solemnly and immediately put it on, shrugging into it, adjusting the drape and preening as he smoothed his hand over the cloth and craned his neck to admire how it hung on him. His wide smile told her everything she wanted to know. He put out his hand and shook hers firmly.

"Thank you, Madame, for the splendid *cadeau*. I am happy to have been of assistance to you. I hope we will meet again under more pleasant circumstances."

As he walked away, back erect, head high, Shay felt a flutter of amusement. She had yet to meet Bossou under pleasant circumstances, but it was a nice hope to cling to for the future. Easing herself to a sitting position she watched dully while Davy tinkered with the engine of the ultralight, muttering to himself about the cretins who had messed with it.

"If they had known what they were doing, we would have been a lot worse off," he finally said, wiping his hands on his jeans and leaving dark black smudges. "As it was they did enough damage. All of it fixable, thank God."

He went back to work, and Shay, despite the pain in her knee and the knife of hunger in her belly, fell asleep. It felt like hours, in the way that deep slumber often does, but was in reality perhaps fifteen minutes. She woke up to Davy's insistent shaking. "It's working, Shay. Let's blow this joint."

He helped her to her feet and into the ultralight, where she clung with anxiety. She never liked flying in this thing under the best of circumstances. In spite of her diligence, thoughts of what might happen if Davy overlooked something nagged her. She tried to force them out. *I will think positive thoughts,* she told herself over the loud buzz of the engine. "I'm putting myself in Your hands, God," she yelled as the little craft picked up speed and bounced jauntily down the makeshift runway.

As soon as they gained some altitude and cleared the jumble of trees and undergrowth that choked out the light of day, the sky lightened. But even Shay knew that it was really too dark for them to be flying. It was dangerous. Still, compared to the danger that awaited them back at the clinic it was the safest route open to them. "Are we going to make it?" she yelled to Davy.

"I don't know," he yelled back. "Keep praying!"

Shay prayed, flinging her words to the wind, feeling them catch and imagining they were swept straight up to God.

Gaius felt gladness in his heart that his charge had responded in a godly way to the challenges set before her. Her faith was stronger now than it had ever been, and he was sure that was why the enemy tried so hard to discourage her. But, praise God, she was not to be discouraged, and all their efforts to destroy her had only met faith in God, which had produced a steadfast spirit and strong faith. No matter what the enemy threw at her, the strength of God was all she needed to weather this or any other storm.

Cindi fought with the lid of her trunk as it crashed down on her arm. With a yelp she dropped the grocery bag she'd been trying to place in the trunk. The trunk light was broken, and in the darkness she had to struggle to place all the grocery bags. She was afraid she'd squashed something important, like the eggs or peaches, but there was no way to see inside the space.

Straightening up she tried to work the kinks out of her back by stretching. She was exhausted. After a long day she had taken Essie grocery shopping. She'd hoped to go alone and leave Essie with Marc, but he had called to say he'd be working late.

"That's what he says," Ogel chortled. "But you know he's not working. He's supposed to be cutting back, remember? He's probably chipped in for a pizza with the boys, and they're sitting around the office gassing. Or maybe he's doing something even worse than that." He'd let her consider the implications of that suggestion.

Cindi felt the creeping fears wriggle into her mind and she clamped down furiously. *No. If Marc says he's working, he's working. I know that. And he wouldn't be working if it wasn't absolutely necessary. He's cutting back. It's only Satan trying to scare me and ruin my marriage. But I won't be scared. Perfect love casts out fear. God, help me to love Marc the way You want me to.*

Her prayer brought a host of angels to surround her as she finished packing the groceries into the trunk and replaced her cart. They sang simple songs, harmonizing perfectly, reaching notes Cindi could not even have heard. Their joy filled her heart and she found herself humming a hymn as she walked quickly back to the car. If she had been a little less self-absorbed she would have noticed the man who stepped out from the shadows and she would have hurried to the safety of her car.

"Cindi!"

She looked up, startled. Her heart hammered in her chest. It was Jared. He was tense with suppressed emotion, but when she looked closer she could see that his expression, beneath the tension, was soft, kind even. "I just, I want . . . what I want to say is that you were right. OK? You were right."

Jared stepped closer to where she was poised, her hand on the handle of the car door. His shoulders slumped as if he'd been carrying a great burden. "I was so angry with you at first. I thought up a million ways to make you see things my way. Then, when I couldn't think of anything else that might work, it dawned on me that it was my way I was fighting for. And deep down inside, where I wasn't willing to look, I knew it was the wrong way. I just wanted it so much I couldn't admit that.

"I don't have many friends; I guess you know that. Krissy was really the only friend I had. When she died, it left this huge vacuum in my heart. When you and I started to become friends it was like you filled her place. But I realize now that you can't fill her place."

Cindi's eyes welled with tears. "No, I can't Jared. But there is Someone who can."

He nodded briefly, struggling to maintain his composure. "I know. God showed me that what I'm feeling is normal. I should feel lonely. I loved Krissy so much, and I miss her every day. But I don't have to stay lonely. I need to make some friends, 'appropriate friends,' as you would say. That's one of the reasons I'm here. In order to have a friend you must first be a friend, right? Didn't someone famous say that?

"Anyway, I'm through moping around wallowing in my own misery. One of the best ways I know to change my focus is to help others. So that's what I'm doing. I signed up for volunteer work at the community shelter and I've joined a Bible study that Pastor Ryan is having, and it's been really great. I'm counting on God to show me who to help and how to be a good friend. And I'm sorry I wasn't a good friend to you. I hope you can forgive me."

He was silent for a moment. "That's all I wanted to say." He started to turn away, but Cindi put her hand on his arm, stopping him.

"Jared, wait." Cindi swallowed hard. Her heart thumped wildly in her chest. "Look, I appreciate your apology, and I accept it. I'm so sorry that we can't be friends. I am, because you are going to be an amazing friend to so many people. I want you to know that I'll be praying for you, and I'm looking forward to renewing our acquaintance gradually even though we'll never be able to share much as friends. Let's start over, what do you say?"

Jared slowly held out his hand with a slow grin. "Hi, my name is Jared Flynn."

Cindi felt relief wash over her, and the sweetness of reconciliation flood her soul. "Cindi Trahan. It's nice to meet you, Jared."

Shania and other angels gathered around Cindi and Jared as they stood talking in the parking lot. Shania's thoughts were bittersweet as she watched the two people interacting. They could have shared so much if they hadn't taken the Master's blessing of friendship and allowed the enemy to twist it into something it was never meant to be. Cindi was learning the hard way that although the Master blessed a righteous response to evil, He could even bless a wrong response following repentance. But, oh, how much pain they could have spared themselves if they had followed the Master's will in the first place.

Shania reached out and took the hand of the angel standing beside her, squeezing it as they both placed their free hands on the shoulders of Cindi and Jared. "Bless this relationship, Lord," Shania prayed. *"Keep it honorable to Yourself and holy in every respect. Guard these two that they will see the attacks of the enemy for what they are and resist him. Keep them strong and wise."*

As Cindi and Jared shook hands in a businesslike fashion, Shania watched them keenly. Jared was perhaps a bit nervous but handled himself well. Cindi was a little harder to peg. Shania knew that this was a tough time for her. She was still having trouble in her relationship with Marc. She knew that Cindi was aware of the danger of going along with this relationship with Jared. She was going to have to guard her thoughts or she would find herself speculating on what a change in relationships could offer her after all. Shania prayed that Cindi would stay strong.

"Not if I can help it," Ogel muttered, sensing the angel's thoughts. "You can bet I won't stop trying on this one either. I'm not going anywhere. Are you?" he taunted.

Shania ignored him, watching Cindi back her car out and drive away. She was strong, that much was certain, but she

*needed to be sure she was getting her strength from the Master
or it would never hold out. Baby steps, she reminded herself, she
just had to take baby steps.*

"Who was that man, Mommy?" Esther asked when she finally
got into the car.

"It's a friend of mine, Essie. A nice man named Jared. He's a
police officer."

"Who were the other people?"

Cindi furrowed her brow. "Other people? What do you mean?"

"The tall people dressed in white," Esther explained. "You know,
they were like the friends that old lady with the really big dog
had."

Cindi glanced at her daughter in the rearview mirror, but
Esther's face was serious. Her voice suggested that her mother
was being dense and she was beginning to lose her patience.
"Esther, I have no idea what you're talking about. There was no
one with Jared."

Esther sighed in frustration. "Mommy," she said, using her
grown-up 'I'm-going-to-explain-this-to-you-if-it-kills-me' voice,
"there were four men talking to you and three of them were very
tall, taller than Daddy, and they wore white clothes. That lady
with the big dog had friends just like them."

Then Esther got excited. "Are they a singing group?" She'd recently gotten interested in a teenybopper band and become interested in the music scene as a result.

"No," Cindi murmured distractedly. "No, they weren't a singing
group." *Could it be?* she asked herself. *Has Esther seen angels?*
The thought sent a shiver down her spine. And then a thought
popped into her head. Had they been there to protect her? Or
Jared? As she drove slowly back home she speculated on the possibility.

Are You trying to tell me something, Lord? she asked in her
thoughts. *What are You trying to say?* Cindi had done a lot of
thinking since she'd seen Jared last. One afternoon, right after
Marc had called to say he'd be home late again, she'd raged
around the house screaming. She hated him, oh, how she hated
him.

After she calmed down she was ashamed of herself. It wasn't Marc's fault that he had to work late. They had agreed that he wouldn't take any more overtime hours than he had to. She'd gotten some temporary work with Meals on Wheels and was bringing in enough for the groceries and best of all, Esther could accompany her and they were having a great time doing it. Cindi knew that deep down it wasn't even the fact that Marc was working late that she felt so miserable about.

What really upset her was that although he was home more, he didn't give her the attention she so desperately craved. The attention that, until recently, had been provided by Jared. And the worst of it was that she found herself wishing for Jared, and she hated herself for that. And she hated Marc for not being what she needed, or, probably more accurately, what she wanted.

How can he know what I need when I never tell him? she thought miserably. How could she say, "Marc, bring me some flowers or take me out to dinner or buy me a present"? How could she say, "Spend time with me, just me. Listen to what I have to say as if you cared"? She couldn't really put all the blame on Marc. She had to take responsibility for her own part.

Wearily she drove on into the night, contemplating Marc and Jared and the angels Essie had seen. When she thought about it, it wasn't so very hard to see what God was telling her. He was warning her to watch her step, and the first step was to guard her thoughts. *God, sanctify my thoughts. Give me honoring thoughts about my husband.*

"Your husband is a good provider and a hard worker," Shania said promptly.

"He works hard, Lord," Cindi said to herself. "And he takes good care of us in his own way. Thank You for giving me such a faithful partner."

As she drove on through the night she began to feel better. The sullen anger that had smoldered since Marc's call to tell her he'd be late was waning. In its place, her heart overflowed with gratitude that theirs was, essentially, a good solid marriage and that Marc was a faithful provider and in that way showed her his love, even if he didn't romance her off her feet.

When she pulled into the driveway she was surprised and pleased to find Marc home. The lights of their house blazed in welcome, and he came out immediately to help her carry in the groceries. "Hi, honey," he said, lightly kissing her.

"Hi. You're home earlier than you expected."

"Yeah, they cancelled the meeting. Some of the guys went out to eat, but I came home. I see those guys all day. I wanted to see my pretty girls." Saying this, he swung Esther up and around, making her squeal with delight.

Cindi smiled and put her arm around his waist as they made their way inside. "I'm glad you're home."

"Me too. It's good to be home more. I was getting so strung out at work. How was your job today?'

"Great. We delivered twenty meals, and Esther distinguished herself by singing a song to Mrs. Hobbes, who is a very lonely widow with fifteen cats."

"Fifteen!" Marc whistled.

"Mrs. Hobbes said that one of the cats howls when you sing," Esther explained, "and I wanted to hear it so I sang 'What a Friend We Have in Jesus,' and the cat sang too. It was very funny, Daddy. And what does *extinguished* mean?"

"I think you mean *distinguished*," Marc said, laughing, "and it means someone who is very important."

"Oh." This seemed to please her.

"What's for supper?" Marc asked.

"Whatever you make," Cindi joked.

"OK, canned beans it is," he quipped smartly.

"Ugh." Esther made a face, and Cindi laughed.

"Actually, I've got some soup cooking in the slow cooker, and we made bread today."

"What a lucky man I am!"

"Blessed, I think you mean."

"Yes, very, very blessed."

Toby heard them first. Ray had finally returned with the Land Rover, and though he took the others back to Niamey with him until the crisis was over, neither Toby nor Don had been able to tear themselves away. Now that the kidnappers were gone, they reasoned, it would be safe enough for them to stay. The first word about Shay and Don would surely be received at the mission, and at the mission they would stay. And now it seemed to have come at long last.

"Get the flashlights," she yelled, feeling a sense of déjà vu.

Don balked. "Flashlights? Why?"

"They're coming in."

"It's your imagination." They were both tired. The tension of the endless hours waiting had worn them both out. Toby felt the weariness throughout her body and for a moment questioned her own hearing. But, no, she heard the unmistakable buzzing of the ultralight.

"I'm telling you, they're coming," she insisted stubbornly, going for the flashlights herself. "Are you going to help me or not?"

Don caught the flashlight she tossed him and began to follow her reluctantly. At the threshold of the door he stopped, cocking his head. "I don't believe it."

"Believe it." Toby sprinted for the runway.

"They can't land in this light," Don was bellowing behind her.

"Yes, they can. We'll help them."

"They'll never make it."

Toby turned on him angrily. "Will you stop being negative! They are going to land. And they're going to make it. Trust God, you always say. Well, I'm telling you. Trust God! They haven't come this far to fail now. Not if I can help it!"

She saw him swallow a retort as he paused to consider what she'd said and then resolution swept over his face. Without a word he stationed himself where she told him to stand and began to wave his flashlight back and forth in sweeping arcs as the sound of the buzzing grew closer.

Toby waved her own flashlight and strained to see the shape of the little plane through the darkness. It really was much too dark to land, and Toby knew Davy would never try it unless there was no other choice. She shuddered to think what might have driven him to take such a daring chance.

When they finally saw it, the ultralight seemed to materialize only a few hundred yards in front of them. It was coming in low. Toby could see the determination in Davy's face. His jaw was clenched, and his concentration intense. There was no wobble of the wings in recognition this time. So hard was he concentrating that he didn't even seem to see who held the flashlights, and he didn't motion them out of the way as he had done before. Toby felt a cold premonition clutch her heart.

Lucien was cold with rage. He had watched his carefully laid plans thwarted at every turn. Relying on the fickle nature of men, he cursed, was a double-edged sword. The men he had commanded had wreaked havoc, but it had all been in their own ranks! He had lost a dozen men, easily. Knowing that they died unsaved was not sufficient enough to ease the bitter gall he felt over his failure to bring down the mission at last.

What were the deaths of a few lost men in comparison to the glorious feat of snatching the Lord's lambs from His very fold? Could he have engineered their destruction, his victory would have been sweet indeed. Now he surveyed the fragile ultralight as it bounced on teasing wind currents and knew he was not finished yet. While they remained in the air he had the opportunity to destroy them.

This time he would take matters into his own hands. Fueled by intense frustration and white-hot rage, Lucien himself sprang to attack the wavering ultralight. With one quick slash he tattered a wing, and the plane dipped precariously to one side. The pilot fought to control it, but Lucien battered it from the side, sending it rocking to the other side. It seemed to observers to be tossed around in the sky.

Afterwards, Lucien couldn't say exactly what happened. At the time he was aware of a sudden blinding light. He was pushed back, screaming in agony as the light bathed him and scorched the backs of his eyes. He fought furiously to get away from it. A host of angels surrounded the plane and helped ease it to the ground.

"No!" Lucien screamed, when he realized what they were going to do. "No!"

"Something's wrong!" Toby screamed. "Hit the deck!" As she threw herself to the ground she tried to track the plane with her eyes. A figure she took for Shay was slumped in the back seat. The wings of the plane were torn and it touched down very unsteadily. For an instant she was sure it was going to plow into the runway nose first, but Davy pulled it up resolutely and it continued to bounce down the runway, jarring its occupants and careening off the runway and toward the mission compound.

Gaius held the nose of the ultralight up as his fellow angels steered it to a stop before it could run into anything. The engine died with a harmless wheeze, and the angel who had his hand on it stepped back to allow Gaius to check on Shay, who had collapsed in the back seat.

Toby was on her feet before Don, who rose looking shaken. "It's Shay," he said in a voice Toby didn't even recognize. "Something's happened to Shay. I think she might be . . . might be . . ."

Before he could finish, they watched the ultralight come to a stop, and Davy leapt out. Reaching into the back seat he scooped up Shay's form and began to make his way to them, staggering slightly beneath his burden. "Help me," he called.

His voice galvanized them to action. Toby ran, but Don was faster. He reached Davy first. "Is she dead?"

"No, I'm not dead," a small voice replied. Shay lifted her head weakly and reached for him. "But I'm very hungry and thirsty, and my knee hurts."

"Oh!" Don gave a strangled cry and took Shay from Davy's arms, kissing her and sobbing so hard that Toby and Davy turned away. Davy held out his arms, and Toby flew into them, astonished at how gaunt he felt.

"I was afraid, I was afraid," Toby said, beginning to weep.

"Me too, Babe," Davy said, stroking her hair and holding her close to his chest. "Me too. But God protected us all."

"Are you OK?" Toby pulled back and studied his face hard. "Are you really OK? They didn't hurt you?"

"I'm OK," Davy reassured her. "Just really hungry and sore." He turned to the ultralight. "I think we lost the old girl, though. She held up better than I ever expected."

"We can fix her," Toby said confidently. "Let's take care of you two first."

Davy jerked his thumb over his shoulder. "Better help Don, then. I'm no doctor, but I think she tore a ligament in her knee. Then you can cook me a feast fit for a king."

Don was crouched over his wife, examining her knee, when Toby approached them. "Hey there, kiddo, I'm glad you're back," she said to Shay, who smiled wanly at her. "Need help?" she asked Don.

He jerked Shay's knee, and she cried out in pain. He looked up, grim. "She tore her anterior cruciate ligament."

"So I see. I'll get some ice packs." As she trotted toward the clinic she felt a surge of happiness that made her almost giddy. Stepping into the dark interior she staggered to her knees, suddenly overcome with a powerful sense of gratitude and profound relief. Everyone was OK. They were all alive. They had been given another chance. "Oh, God, thank You so much for hearing our prayers and protecting us all. Thank You for giving us this chance to work for You. Help us to get it right this time."

CHAPTER

15

Billie Jo straightened up and leaned on the handle of her snow shovel. Her breath came in little white puffs as she panted with exertion and surveyed the snowy landscape around her. Three feet of snow, it was hard to believe. The snow banks towered above her, and she was having trouble heaving the snow high enough to top them. She was thankful that they had kept up with the shoveling all along or they'd be buried by now.

Greta had told her it wasn't unusual to have such a huge snowfall in March. The one good thing about it, she'd said, was that it couldn't last long. Spring was just around the corner.

"Hey! Yoo-hoo!" a voice called. Greta appeared and skidded on a patch of ice. Her down jacket was bulging suspiciously, and she hugged her middle carefully as she approached. "You're almost done, aren't you? I have something to show you."

"What?" Billie Jo hated to be suspicious, but with Greta it could be anything and not necessarily something pleasant.

"Just something sweet," she replied evasively. "Come on into the house and I'll show you. I can't show you out here."

Billie Jo planted her shovel in the snow bank and followed Greta carefully up the steps and into the warm kitchen, marveling again how wonderful it was to be enveloped in warmth coming in from the cold. She took off her wet mittens and hung them by the woodstove. "OK, what is it?"

Greta dramatically unzipped her coat and produced a wriggling, slurping, ecstatic puppy. It wagged all over. "What do you think?"

Billie Jo couldn't help herself. With a squeal, she took the puppy in her arms and buried her face in its soft fur. "Ain't he cunning!" she exclaimed. "And he's got puppy breath!"

"What other kind of breath would you expect him to have?" Greta asked somewhat indignantly. "Isn't he just the sweetest thing you ever saw?"

"Where'd you get him?"

"The Humane Society. I just happened to be going by, so I stopped in." Her expression was completely neutral, but the nonchalance in her voice made Billie Jo look up sharply.

"You were just passing by? How'd you manage that, seeing as how you live on the *other* side of town and ain't got no reason to pass by?"

Greta sniffed. "If you must know, I went on purpose. I was looking for something."

"For a puppy?"

"Not exactly," Greta replied cagily. "I knew I wanted something, but I wasn't sure it was a puppy until I saw him."

"So you wanted a pet?"

"Oh, not for myself!" Greta exclaimed. "I'm allergic to pet hair, all kinds of it in fact. The only kind of pet I can have is fish, and I don't like cleaning the tank when the algae start to take over."

Billie Jo was bewildered. "Do what? Then who'd you get the dog for?"

"Why for you, of course." Greta was all innocence, and Billie Jo wanted to strangle her.

"What on this green earth made you think I wanted a dog?"

Greta shrugged. "I just thought you might, that's all."

"And the Humane Society let you adopt a puppy for someone else? That don't sound right."

"I didn't adopt him, exactly."

"Then what, exactly?"

"It's more like he's on approval. I know it's a bit irregular, but the manager there happens to be my brother-in-law."

"Whose approval?"

"Yours. Do you like him?"

Billie Jo burst out laughing. "You do beat all." She looked at the puppy, which sat quietly in her arms licking her wrist. His whiskered face split into a wide, lazy yawn. "What breed is this anyhow?"

"You do like him!" Greta exclaimed, pleased. "Reg wasn't sure what he was. He thinks some kind of terrier, maybe a little Corgi, and maybe something else too. Cute little fur ball though, isn't he?" She reached over and scratched behind his ears. "If I wasn't allergic I'd take him myself."

"What made you think I needed a dog?"

Greta lifted one slim shoulder. "I thought it might be nice if you had something to take care of. I knew I couldn't ask you to go with me because you wouldn't go. So, I thought, you know, if Mohammed won't go to the mountain, bring the mountain to Mohammed."

"I'm not calling him Mohammed," Billie Jo said firmly.

"You'll keep him?"

Billie Jo stroked the puppy's soft head. "I think I'd like that." She lifted her eyes, swimming in tears, to Greta. "Thank you."

"Don't mention it," Greta said lightly. "What will you call him?"

"I don't rightly know. I'll have to think on it for a bit."

"My work here is done," Greta announced, standing and pulling on her gloves. "I'd better head out. I've got other fish to fry. Don't forget to see Reg about the paperwork." With a twinkle in her eye, she gave Billie Jo a little wave and stepped back outside, picking her way carefully down the driveway.

Billie Jo looked after her, thinking she'd never in her life had such an exasperating, wonderful friend. "Don't that beat all," she said to the puppy, which cocked his head in the most adorable way imaginable. "Ain't you just the cutest thing," she cooed.

She was a little worried about what Jimmy might think, but he took to the new puppy as if he'd been waiting his whole life for a dog. "Ain't he cute," he exclaimed when he saw him. "I mind I had a dog when I was a kid till it run off. I used to wonder if my mother brung him to the pound and then just told me he run off." He scratched the puppy under the chin. "You ain't gonna run off, though, are you? What's his name?"

"Rascal?" Billie Jo suggested tentatively. "He looks like a Rascal, don't you think?"

Jimmy laughed, deeply from his belly. It seemed good to Billie Jo to hear him. "Rascal, I like that. Rascal it is."

The days turned into a blur of playing with Rascal and trying to keep him from living up to his name. He would sink out of sight in the tall drifts of snow that he liked to climb up if Billie Jo turned her back on him for a second. Picking up puppy accidents and making sure he didn't chew Jimmy's baseball hats or something worse, Billie Jo was surprised to discover one day that the puppy had distracted her from her pain.

At first she was devastated and tried immediately to bring back the sharpness of it, tried to recapture the intensity of the feeling, but it had gone. There was still the dull ache of loss, but the sense of despair was gone. As she realized this, Billie Jo found that she could be thankful for the relief of her deepest pain. As if opening her hand in a strong wind and releasing a fistful of leaves, she let go of her anguish and watched it flutter away. The burden had been lifted, and she felt lighter.

"Thank You, God," she said. Rascal looked at her and cocked his head quizzically.

Jewel watched her and felt his heart overflow with happiness. When he'd first learned about the trial that would be allowed in Billie Jo's life he'd been heartbroken and afraid that in her grief and pain she would turn away from the Master. Though she had wavered and staggered under her grief, with Greta's help and the newly discovered spiritual strength of her husband, she had come through. She was battered, but she was not defeated.

Jewel knew that trials such as this were powerful exercises in faith. How often human beings saw only the trial and not what was behind it. They seldom looked for the reason and less often for the good that the Master promised would come from it. Part of this, he knew, was due to their shortsightedness. Human beings lacked perspective.

They had not been around from the foundations of the earth and were not privy to the great counsels that had altered the course of humanity irrevocably. They had not been part of the planning for mankind's redemption even before there was a need for it. They could not see the future, as the Master did, and had no practical experience with heaven. They hoped for a future there but didn't really understand it at all.

There were times when Jewel wondered what it would be like to be a human being. He wondered what it felt like, not to merely take their form, as he had often done, but to actually be one. The Master had done it, and now He would spend eternity in a human body. And He didn't seem to mind. To be connected to the Master in that way, to know Him as a Redeemer, was beyond Jewel's imaginings. He looked forward to talking with some of his charges in heaven to find out what that might be like.

"I'll tell you what it's like," Nog mocked. "It stinks. Who would want to live in one of those fragile vessels? It's constantly breaking down, and that's only if you get one that works properly in the first place."

"They," he sneered, "place too much emphasis on something that started out as a handful of dust and will eventually return to a handful of dust, but that just goes to show you how well our plan is working. They've bought the concept and untold millions will spend more time and energy looking beautiful than will even take the time to get to know your Master. So, tell me, who wins in the end, huh, my friend?" Nog chuckled and didn't bother to wait for a reply to his question. He didn't expect the angel to make a reply and Jewel didn't.

Instead Jewel watched Billie Jo, his sense of satisfaction increasing, and smiled broadly at the antics of her new puppy. He'd had an idea that having something to take care of would help Billie Jo. She needed to be needed. And, as it turned out, he'd been right. He was grateful, truly grateful.

When spring came, and mud season with it, she found she was able to face into the gentle breezes and smile, inhaling all the wonderful promise of new birth and know, not just hope, that she was going to make it through the darkness.

The month of May found Billie Jo and Jimmy at church singing, as lilac-scented air floated in the window. Billie Jo had been surprised to find out that Jimmy had a strong, mellow baritone. When he'd first accompanied her to church after the accident and opened his mouth to sing "Joyful, Joyful We Adore Thee" she came to the startling conclusion that she'd never once, in all their married life, ever heard him sing. Not even snatches of songs from the radio. She wasn't sure which was more of a surprise, that she'd never heard him sing or that he had such a beautiful voice.

Now, standing near him, she marveled at the wonderful sound and that the two of them could be standing side by side in church worshipping God less than a year after the tragic deaths of their children and Jimmy's parents. Only by the grace of God, she concluded. There was no other explanation.

"That's what you tell yourself," Nog shouted from outside the church. The perimeter was the closest he could stand to get. "You're just a heartless monster. You never loved your children if you could forget them so fast. And everyone knows you hated your mother-in-law. It's been great since Helen's been gone, hasn't it? Admit it, you're glad she died."

Jewel could see Billie Jo wince as Nog's thought struck home. Even at that distance he was able to get in under her armor. Jewel reached one powerful wing around the couple to shield them. "Negative thoughts are not from the Master, but the Evil One," Jewel told her. "You loved your children; of course you did. You'll see them again one day. And you didn't get along with your mother-in-law, that's true. But you didn't wish her dead.

"This earth is a place of meaningless tragedy and sin. There is nothing you could have done to prevent it, and you shouldn't blame yourself for it. Your responsibility now is to go on living in a way that pleases the Master. Then, when He comes again to take you home, you'll be ready to go."

Prayer Warriors: the Final Chapter

Jewel saw Billie Jo relax and let out a soft breath of relief. She would be all right, but the battle was far from over. He knew something else that would give Billie Jo reason to rejoice, but the time was not yet right. Still, as he looked into her smiling, hopeful face he couldn't help being a little anxious for the event to take place. It would at the same time make things more complicated, more challenging, and more wonderful than Billie Jo ever hoped they could be again.

Jimmy squeezed her hand, and Billie Jo realized the pastor had stopped praying. Church was over. She tried to recapture the fleeting thought she'd just had, but it slipped away with the lilac air, drifting back out the window. She knew it had been important, a wonderful thought that filled her with gladness, but it was gone.

"Here comes Greta," Jimmy said under his breath. Louder he said, "Hey there, Greta, got any more puppies?"

Greta laughed at his teasing. They got along like sister and brother, and she frequently gave it right back to him. "I'm afraid not, Jimmy. Today all I have is the odd cat or two. Can I interest you in one?"

"Not me, thanks," Jimmy said, twisting out of the pew so Greta could slide in next to Billie Jo. "I'm not a cat person."

"And how is Rascal?" she asked sweetly.

"Fine, just fine," he said, sidling away. "Think he's got some Great Dane in him though. Eats like a house afire."

"What's he in such a rush for?" Greta asked idly, watching Jimmy weave around people in a hurry to get outside.

"I think he's afraid someone is going to ask him to have special music," Billie Jo said.

"No! You didn't tell him!" Greta said accusingly. "Why, Billie Jo Raynard, you weren't supposed to breathe a word! Now look at that. They'll have to chase him down the road."

"I never did tell him," Billie Jo responded placidly. "I might have said, though, that didn't he have a wonderful voice and wasn't it a shame not to show it off some. And I might have mentioned that I wasn't the only one who thought so."

"That's the same thing," Greta scolded. "They'll have some time dragging him up there now. Shame on you, girl."

Billie Jo smiled. "Yeah, well, never weren't nothing special that weren't worth working for."

Greta giggled. "Just for that, I've got half a mind not to tell you what I came over here to tell you."

"What have you got in the other half of your mind?" Billie Jo returned innocently.

"The other half," Greta informed her archly, "agrees with the first half. So, you're just going to have to wait." She made as though she was about to get up and leave.

Billie Jo grabbed her arm. "I'm kidding, Greta, kidding. Tell me before I get eat up with curiosity."

Greta rolled her eyes. "OK, you talked me into it. Guess who has two bus tickets for a garden tour to the Place des Jardins in Montreal in two weeks when everything will be blooming up a storm?"

"The pastor? Jimmy? The town librarian?"

Greta groaned. "You are incorrigible today! Maybe I should bring someone else." She looked around as if searching for someone else to bring.

"No, no, Greta, take me. I want to go to the Place des Thingy whatever it was. What is it, anyway?"

"Just an amazingly beautiful garden, lots of them in fact. You'll love it. I've been before. Nathan took me years ago, and I've always wanted to go back. You spend so much time in your garden that I thought it might give you some ideas. You know, inspire you with things to do in your own."

Billie Jo threw her arms around Greta, all playfulness gone, her eyes full of tears. "You're the most amazingly wonderful friend anyone could ever have. Thank you so much. You got more surprises in you than I could shake a stick at, that's for sure. I never know what you're gonna go and do next."

Greta patted her back. "I like to keep you guessing, that's all. The real Greta said that life would be so wonderful if we only knew what to do with it, but I think most of the fun comes in the not knowing. Don't you?"

Billie Jo pulled back and wiped her eyes. "Yeah, I'd have to agree with you on that. Not knowing the fun and not knowing the pain.

I guess you'd have to have them both. It gets so you never know what's gonna happen next, and I guess that keeps it interesting for sure."

"I know what's going to happen next," Greta said sagely.

"What?"

"You and Jimmy are going to come to my house for lunch. I packed us a great big picnic lunch, and we'll take that little Rascal of yours and go for a long hike up in the mountains and see what we can find."

Billie Jo laughed. "That sounds wonderful. We'll just go home and get changed and meet you at your house."

"Sounds like a plan."

"And Greta?"

"Yes?"

"I love you, you know."

"I know, kid. I love you back."

Jewel smiled with pleasure and a sort of knowing that was beyond the human beings to fathom even if they could have witnessed it. Spontaneity had its place, but for himself, he was glad to know something of what the future held. He carried his knowledge closely, like a child might carry a present painstakingly made for someone he loved. Jewel knew that although there would be trials ahead, that there would always be trials, there would also be good times. In every piece of happiness, he knew, there was a foreshadowing of heaven. He hoped that eventually Billie Jo would find them, as he did, and rejoice in the glimpse of what was waiting just ahead.

Cindi shielded her eyes from the glare of the sun as she scanned the yard for Esther, who she spotted sitting under a tree in the yard having a tea party with her dolls. "Esther, it's time to come in. We have math to do."

"Coming, Mommy," Esther replied, beginning to gather up her things.

Cindi stood for a moment on the stoop of the house and surveyed the scene around her. Off toward the mountains a haze hung low on the horizon. It was already gearing up to be a scorcher, and May wasn't half over. The humidity was oppressive, and she longed for the air-conditioned comfort of the house.

As she waited for Esther she thought ahead through her day. They had to finish up with math, and then there were meals to deliver. Today was special because Esther was going to try out for the local baseball team in the afternoon. She was both excited and nervous.

"Do you think the other kids will like me?" she'd asked worriedly. "Even if I don't go to their school?"

Cindi had tousled her hair. "Sure they will, hon. They'll love you."

She hoped with all her heart that they would because Esther was pretty sensitive when it came to the opinions of others. Fortunately Cindi had found a home-school group early on, so Esther had plenty of friends to socialize with, but going into a new situation with a whole passel of kids had to be a bit daunting.

"Can I wear my baseball hat when we deliver the meals?" Esther asked, her voice coming from the region around Cindi's knees.

Cindi started, not realizing her daughter was standing on the stoop below her. Marc had bought her an honest-to-goodness, genuine Red Sox baseball hat when they'd started practicing out in the front yard every night after work. It was Esther's pride and joy. Even more than that, she enjoyed having her father home more.

"I promised Mr. Collins that I'd show it to him, and my mitt too."

"In that case you best not forget," Cindi smiled, moving aside so Esther could enter the house. But, she didn't follow Esther. She continued to stand on the stoop, looking at the horizon. A trickle of sweat meandered down the back of her neck, but still she stood there, reveling in an intense joy about her life.

"I have a wonderful life, Lord," she whispered. "I'm so grateful to You." For a moment she let herself wonder what might have happened if she had chosen another path, possibly allowed her relationship with Marc to deteriorate, and maybe severed it altogether. She shuddered. How horrible she would be feeling right now, she knew, if she had not given everything to her marriage even when the going got tough. It suddenly occurred to her that this was the very first serious problem she and Marc had ever faced in their marriage. The satisfaction of overcoming was gratifying.

Every now and then she ran into Jared at the community center. He was putting in a lot of volunteer hours; more than Cindi herself put in. He was pleasant and seemed to have moved on, though every now and then Cindi fancied she caught a glimpse of a question in his eyes. To his credit, if it was truly there he had never voiced it. She sincerely hoped that he was not just waiting for her marriage to fail so he could swoop in and rescue her. She hoped he'd given up the idea that they had any kind of future together once and for all.

Though Cindi couldn't know it, the one creature who knew that Jared had indeed moved on in his life had the most reason to dread that very circumstance. Ogel had to admit to himself one day that all hope was gone. It wasn't so much that Jared had become interested in another woman. It was just that his feelings for Cindi had changed. He was fond of her, as of a sister, but he did not wish for her marriage to fail. In fact, he regularly prayed that her marriage would grow even stronger and that she and Marc and Esther would be happy and fulfilled.

No, Ogel couldn't say that he saw a speck of hope from that quarter, and that frightened him even more than he would admit. He remembered the fate Rafe had suffered at the hands of Sparn when he had fouled up their mission. Not only had Rafe suffered unspeakable cruelties at Sparn's hand, but following that he had been banished to a highly undesirable post, one from which he might never return.

Ogel had kept a low profile as the revelation of Jared's complete and utter change of heart became clear to him. He had not seen Sparn, had gone out of his way to avoid him. The way he saw it, the less attention he called to himself the greater the chance that he could avoid the threatened punishment. If he even thought about going through what Rafe had suffered he grew weak in the knees and nearly passed out from fear.

"Ah, so there you are."

Ogel recognized the deep, velvet voice before he saw Sparn regarding him as a cat watches a mouse it's about to catch. A cool, cruel light flickered in Sparn's eyes. So frightening was it to see that Ogel found he had to sit down. He felt paralyzed from fear. "Were you looking for me?" he croaked.

"Didn't you know it?" Sparn purred. "Believe me, I could have found you earlier. It was simply more entertaining to let you sweat it out a little. Did you really think I would forget about our little agreement?"

Ogel wasn't sure if he ought to admit the thought had crossed his mind or deny it strenuously. He opted to keep his mouth shut and let Sparn think what he wanted. "What can I do for you, O Illustrious Leader?" Flattery often worked with human beings. Sadly, it didn't seem to affect Sparn the same way.

He chuckled and toyed with his chin. "I can see you'd rather I forgot about it all, wouldn't you?"

Ogel swallowed hard. It wasn't his nature to be honest, but he found himself nodding eagerly, as if maybe by abasing himself shamelessly he might yet come out of this unscathed. It was a ridiculous hope, he knew, but still he clung to it. "I did try so hard, Your Royal Highness. But, the cursed human wouldn't co-operate. And there were so many angels. Their light burned my hands." He displayed these, the skin of which was in dark tatters and looked dreadful.

"I see." Sparn stroked his chin.

For an instant Ogel thought perhaps he might be spared, and he slumped a little with relief. Sparn reached over and plucked him up with two long bony fingers as if he was no more than a rat. With obvious relish Sparn began to carry him to be tortured, and Ogel wailed as he did not know he could wail. The only response he received was an evil laugh rumbling up from Sparn's chest and exploding very close to his ear. As he was dragged away, Ogel cursed Cindi and everyone connected to her.

Prayer Warriors: the Final Chapter

Cindi felt a vaguely unpleasant sensation, like something you feel when a terrible or irritating thought occurs to you. But she couldn't place it, and she mentally flicked it off like an annoying fly bothering her. Instead she followed Esther into the house and pulled out their math book. She was grateful that she was able to continue home school with Esther. It was her number-one priority, and she was glad Marc recognized that too.

Esther whizzed through the math, and they were done before they needed to leave. Cindi let the little girl have another recess while she worked on A Wing and a Prayer. The list constantly amazed her. And unexpectedly it had spawned a real-time ladies' Bible study group. Every Wednesday ten women in the area got together and studied the Bible and prayed.

Cindi conveyed prayer requests and accepted them in turn, and all were published on the email prayer list. That alone was fabulous, but the most wonderful aspect of it for Cindi was the women she had met. They'd come from all walks of life, from every denomination, but they all loved the Lord and wanted to please Him.

Cindi thought it was slightly ironic that they'd begun a Bible study on marriage as their first study. She'd stifled a laugh when she heard and muttered, "I'm listening, Lord," under her breath. The ways God found to speak to her amazed her every day. Sometimes it was obvious, like the Bible study topic, and other times it was a line from a sermon on the radio or a devotional that seemed written especially for her. Cindi found that on days when she made it a point to seek God out and spend time with Him, He nearly always had something to say to her. It was sobering to think that if she'd pushed her time with Him aside, she would have missed it.

The shrill ring of the phone jerked her out of her reverie, and she sat up with a start in her chair. She was supposed to be working on A Wing and a Prayer, and here she was daydreaming. She picked up the phone. "Hello?"

A static crackle blasted out of the receiver, and a man's voice said, "Sis? Hello? Are you there? Blasted phone!"

"Don? Donny, is that you?" She hadn't spoken to him since he'd left for Africa months earlier, though she'd had many letters and nearly fainted at the reports of the terrorists who had attacked the mission. There had been a lot of prayer activity on the list since then for the safety of everyone who had remained at the clinic. "Don?"

The line cleared up very suddenly. "Cindi?"

"I'm here!"

"Oh, good. I thought we'd been cut off."

"How are you?"

"Fine, just great, actually. I'm calling with some news."

"Good news or bad news?"

His hearty laugh echoed over the phone lines, and for one second was so clear she could have sworn he was calling from around the corner. "Good news! The best! Truth is we've known for some time, but Shay said I had to call and not put it in a letter."

"Well, what is it?" Cindi demanded, getting impatient.

"But, see, we haven't come into Niamey for a while . . ." The static cut in, and his voice broke up. "So, I said I'd come into town and pick up some stuff and call you," he finished.

"Don, will you tell me the news before we lose this connection?" Cindi demanded, running out of patience.

"We're having a—" he practically shouted.

"A what?"

"A . . . —y."

"A what?" Cindi was holding the phone so tight her knuckles were white.

"A baby!" he was yelling now, and laughing. "We're having a baby. Listen, sis, everyone is staring at me now. I'd better hang up before I lose you for good."

"You'll never lose me," Cindi said, laughing herself. "I'm so happy for you, Don. Please tell Shay . . ." But the static came back, and this time he was gone. She hung up the receiver and leaned back in her chair, emotionally exhausted from the exchange. Having a baby. Imagine. She was going to be an aunt again.

"What were you talking about, Mommy?" Esther poked her head around the door into the living room.

"Hey, pumpkin, come here. That was Uncle Donny on the phone."

"Can I talk to him?" Esther asked eagerly.

"No, I'm sorry, we were cut off. We didn't have a good connection this time. But he had some wonderful news. Guess what? Uncle Donny and Aunt Shay are going to have a baby."

"Really?" Cindi could see Esther's eyes light up with thoughts of a real live baby doll to dress up and feed and change and take for walks in the stroller. Then her face fell. "But it won't be born here will it? Will we ever get to see it?"

Cindi tried to squelch her own disappointment at this thought. "No, you're right. Uncle Donny didn't say, but I imagine the baby will be born in Africa, and I don't know how old he or she will be when they come home next."

"Sometimes," Esther whispered, her eyes downcast, "I hate the mission for taking Uncle Donny away. I don't get to see him, and I don't get to play with my cousins ever."

Cindi pulled the little girl close. "I know it's hard. But you have to remember something. Uncle Donny and Aunt Shay and the others at the mission are doing a very important work for God. He called them to go there and to help those people and to teach them about Him. Not everyone gets called to a special job like that. Someday He might even call you."

Esther peeked up through her lowered lashes. "Really?"

Cindi nodded solemnly. "He might. You never know. Or He might call you to do the kind of work we do."

Esther wrinkled her nose. "We don't do any work for God. We only pray for people."

"Oh, yes, we do, young lady," Cindi said quickly. "Praying for people is a very important work. Some of the most important work there is. But we also share Jesus with people we meet by being nice to them and helping them."

"You mean the people we bring lunch to? That's like being a missionary?"

"It sure is. We're missionaries to them. You're being a missionary when you sing for Mrs. Hobbes or when you take the time to bring something special to show someone like Mr. Collins just because he asked. All those little things are the sorts of things that Jesus would do if He were here. We're doing God's work, and when you do God's work you're a missionary."

"Cool." Esther absorbed this. "I guess if God asked me to go somewhere like Africa I'd go," she said at last.

"Would you?" Cindi was amused.

"Yes, but only if you and Daddy could come too."

Cindi hugged her daughter. "Oh, just try and stop us," she said, her voice breaking with emotion.

They were interrupted as the doorbell rang. "I'll get it," Esther shouted, pulling away from Cindi and racing for the door. Cindi lingered behind, saving her document and turning the computer off. It was probably just the postman anyway. He often rang the bell if he had a particularly large package.

"Mommy!"

"Coming." Cindi pushed her chair in and made her way into the kitchen, where Esther was at the side door clutching a massive bouquet of roses and waving at the retreating back of the delivery man.

"Mommy, look what the man gave me. Are they for me?"

Cindi laughed. "Well, let's just see." With trembling fingers she plucked the card from the plastic holder and opened it up. Never, not once in her life, had she ever received flowers at her home. Occasionally Marc would show up with a small bouquet he'd picked up at the grocery store with the milk, and once someone had given her flowers for her birthday, but never had anyone sent flowers to be delivered.

"My dearest Cindi, I love you forever and for always. Marc." Cindi scanned the note and burst into tears.

"Mommy, why are you crying?" Esther wailed.

"I'm happy," Cindi sobbed, trying to smile as she cried to show Esther that indeed it was joy that prompted her outburst and not tragedy.

"Then why are you crying?" Esther demanded.

Cindi stroked Esther's hair and buried her nose in the roses. "You'll understand when you're older," she assured her daughter. "Now, get me some tissues please."

Shania smiled with serene pleasure. It had taken some time for Marc Trahan to listen to them, but once he had stopped over-working himself he'd been more receptive to their pleas to show his wife his love in tangible ways as well as intangible ones. Shania knew their marriage would weather any storms it faced because they relied on the Master and not on themselves.

That wasn't to say they'd never face problems, maybe even some larger than the one they had just come through. But, as long as they put the Master first, their marriage would be strong and sturdy. And she would be here to help them stay on course, Shania thought as she watched Cindi put the roses in a large vase. Yes, she would be here through it all.

Don returned from his trip to Niamey eagerly. Even the sight of the mission as it came into view from the tossing Land Rover only heightened his excitement. There wasn't a hint of fear or anxiety as he drove into the mission compound, laying on the horn and waving carelessly to whomever was standing around gawking at his arrival. And, he convinced himself, his profound confidence had nothing whatsoever to do with the burly technicals who were seated beside and behind him, machine guns at the ready. At least, that's what he told himself.

"You're back early!" Shay exclaimed, limping stiffly down the steps and into his arms. "And you brought company." She smiled brightly at the men. "I'm Shay Germaine."

Don introduced the men all around. "Philip Vassar, Dean Collins, Norm Fields; and this is Sean McCormack. Dorsey highly recommends them, right, guys?"

Philip Vassar, the unofficial spokesman of the group, answered. "Dorsey's an all-right sort of guy. He keeps us in the action."

Shay cocked her head and studied him soberly. "And do you get much . . . action, as you call it?"

His smile was wry and thin on his narrow face. "No, ma'am. Generally speaking, anyone interested in causing any trouble takes one look at our fire power and leaves us alone." He patted the stock of his machine gun meaningfully.

Shay grabbed Don's arm as they walked inside. She was still limping pretty badly, though her knee was getting better. He'd told her that soon she'd hardly know she had torn her ACL except when she tried to pivot and fell down. Consequently she was very careful, but they both knew that eventually, after the baby, she'd be having surgery to replace the destroyed ligament. Until then she had to make out as best she could.

The technicals followed them inside, and Don made new rounds of introductions. Though they'd all been briefed that Dorsey was sending technicals, the staff on the whole was pretty curious about the newest additions to their compound. It seemed that everyone had questions.

"Will you follow us everywhere we go?"

"What happens when we need to leave the compound?"

"Will there be a curfew?"

"What about the plane? Will you come on all our runs, and can you fly if there is an emergency?"

Vassar held up his hands. "One at a time, folks. I'll answer all your questions, but one at a time, please."

As Don listened to the briefing he grew more and more confident. He'd resisted the idea of armed staff for a long time, but the kidnapping had changed his mind fast. When things had settled down and their lines of communication had been restored, he'd called Dorsey immediately and requested technicals. Dorsey had complied promptly and sent them these recruits.

They looked likely enough, probably ex-military and intimidating enough fellows. He was a bit in awe of them and not a little afraid that they might pose a problem in the face of the decidedly spiritual nature of the mission. As it turned out, he was pleasantly surprised and relieved when someone suggested they close their meeting with prayer and even the roughest looking of the men, Sean McCormack, bowed his head, crew cut bristling, his swarthy face relaxed as Davy led them in prayer.

Later he found Shay sitting on the kitchen steps watching the sun set on the horizon. Silhouetted against the setting sun, one of the technicals was making his rounds of the perimeter, his machine gun prominent against the fading light.

"What do you think of them really?" Don asked, reaching for her hand.

Shay was silent for a moment. She shrugged her shoulders. "I'm not thrilled. I wish there was no need for them. I like to think of the mission the way it was when I got here, but everything changes, I guess. We have to expect that it will get worse before it gets better. I just don't like the thought that they might have to kill someone to protect one of us. I'm not sure I agree with that."

"I know," Don said, nodding. "I thought of that too. But maybe the display of strength will keep people from trying to hurt us again. Maybe they'll give us space, and we can get on with the business of helping people, like we want."

"Do you ever think it will be that simple again?"

"No, I guess not. How can I? It was the same in Rwanda. People everywhere take advantage of the less fortunate. It's the way Satan wants it, and he's the boss down here for the time being. The only difference is that this time I'm not running away."

"You didn't run away last time."

"I did. I left."

"You needed a break. What happened was traumatic. Anyone would have needed to get away for a while."

"But I didn't get away for a while, did I? I left for good. I only told myself it was for a little while."

Shay put her arm around his shoulder. "Look, you can't beat yourself up over this. I know you. I know you better than anyone does, and I know you're not the kind of person to run away from anything. If you were, you would have left with the others when you had a chance. Instead you stayed here. You didn't even know if you could help, but still you stayed. That's not the action of a person who runs away.

"Life is tough, and it knocks us down a lot. No one knows that better than you and me. But God is stronger than life. He's stronger than death. He's the road to a better tomorrow. We can only do our best and rely on Him to give us the strength to keep doing it.

"This is our home. You feel it, and I feel it. We've put down roots here, and this is where we're going to stay. Rwanda was an entirely different story. You were unattached and had no real reason to make a commitment there. That's not the case here. Marcus has history here, and so does Madina." Shay took his hand and squeezed it. He felt his heart constrict with something he could only call an overabundance of joy. "We've got history here too. I fell in love with you here."

"I fell in love with you too, kid." He leaned over and kissed her lightly. "I just didn't know it at the time."

"Yeah, well, know it now, Buster," she teased.

"So, you're happy here? You want to stay? Even after everything that's happened?"

She seemed to consider that a moment. "I think it's more because of everything that's happened. I've often thought I could be happy anywhere—anywhere you and the kids are. I still think so. But this place is special to me. It's always had a certain mystique. You wouldn't believe how I romanticized it before I got here." She laughed, and Don could see her again, wide-eyed and naïve, as she had arrived at the mission. "The reality of it is so much harsher, yet so much more beautiful and, I don't know, raw and immediate, I guess, than I ever dreamed it could be."

"I think I understand," Don said. "I've never really been as happy anywhere else. Even when I've been helping people, I have always felt most at home here."

"Care for some company?" Davy asked as he and Toby appeared hand in hand around the corner. They settled themselves on the bottom stair without waiting for a reply. Davy's thin frame still showed the effects of his ordeal. He had been slow to regain his strength and health, often fighting with a dry cough. "What do you think about those muscles, huh?"

"Davy," Toby said, elbowing her husband in the ribs. "They're technicals, not muscles or heavies or hit men. This isn't the mob."

"I'll tell you the truth," Davy said earnestly. "I feel a whole lot safer knowing one of those guys will be flying with me. I don't know about you," he nodded at Shay, "but I only want to go through that kind of ordeal once in my life, and I've filled my quota. All things considered, I think I've had plenty of excitement in my lifetime. I'm happy those guys are here."

"They don't come with any guarantees, you know," Don pointed out.

"Yeah, I know. But, still, I feel safer. Maybe it's just an illusion, but it works for me."

"You'd be better off trusting in God," Toby told him.

Davy sat up straighter. "You think I don't?" he demanded, his voice huffy. "I trust God. I know who was responsible for getting Shay and I out of that whole mess. Believe me, I relied on God plenty. Without trust in God I wouldn't be sitting here today. That doesn't mean I can't feel safer knowing there's someone around to protect me from the chances of that happening again. Besides, a guy can hope can't he? There isn't any kind of a law against that that I know of."

"No law," Toby rejoined mildly. "As long as you put your hope in the right place. That's all I'm saying."

Davy jerked his thumb at her and rolled his eyes at Don and Shay. "You hear that? After all I've been through and me going to get baptized and everything, and this is the grief I get."

"You're going to be baptized?" Shay said. "That's wonderful!"

"Thank you," Davy said with a smile. "I thought so. And I thought someone else would think so too." He stared pointedly at Toby.

"I do think it's wonderful," she protested.

"But not wonderful enough to join me," he countered.

"It's just, well, I kind of have this fear of water."

"And I'd like for us to be baptized together."

Don raised his hands in protest. "The jury's out on this one. You'll have to settle it amongst yourselves. Baptism is a personal thing. But if fear of water is the only issue I'm sure something can be done."

"Yeah!" Davy replied eagerly. "We'll ask. How's that?"

Toby agreed reluctantly. "I guess it wouldn't hurt to ask."

"And when is this blessed event going to take place?" Shay asked.

"Probably the next time we get into Niamey," Davy said. "Unless we get a sudden downpour it'd be hard to get baptized out here. Anyway, Pastor Dimbe doesn't get out this way very often."

Lucien eavesdropped on this conversation shamelessly, his heart growing more and more leaden as it progressed. If there was one thing he hated, one thing he positively abhorred and detested, it was baptism. If Toby got baptized it would ruin everything. When a human being was baptized, the Great Pretender (as he liked to refer to the Holy Spirit) actually lived in their hearts, and Lucien couldn't imagine anything as nauseating as Toby with a heart full of the Holy Spirit.

Plus there was that whole group-support thing. Once a person pledged their life to follow God and joined a church with other people doing the same thing it was harder to get their attention. In groups like that they were more able to resist the temptations thrown at them. They "helped" each other and "prayed for" each other. It was sickening. Just look at the damage it has caused at the mission, and they weren't even a church, he thought.

Occasionally, of course, churches worked in their favor, usually when weak-minded individuals allowed themselves to be swayed by unholy influences. Havoc could be wreaked in that case. But Lucien knew the church Davy and Toby would join, and it was a mighty testament to the power of God. Demons trembled at the thought of that place and did not step foot anywhere near it. No, Lucien reasoned, he'd have his work cut out for him trying to dissuade Toby from being baptized. Already he sensed that she was weakening.

As he looked at the happy faces before him Lucien felt a cold, dreadful anger fill his heart. The worst thing about them was that they were all alive. Not a single one had been seriously harmed. And now they were not only stronger spiritually than they had ever been before, but they were armed to the teeth to prevent a similar situation. They were on their guard, and he would be hard pressed to catch them unaware in the future.

No, all in all, he was in for the long haul. Things here were going too well for them to change anytime soon. He cursed his luck. He cursed the incompetent demons who had bungled everything. He cursed the Prayer Warrior in the United States and all those who prayed with her. Most of all he cursed himself for getting stuck in such a despicable place. Someone would pay for that.

"I'm glad everything is getting back to normal," Toby observed. "And I'm glad we're looking toward expansion." She shot a pointed look at Don, who raised his hands in defense.

"You were right, and I was wrong. I'm sorry already. I can't help it if I'm a little afraid of all this new growth. Part of me is excited about it, and part of me is a bundle of nerves."

"I think we should pray about it and ask God to bless our efforts," Shay said quietly.

"I think that is an excellent idea," Davy agreed.

They bowed their heads. "Lord," Don prayed, "thank You for keeping us safe and sending Your angels to protect us. We know that You have established this mission and that You have a heart for these people, and You've given that heart to us. Please give us strength and courage as we face Your plans for expansion at this mission. Please make us ready to do Your will always, and give us the wisdom to discern what Your will is.

"Thank You for all the people who support this mission with their prayers. Bless them in a special way, especially my sister, Cindi, and her family. Thank You for their faithfulness. I thank You, Lord, for all the people at this mission. Thank You for speaking to their hearts and for helping us all to put aside our differences and work together for You. Please send us Your Holy Spirit and keep us close to You. Amen."

Lucien didn't wait for the last "amen" to sound. With disgust and slight terror, he dove for cover. With a soft roar, the Holy Spirit filled the very air around him, setting it crackling like a forest fire. Screaming with anger and frustration, he bolted away from the intense light that warmed the people and lit every corner of the mission. The Great Pretender had won this round, Lucien admitted to himself, but it was far from over. He would be back. And then . . . well, then it would be a different story. He just knew it would.

Reissa was on her way back up the heavenly staircase. She was on her way to receive instruction from the Master. Below she left tragedy and triumph, loss and gain. To the human beings, she knew, it was sometimes hard to tell which won out over the others. But, to her and to the other heavenly host, the victories were more clear-cut. The events worked together with an unerring design only the Master was capable of forming.

Like the undersides of a great tapestry, what the human beings saw was only the bottom. That side was often ugly and tangled. The tangles occurred when the people took things into their own hands. Rather than ruin the work, the Master tried to help them and eventually reorder the design. The human beings could not see the top, where the Master would toil until He came for them. Then they would see the glorious masterpiece for which their lives had been spent. Only then would it be evident how the dark strands made the light ones stand out.

Reissa knew that even the human beings who understood these things had trouble accepting them. It was hard for them, whose entire understanding was anchored in living on earth, to understand that there could truly be anything better waiting. But there was. As Reissa entered the courts of heaven she breathed a sigh of relief.

Gone were the polluted city streets of earth. Gone were the unspeakable atrocities she was forced to witness every day. Gone was the darkness the human beings lived in that pervaded every area of their lives. Gone were the pinpoints of light, signs of the Spirit, illuminating mostly small areas; here the Spirit's light was everywhere! Reissa raised her arms and sang joyfully at being back, even for such a short while.

"Welcome, sister." Reissa turned and found Noble, his countenance serene, his wings folded majestically and arranged in folds around his shoulders. "How do you find things on earth?"

"Not as here," Reissa mourned, "not as here. But there are yet faithful ones. The humans grow weary at times, but the Master strengthens them, when they will accept His help, and they go on. The time seems long to them."

Noble nodded. "Yet the time is short," he observed.

"Yes," Reissa agreed, "but the humans do not see it so. They allow distractions to occupy their minds. These things take them away from their mission. It is hard to keep them focused because all that surrounds them clamors for their attention. They have many pressures. They could experience victory much more often if they would only keep their eyes on the Master instead of turning away to see to the problems."

"They walk as children, and as children they will grow."

Reissa sighed. "In truth, I grow eager for the end."

"We are all eager for the end," Noble said. "The Master is most eager of all. He wants to bring His children home."

"They will love this place," Reissa said. "They will love it as we do."

"I think," Noble said pensively, "I think they will love it more. We have always had it and so cannot miss it. But they have never had it and cannot imagine the splendor of it. To them, this place will be overwhelmingly beautiful."

"I wish we could show it to them now. I wish we could bring them each, one by one, to the Master. Right now!"

"Soon," Noble said, smiling as he turned. "Soon."

Reissa unfurled her wings and glided above the only home she had ever known. Yes, soon she would lead her charges home, all the human beings she had cared for since the world began who had followed the Master's voice. She would bring them to Him and hear Him say the words, "Good and faithful servant." And the words would be not only for her charges but also for herself. And her heart would fill with happiness.

"Soon," she whispered again, thinking of all the people on earth she loved so well. "Be faithful, my friends. The Master will come," she promised, "very soon."

The trilogy is now complete!

Prayer Warriors, the spiritual fiction saga started by Céleste perrino Walker in 1997, is now complete. All three books in the series, *Prayer Warriors*, *Guardians*, and *The Final Chapter*, give dramatic behind-the-scenes glimpses of angelic activity initiated by the prayers of their charges. The power of prayer comes to life in the pages of these inspiring books. You haven't shared the whole experience until you've read all three.

Prayer Warriors (Book one)
0-8163-1359-8. Paper.

Guardians (Book two)
0-8163-1407-1. Paper.

Prayer Warriors: The Final Chapter (Book three)
0-8163-2001-2. Paper.

The Prayer Warriors trilogy will convince you of the truth that we stand tallest when we are on our knees. US$12.99, Can$19.49 each.

Order from your ABC by calling 1-800-765-6955, or get online and shop our virtual store at www.AdventistBookCenter.com.
- Read a chapter from your favorite book
- Order online
- Sign up for email notices on new products